Trade Winds

Christina Courtenay

First published 2010 by Choc Lit Limited
Penrose House, Crawley Drive, Camberley, Surrey GU15 2AB
www.choclitpublishing.co.uk

A CIP catalogue record for this book is available from the British Library

ISBN-978-1-906931-23-0

Printed in the UK by CPI Cox & Wyman, Reading, RG1 8EX

For my father
Kenneth Brian Tapper
1933–2004

Acknowledgements

First of all, I would like to say an enormous thank you to all at Choc Lit for liking my story and for being such lovely people to work with!

Secondly, I can honestly say I would have given up long ago if I hadn't joined the *Romantic Novelists' Association* (RNA). In particular, I'd like to thank Margaret James and Nicola Cornick (the organisers of the New Writers' Scheme), Katie Fforde, Eileen Ramsay, Rachel Summerson, Hilary Johnson and Mary De Laszlo for their encouragement and kindness.

Some of my friends deserve an extra big thank you – Henriette Gyland and Gill Stewart, my brilliant critique partners, Giselle Green, Victoria Connelly, Catriona Robb and Myra Kersner who all refused to let me quit when the going got tough, and Tina Brown and Caroline Dahlén, who are always there for me. Cecily Bomberg and her writers' circle – Neil, Lorraine, Caroline, Helen and the two Killian's (sorry guys, but I just had to borrow your name for this book!) for valuable critique and encouragement.

At the Gothenburg City Museum Agneta Hermansson and her staff were extremely helpful, making my research time there a very enjoyable experience – *tack Agneta och dina medhjälpare*!

And last but by no means least, thank you to my family and friends and all those who truly believed in me. You know who you are!

Author's Note

This story is loosely based on the Swedish East India Company's first journey to China in 1732 and I have tried to adhere to the true facts as much as possible. Since this is a novel, however, I have had to take a few liberties in order to make it a more exciting story, but the actual travelling and some of the incidents described really happened, notably the capture of the Swedish ship by the Dutch near Batavia.

The Swedish East India Company (the SOIC – *Svenska Ost Indiska Compagniet*) was formed in June 1731, although it was originally named *Henrik (Hindrich) König & Compagnie*. The first ship was called the *Friedericus Rex Sueciae* and it sailed to Canton on the dates given in this novel (leaving Gothenburg on 24th February 1732 and arriving home on 26th August 1733). Although Killian, Jessamijn and their families and friends are fictitious, Colin Campbell was the name of the first supercargo. The other supercargos and crew members named in this novel were also real people.

I have tried to portray Colin Campbell as accurately as possible, based on a journal he kept during this trip (see *"A Passage to China – Colin Campbell's diary of the first Swedish East India Company Expedition to Canton, 1732–1733"*, Edited by Paul Hallberg and Christian Koninckx, Royal Society of Arts and Sciences in Gothenburg 1996, ISBN 91-85252-55-7). A Scotsman born in Edinburgh, he was about 45 years old at the time of this venture and had a wealth of experience of the East India trade. He had sailed as a supercargo to Canton before and was therefore asked to help form the Swedish OIC, of which he became one of the first directors. He decided to go along as the first supercargo to show others the way and thanks to him the venture was a success. Other SOIC ships were able to carry on the very profitable trade with China.

During the first few years of the SOIC, a lot of Scotsmen and Englishmen were employed, especially as supercargos, since they had more experience than the Swedes. Gradually this changed. To protect any foreigners who sailed with the Swedish ships, however, everyone was given Swedish nationality (as other countries were not keen on the competition). Campbell became a naturalised Swede at the same time as the first charter of the SOIC was approved in 1731 and was made the first ever Swedish envoy (Minister Plenipotentiary and Envoy) to the Emperor of China. On his return, he was summoned to meet King Fredrik I in person and given a miniature of the king surrounded by diamonds as a gift. Campbell stayed on in Sweden and lived in Gothenburg until his death.

For anyone interested in learning more about the SOIC, the Gothenburg City Museum houses a collection of artefacts and much research material such as journals written by the intrepid SOIC employees. As mentioned in the Acknowledgements, I am greatly indebted to Agneta Hermansson and her staff at the Museum for their assistance in helping me to find the documents I needed and for being so kind and welcoming.

Chapter One

Edinburgh, Scotland
August 1731

'You have the devil's own luck, Kinross, but it can't last. Just one more throw of the dice and you'll see I'm right.'

Killian Kinross stared at the man sitting opposite him and weighed up the risk. On the table between them lay the money he had won so far and it was a fair amount. He was too canny these days to trust the fickle Lady Luck completely though. As usual, he had taken the precaution of slipping some of his coins into his pockets when the others weren't looking, just in case of an emergency.

He glanced at the winnings again. It was very tempting to just pick it all up and leave, but gambling was his only income and he was known as a man who rarely refused to play. For the sake of future earnings, he wanted it to stay that way.

'You've nothing left to play with, McGrath,' he drawled. 'Shouldn't you go home and lick your wounds?'

The other two men sharing the table muttered in agreement, their words slurred from too much wine. McGrath wasn't as far gone and glared back. 'There's still my ship. I'll wager that against your entire night's winnings.'

'That old sieve?' Killian scoffed, even though he'd never actually seen it. 'What would I want with that? Besides, you'll need it yourself now I've cleaned you out. How else will you make a living?'

Although McGrath was an uncouth man who deserved no consideration, Killian didn't want to bankrupt anyone he gambled with. It would be stupid to acquire a reputation for such things, then others might refuse to play with him. That would be nothing short of a disaster.

'If I don't win back what I've already lost, I can't afford to buy a cargo in any case,' McGrath growled. 'So I might as well take the chance.'

Killian studied the man for a while longer, considering his options. He could lose a huge amount of money. On the other hand, if he refused, McGrath might think him a coward and spread rumours to that effect. He made up his mind.

'Very well, if you're hell-bent on destroying yourself, so be it.' He sounded more confident than he felt. The odds really were in McGrath's favour and they both knew it.

McGrath smiled, a wolfish grin that showed Killian just how sure he was of winning this time. 'Excellent, but first, some more wine. You there, girl,' he shouted at a serving wench who was passing by, 'bring some more of that piss you call Burgundy.'

The girl threw him a look of acute dislike, but did as she was told. When she returned, she made a point of standing next to Killian rather than McGrath. She leaned over at just the right angle to give him an eye-full of her assets. Straightening up, she touched him on the arm and said, 'Anything else for you, sir?' Killian shook his head with a smile and watched her sashay away to the next customer.

'You're too damn handsome for your own good.' Rory Grant, his long-time friend and gambling companion, cuffed him jokingly on the shoulder. 'Should leave some ladies for the rest of us.'

'And you shouldn't drink so much, then they might look twice at you too. You're not much use to them in that state,' Killian shot back.

'Rory's right though.' The fourth man at the table, Dougal Forster, nodded in exaggerated fashion. 'With you around, the rest of ush don't get a look-in. Sh'not fair.'

Killian didn't know whether to be amused or exasperated. He was well aware the ladies seemed to like what they saw when they met him. He had always refused to wear a wig and his thick auburn hair, bright blue eyes and even features usually made women stare at him with longing. It was something he'd become used to and he rarely gave it a thought. Besides, Rory and Dougie had their fair share of amorous adventures, even if they couldn't compete with Killian when it came to looks. Tall, blond and easy-going, Rory could charm most ladies if he had a mind to, and although Dougal was shorter, with dark hair and eyes, he was so good-natured it was impossible not to like him. Killian let their comments pass. No doubt they'd have forgotten the conversation by morning in any case.

'Are we playing or not?'

McGrath's petulant voice brought Killian back to the matter in hand. He nodded. 'Do you want to go first?'

'Aye, I do.' The man picked up the little container and rattled it, but stopped abruptly. 'I say we ask for new dice first though. Just to make sure.'

Killian frowned. 'Are you accusing me of cheating?'

'No, no, but I'm not taking any chances. Why, do you refuse me the right to change them?'

'Go ahead, it makes no difference to me. Just takes longer, that's all.' Killian shrugged, but inside he was seething. He had never cheated in his life, and he wasn't about to start now.

After a lengthy delay, new dice were found, and McGrath picked up the container once more. He muttered some incantations for good luck in Gaelic, then shook the dice as hard as he could before rolling them onto the table.

'A four and a six,' Rory commented, as if they couldn't see that for themselves. 'You'll have a hard time beating that, my friend.' He tried to cuff Killian's shoulder again, but missed and almost fell off his chair.

'For heaven's sake, Rory.' Killian took a deep breath, trying not to let on that he felt as rattled as the bones they were playing with. He had already thrown double sixes twice this evening. There was no chance they'd come up again unless a minor miracle happened. He cursed inwardly. *I should have walked away with the spoils while I had the chance and to hell with the consequences!*

But it was too late for regrets.

Scooping up the dice, he put them back in the container and began to shake it in his turn. The sound was familiar, almost soothing, but he knew it was a stupid way of earning a living. Sometimes, like right now, he wished that he had found some other means of supporting himself. He pushed the thought aside and spilled the dice onto the table with a flourish.

'Hell's teeth!' Rory blinked and rubbed his eyes. They were probably smarting as much as Killian's from the unwholesome atmosphere inside the tavern, a mixture of cheap, smoking candles and a fire made up with unseasoned wood that belched grey clouds into the room.

'A six and a five? I don't believe it.' With a roar of rage, McGrath upended the table. Dougie, who'd been on the verge of falling asleep, crashed to the floor and sat there staring around him with an expression of total confusion. Most of the coins ended up on his lap, but he seemed not to notice.

'You just can't have that kind of luck, Kinross, it's impossible!' McGrath bellowed.

'Meaning what?' Killian narrowed his eyes at the man as righteous anger surged through him. He'd had more than enough of McGrath's insinuations. 'Be careful what you say,' he warned. 'I'd never seen those dice before and you know it.'

But McGrath was beyond listening to reason. His face was purple with rage and his throat worked as if he was having trouble making any sounds at all. Instead of replying, he launched himself at Killian, fists flying.

Throughout the taproom there was a mad scramble across stools, tables and benches as everyone realised there was a fight going on. No one wanted to miss such entertainment and a circle quickly formed round the two combatants. The crowd began to egg them on, shouting out advice and abuse in equal measures. Most of the spectators probably didn't know what the fight was about, but they didn't care. The thrill of it was all that mattered.

Killian ignored the onlookers and concentrated on the man in front of him. He side-stepped the first onslaught with ease, feinting left, then right, and lashing out with a quick fist. This wasn't the first time he'd been challenged and he'd learned the hard way how to defend himself.

McGrath charged at Killian several times, but despite the rage that lent the man extra strength, Killian's fast reflexes kept him at bay. Time and again, Killian's punches hit their target, while McGrath's mostly went wide. With a snarl of fury, McGrath finally stepped back and produced a lethal looking dirk from inside his sleeve.

'Now we shall see,' he muttered and with a triumphant smile he tossed the knife from one hand to the other, showing off his skills with the blade. Killian drew in a sharp breath and felt a shiver of unease snaking up his back. Fisticuffs was one thing, a knife fight quite another. He had to end this, and quickly.

When McGrath attacked, Killian danced out of reach of the flashing steel. Before his opponent had time to even blink, he retaliated with a lightning strike, faster than a viper's bite. His knuckles connected with McGrath's left temple, all the strength of his powerful arm and shoulder behind the blow. While the man was temporarily stunned, Killian reached for his wrist with both hands and twisted it until the dirk clattered to the floor.

McGrath tried to fight back, but with his flabby girth and a gut full of wine he was no match for the much younger and fitter man. Killian punched him once more and McGrath fell backwards into the crowd. With a cheer, they pushed him back into Killian's path and Killian grabbed him by the throat with both hands and shoved him up against the nearest wall.

'I never cheat,' he hissed. 'Do you yield?'

McGrath struggled for breath, glaring at Killian with murder in his eyes, but said nothing.

Killian slammed him against the wall once more and tightened his grip on the man's windpipe. 'You changed the dice yourself,' he insisted.

McGrath's only reply was to try and land a few punches to Killian's ribs and back, but without enough air, his efforts lacked the necessary strength to do much damage. He soon ran out of breath, his face turning ever more puce. 'Fine. Let ... me ... go,' he croaked at last. Killian took his hands away, but just to be on the safe side, he pinned McGrath's arms to the wall instead.

'Well?' he prompted.

'I said fine,' McGrath growled. 'The damned ship is yours. Have someone fetch me a piece of paper. And a quill and ink.'

Killian waited a moment longer, staring McGrath straight in the eyes, then judged it safe to let the man go. He nodded at a nearby servant. 'You heard the man. Some writing implements if you please.'

The crowd began to disperse and a few of them congratulated Killian on his successful tactics, clapping him on the back. He only nodded his thanks. The entire episode seemed so unnecessary and he certainly hadn't meant to provide the evening's entertainment.

While McGrath massaged his bruised throat, Killian and Rory righted the table, then bent down to pick up the coins on Dougie's lap and some that had scattered onto the floor. A few had probably been lost as they rolled under the feet of the onlookers, but he didn't care. He just wanted to leave, and fast.

The stench of unwashed bodies, mixed with the acrid smoke from the fire and candles made him gag suddenly. The cheap vinegary wine he'd drunk didn't help either, and he swore this was the last time he spent an evening in a place like this. There had to be more to life.

He waited while McGrath wrote him a note, ceding all rights to his ship. 'I need witnesses to my signature,' the man said, tight-lipped and ungracious, but in control once more. 'Anyone here who can sign their name?' Two men came forward and witnessed the deed, then McGrath thrust it at Killian. 'I hope you get what you deserve one day,' he spat, before storming out, slamming the door behind him.

Killian stared after him for a brief moment, then bent down to pull Dougie off the floor, where he had stayed since sliding off his stool. 'Rory, help me get this fool out of here. I've had enough of this place.'

Rory did his best, but it was mostly Killian who half dragged, half carried his friend out. Relieved to be outside, he drew in huge breaths of the cool night air.

'I need to get away from here,' he said to no one in particular.

Rory hiccoughed, then laughed. 'Well, you can always be a ship's captain now. When do we sail?'

Chapter Two

Gothenburg, Sweden

Jessamijn van Sandt entered the room which had been her father's study and her heart contracted painfully. If she closed her eyes, she could picture him sitting there in his quiet haven, greeting her with that beaming smile he reserved just for her. Sadly, he was gone for ever. In his place sat Robert Fergusson, the stepfather she'd never wanted and cared about even less. A man who, in her opinion, didn't belong there.

The usurper.

'So you're back,' he commented.

Jess only nodded, since he was stating the obvious.

'I trust you've had a nice stay in the country?' His voice was bland, as if she'd gone away for pleasure instead of being banished at his command nearly a year ago.

Jess had to bite back a sharp reply. His mild expression didn't fool her for a moment. Instead it reminded her just how precarious her situation was. Robert had ignored the countless letters she'd sent, begging to be allowed to return, but now he'd relented at last. She had no idea why, but was only too aware he could reverse his decision in the blink of an eye if she put so much as a foot wrong.

'Yes, thank you,' she replied. 'And it was kind of you to send Mrs Forbes to keep me company.'

Robert frowned, as if he wasn't sure whether she was being facetious or not. She looked him straight in the eyes to convince him she was sincere and he relaxed. It was partly true in any case, she thought. His relative Mrs Forbes had been acting as her gaoler and wasn't what anyone would call stimulating company. However, without her the months of incarceration would have seemed even longer.

'She tells me you've been a model of propriety.' Robert steepled his fingers together and looked at her over the top. His dark, deep-set eyes were fixed on her from under shaggy brows, his gaze penetrating in a way Jess found most uncomfortable. 'Make sure you continue to behave here in Gothenburg.'

Jess nodded again. She didn't trust herself to speak in case she gave her true feelings away.

'Just a word of warning. I believe everyone has forgotten all about your ill-advised attachment to young Mr Adelsten last year. Still, it might be wise if you don't seek him out.'

'I have no intention of doing that,' Jess answered, without looking at him this time, since it was precisely what she had planned.

Karl Adelsten's ardent courtship of her had come to an abrupt end on the day he had gone to ask Robert for her hand in marriage. This puzzled her and she wanted to know what had made him change his mind so suddenly. It was obvious it had something to do with Robert. What exactly had he said to the young man? The more she thought about it, the more she suspected Robert had an ulterior motive in wanting her to stay unwed.

She recalled her conversation with him at the time of her banishment. It was etched into her memory, word for word.

'There was a young man here this afternoon, asking to marry you,' Robert had said. 'I sent him away, I'm afraid. Most unsuitable.'

'What do you mean, unsuitable?' Jess had felt her spirits plummet and disappointment made her blurt out, 'That's not true. I *want* to marry Karl. I love him!' Hearing herself saying the words out loud for the first time, Jess was suddenly unsure. She did love him, didn't she? And he had said he loved her.

'Pah, love,' Robert waved his hand dismissively as if such a thing didn't exist. He smiled. 'A youthful fancy, that has nothing to do with the matter. No, marriage is a serious business, as I'm sure you know. In any case, the boy is too poor.'

'Surely not? He's a nobleman.'

'I happen to know that Mr Adelsten's father is in financial difficulties, noble lineage or not. Trust me, there are better fish in the sea.'

'Not here in Gothenburg. In fact, nowhere in the whole of Sweden.' Jess clenched her jaw and suppressed the angry words she wanted to hurl at her stepfather. How could he be so blind? Karl was perfect in every way. His family had been prominent in the area for generations. Why couldn't Robert see the advantages of that?

'Nonsense,' he said. 'Besides, you should be marrying a foreigner like yourself, not a local. It's what your mother would prefer.'

Jess frowned. It was true that her father had been Dutch, but the family moved to Sweden when Jess was just a baby. She had never lived anywhere else and didn't feel like an outsider, even though she spoke both Dutch and English in addition to the native tongue. And Robert himself had been here some ten years now. He'd even taken on Swedish nationality, although she knew that was probably only because it was expedient from a business point of view.

'Mother has never mentioned anything about that to me. I thought she just wanted me to marry well, and Karl is the third suitor you've sent packing in as many years.'

Jess could feel the frustration swirling inside her. She'd been glad when the other two young men were refused, since she had no interest in either of them. But Karl was a different matter. He made her feel desirable, beautiful even, despite knowing herself to be only passably pretty at best. Her white-blonde hair and clear grey eyes didn't draw anyone's attention. Nor did her small stature or a figure which was pleasing but nothing out of the ordinary. And yet Karl had pursued her with a single-minded determination that persuaded her of his sincerity.

He was also practically her last hope. She was nearly twenty and if Robert refused any more suitors on her behalf, she was afraid they would stop asking and she would end up an old spinster.

She decided to try a different tack. 'Surely marrying into a noble Swedish family is better than a Dutch or Scottish merchant's son whether he's rich or not? Think of the connections, the commercial possibilities.'

Robert shook his head. 'I doubt he'd be of much use in that respect. And we wouldn't want to hand over your dowry to just anyone. High-born people like that simply spend money, without any thought for the future. They have no business acumen whatsoever and no idea how to earn money. Ask him. I'm sure he'll tell you he's not interested in such things.'

Jess narrowed her eyes at him, thinking furiously. She sensed there was more to this matter than met the eye. Her father had educated her beyond what was normal for a girl and she was far from stupid. Lately, she had begun to suspect Robert was trying to keep her under his thumb for as long as possible. There was only one reason why he should want to do that – by keeping hold of her share of the business he could use it for his own ends. Was he investing her money in ventures that would never benefit her?

He had no right.

'Isn't that a moot point though?' she dared to ask. 'When I marry, my dowry will consist of most of the business. I know, because Father told me I would inherit everything.

If my future husband has no interest in such things, he can always sell it.'

Robert looked surprised. 'I'm afraid you're mistaken. Your father's will said nothing of the kind. He left everything to your mother and since I'm now her husband, her assets have naturally passed to me. There was an instruction she should pay your future husband a dowry of three thousand silver *daler*. Of course I'll honour your father's wishes in that regard, but I can assure you such a sum isn't large enough to support the kind of lifestyle Mr Adelsten is used to.'

Shocked to the core, Jess stared at Robert in disbelief. She shook her head slowly and tried to assimilate his words. It simply didn't make sense. 'That can't be,' she murmured. 'That's not at all what Father told me. Are you sure you had the right will?'

Robert regarded her calmly. 'There was only one, as far as I know. It was legal, signed by your father and witnessed. Whatever he may have told you, we have to follow his written wishes. They take precedence over any foolish promises made.'

'Could I have a look at the will, please?'

Robert stiffened, obviously not pleased by her persistence. 'That won't be possible. It was retained by the magistrate, after it was proven. I doubt he'd still have it after all this time.'

Jess was far from convinced, but realised she had no proof of any wrong-doing, just a niggling sense of unease. The way she had been banished soon afterwards, despite fighting tooth and nail to be allowed to stay in Gothenburg, only made her even more suspicious. Robert had claimed she was being sent to the country to heal her broken heart, but Jess knew that was just a convenient excuse.

Now, a year later, she still couldn't shake the feeling of having been duped. Her father had said she was to receive everything except a ten percent share already owned by Robert. Although as a woman she couldn't run the business herself, he had taught her enough to be able to oversee whoever she employed.

'I wouldn't want you to be cheated,' he'd said. 'You have to be the one making the decisions.'

They both knew very well that Jess' mother Katrijna would never be able to cope with such a burden. Why then should he suddenly have changed his mind and bequeathed the company to her? It was most unlike him.

No, Robert was up to something and she was determined to find out what that was. For her father's sake as well as her own. She could read between the lines, however, and recognised the threat implied in her stepfather's words. If she didn't do as she was told, she would be punished again.

'Very well, you may go then,' he said. 'I hope you've learned your lesson. Men will declare their love for you one minute, then change their mind the next. It's the way of the world.'

'Oh, yes. I have definitely learned my lesson. I'll guard my heart in future.' *And my thoughts, especially from you.*

She walked out of the study with her head held high and closed the door behind her as quietly as she could. She suppressed the urge to slam it hard instead.

Insufferable man, she thought. Well, she would show him. He might think he had the upper hand, but she wasn't beaten yet.

Chapter Three

Edinburgh, Scotland

What on earth did he want with a ship?

Killian mulled this over as he made his way back to his lodgings, after he'd made sure his friends arrived safely at theirs. A change of scene was necessary, that was for sure, but he knew next to nothing about seafaring or trade. Whenever he had thought about it, he'd imagined something slightly less drastic than captaining a ship. A long visit to London perhaps.

Most people had heard of the fashionable gaming salons to be found in the capital and Killian thought he could do worse than try his luck there. That would mean continuing his present occupation in a different place though. He sighed. It was a shame he hadn't won himself a country estate or something more useful. Most landowners weren't stupid enough to gamble away their property, more was the pity. Perhaps there were Sassenachs who were that gullible?

His footsteps echoed on the cobbled stones of the narrow wynds and closes. It was late and not many people were out, but he kept his wits about him, looking out for cutpurses and pickpockets. It was dark between the houses and he didn't fancy being caught unawares, especially not with his pockets full of silver.

He reached his lodgings, two cramped rooms on the first floor of a building that had seen better days. It was situated in the less salubrious part of Edinburgh, not too far from Holyrood. Although it was a dreary place smelling vaguely of mould and dirt, he managed to ignore that most days. It wasn't the kind of accommodation he would really like, but he was reluctant to move. The elderly landlady had a soft spot for him and had agreed on more than one occasion to wait patiently until he could pay the rent. There were times when he didn't have enough money to eat, let alone pay her, but kind Mrs MacIver never nagged him. She was a rare gem.

Stepping through the door, he tripped over a soft bundle on the floor, which uttered a muffled squeak. Killian swore. 'Adair, what the devil are you doing there?' he growled, while fumbling his way to the table to light a candle.

Adair, a grubby youth with a mane of wildly curling black hair, stood up and rubbed at his ribs. 'Tha's sore,' he muttered, blinking and yawning hugely. His amber eyes, which as yet seemed too big for his small face, sent Killian an accusing glance.

'Well, what on earth made you to go to sleep by the door? You have a perfectly good mattress over there by the fire.' Killian glared at the boy and curbed the desire to throttle him. He wanted to do that at least ten times a day, so it was nothing new.

Adair was a most unsatisfactory servant. He performed only those tasks specifically set him each day and nothing more, but he was loyal in the extreme. He was also very useful when it came to slightly shadier business. Before working for Killian, he had been a pickpocket and a thief. Killian had first come across him in a dirty tavern where he observed him going about his business. He'd been fascinated by the boy's dexterity and skill, and after he finished his gambling for the evening, he'd gone in search of him.

He found him in the courtyard at the back, being beaten to a pulp by the landlord. The boy yelled blue murder, while the man was shouting and swearing.

'I'll no' hae the likes of you in here. Haven't I told ye afore? Robbin' my customers, it's bad fer business. How're they goin' tae pay fer their ale if ye steal their purses? Dirty little thief! I'm goin' tae hand ye over tae the magistrate and then I'll …'

Killian intervened and pulled the large man away from the boy, who by then had a black eye and was bleeding profusely from a cut lip. 'Leave him be, landlord. He's with me. Here, I'll pay you for lost earnings and I guarantee he won't come back. Will that satisfy you?'

The landlord glared at him, his face still suffused with rage, but the sight of the silver coins in Killian's outstretched hand calmed his temper. 'Very well, sir, but I never want tae see him agin, ye hear?'

Killian nodded. 'You have my word.'

As soon as the man had gone, he dragged the little thief back to his rooms. There he cleaned him up and gave him a meal, then sat him down for a talk.

'What's your name, boy?' he asked.

'Adair.'

'Adair what?'

'Dinnae ken, just Adair.'

Killian stared at the youth. It seemed to him a very sad state of affairs that Adair didn't even know his full name. It tugged at a heartstring he hadn't known he possessed. 'I see. You do realise you're going to get caught eventually, don't you?' he said, mildly. 'The punishment for thieving is severe.' He made a slashing gesture across his throat.

The boy nodded and wiped his nose on the sleeve of the clean shirt Killian had given him to wear. It was much too big for him and he looked as though he was drowning in a cloud of white linen. 'I have tae eat. I dinnae ken whit else tae do,' he muttered.

'I understand that, which is why I have a proposition for you. How would you like to work for me? You can be my servant, but mostly I need you to keep your eyes and ears open. In my line of business, it never hurts to know your opponent's strengths and weaknesses.'

'Never bin a servant afore.' Adair sounded doubtful.

'Well, I'm sure you can learn. Are you willing to try?'

The boy nodded. 'I s'pose. And I'd bide here?' He looked around, his eyes resting longingly on the fire that smouldered in the hearth nearby.

'Yes, you can sleep on a mattress on the floor. You'll get food every day and I'll buy you some new clothes and shoes.'

'Aye well, I'll gie it a try.'

That had been the start of an unlikely relationship, but Adair proved extremely useful. He warned Killian away from potential gambling partners when he heard rumours of them being in financial straits. On at least one occasion he also picked the pocket of a man who had fleeced Killian by cheating. He was unable to keep either himself or Killian's rooms clean and tidy. Still, Killian became fond of the youth and he knew Adair hero-worshipped him in return. Although he frequently wanted to beat him to within an inch of his life, he never laid a finger on him. Adair's unusual talents more than compensated for his other shortcomings.

He sighed now. 'Explain yourself.'

'Well, I noticed ye've bin on a winnin' streak lately. There's a fair bit o' money in yer hidey-hole.' Adair nodded towards a corner of the room where Killian usually hid his loot underneath a loose floorboard. 'An' I thought, if I'd noticed, mayhap other people aye had too. Someone might come an' try tae steal yer siller.'

'I see. And you think that sleeping across the threshold would stop them?' Killian asked with an edge of sarcasm in his voice. Adair didn't reply. Instead he produced a razor-sharp knife from the waistband of his breeches. Killian frowned at him. 'Ah, now I understand. Where did you get that?'

'Found it,' Adair said, although he wouldn't meet Killian's eye.

'Adair ...'

'I ken, I ken, ye said tae stop pickin' pockets, but this man was so drunk, he'd not hae kent if I'd taken the coat frae his back. I swear. And there was nae one aboot.'

Killian shook his head. 'Well, thank you for your concern. Perhaps it's time I found another hiding place, especially now I've got this to add to it.' He pulled his winnings from that evening out of his pocket and jingled the leather pouch slightly. Adair whistled.

'Ye *are* on a guid streak, are ye no, sir.'

'It would seem that way.' He grinned and pulled out the note McGrath had written. 'I'm also the proud owner of a ship.'

Adair goggled. 'A wha'?'

'The *Lady Madeleine*, to be precise.' Feeling suddenly restless, Killian was seized by an urge to go and see the ship. 'How would you like a little outing to the harbour?' he asked. 'Come on, let's go for a walk.'

'Now? It's the middle o' the bluidie night.'

Killian stowed the pouch and note under a different floorboard, just in case Adair was right, and turned for the door. 'Now is as good a time as any. I want to see my ship.'

Adair scratched his head, making the black curls look even more tousled than usual. 'If ye say so, sir.'

Killian retrieved his cloak from the chair where he had flung it earlier, and put it back on. Leading the way out into the street, he looked for a conveyance, but because it was so late, there was none to be found.

'Let's walk,' he told Adair. 'It's only a couple of miles to the port at Leith after all, and it's downhill most of the way. The fresh air might clear my head.' Adair grumbled, but followed nonetheless.

It seemed even darker outside than before. Killian ordered the boy to walk slightly behind him so he could warn him of any danger. This had the added bonus of peace and quiet since Adair was unable to chatter in his usual fashion while keeping watch. Killian needed some time to mull things over.

His lungs filled with salt-tinged sea air and his thoughts became more ordered as he strode along. The physical exercise proved a great outlet for the restless energy that had him in its grip. As he came closer to the port, Killian felt his heart beating faster and realised that he was excited at the prospect of seeing his ship. He had never owned anything as substantial in his life. It seemed fate was taking a hand, showing him the direction he ought to go.

What had happened during the evening had triggered something inside him too, a cataclysmic change of view that startled him with its intensity. For several years now, he had supported himself solely by gambling. Against the odds, he'd succeeded fairly well. Tonight, however, he had suddenly and unexpectedly come to the conclusion that he simply couldn't go on like this. He needed a proper income.

'You should marry a rich girl,' Rory said, when Killian mentioned it on the way home. 'It's the only thing to do. M'father told me, solves all problems.'

Killian snorted. 'And where will I find one of those? I haven't noticed them queuing up to wed me.'

By rights, they should have done. As the grandson of Lord Rosyth, he ought to have been welcomed everywhere. Unfortunately, this was not the case. Lord Rosyth was a rich Highland laird who had somehow managed to hold on to his estates during the recent troubles with the English. He had been less successful when it came to keeping the peace with his grandson. Killian and his grandfather clashed, for various reasons, and the old man had let it be known that Killian was to inherit nothing more than the title. He considered him a 'profligate wastrel' and a 'good-for-nothing lazy layabout', among other things. No parent worth his salt would accept him as a suitor for their daughter, certainly no one with an heiress to marry off.

Either way, Killian didn't feel ready for marriage and the last time he looked, all the available heiresses were either old or ugly. ('A desperate lot' was how Rory had described them with a guffaw.) He didn't much fancy being leg-shackled to any of them. No, he was sure he could do better than that on his own.

'My ship.' He savoured the words on his tongue as he walked and decided he quite liked the sound of that. He was the owner of something solid at last, not just a future title that meant little or nothing. He had something to his name other than gambling gains. It felt good.

Once at the port, it took them a while to find the *Lady Madeleine*, but when they finally did, they were both amazed.

'Gor!' Adair squeaked, his voice still at the stage where it shifted regularly between high and low. 'Tha's massive.'

'You're not wrong there.' Killian stared at his acquisition with awe, feeling suddenly very small.

Far from delicate and ladylike as the name suggested, she was huge and bulky, like a floating behemoth: a sea-going vessel with more masts than he could count in the faint moonlight. Killian hadn't realised McGrath owned anything so enormous and he swallowed hard, shocked at the thought that it was now his. No wonder the man had been so angry at losing.

The ship wasn't perfect, by any means. Despite the darkness of the night, he could see that she was in need of repair and there were obvious signs of wear and tear. All the same, a feeling of hope began to build up inside him. This really was his future.

'I thought ye meant a wee boat, like fer sailin' in.' Adair

blinked and gazed up at the tall masts.

Killian grinned at him. 'To tell the truth, so did I, but this is so much better. Absolutely perfect, in fact.'

He debated whether to try and go on board for a quick inspection, but before he had time to decide, he was suddenly grabbed from behind by strong arms.

'Got him,' someone crowed triumphantly.

'What the ...? Let go of me. Adair, run for the watch!'

Killian kicked backwards and bucked at the same time. He succeeded in freeing himself, but there was more than one man and they were coming at him from all sides. Out of the corner of his eye, he saw Adair avoid being captured and make a run for it. He began to fight back, hoping the boy would soon return with help, but he knew it might take a while. He was thankful he had left his hoard of money at home, but wished he'd brought a weapon of some kind. However, as he had proved earlier that evening, he could beat most opponents with his fists given half a chance. He set about trying to do just that.

The odds were against him from the start – he counted five men, hell bent on capturing him. Although he gave a good account of himself, in the end their sheer numbers got the better of him. With one of his eyes rapidly closing, and blood pouring from a cut on one cheek, he continued to fight until they jumped on him as one. They held him down until one of them managed to land a punch to the side of his head.

He still had no idea who they were or what they wanted when the world went black.

Chapter Four

Gothenburg, Sweden

'There you are at last, thank goodness! I could really do with some help, I tell you. These two are such a handful and with the nursemaid sick, I'm at my wit's end.'

Jess stopped just inside the door of her mother's little sitting room, disappointed by such an un-effusive greeting. After all, they hadn't seen each other for nearly a year and Jess had thought she'd been missed. Unlike Robert, Katrijna had replied to her daughter's letters, although mostly with long rambling accounts of her two youngest children, Jess' half-brothers Ramsay and James. Aged four and one respectively, it was only natural they should take up a lot of their mother's time. Even so, Jess had expected Katrijna's help in persuading Robert to let her return, but there had been only vague promises.

Now that she had finally been allowed back to Gothenburg, she had hoped for a much warmer welcome. Her joy at being home again faded a little, but she forced a smile. She knew her mother loved her and told herself Katrijna was just distracted by the younger children. Jess was here at last, which was all that mattered for the moment.

'It's lovely to see you, *Moeder*,' she said, speaking Dutch the way they always did when they were alone together. She couldn't help but notice that Katrijna seemed tired and drawn. The corn-coloured hair, usually so neat and tidy, had been twisted into a messy bun on top of her head, with tendrils escaping to hang round the pale cheeks. It seemed to Jess that her mother had aged considerably since she'd last seen her, with new lines furrowing her brow. Jess went over to embrace her. It was slightly awkward, since Katrijna was holding little James in her arms and he had to be included, but that didn't matter. 'I've missed you,' she murmured.

'We missed you too, dear,' Katrijna replied and returned the hug with one arm. Most of her concentration seemed to be focused on James, who was whining non-stop. His cheeks were flushed and his lower lip stuck out as if he was on the verge of proper crying. Jess could understand having to listen to that all day would be very trying, but surely her mother had other servants who could be put in charge of him?

'Ramsay, greet your sister,' her mother nudged the other little boy forward, but he hung back, hiding his face in her skirts.

'Perhaps he doesn't remember me,' Jess said. 'He was only three when I left after all.'

'Nonsense, of course he does. He's been talking about you all morning. He's just a bit shy, that's all.'

Jess wasn't convinced, but didn't comment. A year was a long time to someone Ramsay's age, but she knew he would soon warm to her when he became used to her being back. They had always got on well before, she just needed to give him time to get to know her again.

'Is James ill?' she asked instead, changing the subject.

'No, I think he's just teething. He won't settle though, it's driving me insane. Didn't sleep a wink last night.'

'Here, let me take him for a while.' Jess held out her arms and Katrijna handed James over with a sigh of relief. She bent to deal with Ramsay, who was still clinging to her skirt and repeating 'Mama' over and over again in a never-ending bid for attention.

'Yes, darling, what is it?' Ramsay whispered something in her ear. 'No, not now, dearest, perhaps a bit later. Now do stop bothering me. You two are enough to try the patience of a saint.'

Jess wasn't really listening. Instead she gazed at the small boy in her arms who was squirming and whining even louder now. He held his arms out towards his mother. 'Shh, little one,' Jess crooned, hugging his little body close. He was as soft and light as thistledown. 'Mama will take you in a moment. She needs a rest. Let's look out of the window, shall we?'

She tried to pat his back in soothing motions to stop his fretting, but he refused to be comforted. Jess looked at his screwed up face, wondering why she didn't hate him. She ought to at least dislike him, since he was a reminder of her unofficial status as the cuckoo in the nest. He was so small and helpless though, her heart ached with the need to love and protect him.

'Is he eating well, Mama?' she asked, worried by the thinness of little James's arms and legs. They were like the sticks of a bird's nest, bony and pale. His older brother, who was now sturdy and tall for his age, had been a big, fat toddler. Nothing like this scrawny scrap of humanity.

'Yes, he's normally as greedy as Ramsay was,' Katrijna said, 'but nothing pleases him at the moment.' She sighed and sat down on a rocking-chair, leaning back onto the fat cushions. As James continued to whine and fidget, she held out her arms for the child, an expression of resignation and weariness on her face. 'Oh, you'd better give him back. He wants no one but me at the moment. So tiresome, but what can I do? You were the same at that age.' Jess bent to put James on her mother's lap.

'What about you, Ramsay, would you like to come with me?' She glanced at her other brother, who was still standing next to his mother. He held onto Katrijna's gown as if he wasn't going to let her go long enough to pay attention to his brother. He was clearly jealous and Jess wasn't surprised when he shook his head.

'Don't be silly, Ramsay, go with your sister now.' Ignoring his pleading look, Katrijna pushed him in Jess' direction without really noticing him. The little boy's face fell. His mother's concentration was all for James as the baby's whining became louder by the minute. Katrijna looked up briefly at Jess and said 'Thank you', then added as if she had finally realised that Jess had only just returned, 'It *is* good to have you back.'

Yes, but is it only because you need another pair of helping hands and not a beloved daughter to keep you company, Jess wondered, feeling unwanted despite her mother's words.

Disappointment churned inside her, but she took Ramsay's hand and pulled him towards her for a quick hug. She couldn't bear to see the hurt in his dark eyes, which must mirror her own. He was so like his father with those eyes and his thick, brown hair, but he had an air of vulnerability that she couldn't imagine Robert had ever suffered. 'Shall we go to my room for a while?' she whispered. 'It may be I have a little surprise for you.'

Ramsay's face brightened. 'A present?' Jess smiled and nodded. 'Oh, what is it, what is it?'

'I'm not telling. You'll just have to come and see, won't you?'

But as she towed him away, he dragged his steps and looked back over his shoulder. 'Is Mama coming?'

'Not right now, but don't worry, you'll soon be back with her,' Jess told him. 'And when James has gone to sleep, she'll have more time to talk to you.'

Despite the reassuring words, however, she doubted she was right. Like her, he had been usurped and although they both still had their mother's affection, Katrijna only had time for her youngest. It made Jess furious on Ramsay's behalf. Unlike her, he wasn't mature enough to accept that Katrijna had a new chick to worry about.

If I ever have children, I swear I'll love them all equally, she thought savagely. Even if one child was being difficult, it must be possible to spare some time for the other.

She closed the door behind her with a distinct snap, then tried to calm down. At least she wasn't in the back of beyond any longer. For what it was worth, she was home.

When Killian woke up the first time, he heard waves lapping against a hull and somewhere nearby a seagull's harsh cry rang out. He guessed he must be on a boat, but his fuzzy brain couldn't work out why. It was too dark to see anything, so he gave up thinking about it and drifted back into oblivion.

The second time he came to, he was rattling along in some sort of conveyance. He blinked and tried to avoid the light spilling through a chink in the door. Pain knifed through his head whenever he looked at the brightness of the sun outside. It had to be at least midday, if not later, so he must have been unconscious for some time. His stomach growled as if agreeing with this and he realised he was starving.

Where was he? And more importantly, where was he going?

He was lying on the floor of an ancient carriage, its faded red leather seats moth-eaten and smelling none too fresh. It seemed to possess no springs whatsoever and as the vehicle bumped over a rut in the road, his head bounced against the floor and he winced. Thankfully his hands were bound in front of him, so he was able to put them up to protect his aching skull. He cursed under his breath.

'They'll pay for this,' he muttered. 'Whoever they are.'

He tried to think who could have done this to him, but no one in particular sprang to mind. There were no outstanding gambling debts, no one he had offended or who thought himself cheated. Except McGrath, of course. Was this his doing?

As the pounding inside his head increased with every stone the carriage encountered, he decided to give up thinking about it for now. He needed to rest so that he would have his wits about him when they reached their destination. He closed his eyes and curled up as best he could.

He was asleep within seconds.

Some time later, he woke to find himself being blindfolded, and then yanked into a standing position. Rough hands pushed him along stone paving, up some steps and then into a dwelling. He could tell they were in a grand house of some sort, since their footsteps on the creaking floorboards echoed in what sounded like a cavernous room. He breathed in the musty smell that was vaguely familiar, as if he had been here before, but in his slightly befuddled state he couldn't place it. There was still a dull thumping inside his skull and his legs were unsteady. He felt nowhere near as bad as before though and was able to grit his teeth against the discomfort.

'Where am I?' he asked. 'What do you want?'

'You'll find out soon enough,' came the reply and this was the only answer he received before he was forced to stumble on. His captors took him through several rooms, judging by the number of times he bumped into door frames along the way, and finally pushed him into a chair.

'Stay there,' the voice ordered, as if Killian had a choice in the matter. He supposed he could have tried to explore his surroundings by feeling his way round the room like a blind man, but he didn't think he'd get very far. And someone was bound to be standing guard outside. Far better to conserve his strength for whatever was coming.

Footsteps echoed in a seemingly large room, and a door slammed shut, leaving him in silence for a moment. In the distance, he could hear raised voices, but he couldn't make out what was said. He ground his teeth in frustration.

Ages later, the door was thrown open and someone approached his chair from behind. He braced himself for a blow, but instead he felt fingers tugging at the blindfold. It was torn off with an angry growl. He opened his eyes and stared into the furious red-tinged face of his grandfather.

'What in blazes ...?' Killian blinked and anger welled up inside him. He stared at the old man who stood before him, looking for all the world as if it was Killian who had done something wrong. He had no idea why and didn't particularly care. 'If you'd like me to visit, you have only to ask, you know,' he pointed out, his voice dripping sarcasm while he seethed with fury. How dare his grandfather have him kidnapped in this way rather than command his presence in his usual fashion? They may be at odds, but Killian wouldn't have refused a meeting if the request was reasonably polite.

Kenelm, Lord Rosyth, was a formidable sight. Still very upright despite his age, with a shock of white hair over steely grey eyes and darker brows, he had an air of command few quarrelled with. Like his grandson, he couldn't be bothered with wigs unless it was absolutely necessary, and he certainly didn't need one. His nose jutted out proudly and there was a determined set to his thin mouth. Most people thought twice before crossing him, but right now Killian couldn't care less.

Lord Rosyth didn't reply straight away, but bent to untie the knot on the rope that bound Killian's hands. Having nearly reached the venerable age of seventy-five, it took the old man a while. His fingers, as gnarled as ancient tree branches, were clumsy when faced with such a delicate task, and this seemed to annoy him as he 'tsked' several times. 'As if I'd want to see you,' he muttered after he had finally succeeded. 'Good for nothing son of an Irish whore.'

'Can we leave my mother out of this please?' Killian's request was politely phrased, but carried an overtone of menace that only a fool could have missed. He knew his grandfather's views about his mother. The old man may have cause to dislike his daughter-in-law, but Killian was sure Lord Rosyth had somehow engineered her downfall. It had been a bone of contention between them for a number of years now. He rubbed his sore wrists with jerky movements.

'Couldn't even give you a decent Scottish name,' the old man continued, as if he hadn't heard his grandson.

'For the love of God, tell me why I'm here so I can leave as soon as possible,' Killian demanded, not bothering to hide his anger now. 'I don't have to stay to be insulted.'

Lord Rosyth went to sit down in a chair at the opposite end of the long table at which Killian had been seated. He stared down the endless, polished length of it with a grim expression. 'Oh, I'll tell you all right, and when I'm finished, I want you out of my sight. You've really done it this time.'

'Done what? I wish someone would just explain what this is all about,' Killian complained, exasperated beyond belief. His head had started to pound again, a steady rhythm of painful blows against his brain. That didn't exactly help his thought processes. 'Has cousin Farquhar been carrying tales again?'

His saintly cousin, with his pure Scottish blood and fawning ways, was all Lord Rosyth appeared to want in a grandson. He had caused most of Killian's problems, or so it seemed to him. Farquhar was forever poisoning the old man against him and had succeeded all too well so far.

'This has nothing to do with Farquhar. Out there in the hall, I have half of clan Cameron baying for your blood. They tell me you've ravished young Iona, Ruaridh's daughter, and left her with child. They want me to make sure you marry her as soon as possible. In fact, they were all for dragging you straight to the altar, but I got wind of their plans and persuaded them to bring you here first. They'll be fetching

Iona later today so you can marry her in Rosyth kirk.'

'The hell I will!'

At last, this entire charade was beginning to make sense and Killian breathed a sigh of relief. It had nothing to do with McGrath or any of his other gambling partners, thank the Lord. A girl he could handle, this one in particular.

'And why not?' his grandfather asked in icy tones. 'Are you so far gone in debauchery that you can't do the decent thing by an innocent girl when you get her into trouble? I should have known this was going to happen. Actually, I'm surprised it hasn't done so before, given your reputation with the ladies.'

Killian took a deep breath and counted to ten. If the old man had been anyone other than his grandfather, he would have been lying on the floor by now with a broken nose.

'For your information,' he hissed, 'Iona Cameron is far from innocent and wouldn't need to be ravished. I doubt very much that I'm the father of any bairn she's carrying.'

'Then who is?'

'I'd put my money on young Hamilton, who's been hanging around her since June, but it could be any number of other men from what I hear.'

'That's a scandalous slur.'

Killian shrugged. 'I'm not marrying her and that's final. Unless, of course, you really want someone else's bastard to inherit the title?'

His grandfather glared at him. 'Why should I believe you? I hear rumours that you've bedded everything in a skirt. Ruaridh Cameron is my best friend, he'd not lie to me.'

'And I would?' Killian shook his head. 'No, don't answer that. I know you prefer to think the worst of me, but this time at least, you're wrong.'

Lord Rosyth snorted. 'I doubt it.'

Killian held on to his temper by a thread. 'I think you'll

find that even the young lady herself will admit I only slept with her once.'

'That's not what she says.'

'Well, it's the truth. It was last year and I certainly wasn't either the first or the last. I'd bet she wants to be Lady Rosyth, rather than plain Mrs Hamilton. She has her father twisted round her little finger, everyone knows that. He'll believe anything she says.'

The old man was silent while he considered what Killian had said, then he appeared to make up his mind. 'Very well, for once your words ring true and we've certainly had enough whores in this family.' He ignored the threatening noise Killian made. 'I can't allow someone who may not be a Kinross to inherit. I'll have to tell those fools out there you hit me over the head and then escaped somehow. Also that they might do well to have a word with young Hamilton.'

'Oh, wonderful. Now I'm the kind of man who batters his grandfather as well,' Killian muttered. 'Will that be all then?'

'No. I've decided you'd best disappear for a while, make yourself scarce as it were, just in case.'

'*You*'ve decided?' Killian asked, but sarcasm was wasted on the old man.

'Aye, I have. If you wait a moment, I'll prepare a letter for you to take to a distant cousin of mine in Sweden. Robert Fergusson lives in the town of Gothenburg on the west coast, where he's a successful merchant. I'll ask him to take you in for a few months. You'll probably have to make yourself useful in return. Might even learn a thing or two, although no doubt the locals gamble as much as the next man.'

'Sweden? You must be joking.'

'No one will think to look for you there.'

'Well, as a matter of fact, I had plans to go elsewhere.'

'You'll do as I say or I won't give you the wherewithal to

go anywhere.'

Killian stared at the old man in disbelief. His grandfather offering to give him money wasn't something that happened every day. In fact, he'd not received so much as a penny in three years. 'You're giving me something? Of your own free will?'

'Don't be impertinent or I'll change my mind.' Lord Rosyth pulled a pouch out of his pocket and slammed it onto the table, then went to a cupboard and came back with a piece of paper and writing materials. Killian waited in silence while his grandfather scratched out a lengthy missive, wondering at this new turn of events. The old man must want him out of the way badly, or he'd never consider going to all this trouble.

'Are you indebted to Ruaridh Cameron?' he wondered out loud.

'I don't owe anyone anything,' his grandfather spat. 'I told you, Ruaridh is my best friend. He'd likely counted on our friendship to net his daughter a noble husband, even if he is aware of her lies. Though where he got the idea that you fitted into the category of "noble", is beyond me.'

Killian sighed and closed his eyes. He wished things could be different between them, but the old man had been prejudiced against him from birth. Nothing he ever did could change that and the frustration and unfairness of it ate away at him constantly, like a maggot gnawing a rotten apple.

He knew Lord Rosyth had doted on his older half-brothers Brice and Blake, particularly the former. They had been the product of his father's first marriage to a Scotswoman, and his lordship had been very sad when the lady in question died giving birth to Blake. After mourning her for two years, Killian's father Fraser had gone off to fight the English in Ireland, on behalf of James III. He was wounded at the battle of the Boyne and taken in by a kind, but poor Irish nobleman, whose daughter Niamh he promptly fell in love with.

He married her as soon as he recovered. Lord Rosyth hadn't been pleased to be presented with a new daughter-in-law who was not only penniless, but Irish as well. The lovely Niamh had nothing but her beauty to recommend her, and Lord Rosyth never forgave her. That she eventually produced a healthy grandson, after numerous miscarriages, did nothing to endear her to him.

When Killian's half-brothers both died ten years later at the battle of Sheriffmuir, together with their father, again for the Jacobite cause, it was as if the old man blamed Niamh and her child. He made their lives unbearable with his constant criticism of Niamh's mothering skills and Killian's behaviour, as well as a whole host of other things.

It was no wonder Niamh couldn't stand it in the end. But Killian had been left to suffer on his own and ... *No, I won't think about that.* He clenched his fists and turned his thoughts back to the present.

'Here,' Lord Rosyth said curtly, holding out the sealed letter and pouch. 'Now get out of my sight and stay away for at least six months. By that time, young Iona will have had to find another man to wed if she doesn't want to bear a bastard. It should be safe for you to return by April.'

'Don't worry, I have no intention of returning at all. You've made it clear I'm not wanted here, so I'll make my own life elsewhere. I hope Farquhar never shows you his true colours, or you might actually have to admit you've been wrong about me all along. God forbid! Goodbye.'

Killian shoved the heavy pouch into his pocket and picked up the letter, then strode over to the panelling next to the huge fireplace that sat in the middle of one wall. Pushing his finger into a small hole invisible to anyone who didn't know its exact location, he opened a secret door and slipped into the draughty passage beyond. He looked at his grandfather one last time and saw the surprise on the old man's face. Lord Rosyth had probably thought he was the only person who knew about the secrets of the house, but Killian had been an inquisitive child who kept his eyes and ears open.

I hope that gives him something to think about, he thought with satisfaction. *With a bit of luck, he'll wonder what else I know, and that might keep him awake at night. Good! Let him suffer for a change, sanctimonious old curmudgeon ...*

He closed the door behind him with a soft click and set off towards his new future with quiet optimism.

At least he wouldn't be lacking in funds.

Chapter Five

Rosyth House, Scotland

Farquhar Kinross was not in a good mood, and if there was one thing he really hated, it was waiting patiently. This, however, was exactly what he was forced to do on this occasion. Sitting still was out of the question since his nerves were as taut as fiddle strings. He therefore paced back and forth across the private sitting room he shared with his wife and children in the north tower of Rosyth House.

Having set up the kidnapping of his cousin Killian and the false charges against him, he couldn't be seen to have anything to do with the matter now. He had to trust that all his hard work would have the desired effect – the utter ruin of Killian. For years he'd been waging a smear campaign against his cousin, but still his grandfather refused to disinherit Killian completely. This wasn't something Farquhar could tolerate.

He was the rightful heir.

Killian was nothing but a half-Irish bastard, an outsider who didn't belong in the Highlands. The estate and the title ought to be in the hands of a true Scotsman. A man like himself. Only he would make a fitting laird.

'Is something the matter?' Ailsa, his wife, had been sending him apprehensive glances as he paced in front of her, and she couldn't keep quiet any longer. She was as twitchy as a mouse, and had a tendency to blurt things out in a cringing manner. He found this supremely irritating, but gritted his teeth in order to stop himself from striking her. It would only give him temporary satisfaction and it usually made matters worse in the long run as he couldn't stand her endless crying. Besides, their two young daughters Flora and Kirsty were watching from under lowered lashes. He preferred not to hit their mother in front of them.

'Nothing that concerns you,' he snapped and strode across the room once more. He knew he was being unkind, but he couldn't seem to help himself. Ailsa brought out the worst in him and he wondered what he'd ever seen in her. True, she'd been pretty once, but her ash-blonde hair had faded to a mousy colour and her eyes, once sparkling and bright, were now forever fixed on him with an anxiety that drove him mad. He sighed inwardly. The useless woman couldn't even give him a son, although thankfully she was expecting again, so there was still hope.

What was happening downstairs? Why was it taking so long?

He decided he'd had enough of waiting and there was no harm in going down on the pretext of looking for something. Without so much as a glance at his family, he left the room and made his way towards the main hall.

As he rounded a bend in the stairs, he heard the sound of voices raised in anger. These were interspersed with the firm, but calmer tones of his grandfather. Curious, he crept further down, but the words he caught were not quite what he'd hoped for.

'What do you mean, he escaped? How could he have escaped? There is but the one door, isn't there?' That was one of the Camerons speaking; Farquhar recognised the voice.

'How should I know? I told you, he hit me over the head, the ingrate, and got out somehow. Probably through the window, he was always a resourceful lad,' he heard his grandfather reply.

Farquhar gritted his teeth and decided it was safe for him to continue downstairs. He swore under his breath, not wanting to believe what he was hearing. Killian had escaped? It simply couldn't be true. Grandfather should have allowed the Camerons to beat Killian to a pulp by now, before marrying him off to a young lady as penniless and ill-bred as himself.

'Grandfather, what is happening here?' He smiled urbanely, trying to look as if he found large groups of angry men in the castle's main hall every day and thought nothing of it.

'Your cousin has got our Iona with child and we came to see he did the decent thing and married her,' one of the Cameron clansmen informed Farquhar, 'but he's escaped somehow.'

'Really? How very unfortunate. He shouldn't be too hard to find though.' Farquhar tried to appear unconcerned, when in fact he wanted to scream at the dolts to run after his cousin without wasting another minute. What in the name of all that was holy were they waiting for?

'He's long gone, no point pursuing him,' Lord Rosyth stated firmly. 'And as I was just saying to these gentlemen, I have my doubts about young Iona's claim. I saw her earlier in the year, shamelessly flirting with all and sundry. It wouldn't surprise me to find that she'd been the one to throw herself at Killian. What girl wouldn't?'

Farquhar clenched his fists behind his back. He knew his grandfather was right. Killian had the kind of looks that drew the eye, no matter what he did, with those startlingly blue eyes and irritatingly handsome face. His mother possessed the same allure, which was no doubt why his fool of an uncle had fallen for her. Killian also exuded the sort of latent power that ensnared women without him even trying. It had always infuriated Farquhar, who was himself plain and sturdy, with a mop of uninteresting ruddy hair that attracted no one. He was also shorter than Killian by several inches, something he'd always resented.

'You can't dismiss this claim out of hand, Grandfather,' he said, striving for an even tone. 'Just because the girl fancied herself in love with him, that's not to say Killian didn't take advantage of her.'

'No, but I've heard rumours of her being seen with young Hamilton lately. Although he's well connected, he has no prospects. Perhaps she thought she would prefer to be Lady Rosyth, rather than plain Mrs Hamilton?'

'That's a slanderous suggestion,' one of the Camerons muttered and the others murmured angry assent.

'I know it's plain speaking, and I apologise if I'm wrong, but it might be prudent for you to have a word with Hamilton first, before going after my grandson. I shall pay a visit to Iona's father myself to discuss the matter. I've no wish to fall out with my oldest friend. In the meantime I would suggest you find the young lady's other *beau* and question him carefully. Killian may be a scoundrel, but I very much doubt he'd lie to me and he swore he wasn't responsible for Iona's condition.'

'Surely you didn't believe him, Grandfather?' Farquhar said, taken aback by his grandfather's defence of Killian. 'You know he's a liar *extraordinaire*.'

Lord Rosyth sent him a glance he couldn't quite understand and which made him feel more than a little uncomfortable. 'As a matter of fact, I did believe him for once. Do you doubt my ability to tell truth from falsehood, Farquhar?'

'No, no of course not, I just wondered ...'

'Well, don't.'

Farquhar refrained from answering back although it went against the grain.

There was a lot of muttering amongst the Cameron men, but at last they appeared to come to an agreement. 'Very well,' the spokesperson said, 'we'll go have a wee word with Hamilton, but if you set eyes on that grandson of yours again, don't let him escape a second time.'

'I didn't *let* him escape,' Lord Rosyth said, his patience obviously wearing thin, 'he hit me over the head. I'm an old man, what chance did I stand? But naturally, I'll have him watched, should I set eyes on him again. I give you my word.'

When the Camerons had trooped off, Farquhar blurted out, 'You don't expect to see Killian for some time, do you?' It wasn't really a question, but his grandfather replied nonetheless.

'No. I've sent him away.'

'Why? Shouldn't you have made him stay to face up to his crimes?'

Lord Rosyth sent Farquhar another quizzical look, his grey eyes boring into his grandson's. 'Are you so sure he was responsible, then? I told you, I don't believe he is.'

'But it's as plain as a pikestaff. He's forever seducing young women, why not Iona? I've told you before of the rumours circulating about him. You must have heard them yourself?'

'To be sure, I know he has a reputation with the ladies, but I was given to understand he normally sticks to more, shall we say, mature females. Not young virgins, which incidentally I don't believe Iona to have been. He may be reckless, but he's not stupid.'

'I thought you disapproved of Killian's way of life.' Farquhar couldn't believe his grandfather was suddenly condoning his cousin's behaviour. It was the outside of enough, after all his efforts to foster enmity between the two men.

Lord Rosyth turned thoughtful. 'Well, it's been a few years since I've seen him, and I have to admit I found him changed.'

'Changed? How can you say that? He's as debauched as ever. No, worse, in fact.' Farquhar felt as if he was grasping at straws and all his schemes were rapidly slipping out of his hands.

'Perhaps,' Lord Rosyth conceded, 'but although he's as insolent and full of himself as before, I detected a subtle difference. He looked wary, as though he didn't trust anyone. There was a sharp edge to his voice, showing steely resolve perhaps, although why, I'm sure I don't know.'

'It's what you need as a hardened gambler.'

'Yes, yes, I know.' Lord Rosyth sighed and suddenly looked his age. 'Maybe I shouldn't have been so hard on him though. I can't in all conscience blame him for being alive when his brothers are not and a man doesn't choose who gives birth to him.'

'Brice was a good man, and so was Blake. A completely different sort altogether,' Farquhar lied. He hadn't liked Killian's older brothers any more than he liked Killian himself, but at least they'd had the sense to get themselves killed while fighting for the Jacobites in the '15. And the old man's love for his oldest grandson, the oh-so-perfect Brice, had worked to Farquhar's advantage. His death had made Lord Rosyth resent Killian all the more. Was he changing his tune now? Farquhar couldn't allow that to happen. Being the only other surviving grandson, he had always tried his best to fill the void left by Brice and Blake, doing everything his grandfather asked of him and more. Compared to Killian, he'd been a veritable saint, at least outwardly.

'Yes, he was – brave, fearless, strong and loyal – they both were, but they're gone, never to return, killed by the damned Sassenachs.' The old man sighed again. 'Perhaps because of them I haven't given Killian the benefit of the doubt? He never bothered to deny the accusations after all, but I'm beginning to wonder if all these stories about him can really be true.'

'Believe me, they are.'

Lord Rosyth sent him yet another appraising look which made Farquhar want to squirm like a worm on a hook. He quashed the impulse and nodded for emphasis. 'I hear tales about him I would blush to tell you.'

'Hmm, well be that as it may, I think it's time I made my own enquiries rather than rely on hearsay.'

'What, you're going to Edinburgh?' Farquhar was stunned.

'Yes, I believe I shall.'

'But, your health ... Surely that isn't wise?' Lord Rosyth never ventured that far normally. Travelling was an ordeal for him and he considered the capital a den of iniquity, not to mention a disgustingly dirty place. 'Auld Reekie' was just that – full of smoke and as filthy as any chimney, overcrowded and malodorous. There was no doubt the city deserved its nickname. This had been a godsend to Farquhar, who could pick and choose which tales to tell and which to suppress. 'Really, Grandfather, this isn't necessary. You have loyal servants who can be trusted to use their eyes and ears on your behalf.'

'No, I want to see for myself. I shall pay a visit to my friends, they'll not lie to me. You're welcome to accompany me if you wish?'

'Of course I'll come, if you're dead set on going, but I still think ...'

Lord Rosyth held up a hand. 'Enough, lad. When I want your advice, I'll ask for it. Now kindly order the servants to make everything ready for the journey.'

'Very well, if that's what you want.' Farquhar made himself smile as if the proposed trip was something he was looking forward to already. In truth, nothing would stop him from going. He had to make sure Lord Rosyth didn't accidentally hear anything bad about himself. He shivered. Now that really would be a disaster, although after today, he didn't know how matters could possibly get any worse.

His plan had failed and now there was only one course open to him – Killian, damn him, had to be eliminated altogether, and soon.

Chapter Six

Gothenburg, Sweden

Jess soon settled into life in Gothenburg once more and in some ways it felt as if she'd never been away. There were subtle differences, however, and the most obvious one was that Robert ruled the household with an even firmer hand than ever before. Katrijna had never been a strong-minded woman, but now she deferred to her husband in all things. It was as though she had no will of her own at all, and Jess began to see why her mother hadn't been able to do anything about her daughter's banishment.

Although Jess knew a woman's duty was to be subservient, she had always thought that in a marriage there would be some give and take. That wasn't the case here and she found the situation unbearable, while her mother seemed not to mind or even notice.

Robert had been her father's junior business associate and had proved himself a pillar of strength when Aaron died. He'd taken on the burden of running the family's merchant company, as well as sorting out all the legal and practical details. Jess was grateful to him for that. The fact that he had also made himself indispensable to her mother had been an unexpected and unwelcome surprise. Their marriage, only six months after Aaron's death, seemed nothing short of sacrilege to his grieving daughter.

It wasn't unusual for a widow to remarry though, and even Jess had to admit Katrijna wasn't the type of woman who could cope without a man to take care of her. Her mother was also ecstatically happy with her new husband, which made Jess swallow any protests, but secretly she felt it was all wrong.

He has no right to be here.

Jess tried to stop herself from thinking such thoughts. She knew they were probably just born of her resentment that Robert had so easily insinuated himself into their lives. The truth was she couldn't fault his behaviour in any way. She also knew his efficiency and orderliness ought to be praised, not criticised.

Her suspicious mind had other ideas. It refused to let her rest and what she needed was some kind of proof of wrong-doing. *If only I could find a way of showing that Robert's been using money which is legally mine*, she thought, *then I might be able to take my claim to the magistrate.* It was her only hope, unless she could find someone to marry her, which seemed unlikely.

Her lack of marriage prospects was confirmed beyond doubt the very first time she went out with Mrs Forbes. As luck would have it, in the market square she ran into Karl Adelsten, the man she wanted to speak to. She had wandered a little way off from her chaperone, who was busy trying to haggle over a purchase. Swerving to avoid someone, she almost walked into Karl instead. She gasped and he stopped dead and stared at her, clearly flustered.

'M-Miss van Sandt,' he stammered. 'I, er, didn't expect, ... that is to say, a pleasure to meet you as always.' He bowed and Jess curtseyed, while studying him carefully. He was dressed in dark blue, with ostentatiously large silver buttons adorning both his coat and waistcoat. There was nothing in his demeanour to suggest he'd been pining for her. On the contrary, he had the air of a man who had everything he could wish for in life. It seemed inappropriate to raise the subject of their failed engagement, but Jess felt she had no choice. As time was important, she decided to come straight to the point.

'It's nice to see you too, although I had rather hoped to hear from you before now. What did my stepfather say to put you off marrying me?'

Karl, who was a handsome blond giant, flushed to the roots of his hair. 'Really, Miss van Sandt, I don't think we ought to discuss such matters here.' He looked around, as if he expected everyone to be watching their every move. Fortunately, no one was paying them any attention and Mrs Forbes was still occupied.

'I'm sorry, but I have no option, Mr Adelsten.' Jess gritted her teeth. 'I was under the impression you were very keen to marry me last year. Yet your proposal came to nothing once you had spoken to my stepfather. As there couldn't have been any reason for him to reject such an exalted man as yourself, I can only assume he told you something about me which put you off. I need to know what that was.'

'This is plain speaking indeed.' Karl tugged at his neckcloth as if it was too tight for him. 'The thing is, uhm, well, you see, my father wished me to wed someone else. I'm now married to Elsa Leijonberg. I'm sorry if you thought there was more to our little flirtation than I meant.'

Jess threw him a scornful glance. *Little flirtation, was it?* Less than a year ago, Karl had proclaimed his undying love and couldn't take his eyes off her whenever they met. When she was packed off to Askeberga Manor, he had never so much as tried to contact her though, at least not to her knowledge. *Some grand passion that turned out to be,* she thought.

She looked the fickle man up and down, noticing for the first time that despite his good looks he had a rather weak chin and a tendency to plumpness round the middle. The sight of him no longer made her go weak at the knees. Perhaps Robert had actually done her a favour, but it still annoyed her that her stepfather had the power to ruin her life.

'Mr Adelsten, I'm neither stupid nor blind and I would appreciate it if you'd have the courtesy to tell me the truth. I know my stepfather influenced your decision. I only want to know what he said so that I can prevent it happening again, if someone else should want to marry me. It's a reasonable request, don't you think?'

Karl now desperately scanned his surroundings as if searching for a way out, but when he couldn't find one, he mumbled, 'Oh, very well, I may as well tell you. He said that although your father wished you to have a dowry, the business was in deep trouble when he died and Mr Fergusson was still trying to put it back on an even keel. Therefore he couldn't see his way clear to paying more than a very small amount, although he did say he might be in a position to remedy this some time in the future. In short, you have no dowry to speak of at the moment and, uhm, my father would never have agreed to a match on such terms.'

'What, none at all?'

'Well, a paltry sum. A few hundred *daler* ...'

'A few hundred?' Robert had told her three thousand, if she remembered correctly. Jess took several deep breaths as anger threatened to choke her. She knew none of this was Karl's fault and she had pushed him far enough as it was.

'Thank you,' she said curtly. 'I bid you good day then, and wish you and your wife all the best for the future.'

She turned away just as Mrs Forbes came striding over with an angry expression on her face. 'What do you think you're doing, talking to that man?' she hissed. 'My cousin told me that he specifically asked you not to.' Mrs Forbes was small in stature, but she made up for it with a very forceful manner. Her eyes, deep-set like those of her cousin Robert, although hazel rather than brown, were now flashing with suppressed fury and Jess hurried to defend herself.

'I'm sorry, Mrs Forbes, I couldn't avoid greeting him as a former acquaintance. It would have seemed odd otherwise. Mr Adelsten just stopped briefly to tell me about his marriage to Miss Leijongren. I wished him happy and that was all.'

Mrs Forbes threw her a suspicious look, her small mouth tightening in disapproval, and steered her charge away with a rough hand under the elbow. 'You're not to speak to him ever again, do I make myself understood?' she said in a savage undertone, while smiling a greeting across the street to a lady of their acquaintance. 'Robert would have my head.'

'Believe me, I wouldn't want to,' Jess replied with feeling.

'You're going where?' Rory stared at Killian with eyes that could barely focus, having been woken by his friend only a few moments previously.

'To Sweden.'

'In the far north? Where it's always dark?' Rory rubbed at his eyes and blinked.

'Of course it's not always dark, you imbecile. And Sweden's not much further north than we are, as far as I can tell, at least not the part I'm heading for.'

'No need to be so prickly, only asking,' Rory grumbled. 'Pass me some clothes, there's a good fellow.' He pointed towards a pile of clothing that looked as if it hadn't been near a laundry maid for weeks.

'This place is a mess, Rory. What's got into you lately? You do nothing but drink. Is something bothering you?'

'Unrequited love,' Rory said, doing his best to look tragic.

Killian wasn't impressed. 'Again? Who is it this time?'

'No one you know, unfeeling brute,' Rory muttered. 'I'm dying of thirst. Is there anything in that bottle?'

'Water is all you're having for now.' Killian ignored Rory's wounded look and poured some into a dirty glass, which he handed to his friend.

'What happened to your eye? It's a very pretty shade of purple.'

'It's a long story.'

Rory squinted at him. 'Tell me, I've got all day. Might cheer me up to hear all about you being beaten black and blue.'

Killian closed his eyes and sighed. 'Not now. Look, Rory, I really haven't the time. I need to leave the country, and fast, or I'll be leg-shackled to Iona Cameron. She claims I've got her with child.'

'The devil she does!' Rory's eyes opened wide, then he winced as the morning light caught him full in the face. 'Do you really have to go as far as Sweden to escape her clutches though? Doesn't make sense to me.'

'Me neither, but it doesn't really matter. I've been given a letter of introduction to one of grandfather's relations who lives over there. The man's a merchant, and I've decided I might as well make use of the connection and learn all I can about trade. Now that I own a ship, what better time to set up in business for myself? I'm sick and tired of gambling. I want some security, a proper income of my own.'

'You should have stopped after the word "sick",' Rory commented with a lopsided grin. 'Sounds to me like your brain's addled. Security indeed.'

'You've got your father's money to fall back on whenever you lose, I don't. I think it's time I tried to make my way in the world without the help of a pair of dice or a deck of cards.'

Rory chuckled. 'I'll give it three months, if that, then you'll be back to your old ways, see if you're not.'

Killian clenched his jaw, not wanting to argue with his friend. Rory had no idea how serious he was this time. It wasn't a new game.

'So shall I come with you then?' Rory offered. 'Keep you company in the not so dark north? The women are pretty, I hear.'

'Much as I'd like to take you with me, I'd prefer it if you stayed here.' Killian fixed his friend with a serious stare. 'Listen, Rory, I need someone I can trust to keep an eye on my cousin. He's up to something, and I want to know what it is.'

'Farquhar? What do you mean?'

'I'd bet anything he set this whole thing up. He wants me out of the way, probably for good, because sooner or later grandfather is going to see him for what he really is. Then he won't get so much as a penny. I wouldn't put it past him to get rid of the old man too. You'll need to watch him whenever you can.'

'Surely not? I know he's a conniving whoreson, but murder? He's too weak for that.'

'Oh, he'd find someone else to do his dirty work for him no doubt, and then he'll make it look like it was my fault. He always did when we were young boys, playing pranks. Don't think he ever got punished. Now, will you help me or not? You're still welcome at the sort of functions he attends, so you could keep a discreet eye on him for me. Ask Dougie to lend a hand too. I'll write to you, once I know where I'll be staying, so you can keep me informed.'

'If that's what you want. I'd much rather go with you though.'

'No, I need you here. You're one of the few people I trust, apart from Dougie of course, but he hasn't got your brains. There's Adair too, and I've told him to follow Farquhar whenever he's out and about. You and Dougie can keep an eye on him when he's socialising.'

'Don't feel like I have any brains myself at the moment,' Rory complained, putting his head into his hands, 'but I'll do my best, you know that.'

'Thanks. You're a true friend.' Killian smiled, then couldn't resist adding, 'Besides, keeping an eye on my cousin will stop you from brooding over worthless women.'

'Worthless! I'll have you know this one's special,' Rory protested.

Killian laughed. 'That's what you say every time. You'll get over it. There are plenty more where she came from.'

'You don't understand, you've never been in love.'

Killian grinned. 'And neither have you.' He walked to the door. 'Now I really must go. A word of advice though ...'

'Yes?'

'Do something about this pigsty and yourself. A bath and some clean clothes might be an improvement. Maybe the poor girl just couldn't stand the smell of you.'

Rory threw a dirty pair of breeches at his friend, but grinned broadly. 'Get out. Go, I say!'

Killian did so, laughing all the way down the stairs.

There was another visit he ought to make that morning, one he wasn't nearly as keen on. In fact, he thought he was probably a fool to even consider it. But since he was leaving the country indefinitely, he was reluctant to leave unfinished business behind.

He hadn't seen his mother since he was ten.

Or rather, he had seen her occasionally when attending functions in town, but had neither acknowledged her existence nor spoken to her. Now he stood on the opposite side of the street outside her tiny house, debating whether to go and knock on the door and demand some answers. He wasn't sure if he really wanted to know. Wasn't it better to let sleeping dogs lie?

Some months after her husband's death, Niamh had gone to live in Edinburgh. She left Killian behind and although she tried to explain her reasons to him, he never understood why. Much later, he heard rumours that she preferred to live openly as the mistress of a married man, rather than staying on at Rosyth. He had no idea if it was true and he wasn't about to ask anyone.

'Your grandfather has told me I have no right to take you away from here,' was all she'd said before leaving. 'As the future heir, you need to stay and learn about the management of the estate.' Killian didn't believe her. He felt betrayed by the only person in the world who should have loved and protected him. If she'd wanted to, he was sure she could have found a way to keep him with her, but she didn't.

In childish retaliation, Killian had sworn never to speak to her again. He hadn't changed his mind by the time he reached adulthood and finally escaped his grandfather's clutches to move to the city himself. That was over five years ago, however, and recently he'd begun to wonder if he hadn't been too hasty. Lord Rosyth was, after all, a very overbearing man. Killian could well believe that he may have bullied Niamh into leaving, whether she wanted to or not. Perhaps it was time to listen to her version of the story?

But what difference would it make, he wondered. *What's done is done. I don't need her now. I'm not a ten-year-old yearning for his mother's affection.*

Still, he would have liked to know her reasons.

As he stood there, torn by indecision, the front door of the house opened. Niamh came out and stopped for a moment to check for something in her silk draw-string bag. Killian tried to look at her dispassionately and saw a middle-aged woman, well-dressed in a gown of striped green silk with a matching feather in her bonnet. She was still beautiful, her auburn hair only lightly streaked with silver, but there were lines of sadness etched around her eyes and no animation in her face. From a distance she seemed to him an empty shell, with no spark of life, no joy in her existence. Was that the truth? Had he contributed towards this state?

A twinge of guilt made him wince, but he hardened his heart. *She* had left *him*, not the other way around. If anyone should feel guilty, it was his mother.

In that moment she looked up and their blue eyes met across the street, clashing momentarily. Hers widened, whether in surprise or dismay, Killian didn't know. He stared back without blinking, but remained rooted to the spot. The distance between them was as wide as it had ever been and there was no reason to bridge the chasm. It was all in the past. Relief flooded through him, he had made his decision at last. He turned to walk away, but had only gone a few steps when he heard her voice behind him, slightly breathless.

'Killian, wait. Was there something you wanted?'

He swivelled round. 'No, nothing,' he said, keeping his expression neutral.

'Oh, I see.' She frowned, obviously confused and disappointed and Killian felt awkward. *Damn it all!* It had been madness to come here, he thought, stirring up emotions best forgotten.

'I thought perhaps ...,' she hesitated, then shook her head. 'Well, never mind.'

A shard of guilt prodded him once more and he felt obliged to say something, anything, to justify his presence outside her house. He blurted out the first thing that came to mind.

'Why did you name me Killian? Grandfather seems to take it as a personal insult for some reason, although why an Irish name should irritate him so much I have no idea.'

Niamh blinked. 'Why, you were named in honour of your uncle, my brother, who died at the battle of the Boyne. Since your father fought there too, he agreed with me you should have that name, no matter what the old man thought. My brother died for a just cause, exactly like your older brothers.'

Killian nodded. 'Thank you, then I shall carry it with pride,' he said and turned on his heel, walking away without looking back.

He shouldn't have come, but at least now he had one answer.

Chapter Seven

Gothenburg, Sweden

'I hear you've been seen speaking to young Adelsten. Didn't I tell you that would be unwise?' Robert's voice had a steely undertone to it that made Jess' palms feel suddenly clammy. She suppressed a shiver.

Once again she was facing the man she had come to think of as her Nemesis in his study. She had to bite her teeth together hard in order to hold back the angry words that welled up inside her. Robert wore a look of disappointment, as if he had expected better of her. Jess was sure the matter was much more serious than that. She also knew she had to stay calm if she was to have any chance of putting on a convincing performance.

'I'm afraid I couldn't avoid him this time. I almost literally ran into him in the market square,' she said, trying to control her breathing so that her voice wouldn't give her away. 'It would have been very rude of me not to acknowledge him as an acquaintance, and we merely exchanged greetings. Besides, Mrs Forbes was nearby, so there was no impropriety, I assure you.'

Robert gave her a measuring stare, but she opened her eyes wide and gazed back in pretended innocence. It was true, after all, nothing improper had happened. As for what else had been said, her stepfather didn't need to know that.

'You didn't try to engage him in conversation then?' he asked, sounding sceptical.

'No more than the usual "how do you do's". He told me he was very well and extremely happy as he's now married to the former Miss Leijonberg. I congratulated him and that was the extent of it.'

Robert kept his gaze on her, as if he didn't believe her for a second. She maintained her guileless expression and after a while longer, he grunted and waved her away.

'Very well.'

She made her way upstairs, mulling over what she had learned from Karl. Robert had claimed the family business was in trouble at the time of her father's death, but she was sure that couldn't be true. She would have found out about it, one way or another. Even if her father had chosen not to tell her, he couldn't hide his feelings from her. She always knew if he was worried about something, but he'd been as happy and content as always until the day he suddenly died.

A terrible thought struck her. Aaron had died in an accident at the warehouse when a shelf stacked full of iron ore had tipped over and crushed him. But what if it wasn't an accident at all?

Her body went cold all over and she couldn't stop a shiver from snaking up her spine.

No, surely Robert couldn't have done away with her father on purpose? She shook her head to get rid of such thoughts. She was turning into an overwrought, hysterical female instead of the intelligent one she knew herself to be. Just because she disliked Robert and resented his hold over her, it didn't make him a murderer. Nor did the fact that he'd lied to keep her under his thumb. And Robert had been at a meeting when the accident happened, or so she'd been told.

Jess pulled herself together. She had to deal in facts, not flights of morbid fancy. If Robert was telling people she was virtually without a dowry, there was no chance anyone would want to marry her. Therefore, she had somehow to find a way of changing his mind or forcing him to come up with the money her father had stipulated. That was all.

And once she had that, she would marry the first man

who asked, because she simply couldn't stay in this house.

It didn't feel like her home any more.

'Do I hae tae bide here? I'd liefer go wi' ye,' Adair whined for about the tenth time. Killian sighed and took a deep breath, praying for patience. The boy had been on edge ever since he'd been told about Killian's proposed stay abroad. It was obvious he was scared of losing the only person in the world who cared about him.

'Adair, listen to me. You know my cousin is always up to mischief and he bears a grudge against me bigger than a mountain. Things have gone so far now that I believe he's getting desperate and I've no idea what he'll do next. I really need you here to follow his every move and the instant you see anything suspicious, you report it to Mr Grant. Understand?'

Adair nodded, albeit still with a sullen expression. Killian gripped the boy's thin shoulder. 'You're the only one I can trust to do it without being noticed. You're stealthier than a fox. I swear I'll send for you as soon as you're no longer needed here. Look, I'm leaving you more than enough money in the hidey-hole to live on for months. Doesn't that please you? You can come and go as you like and you won't have any other duties, except perhaps keeping this place tidy.'

'Aye, I'll dae it, but if Mr Farquhar doesnae get up tae ony tricks, I'll come after ye.'

'Please, Adair, just wait until I tell you it's the right time. I'm not abandoning you, I promise. I'll send you a letter and as soon as you receive it you can come to Sweden on the *Lady Madeleine*, but not before. Is that clear?'

Adair made a face, but nodded. Then he grinned suddenly, back to his normal self now that he'd been reassured. 'Guid thing ye taught me tae read then, is it no. Else how would I ken wha' yer letter said?'

Killian rolled his eyes, remembering all too well the struggle he'd had in trying to persuade Adair to learn, but also the joy and pride he'd felt when he succeeded. 'Varmint,' he said and cuffed the boy playfully on the arm. 'Now keep out of trouble. Though I don't understand why myself, I'll miss you and would prefer to see you in one piece next time we meet.'

The North Sea was rough and Killian's first voyage on board his new ship was a baptism of fire, if ever there was one. However, he was pleased to find he had a cast-iron stomach that didn't even quiver from the rocking motion of the waves. As long as he didn't lie down in his cabin he was fine, and the captain of the *Lady Madeleine* was impressed.

'You're a lucky man, Mr Kinross, and no mistake. Most folks go green at the gills just looking at the sea. You must have seafaring ancestors I reckon.' Captain Craig himself was a robust, ruddy-cheeked man in his early forties who looked as though he'd never suffered a day's illness in his life and certainly not seasickness.

'I don't know about that, but I'm very glad not to be suffering from *mal de mer*, that's for sure.'

It also helped not to be incapacitated when there was so much to learn. To the captain's surprise, Killian was constantly at his side, asking questions, watching and learning. 'You want to be a sailor, then, Mr Kinross?' he asked.

Killian smiled. 'Not exactly, but I like to do things thoroughly. If I'm to own a ship, I want to know how it works, where everything is, what it's called. I think knowledge is power.'

Captain Craig nodded. 'Very wise. That Mr McGrath what owned the ship before you never set foot on it. Just arranged for the cargo and told me what to bring back instead. I'm very pleased to be working for you, Mr Kinross. Makes a nice change.'

'Not just *for* me, Captain, but *with* me,' Killian replied.

'How so?'

'If you continue to help me find the best goods to trade with between the two countries, I'll give you a share of the profits.'

The captain's eyes widened as he took in Killian's meaning. 'No! Truly?'

Killian nodded. He'd considered this carefully and thought it would be in his best interest. Hopefully, with such an incentive, the man would work harder and they would both gain. He didn't want a surly employee. What he needed was someone he could trust.

'Well, I don't know what to say.' Captain Craig still looked dumbfounded. 'I mean, I shall certainly do my best. Not that I wouldn't have done otherwise, of course, but ... really, Mr Kinross, you've stunned me.'

Killian smiled. 'The arrangement will be to both our advantage, I think. I hope we can work well together.'

'Absolutely.' Craig beamed at him. 'You won't regret this, I promise you.'

With the captain's help, Killian had already managed to buy a high-quality cargo to take with them. Mostly they bought salt, which was much sought after in Scandinavia, but also superior cloth, wheat, butter, coal and some luxury goods from the Americas, such as tobacco. He paid for it with the money he had won at gambling. The captain assured him these were the kind of goods that would sell well in Sweden and Killian had no reason not to believe him. Any profit would be good, the more the better. It was a start, and he knew that iron ore, copper, wood, tar and pitch were good things to ship back to Scotland from Sweden. He planned to send the captain back and forth while he was there, making as much money as he could.

He had well and truly embarked on his new career and he intended to make a success of it.

Sailing in through the archipelago towards Gothenburg, on the west coast of Sweden, Killian was amazed what a small town it was when he finally set eyes on it. He had expected something larger, but compared to Edinburgh it was a mere village. Situated at the mouth of the river Göta, it seemed to be all on flat, even ground. There were just a few small hills sticking up, the largest on the right hand side.

'The town was built by Dutchmen,' Captain Craig informed him. 'This place was nothing but a quagmire before apparently, so the Swedes knew the Dutch were the best people to help them with the construction. They had enough practice with their own wet landscapes, didn't they.'

Killian had never been to Holland, but had heard of the way the Dutch dammed water and built beautiful cities criss-crossed by canals. 'So it's like a miniature Amsterdam then, is it?'

'You could say that. There's certainly a canal or two, as you'll soon see. It's fortified though, with two redoubts they call *The Lion* and *The Crown*, as well as all those walls with sharp angles sticking out in several places and a moat all around.'

The *Lady Madeleine* had to drop anchor some way outside the city ramparts, and everyone was brought to shore by stevedores. They had the exclusive rights to ferrying people around on the canals and to and from the large ships.

'They'll also see about transporting the cargo,' the captain assured Killian. 'It'll be taken onto dry land as soon as we've found someone who wants to buy it, seeing as you haven't got any storage, Mr Kinross,' he added. Killian made a mental note to try and rent some storage space as soon as he could.

As they were rowed towards the city, Killian saw the strong ramparts and bastions close up. Over the top, as they came nearer, he glimpsed the roofs of houses and the spires of two churches. The entry to the main canal was roughly in the middle of the town. It was flanked by rocky little hills and they passed a huge wooden bar, which according to the captain was lowered each night.

'It's called *Stora Bommen* and they only keep it open during the day. Best for defensive purposes, I would hazard a guess.'

Killian wondered who the Swedes' enemies were. Presumably the Danes or Norwegians, who were their closest neighbours, at least on this side of the country. He knew very little about the political situation and resolved to find out more as soon as he could. If he was going to make this his home for the foreseeable future, it would pay to be well-informed.

They continued along a canal flanked by buildings mainly built from wood. Most of them were painted either red or yellow with white or blue window frames. One or two of the houses were made of stone and seemed sturdier, but they were the exception. The streets looked to be laid out in a regular, straight grid pattern, at right angles to each other, from what Killian could make out, although the canal itself wasn't quite straight. It had a kink at the end where it veered to the left. He could also see some sort of an island in the middle of it further up ahead.

'For some reason they call this canal *Stora Hamnen*, which roughly means "the big harbour",' Captain Craig told him, 'on account of it being the place where everything is loaded and unloaded, I suppose.'

They passed under several bridges, all arched and quite pretty, and came to a stop next to a large square. It was at roughly a man's height above the level of the canal. They had to climb up a few steps to reach the street, where the noise and bustle was almost deafening. Killian stopped for a moment to look around, and liked what he saw. He drew in a deep breath and was pleased to find the air not too noxious either. Compared to Edinburgh, it was positively sweet-smelling, despite the inevitable stench from the canals.

The square was cobblestoned and had trees planted at intervals along the canal. It gave a pleasing sense of space, despite the many people who were going about their daily business. Hawkers, vendors, street entertainers and workers, mangy dogs, horses and carts – all contributed to the scene, but it wasn't nearly as crowded as the streets of Edinburgh. Neither was it as colourful. Most of the inhabitants seemed to be dressed in greys, browns or black, although there were the odd splashes of colour from more exalted persons that drew the eye. Killian was glad he had put on a fairly sober coat of grey silk, so he didn't stand out too much.

'How many people live here?' Killian asked Captain Craig, as he followed him along one of the side canals towards a hostelry. It seemed preferable to spend the night at an inn, rather than go straight to Mr Fergusson. He didn't want to be beholden to the man, after all, and wanted to wait and see whether he would be invited to stay with him or not. First, he needed to get his bearings.

'Not sure. Five, maybe six thousand? Could be more though.'

The landlord of the *White Hart* – or *Vita Hjorten* as it was called in Swedish – was a jovial, rotund Scotsman by the name of Murdoch, whose face split into a welcoming grin at the sight of Captain Craig. 'Ah, so you're back then?' He beamed. 'And you're wanting rooms I presume?'

'Aye, indeed we are.' The captain introduced Killian and entered into negotiations regarding the room charge. While he did so, Killian listened intently to a group of people speaking Swedish nearby. It sounded like a very guttural language and contained some strange noises, but one or two of the words seemed familiar.

'I'll have to learn to speak Swedish,' he told Craig. 'It shouldn't be that difficult. I managed to learn French and Latin after all, and Latin's the very devil to get the hang of.'

'Swedish is easy, so they say, but then I've never tried more than a few words, Mr Kinross. Good luck to you, I say,' Craig laughed.

Killian wasn't sure if luck was what he needed, but thanked the captain all the same.

Walking into the taproom some time later, Killian was astonished to hear Scots-accented English spoken almost all around him. Captain Craig was seated in a corner and beckoned him over.

'There you are, Mr Kinross. Come and meet some fellow countrymen. These kind gentlemen are buying the drinks.'

'That is indeed very hospitable.' Killian joined them at their table and introductions were made.

There were two young men, James McEvoy and Graham Frazer, who worked as assistants to Scottish merchants. One was dark-haired and swarthy, the other fair and fresh-faced, but both looked like they enjoyed life to the full and had no particular cares at the moment. The fourth person at the table was an old sea captain. His name was Muir and apparently he had known Craig for many years. They soon had Killian provided with a large tankard of ale and a heaped plate of food, which gave off an appetizing aroma.

'Plain fare,' Muir said, 'but plenty of it and well cooked, to my mind. Though Murdoch's wife can oblige with Scottish victuals if you prefer?'

'No, no, this is fine, thank you.'

Killian had to agree that the food was plain, but although he'd been served only mashed turnips and salted, fried pork with onion gravy, he found nothing to complain about. He'd never been fond of fancy food and preferred to eat anything that kept hunger at bay for as long as possible. During the past three years there had been quite a few occasions when he hadn't been able to afford to eat, so he was always grateful when he could.

'So you're learning to become merchants?' Killian said to the two younger men. 'That's what I'm hoping to do. Eventually I'd like to set up in business for myself, but I need to learn the ropes.'

'You've come to the right place then,' McEvoy smiled. 'But be prepared to work like a slave, isn't that right, Frazer?' His companion nodded in full agreement and rolled his eyes.

'And how! Never a moment's peace, but at least it's not dull and at the end of the day, there's always convivial company to be had here at *Vita Hjorten*.'

'Glad to hear it.' Killian had expected to have to work hard, so the two men's warnings didn't faze him. It was good to know he wouldn't have to spend his evenings alone once Captain Craig had left for Edinburgh.

During the conversation, Killian looked around him and noticed that the inn was very sparsely furnished, with the bare minimum of tables and benches. There was no decoration to speak of, simply bare wooden walls. However, the large fireplace, very broad at the bottom and tapering up to a thin point near the ceiling, gave out plenty of heat and added cheer to the otherwise stark room.

'Fancy a game of dice?' McEvoy asked hopefully. 'No one will play with me this week as I have the devil's own luck.'

Killian hesitated for a fraction. He really did want to put his old life behind him. On the other hand, if he was to set up in business he would need all the funds he could get. Unless Lady Luck had deserted him for the young man sitting opposite, here was a way of acquiring additional capital. To refuse would seem churlish and if he wanted to make friends in this foreign country, he couldn't afford to offend anyone. To clinch the matter, he promised himself he would stop before he either lost too much or fleeced his companions.

He smiled. 'That sounds like a challenge I can't refuse.'

Chapter Eight

Robert was becoming more openly critical of Jess every day and she found herself being reprimanded for the slightest thing. Her mother, wrapped up as always in her toddlers, appeared not to notice. The few times she did, she only frowned at Jess and sighed. It was as if the additional strain of strife between her husband and her daughter was just too much to bear on top of her other burdens. This made Jess feel more and more isolated and increased her determination to find a way to escape.

'I hear you insulted Mrs Forbes this morning,' Robert said with a frown.

Jess had been called into his study yet again, this time because she had been rude to his relative. In his mind, that was probably an offence punishable by death, Jess thought sarcastically. Outwardly she tried to keep her emotions under control, although her jaw was clenched as tight as a vice.

'Not intentionally. I just pointed out that since Mother was suffering from a headache, my time could be better spent helping her instead of wasting it on useless embroidery.'

This wasn't quite how she had phrased it, as Jess well knew, but it was what she'd meant. Not that she didn't enjoy embroidery occasionally, but she much preferred to spend time with her brothers, Ramsay in particular. Their former rapport had been well and truly re-established, and she played with him as often as she could.

Apparently Robert had been told the unedited version of events. This was all the excuse he needed to give Jess a very long lecture on the evils of not minding her elders or doing as she'd been told. He never once raised his voice, but she still felt like a five-year-old caught doing something heinous. Throughout his diatribe there lurked the underlying menace of possible banishment. She heard him out in seething silence, knowing her face was becoming suffused with a flush of anger she couldn't hide.

When at last he ran out of breath, she walked out of the study with her head held high. As always, she closed the door behind her as quietly as she could, instead of slamming it hard the way she'd like to do. Gritting her teeth, she ran towards the stairs, only to barrel straight into someone who was just coming in from the hall.

'Ooof! I beg your pardon.'

Disconcerted, she took a step back and was about to apologise again, but as she looked up the words died on her lips. In front of her stood the handsomest man she had ever seen and she couldn't do anything except stare at him for a moment. He had shining dark auburn hair, pulled back into an untidy queue, cornflower-blue eyes surrounded by sweeping black lashes, and impossibly perfect features. She blinked and wondered if he was real. Perhaps he was one of the archangels spoken of in the Bible? She shook herself mentally. What a ridiculous thought.

'No, it is I who should apologise. Miss Fergusson, is it?' He bowed. 'Killian Kinross at your service. I've come to see your father and was told to wait over there.' He indicated a chair obviously placed for this purpose against the wall outside Robert's study. 'I should have looked before entering this hallway. My mistake.'

'He is *not* my father,' she hissed, reminded again of the recent encounter and ignoring the rest of the man's sentence. 'He is the devil reincarnated.' This was perhaps a gross exaggeration, but saying the words out loud gave vent to her pent-up frustration and made her feel a whole lot better.

Mr Kinross raised his brows a fraction and a slow smile spread over his features. Jess almost gasped as the effect of it was like a physical blow to her solar plexus. 'Riled you, has he?' he enquired with amusement in his voice. 'Ah, but of course, he's related to my grandfather. Stands to reason.'

Jess didn't follow the logic of this statement. In fact, she had trouble thinking coherently at all with that devastating smile dazzling her, but she closed her eyes and gathered what few wits she had left. 'I don't wish to discuss it. Good day to you, Mr Kinross.'

And with that parting shot, she stepped around him and ran up the stairs, lifting her skirts to take the steps an unladylike two at a time. Glancing down from the first floor landing, she saw him staring after her with a thoughtful look on his face. When he noticed her pause, he smiled again and bowed in a lazy, almost insolent salute.

Jess ignored him and continued upstairs. She'd had more than enough of men to last her a lifetime and she wanted nothing to do with any of them, handsome or not.

Killian stared after the tiny blonde who had just rammed him in the chest, a not un-enjoyable experience in itself. She seemed to be in a terrible temper, which made her grey eyes flash with quicksilver spirit and her cheeks blush becomingly. Although she wasn't a beauty in the normal sense of the word – she was too petite for that and her colouring a little insipid – Killian had nevertheless felt a pull of attraction which took him by surprise. Normally he preferred his women well rounded, dark and pliant, but he reflected that it might be interesting to try a fair-haired miniature Valkyrie for a change.

He smothered the thought before it took root. She had been at odds with Mr Fergusson, the man he was here to work with, and it wouldn't do to antagonise him from the start. He wondered at the relationship between them since the girl clearly lived in this house. Whoever she was, she was most definitely out of bounds at the moment. Besides which she had 'untouched' all but engraved on her forehead. Killian smiled to himself. Years of experience had taught him to recognise the innocent among the girls he met. Nothing would induce him to break his rule about not bedding young virgins. They were more trouble than they were worth.

As the door opened and he was ushered into the office of his grandfather's relative, he put the episode behind him. Time enough to find out more about the strangely delectable young lady later.

'Come in, come in, young Kinross.'

Robert Fergusson was all smiles. He didn't show by as much as a flicker of annoyance that he had just had an altercation with the little Valkyrie. A thick-set man with a craggy face and bushy eyebrows, he was half a head shorter than Killian. He had wavy dark brown hair, liberally shot through with grey, and brown, almost black eyes. An aquiline nose gave an impression of hauteur, despite the outwardly friendly manner and his presence was such that anyone meeting him for the first time felt latent power ooze from his every pore. Killian suppressed a shudder. This man was ruthless, he knew it instinctively. He would have to be careful.

He handed Fergusson the letter from his grandfather. 'Thank you for receiving me so soon, sir,' he said. 'Grandfather didn't have time to send you word of my arrival, but here is his letter of explanation for my presence here. I warn you though, it might make tedious reading. I expect he'll be giving you a blow by blow account of my character.'

Fergusson smiled briefly. 'I take it the two of you don't see eye to eye? Well, Uncle Kenelm was always a touch domineering. I'll take his words with a pinch of salt.' He read through the missive quickly, and Killian waited in silence until he had finished. Fergusson nodded. 'It's as I thought. He wants you to have some "gainful employment". I think I can manage to supply that. What do you know of trade?'

'Not much. I picked up a few hints from the captain of the ship I arrived on, but I think it would be best if you treated me as a complete novice.' Killian decided not to tell Fergusson the ship was his. Time for that later perhaps. 'I'm willing to work hard and I learn fast. I'll be happy to perform whatever tasks you set me.'

'Sensible words. I see you don't lack brains.'

'That's not what grandfather says.' Killian smiled and shrugged.

Fergusson's mouth twitched again. 'As to that, you'll have to prove him wrong then.'

'I certainly hope so.'

'Have you anywhere to stay?'

'I've taken a room at *Vita Hjorten*, near *Smedjegatan,* for the moment, but I'll be looking for lodgings as soon as possible. I wanted to get my bearings first.'

'Of course. You're welcome to stay here if you wish, but it's a household of women and children. Not ideal for concentration of any kind.' A look of impatience crossed Fergusson's face, but was quickly smothered and the urbane expression returned. 'Do come for supper tonight though. The children will be in bed by then.'

Killian wondered vaguely if that included the blonde girl, but hoped not. He would enjoy meeting her again. It might prove amusing, especially if she was still at odds with Fergusson. 'Thank you,' he said and bowed. 'I'll return later then.'

'Good, good, then on Monday morning I'll take you to my business premises where I'll introduce you to Albert Holm, my chief assistant. He can show you the ropes at first, he's very knowledgeable. You could do worse than listen to him.'

'Thank you again. That sounds ideal.'

As he left the house, Killian wondered whether Fergusson was palming him off on his assistant in order to be rid of the responsibility. Only time would tell. Whatever happened, he was determined to learn as much as possible, in as short a time as he could.

The sooner he could set up his own business, the better.

The atmosphere in Lady Brabury's ballroom was stifling and the air barely fit to breathe. Feeling decidedly irritable, Farquhar positioned himself behind a convenient pillar and loosened his neckcloth a fraction when no one was looking. He couldn't understand why it was necessary to invite more people than the room could actually accommodate, just to show the world that one's gathering was a social success. This seemed to be the norm these days and it was deuced uncomfortable.

His main concern was not the lack of space though, but keeping an eye on his grandfather, who had insisted on attending this function. The old man was sitting nearby talking to his old friend Ruaridh Cameron, who seemed to be in remarkably good spirits for someone whose daughter was facing imminent ruin. He was also not glowering at Lord Rosyth, which could only mean the two men had come to some agreement regarding Killian. Farquhar suspected Lord Rosyth had rescued the undeserving scoundrel from his just desserts. What made Farquhar's blood boil the most was the fact that his grandfather didn't seem too concerned this time. He should have been furious.

Blaming Killian for the Cameron chit's predicament had seemed like such a good plan when he first hatched it. Farquhar realised now he should have picked the girl with more care. He hadn't had any dealings with young Iona himself and hadn't paid attention to the gossip circulating about her. That was a mistake. He really must be more careful. Not that he'd had much choice; she was the only pregnant girl who Farquhar knew for sure that Killian had slept with. He'd ignored the fact that the encounter had taken place the previous year and therefore ruled Killian out as potential father of the child.

Farquhar shook his head. What was done, was done. No use repining. The thing now was to move forward and he could only see one way of settling the matter once and for all: Killian had to be eliminated. Until that happened, Farquhar could never be sure of his position. Lord Rosyth was liable to change his mind whenever he saw fit.

Farquhar threw the old man a glance. Perhaps he should rid the world of his grandfather as well while he was at it? A convenient accident shouldn't be impossible. It would be a shame though and since what Farquhar really wanted was his grandfather's approval, bumping the old man off would take away half the satisfaction of being the heir. Still, it was something to think about.

First, he needed to find out where Killian had gone, and there seemed no chance of that here. He couldn't hear a word the old man was saying either with all the noise going on around them. Tiring of this spying game, Farquhar looked about for a servant with a tray of drinks. Instead his eyes fell on one of Killian's cronies, Dougal Forster, who was lounging against the opposite wall. He looked as miserable as Farquhar felt. No doubt he was missing his debauched companion, but perhaps that could work to Farquhar's advantage. In the hope that he might glean some information from him, he strolled over.

'Evening, Forster,' he said.

'Good evening.' Forster looked slightly taken aback to be

addressed by Killian's cousin. The two had never been more than nodding acquaintances before.

'Dreadful squeeze, isn't it?' Farquhar glowered at the occupants of the room in general. 'Didn't think this was your kind of scene. Not out carousing with my cousin tonight?'

Forster threw him a confused glance, but answered evenly. 'No, he left for Sweden a few days ago, remember?'

Farquhar hid his surprise. 'Oh, I thought he wasn't leaving until the end of the week.'

'Well, the matter was rather urgent.' Dougal looked across the room to where Farquhar now spied Iona Cameron simpering at young James Hamilton. The young man's expression was that of a cornered rat since there was a Cameron relative on either side of the couple. They seemed intent on thwarting any possible escape attempts on the part of the intended groom.

Farquhar would have laughed at this sight, if he hadn't remembered it should have been Killian at the girl's side, looking every bit as uncomfortable as Hamilton did now. He drew in a steadying breath to suppress the anger. 'Yes, so I gather. Sweden seems a drastic choice though, just to avoid parson's mousetrap. Nasty, cold place, from what I hear.'

'No more so than here,' Dougal said. 'And Gothenburg is in the southern part, Rory said, so perhaps not as cold as all that.'

'We must hope not, for Killian's sake. …'

'Farquhar Kinross, fancy meeting you here.' The cold voice of Rory Grant sliced across Farquhar's words. 'Doing the pretty with your grandfather, are you?'

Farquhar studied Killian's closest friend through narrowed eyes. Grant didn't look pleased to find him talking to Forster, and this made Farquhar smile. 'Someone has to take care of the old man,' he replied ambiguously and couldn't resist adding, 'I've just been informed by your friend here,' he nodded towards Forster, 'that my cousin has deserted us for the delights of Sweden.'

Grant sent his companion an accusing glare, and Forster blanched, obviously realising his mistake. Farquhar's smile widened. 'Well, I'm off. Can't stand another moment of this purgatory. Good evening to you both.' He gave them a slightly mocking bow, which was returned as the merest nod by Grant and not at all by the flustered Forster. He sauntered off, trying to suppress a shout of laughter. Killian really should choose his friends with more care, he thought. Forster might be a nice enough man, but when it came to wits, he definitely hadn't been blessed with his full share.

Still, Farquhar wasn't complaining. If only all Killian's cronies had been as stupid, it would have made life a lot easier. Stopping by the door, he stared across the room to where Forster and Grant seemed to be exchanging angry words. When they glanced his way, Farquhar gave them one last mocking bow before leaving. In return, he received only icy glares, but he didn't care.

He had all the information he needed.

Chapter Nine

'Please may I be excused from dinner, *Moeder*? I have a dreadful headache.'

Jess hovered just inside the door of the nursery. She was hoping for a quick reply so she could flee back to her bedroom before Robert came upstairs to change. She really did have a headache, although it was more of a nagging sensation at the back of her head than anything else. Either way, it was as good an excuse as any.

Jess had spent the afternoon fuming about Robert's unfair treatment of her. The last thing she wanted was another evening making strained conversation with him and Mrs Forbes. Her mother hardly ever contributed. She was usually too tired from running around after her sons all day, so it was up to the other three to make small talk, something Jess couldn't stand.

When Jess entered the room, her mother had been in the middle of helping the nursemaid make the boys ready for bed. It was a task the servant could very well have done on her own, but which Katrijna insisted on supervising every evening. There didn't seem to be a single aspect of her younger children's daily routine she didn't want to be involved in, Jess thought resentfully. *She never asks how I spend my time except when she needs me for something.* Jess knew that was unjust though. Katrijna was merely a mother hen, forever anxious about her smaller chicks.

Katrijna struggled to pull a clean nightshirt over the head of a recalcitrant James. She looked round at Jess with a frown, her face flushed with irritation and effort. 'Not today, dear. We have a guest coming, Robert said. He won't be very pleased with you if you don't attend. Why don't you ask cook for a tisane? I'm sure if you lie down for a short while you'll be as right as rain.'

Jess' heart sank. She very much hoped the guest wasn't the man she had encountered in the hall, but it seemed more than likely. Had he told Robert about her rude remarks? *That's all I need!*

'Please, Mama? I'm sure Robert's guest would rather discuss business and such matters with him. With Mrs Forbes at the table you'll be an even number, you don't need me.'

Katrijna shook her head. 'No, I'm sorry, but I'm too tired to make proper conversation. Robert will need your help. You can talk about sensible things, while you know Mrs Forbes does nothing but gossip.' She noticed Jess' look of distress and came over to put a hand on her daughter's arm. 'Come, my dear, our guest might be an eligible young man. Didn't you say just the other day you were longing for a husband of your own? You'll never catch one hiding yourself away in your room.'

I have no chance of catching anyone, Jess wanted to scream, but something made her hold back. She couldn't tell her mother about her lack of dowry and Robert's part in that. It would only upset her and no doubt there would be a terrible scene. Somehow, it would all end up being Jess' fault and she'd be no better off than she was now. No, she had to find a way out of her predicament by herself.

'Very well,' she sighed. 'If you need me, of course I'll come down. I'll go and see cook now.'

'You do that. And while you're there, can you make sure she's warming some milk for the boys? Please check that it's not boiling like yesterday, they really don't like it lumpy. I'm forever telling cook to heat the milk slowly, but she won't listen.'

'Yes, *Moeder*.'

Her mother's thoughts had returned to her boys and Jess was on the outside once again.

Killian knocked on the front door to the Fergusson house for the second time that day with a slight feeling of anticipation building up inside him. It had been a long time since he'd felt anything other than bored with his existence. Somehow, coming to Sweden had changed all that. It was as if he had turned a corner and the past was no longer important. He intended to make the most of his new life, learning as much as he could in record time. He was tired of living on the fringes of society, scraping by. He wanted to make his way in the world and show his grandfather he didn't need him or his inheritance.

He needed no one.

Knowledge was power, as he'd said to Captain Craig. Therefore he had spent the afternoon trying to find out more about Gothenburg in general and the Fergusson family in particular. Fortunately Murdoch, the Scottish landlord at *Vita Hjorten*, was a gregarious fellow who was very happy to spend time chatting with his guests. He accepted a tankard of ale with alacrity and after a few sips, there was no stopping him. He was an absolute fount of useful information. For the moment, however, Killian was mostly interested in details about the Fergusson household, so that he would know who he was dealing with. He steered the conversation in that direction with a couple of innocent questions.

'Fergusson is a canny one,' the landlord said, tapping a fat finger on his nose. 'Keeps himself to himself mostly and doesn't mix much with the rest of us.' He looked around in a furtive manner and lowered his tone. 'I've heard tell he's ruthless when it comes to business dealings. There've been rumours of clashes with other merchants, but no hard facts. He wasted no time in hitching himself to the grieving widow when his partner passed away. Didn't even wait a year for proper mourning, but then I suppose the lady needed looking after. Her and her daughter both.'

'Daughter?' Killian prompted, very interested in this tale.

'Yes, Miss van Sandt. Pretty little blonde girl, Fergusson's stepdaughter. Well, I say girl, but she must be all of nineteen or twenty now. Little heiress I suppose, seeing as she was her father's only child. Fergusson'll be looking after her inheritance until she marries though and that may not be any time soon.'

'Why not?' If Miss van Sandt was the girl he'd met that morning, as he assumed she must be, Killian saw no reason why she shouldn't marry. There had been nothing wrong with her that he could see. In fact, coupled with a substantial inheritance she would be quite a temptation to any man.

'Ah, well, now here's a story.' Murdoch smiled knowingly and lowered his voice again, making sure no one was listening. 'It was the talk of the town last year, so it was. Her and a young Swedish nobleman, madly in love they were the pair of them, inseparable at any gathering apparently. Then suddenly she's gone, disappeared into thin air.' The landlord clicked his fingers together to emphasise his point. 'Turns out he didn't love her after all, had only been toying with her feelings to get at her dowry. Someone spilled the beans and she, poor girl, suffered from a broken heart. Had to go and nurse it in the country for nearly a year. And her such a lovely young lady, fair boggles the mind, don't it?'

'Indeed. But now she's back?'

'Yes, been seen out and about. Saw her myself a few days ago, but didn't look too happy to me. Perhaps she's still suffering, poor mite? Love is a strange thing.'

Killian was sure there must be more to it than that. Miss

van Sandt certainly hadn't looked the sort of young lady who'd suffer from a broken heart for a whole year. She was much too spirited for that. And why had she been at loggerheads with her stepfather? An enigma, to be sure, but Killian liked a challenge. He decided to keep his eyes and ears open.

As he waited for the door to the Fergusson house to open, Killian wondered again whether Miss van Sandt would be present at supper. It would certainly make for a more interesting evening, particularly if she was still in a temper. The thought made him smile just as a maid opened the door, and the poor girl jumped and stared wide-eyed at this sight before recalling her duties.

'*God afton och välkommen, Herrn.*' She lowered her gaze and curtseyed, then took his cloak before showing him into the parlour. This was a large room at the back of the house dominated by an impressive floor-to-ceiling stove made of blue and white Delft tiles. The brass hatch at the front was open, allowing the heat from the fire to penetrate the room, but Killian still felt a chill in the air. He guessed the parlour wasn't used very often and the fire had only just been lit. A slightly musty odour wafting through the room seemed to confirm this.

The room itself was otherwise fairly plain. The walls were painted a muted grey and the floorboards sanded and scrubbed until they were almost white. A great deal of furniture – too much Killian thought – was crammed in seemingly without purpose. There were massive ornately-painted cupboards, a lot of high-backed chairs that looked uncomfortable and several tables covered with linen cloths. The walls held a mirror in a carved and gilded frame as well as some dark paintings and wall hangings. A brass chandelier illuminated the gloom of the early evening.

Apart from his host, the room also contained three ladies,

all dressed in plain gowns in shades of brown or grey. Killian was pleased to see that one of them was the little Valkyrie he had met earlier. He didn't look at her, however, but concentrated on greeting Fergusson. 'Good evening. I hope I'm not late?'

'Not at all, Kinross, we sup at six as I told you. Come and meet my wife.' Robert Fergusson ushered him towards the ladies, who all stood up to greet him. 'Katrijna, my dear, this is a distant relative of mine, Killian Kinross, the grandson of Lord Rosyth. You remember I told you about him? Rosyth is my mother's cousin.'

'Yes, of course.' Katrijna Fergusson was a small, slightly plump woman with hair the colour of ripe corn. Although she must have been pretty once, her beauty had faded and there were lines of tiredness and worry etched into her face. The pale blue eyes, fringed with sandy eyelashes, were dull and unfocussed, as if she was forever thinking about something other than the present. Killian bowed over her hand and murmured 'How do you do, Ma'am?'

'This is Jessamijn van Sandt, my stepdaughter,' Robert continued.

Killian immediately detected a slightly harder edge to the man's voice when he said the girl's name. Obviously the antagonism she felt for Fergusson was mutual, which was interesting. 'A pleasure to meet you, Miss van Sandt,' he said and bowed over her hand in the same way as he had her mother's. Instead of merely pretending to kiss the back of it, however, he allowed his lips to graze the soft skin. He hid a smile when he heard her quick intake of breath.

'Mr Kinross,' she said in a voice as cold as the icy depths of her grey eyes. Killian just nodded politely and moved on to the next lady.

'And this is Mrs Oona Forbes, another relation of mine, but on my father's side,' Fergusson said. 'She is Jessamijn's companion.'

Poor girl, guarded by an old dragon, Killian thought, but out loud he made the usual polite noises. Mrs Forbes was tiny, but looked decidedly pugnacious with sharp eyes and a jutting chin. Her grey hair was pulled into a hairstyle as severe as her expression. He wondered if her presence had anything to do with the love affair and the young nobleman the landlord had spoken of. Had the young lady perhaps been a little reckless? Another interesting thought.

'*Middagen är serverad, Herr Fergusson.*'

The maid had returned to announce supper, and the company went through to another equally plain room which was linked to the parlour by an archway. Killian was seated on the right hand side of his hostess. Miss van Sandt was opposite and her companion next to him. He did his duty and made small talk with both the older ladies while the first course was served, then turned to his host.

'What made you come to Sweden, of all places, Mr Fergusson?' he enquired.

'Well, Scotland was a dismal place after the '15, especially for anyone suspected of sympathising with the Jacobites. I thought it wise to go abroad for a while. A friend of mine told me there were great opportunities in Gothenburg for anyone with experience of trade, so I made my way here.'

'And were there?' Killian asked.

'Oh, yes. At that time, exports of timber and iron ore were on the up, so business was booming. I quickly became a partner in the firm of my wife's late husband, who had been here longer, and I was therefore in a position to invest my money wisely. When he sadly passed away five years ago, I took over the running of the company.'

And his wife, Killian added to himself. He wondered how Fergusson had bamboozled the recently-widowed lady into marrying him so quickly. She seemed meek and biddable, so perhaps it hadn't been such a difficult task. She also threw her husband adoring glances from time to time, proving the match had been one of love, at least on her part. Killian saw Miss van Sandt glare at her stepfather, looking as if she wanted to say something even though she remained silent. He felt sure the daughter had been less easy to convince. She obviously still harboured some resentment.

'I see,' was all he said, not wanting to stir up any quarrels, but then decided to probe just a little further. 'I take it Miss van Sandt had no brothers to take their father's place?'

'No.' Fergusson's answer was curt and he glanced at his stepdaughter. 'And naturally a girl can't have anything to do with running a business, no matter how capable she may think herself.'

'Of course not,' Killian said and earned himself a scowl from the young lady. Another interesting tit-bit. So she had thought herself her father's successor? Killian wondered why. Fergusson was right, girls didn't normally have anything to do with such things. He would have to find out further details. 'Do please tell me more about the sort of goods you trade in,' he added to divert Fergusson's attention from a subject which seemed contentious in this household.

He listened with half an ear to Fergusson's rather boring account of his various business interests, while keeping an eye on the young lady opposite. She concentrated on the food in front of her, but he noticed she didn't actually eat much, just pushed it around on her plate. He tried to attract her attention, but she didn't look up once, a novel experience for him. Usually any young lady in his vicinity would have her eyes glued to him. Not this one.

He should have been grateful, since he'd already decided she was out of bounds, but some perverse streak made him want her to notice him. Throwing caution to the wind, he stretched out his legs under the table, which wasn't very wide, and allowed his feet to accidentally brush her skirts. This provoked an instant reaction. She raised her eyes and shot silver daggers at him, which he found infinitely preferable to being ignored. With an inward smile, he wondered if she'd always had a hasty temper, or if it was provoked by her stepfather's arrival on the scene. Either way, she was easy to tease in her current state. Like a powder keg ready to blow up at the slightest sign of fire.

'And why have you come to Sweden, Mr Kinross?' She interrupted her stepfather in mid flow, and Fergusson frowned at her rudeness.

'Really, Jessamijn, where are your manners?'

Killian was tempted to laugh, but kept a straight face. He knew, of course, that Fergusson was objecting to being cut off, not the abruptness of the question. He pretended it was the latter. 'I don't mind answering Miss van Sandt. It's a reasonable query after all.' He smiled at her, but her expression remained stony. 'My grandfather sent me over here because he thought I should learn something useful. Perhaps find a way to fill the family coffers before I take over as laird.'

'You're going to be a laird?' Her disdain was clear and Killian's good humour evaporated.

'Yes. You find that hard to believe?' He stared her straight in the eyes and she had the grace to look ashamed.

'No, I mean, it was just ... you seem too young for such a role.'

'No doubt Grandfather will live a good many years yet. He's as tough as old boots, as I'm sure you can attest, Mr Fergusson.'

'That he is. Never knew a man in better health.'

The conversation turned to other things and Killian decided to leave Miss van Sandt alone for now. He didn't want to cause any further friction between her and her stepfather until he knew more about the situation. It seemed wiser to observe and concentrate on his food.

He had been surprised, when they sat down earlier, that all the food was carried in and left on the table. They had to help themselves, passing the dishes from person to person. Although there were plenty of servants, it didn't appear to be their job to actually serve, which seemed rather odd to him. He reflected that he obviously had a lot to learn about Swedish customs.

The fare was plain, just like at the inn, and somewhat stodgy. Cabbage soup with some sort of meatballs floating in it came first. This was followed by a choice of fatty roast mutton, fillet of veal with mushroom gravy, and black pudding with something that looked like miniature cranberries. 'What are these?' he asked, curious to know everything about this country now he was here.

'*Lingon* berries. They're a bit sharp, but make a nice contrast to the sweet taste of the black pudding. It's made from pig's blood, as I'm sure you know. A bit different from the Scottish variety, but not bad.'

Mrs Fergusson looked alarmed at her husband's words, as if she was afraid that Killian would refuse to eat the food if he was told what it consisted of. Killian smiled at her to reassure her this wasn't the case. He was neither squeamish nor a fussy eater. He tried everything, found that he enjoyed it all and ate with relish.

'I like it. In fact, it is all delicious, Ma'am,' he said to Katrijna, who smiled back at the compliment. She was a difficult woman to talk to, since she often stopped in the middle of a sentence to listen to muffled sounds coming from upstairs, her pale gaze clouding over. When he finally hit on the idea of asking her about her younger children, however, she suddenly became very talkative indeed. So much so, that Fergusson interrupted her in the end with a mild reproach.

'I'm sure young Kinross, who doesn't yet have children of his own, has heard enough tales of our two little scoundrels, my dear. Won't you ask for dessert to be brought in?'

'Oh, yes of course, do forgive me.' Katrijna became flustered and withdrawn once more and Killian felt sorry for her. At the same time he was grateful for the intervention. One more tale of little Ramsay's precociousness or tiny James's attempts at walking would have made him run screaming for the door. Babies and toddlers didn't interest him at all.

Dessert turned out to be apple pie served with thick whipped cream, and Killian enjoyed this dish so much he had a second helping. Miss van Sandt frowned at him from across the table, where she had continued to pick her way through the food put in front of her with the appetite of a bird. He raised his eyebrows at her in an unspoken question. Just because she had no wish to eat, did that mean he couldn't enjoy the meal? She blushed and looked away and he couldn't resist the opportunity to tease her one last time. He stretched his legs out and deliberately caressed her shin with his foot. She jumped and her eyes returned to glare at him once more.

Killian adopted an innocent expression and began a conversation with his host about the natural resources of Sweden.

He had a feeling he was going to enjoy his time in Gothenburg.

Chapter Ten

'Is that man going to stay in Gothenburg for long?' Jess couldn't resist asking her stepfather after their guest had left. 'He was insufferably conceited.'

Robert threw her a puzzled look. 'He seemed perfectly amiable to me.'

'Yes, lovely manners,' Katrijna put in, happy now she had at last been able to check for herself that her two little boys were fast asleep upstairs and all was well. 'And so handsome.'

'Handsome is as handsome does,' Jess muttered. After her experiences with Karl, she had decided that what a man was like on the inside was more important. And a little steadfastness in the face of opposition would be nice too. She, for one, would certainly not be falling for anyone with good looks again. *Not that I'll be given the opportunity.*

'Well, he's staying here for as long as his grandfather thinks it necessary,' Robert stated firmly. 'So you will please be polite to him at all times. Lord Rosyth is my relative and he's too important a man to offend. We have to treat his grandson with respect.'

'Why is he here though? He didn't look like he'd done a day's work in his life.' Jess was feeling on edge. Mr Kinross had unsettled her with the strange game he'd been playing under the table. Not to mention his knowing glances. It wasn't something she'd ever encountered before and she had no idea how to deal with it. With Karl and her other suitors, there had been straightforward demure flirtation and courtship. No subtle teasing, only admiring gazes and polite requests for dances or conversation.

'He's to work with me and learn to be a merchant. That shouldn't be too difficult, the lad seems bright enough. Not a dullard by any means. Speaks Latin and French too, so I understand.'

Jess wasn't convinced. Mr Kinross had the look of a man who'd spent his time pursuing nothing but pleasure and probably trading on his good looks to achieve whatever he wanted. She had mistrusted him from the moment she set eyes on him. An evening spent in his company hadn't changed her view. She sincerely hoped her stepfather would make him work really hard, then perhaps he'd decide being a merchant wasn't for him and leave.

Jess rather thought that would be the best thing for her peace of mind, although why he bothered her so much she had no idea. She ought to have been pleased that a man – any man – paid her some attention, but she knew instinctively Mr Kinross had not had marriage in mind. He didn't look like the marrying kind.

The following day was Sunday. Although Killian hadn't set foot in a church for years, he had thought it politic not to refuse Fergusson's invitation to join his family for the morning service.

'If only you could see me now, Grandfather,' he muttered as he hurried along the cobbled streets towards the church and slipped in just before the doors were closed. 'Close to sainthood, at the very least.'

It had been a struggle to rise so early. His head pounded from the after-effects of several bottles of wine shared with McEvoy and Frazer, who had greeted his return to the inn with cries of welcome. Even though Killian had soundly beaten McEvoy at dice the evening before, they didn't seem to bear him any ill-will.

'Come and join us for a game of cards,' they shouted

across the tap room. Their good humour was infectious and Killian was happy to oblige. After an evening of stilted polite conversation, he definitely needed some diversion. He was paying for it now and flinched as a shaft of sunlight streamed in through a particularly red pane of glass in the stained glass windows and hit him square in the face.

Squinting, he saw Fergusson sitting in a pew near the front, waving at him. Killian made his way up the aisle, squeezing into the end of the row next to Miss van Sandt. The girl moved her skirts as if she couldn't bear for them to touch him, but this only made him want to provoke her again. Deliberately, he shuffled closer and whispered, 'Good morning, Miss van Sandt. You're looking particularly lovely today.' Actually, it was nothing but the truth – her hair glinted in the sunlight like gilded silver and although her eyes were grey storm clouds, her cheeks were stained a becoming shade of pink.

He received only a curt, 'Good morning' in return and from then on she kept her gaze firmly fixed on the front of the church.

Killian wasn't much interested in listening to the sermon and he couldn't understand it anyway since it was in Swedish. As soon as the first hymn had been sung and the minister began to speak in a loud, carrying voice, he decided this was a good opportunity to get to know Miss van Sandt a bit better. 'I gather you don't like me,' he whispered. 'Why is that?'

At first it didn't seem as though she was going to answer such a direct question, but finally she hissed, 'You're related to him.' She nodded towards her stepfather, who was thankfully at the other end of the pew and therefore out of earshot. Mrs Forbes was seated next to her charge, but she was busy helping Mrs Fergusson. The two little boys were placed between them and had to be kept in check. One of them had a loud hacking cough and both were fidgeting and whining about something, creating a useful diversion.

'Only very distantly,' Killian protested. 'I barely even know how myself.'

'Well, if not by blood, then probably in other ways.' Miss van Sandt raised her chin a notch, as if defending her views.

'You shouldn't judge people before you know them. Why should I be like your stepfather?' Killian was intrigued by her reasoning.

'You have the same look of assurance. Swagger, in fact. I know your type and I will not be taken in again.'

Killian raised his brows at her, but she still wouldn't look at him. 'You've been taken in by your stepfather?'

'No, I meant … that is, it's none of your business. Kindly pay attention to the sermon and leave me in peace.'

Killian did as he'd been asked, but he was more determined than ever to find out what Fergusson had done to earn the girl's enmity to such a degree. It couldn't just be because he had usurped her father's place in her life and married her mother. And with a tongue as sharp as that, he believed even less in the story about her broken heart. There was a mystery here and he wanted to get to the bottom of it, but he'd have to be patient for now.

Meanwhile, he could amuse himself by ruffling her feathers, which seemed all too easy to do. He knew she was as aware of him as he was of her. Fidgeting just like her half-brothers, he took up the largest amount of space possible on purpose. This meant their thighs came into contact whenever either of them moved, which sent a frisson through him and hopefully her as well. He didn't know what devil prompted him to act in this way, but he felt more alive than he had in ages. Never had a visit to church been so enjoyable.

As they made their way out into the autumn sunshine at last, Miss van Sandt whispered under her breath, 'I shall take care not to sit next to you again, sir.' She made to move off, but under cover of the throng of people, he grabbed her wrist to detain her.

'And I shall make sure you do,' he whispered back.

Jess unconsciously held her wrist, which seemed to burn from his touch. She couldn't help but stare at Mr Kinross' broad back while he stopped for a word with her stepfather. She felt shaken again, just like she had the night before, but she wasn't sure if it was outrage at his behaviour or excitement from the unusual sparring between them. A little voice inside her head dared her to admit that she had enjoyed the encounter, but she quelled it ruthlessly.

Before she had time to think about it further, the daughter of another Dutch-born merchant came over to greet her. Jess hadn't seen Margreet Jansen since her return, even though they had known each other for years. She'd had no opportunity to rekindle friendships, because Robert had discouraged her from going out. So far there hadn't been any invitations to social gatherings either. Since she felt like she was treading on eggshells most of the time, Jess hadn't dared to contact any of her former friends of her own accord. It seemed safer to wait for them to call on her.

'Jessamijn, you're back at last! I thought you lost to us forever, you were gone so long. Did you find a handsome prince in the forest to marry?' Margreet was small and dark, and known as a great flirt, but she had a kind heart. Jess knew she was only teasing, so she shook her head with a smile.

'No, nothing as exciting. I just had a great deal to do and became caught up in the running of the manor for a while,' she lied.

Margreet made a face. 'How boring.' She glanced in Mr Kinross' direction. 'But it seems you've found something better here, eh?'

'What? Oh, you mean Mr Kinross. No, he's just my stepfather's new apprentice.'

Jess pretended indifference, but her eyes followed Margreet's. She studied the stylish cut of Kinross' black silk coat, which seemed moulded across his wide shoulders and fell in perfect pleats to just above his knees. He couldn't be accused of ostentation as he had dressed in the best possible taste. His coat had only a moderate number of silver buttons down the front and on the cuffs, but its very plainness enhanced his good looks. It also contrasted beautifully with his auburn hair.

'I wouldn't mind having him as my apprentice,' Margreet giggled.

'Oh, I don't know. He's very full of himself.' Jess didn't really want to talk about Mr Kinross any more. Just looking at him from a distance made her feel distinctly odd and she knew she had more important things to do. She took Margreet's arm and began to walk in the opposite direction. 'Now please, won't you tell me what I've missed while I've been away? There must be some interesting gossip, surely? How many young men's hearts have you broken in a year? Hundreds?'

Margreet laughed, then obliged good-naturedly with the latest tales of Gothenburg society. As they promenaded back and forth outside the church, however, Jess found her eyes kept straying to Mr Kinross. It was impossible not to notice how his hair shone with copper highlights in the sun and his laughter carried on the wind.

He was altogether too much of a distraction.

Killian spent the rest of the Sunday with Captain Craig and the group of other Scotsmen gathered at *Vita Hjorten*. He was introduced to a whole host of new people and they all seemed only too happy to welcome another fellow countryman. Several of them extended invitations to dinner even though he barely knew them. Killian gathered they stuck with their own kind as much as possible.

'Not sure the Swedes really want us here any more,' one man commented. 'But they needed our expertise and the money we bring in, so there's no going back now.'

'Expertise in what exactly?'

'Well, it was really the Dutch they needed most to build this place. But we're every bit as good at trade and seafaring, not to mention our contacts in England and Europe, so they welcomed us too. You'll soon learn.'

This was Killian's intention, but he didn't plan to be quite as insular as some of his compatriots. In order to really take advantage of all the opportunities that Gothenburg could offer him, he knew he had to forge links with the natives as well. With that in mind, he asked the landlord's fifteen-year-old son Jamie to teach him the Swedish language, starting immediately.

'I hate not knowing what everyone is saying, it makes me feel at a disadvantage,' he told the boy. 'So the quicker I can learn, the better. Will you help me, please?' The boy took one look at the silver *daler* Killian held out to him and nodded with a smile.

Killian found it difficult to get his tongue round some of the sounds the boy made, but other than that he discovered it wasn't a complicated language. Quite a few words were similar to English ones, which made it easier. Young Jamie was only too pleased to earn some extra money. As soon as he noticed that Killian treated him well, he even dared to assert himself more and correct any mistakes his pupil made.

'You'll soon catch on, sir, I'm sure of it,' he said with a cheeky grin, having just laughed at Killian's particularly bad pronunciation of the Swedish word for seventeen – *sjutton.*

Killian was determined to prove him right.

'Just you wait, you little scoundrel,' Killian smiled good-naturedly. 'Now go through those numbers again, please, and I'll get it right this time.'

Fergusson introduced him to his chief assistant early on the Monday morning. Albert Holm proved to be a quiet Swede of indeterminate age who seldom smiled. His face was plain, but pleasant, his thinning fair hair tied back neatly and his expression open and honest. Killian decided the man also had kind eyes. He spoke English, but it was heavily accented.

'Please to meet you,' he said. He pronounced the words as if he was still speaking in his native language, which made them seem flat and toneless. He bowed politely and Killian bowed back.

'*God morgon, herr Holm,*' he said, trying out his best newly-acquired Swedish. '*Hur mår Ni?*'

Fergusson laughed. Holm's eyebrows rose a notch and he nodded, as if he approved of Killian's attempt, but the man gave no other sign of surprise. '*Bra, tack*,' he replied.

'Been listening to the natives, have you?' Fergusson cut in. 'Good, good, always pays to keep your ears open. Well, I'll leave you in Albert's capable hands then. I've got some people to see about a cargo.'

Killian was left with Holm, feeling slightly awkward as he had no idea what was expected of him. Although he had spent some time with Lord Rosyth's steward learning about the running of the estate, he had never held a job as such. There was an embarrassed silence, then he decided he might as well try to break the ice. 'Er, what would you like me to do this morning?'

'Perhaps some sums?' They had been standing inside the doorway of a huge warehouse. Holm now led the way up to a smaller room on the first floor, reached via a rickety staircase. Holm's spare, but wiry frame moved without haste, but always with purpose. Killian soon understood that the man only spoke when he had something important to say, which meant it was best to listen carefully and take note.

The office, which was what the room proved to be, was covered in shelves from floor to ceiling. Ledgers and other papers were stacked in orderly heaps on just about every surface. There were two tall sloping writing desks at right angles to each other with writing materials neatly laid out at the top of each. 'Sit here, please. You can add?'

'Yes.' Killian hadn't exactly been a diligent pupil and most of his and Farquhar's tutors despaired of him. Still, he had a quick mind and they had never been able to complain about his aptitude. Learning came easily to him, as long as the subject in question interested him, and numbers was one of his *fortes*.

Holm placed a fat ledger in front of him and opened it at the latest page. He indicated a piece of clean paper on the desk and said, 'Add on there first, please, I want no mistake.' Killian nodded and got on with it.

There were only a few pages of sums needing attention, and he had soon finished. Holm sat at the other desk and was busy writing letters, but when Killian placed the finished sums in front of him, he looked up.

'You finish already? I check.'

While Holm went through the sheets, Killian paced back and forth in front of the windows of the office, which overlooked the coast. He could see his own ship anchored in the distance, as well as a large number of other vessels of various sizes. A warm glow spread through him at the thought that he was the owner of one of them. He hoped the cargo he and Captain Craig had decided on would make a good profit. The captain was off at this very moment negotiating with the local merchants to sell the goods they had brought and ask for a favourable price with regard to the cargo they wanted to buy.

'This is right,' he heard Holm say, and turned back to face the man.

'I know,' Killian said and smiled. The corners of Holm's mouth grudgingly turned upwards.

'So you know how to add, that is good. Now you do it in the book, then we go downstairs.'

'Fine.' Killian quickly finished this task as well, and then the two of them went back down to ground floor level.

Holm took him on a tour of the warehouse. 'All these things we trade,' he explained. 'Iron, tar, copper ...' The list went on, but Killian gathered those were the main items, or at least the ones that gave the most profit.

'*Vad är det*?' Killian pointed to a stack of sacks piled up against a wall.

'*Havre,* oats,' Holm said. 'Going to Scotland. Your people like ... er, *gröt?* What's it called in English?'

'You must mean porridge. Yes, we do. Did I say the question right? I've only just started learning.'

'You did in a way, but there are more polite ways of asking.'

'Will you teach me, please? As well as everything else?' Killian spread his hands to encompass the entire business of Messrs. Van Sandt & Fergusson.

Holm hesitated only a fraction before nodding. '*Ja*, I will. But only if you really want to learn.'

'Believe me, I do.'

'Good.'

And with that one word, Killian somehow felt he had received Holm's seal of approval.

It was the start of a friendship of sorts, although Killian

always felt as if the other man was holding back somehow. Holm never offered any comments about anything other than business. The few times Killian dared to ask a personal question, he was given a non-committal answer. He learned only that Holm was unmarried, lived alone in rented rooms and liked reading for pleasure. The older man helped Killian in many ways, however, such as with the problem of accommodation.

'Are you staying with Mr Fergusson?' he asked on the second morning.

'No, I'm still at the inn, but I would prefer some sort of lodging of my own. I really don't want to impose on Mr Fergusson and his family, although he did offer.'

Holm gave a small smile. 'Too many babies in that house,' he said and Killian grinned back at his perspicacity. 'I know a widow with two rooms to rent out. Respectable. You interested?'

'Definitely. Thank you, that was just what I had in mind.'

'Very well. I take you there after work.'

Fru Ljung proved to be a relative of Holm's, some sort of distant cousin from what Killian could gather. Friendly and chatty, she was pleased to let him have two connecting rooms on the first floor of her modest house. It was in a narrow street on the opposite side of town to the warehouse, but as Gothenburg wasn't very large, Killian didn't mind. A walk every morning would do him good.

Although it was only early autumn, the evenings were cold and he was grateful the sitting room had a tile stove similar to the one in Fergusson's house, although much smaller. *Fru* Ljung kindly lit it for him before he came home from work each day. She also agreed to cook him supper for a few extra *daler,* which saved him a lot of bother.

Next, Killian arranged for young Jamie to come to his lodgings as often as he could, and he was soon progressing with his Swedish speaking.

'Your pronunciation is atrocious,' Holm told him with an unaccustomed grin.

'Oh, yes?' Killian grinned back and didn't take offence since Holm said it in a good-natured fashion. 'Guess I'll just have to try harder then.'

Halfway through his second week, he was surprised to find Miss van Sandt outside the door to the warehouse one afternoon. He had answered her knock, since Holm was out at a meeting, and no one else seemed to be about.

'Miss van Sandt, what an unexpected pleasure,' he said and smiled.

She looked startled and tried to peer around him into the warehouse, as if she was searching for someone. 'Er, I came to see Mr Holm. Is-is he here?'

'No, but you're welcome to wait for him upstairs if you want.'

'Uhm, no thank you. I was only passing and don't have much time.'

He looked past her to see whether the formidable Mrs Forbes was in evidence. All he could see was a maid with a bored expression on her face waiting nearby. 'You were allowed out on your own? Tut, tut, your gaolers are slacking,' he teased.

'What do you mean? I'm not a prisoner. Whatever gave you that idea?' Her protest came rather too quickly, proving that he had hit the mark. She scowled at him, which made him want to reach out and smooth her brow. He resisted the urge.

'Aren't you? It seems to me that most girls are prisoners until they marry, forever guarded against any passing man.'

'Only against men like you, I should think,' she shot back.

'Perhaps,' he conceded with a grin. 'Why don't you come

inside and we can put it to the test? I presume that little maid is meant to defend your virtue, but we can leave her there.'

Miss van Sandt drew herself up to her full height, which wasn't very much since she didn't reach any further than the bottom of his chin. 'Thank you, but I don't need to test that theory. I'm fairly sure I wouldn't be safe anywhere near you.'

'You're probably right. Does it scare you?'

'No. I can deal with men like you. My father taught me.'

'I see. And what else did he teach you? How to do sums? How to trade?'

A wary expression crossed her features. 'Who told you that?'

'No one. Let's just say it was an educated guess.'

'Have you been talking to Albert?'

'Who? Oh, you mean Mr Holm. No, he's quite the clam. He only talks business. Is that why you came, to talk business?'

'Yes, I mean no ...' She tailed off, looking thoroughly flustered. 'You ask too many questions.' A frightened look entered her eyes. 'I would be grateful if you didn't mention to my stepfather that you have seen me here today. I, er, ... he wouldn't be pleased.'

'No, I don't suppose he would. Does Mrs Forbes know you're out?'

'She thinks I'm at the market. And I was. I just thought I'd pay Albert a quick visit while I was out. He was my father's friend, you know.'

'Just on the spur of the moment. Of course, I quite understand.' She opened her mouth to say something again, but before she could utter another word, he pulled her inside the door, out of sight of the maid. 'I'll keep quiet on one condition.'

'What?' Suspicion lurked in her eyes now.

'You give me a kiss.'

'How dare you?' Her grey eyes flashed like slivers of diamond ice and she took a step backwards, her chest heaving with indignation. But Killian noticed she didn't flee entirely. He took that as a good sign and followed her.

'I dare anything,' he said, then without further ado he pulled her close and covered her lips with his in a swift kiss. He didn't hold her for very long, but he had time to register that she felt soft and just right in his arms and she smelled of summer flowers. She blinked up at him, as if she couldn't believe what had just happened and he almost felt bad for taking advantage of her like this. Almost, but not quite. How could he regret something so enjoyable?

'There, now you have my word I won't mention a thing. *Adjö, Fröken* van Sandt,' he said, and took the stairs up to the office two at a time, resisting the temptation to look back.

He had definitely won that round.

Chapter Eleven

It was over before she even had time to blink, but the imprint of his mouth stayed on Jessamijn's for the rest of the day. It was as if he had branded her. She walked back to the house in a daze, looking neither right nor left. Once home, she went straight up to her room and sat down on her bed.

'Dear God,' she muttered, wondering why a simple kiss could have such an impact on her when she didn't even like the man.

It had seriously shaken her, there were no two ways about it. Her entire body was tingling, as if he had done much more than touch her lips with his own for such a brief space of time. It was ridiculous. The man was a rogue and he was just playing with her for some perverse reason only he knew. He couldn't possibly have any interest in courting her, or he would have come round to the house again without being invited. They hadn't seen hide or hair of him since that first supper and her stepfather claimed he kept the young man busy.

So why had he kissed her?

Jess could only assume he acted out of habit. A man with looks like that must be used to the attentions of women and perhaps flirting was as normal to him as breathing was for everyone else. There could be no other reason. He seemed to delight in teasing her. It worried her that he had been astute enough to ask about her interest in the business. What had he found out? Did he know she still kept in contact with Albert from time to time? That Albert was in fact loyal to her and tried to keep her up to date with matters relating to the company so that she wouldn't forget the things her father had taught her?

No, he couldn't know that. Albert would never tell a soul. Besides, that was before her banishment to Askeberga. She hadn't seen Albert since her return, which was why she'd jumped at the chance to seek him out today when she was finally allowed out without Mrs Forbes.

Albert was the only one who could answer her questions about whether the business had really been in trouble when her father died. He'd be able to tell her if that was yet another lie which had conveniently tripped off Robert's tongue. Albert would also know the best way of discovering what had happened to her father's will. Jess felt sure there must be some way of finding out about its contents, someone who remembered. Even if the document itself had been destroyed.

But Albert wasn't there. Instead she'd met Kinross and that penetrating blue gaze of his had almost made her forget why she had come. Unless he was a mind reader, he couldn't possibly know anything. Her secrets were safe.

But was her heart? Jess shivered. She had to make sure that it was.

'There's a gentleman to see you, sir. Says he has information for you.' The butler at Lord Rosyth's town house was wearing an expression of acute dislike as he made this announcement to Farquhar. He looked as if the individual in question smelled badly. 'I've put him in the morning room.'

Farquhar looked up from the broadsheet he'd been reading in the peace of his grandfather's study. He had retreated there, since he knew the old man was still asleep. 'Thank you, I'll go and see him in a moment.'

Farquhar had a network of spies working for him, but as Killian was now out of the country, he hadn't expected to hear from any of them. His curiosity piqued, he made his way to the morning room. There he found his most trusted, but also scruffiest, informant waiting for him.

'Allan, I didn't expect to see you today.' He indicated the man was to stay seated and he took a chair on the opposite side of the room. The butler had been right in his opinion. Allan was none too clean and stank to high heaven, but then personal hygiene wasn't what Farquhar paid him for.

'No, don't suppose you did, sir, but I heard a very interesting piece of information and I said to myself, I said, I bet Mr Kinross would be very pleased to hear about that.'

'And what was this interesting information?' Farquhar often became impatient with Allan's long-winded way of reporting, but he knew he couldn't show any outward signs of this or the man would demand a larger payment than necessary.

'Well, I was in a tavern drinking, and there was this man called McGrath. Drownin' his sorrows he was. Tellin' everyone in sight as how he didn't have nothin' to live for no more because your cousin, that's Mr Killian o' course, had robbed him of his only means of earnin' a living.'

'Robbed him?' Much as he disliked him, Farquhar didn't think Killian would stoop quite that low.

'Well, a figure of speech really. What he meant was, he played a game o' dice with your cousin and nat'rally he lost, like everyone else.'

'Of course.' Farquhar ground his teeth. It had always been a mystery to him why his cousin should have been blessed with such luck when he never won anything himself. So unfair. 'And how much did this McGrath lose?' He wished Allan would get to the point.

'Not how much, sir, but what. A ship, it were. The *Lady Madeleine* by name. Big one 'parently. Your cousin sailed off in it hisself, so I heard. Not sure where he was headed though.'

Allan finished his tale, looking hopeful. Farquhar dug in

his pocket and brought out a couple of silver coins, which made the man's eyes light up. 'You're sure my cousin now owns this ship?'

'Oh, yes. No doubt about it. McGrath signed a note and everythin' in front o' witnesses. I asked one o' his mates and it was all above board.'

'Right. Well, thank you, Allan, that is most useful. Do you think you could keep an eye out and let me know if the ship returns?'

'O' course, sir. Thank you, sir.'

Farquhar showed Allan out, deep in thought. So Killian had acquired a ship, he mused. That was bad news and something would have to be done about it. He couldn't possibly allow Killian to keep such an asset for long. That would be sheer madness.

'Damn his eyes,' he muttered. Killian was like a cat, always landed on his feet, but Farquhar was determined to put a stop to it. Even cats only had nine lives and he was sure his cousin had already used up a fair number of them. It was past time he lost the rest.

'Miss van Sandt came to see you,' Killian told Holm when the man returned. He kept his tone neutral to show him he hadn't thought this strange in any way. Despite this, a wary expression crept into the Swede's eyes and he frowned slightly.

'Did she? I knew her father well. She sometimes comes to talk about him and to ask after my health. Very kind-hearted, she is.'

'Yes, so she said. Well, I'm sure she'll come again another day.' Killian decided not to push his luck by probing deeper, although he was sure this was nowhere near the whole truth. There were still a lot of things he needed to learn. Finding out Miss van Sandt's secrets was only one of his goals.

Without further comment, he went back to adding up sums.

The most important documents in the office, together with any cash, were kept in a strongbox. A short while later Holm asked Killian to search through this for a particular agreement which the chief assistant wanted to look at. The box had a hefty lock and only Holm and Mr Fergusson had a key. Holm gave his to Killian, then went to speak to one of the workers employed to load and unload cargoes down in the warehouse.

Killian had no difficulty opening the box. It took him a while to find the required document, however, and he had to riffle through most of the contents before he came across it. On impulse, he quickly sifted through the rest of the papers inside to see if there was anything of interest.

He was intrigued by several official-looking documents relating to house purchases. It would seem that Fergusson was buying up property in Gothenburg. Was he trying to increase his wealth by renting them out? It was likely, although the houses were all bought on behalf of the company.

So far, Killian hadn't come across any rent payments in the accounts he was given each day. This made him wonder if the rents were going straight into Fergusson's pockets. It was certainly something he would have to investigate. He memorised the addresses of the properties in question so he could make discreet enquiries at a later date.

He gave Holm the document he'd been asked to find.

'Thank you.' Holm nodded. 'You can put the rest back now. We don't want any of the workers to see its contents.'

Killian replaced the papers and locked the box, then sat down again. For some reason, his thoughts returned to Miss van Sandt. He decided to try to fish for at least a few answers, just to see where it might lead him.

'Mr Holm,' he began, trying his best to look as if he was just curious, 'does Miss van Sandt own shares in this company?'

Holm looked up and narrowed his eyes. 'No, why you ask?'

'I just wondered. I heard some gossip about her and a young nobleman who was after her dowry. I thought perhaps it was the company he wanted. Not that she isn't pretty,' he added quickly, since it was obvious Holm was very fond of her.

'Well, he wouldn't have had any part of it,' Holm said, ignoring Killian's comment about Miss van Sandt's looks. 'Mr Fergusson owns it now. Everything was left to Mrs van Sandt and as her new husband, of course it all came to Mr Fergusson when he married her.'

'Did you see the will?' Killian smelled a rat, but couldn't quite put his finger on it.

'No, why should I? Mr Fergusson gave it to the local magistrate as is the usual way.' Holm gave him a speculative look. 'Why you want to know these things? You want to marry the girl yourself?'

'Me? No, heaven forbid. I don't have the time for marriage just now, there's so much else I have to do first.'

Holm nodded, seemingly satisfied, and Killian thought it best not to ask any further questions. At least not openly.

Killian had spent an afternoon in the warehouse, learning from one of the foremen exactly how everything was stored, and was making his way up the stairs to the office when he heard raised voices. Or rather, one raised voice and a few muted replies. He tip-toed up to the top and stopped just short of the door, listening intently.

'And I must've told you a hundred times not to encourage that girl to meddle in matters she has no right to know anything about. She was seen entering this building and I won't have it, you hear? This is *my* company now. I don't hold with females doing anything other than keeping house. I don't care what nonsense her father taught her. The man was a deluded fool who obviously couldn't cope with the fact he'd bred no sons. No one in their right mind would expect a female to know anything about a business, even if she had inherited it, which she didn't. And besides ...'

Fergusson, whose outraged voice could be clearly heard through the thin wood of the door, continued in this vein for quite some time. Occasionally, Holm tried to inject a comment or two. He protested that Miss van Sandt had only come to pay him a courtesy visit because of his friendship for her father. Inevitably, he was shouted down and soon stayed silent.

'From now on, if I catch that girl in here again, or if I hear she's been within a mile of the warehouse, she'll be sent back to live in the deep forests again. And this time she won't be coming back. Is that clear? I shan't speak of the matter with her, because she knows my views on this subject, so it's up to you to tell her. No doubt she'll listen to you more readily, since she never seems to take any notice of the slightest thing I say.'

Fergusson stomped towards the door and Killian only just had time to scoot down to the bottom of the stairs. He pretended to be on his way up when the door was yanked open. As he opened his mouth to greet his employer, Fergusson barged past him without a word, his dark eyes blazing. He slammed the door to the warehouse with as much force as he could muster. Killian looked after the man and shook his head. When he began to climb the stairs again, he found Holm standing at the top, frowning.

'You hear any of that?' he asked curtly. His usually placid expression had been replaced by one of deep worry.

'A few words,' Killian admitted. He couldn't very well deny it, since it was likely anyone within a hundred yards had heard Fergusson yelling.

'Well, keep it to yourself, right?'

Killian nodded. 'Won't breathe a word. But what of the young lady? Will you warn her?'

'*Ja.* I already tell her in church, but she's stubborn, so I don't know if it will be of any use.' Holm sighed. 'Let's forget it now, is not our problem.'

Killian followed him into the office. He knew Holm was right, but he had a feeling he hadn't heard the last of the matter.

Chapter Twelve

Jess received the terse note from Albert that same afternoon and gritted her teeth in frustration. He told her in no uncertain terms to stay away from him and the warehouse for now. But how was she to learn anything about Robert's activities? She needed answers.

She had managed to have a brief word with him after church the previous Sunday, but this had only reinforced her feeling that something wasn't right.

'As far as I know, the company has never been in trouble,' Albert said, frowning in concern when she asked about this. 'When your father died, all was in order and business was fairly brisk as I recall. I don't know why Mr Fergusson should have claimed otherwise. Unless it was to discourage the young man from courting you? Most parents tell small lies in order to protect their children.'

Jess didn't think protection of her had been Robert's motive at all, but she couldn't prove it. 'Is he investing heavily in anything? Is there something underhand going on he wouldn't want me to know about?'

Albert shook his head. 'I've not seen or heard anything out of the ordinary. Besides, it's his business so why would he be worried about you finding out? You have no say in such matters.'

That was precisely what annoyed Jess, but she knew he was right. 'Well, all the same, I'd be grateful if you could be vigilant, please.'

'Very well, I'll keep my eyes and ears open, but please bear in mind that although your stepfather is not well liked, it doesn't mean he's dishonest. I really don't know what it is you expect me to find.'

Jess didn't know either. She only had a vague feeling that somehow Robert had cheated her, and she had to get to the bottom of it.

The question was how, if she wasn't even allowed to see Albert? She had been so careful when she went to the warehouse, bringing only a maid. Either the girl had been bribed to tell her employer where Jess had gone, or he had set someone else to spy on her. It made her furious that she couldn't do anything without him knowing about it, but didn't it also confirm he had something to hide? If he didn't, surely there would be no need to keep tabs on her or to prevent her from seeing Albert?

Well, she refused to let this stand in her way. She would just have to be even more careful in future.

As autumn arrived with a vengeance and the weather grew progressively colder, the foreigners living in Gothenburg began to congregate more often at Murdoch's inn. Killian was told that Sweden was a bleak and godforsaken place for more than half the year, but as far as he could see, it wasn't all that different from Scotland. The coming of winter didn't bother him. He'd always enjoyed the wild weather and sudden snowstorms at Rosyth House, and looked forward to the freezing months ahead.

Darkness fell earlier each day and the cosy atmosphere of the taproom became a haven of light and leisure pursuits, including gaming. Killian had been careful not to overdo it with the cards and dice since his arrival in Gothenburg. However, he knew that if he wanted to be able to buy better cargos for his ship, he would need more money. Therefore, although he never initiated a game of any kind himself, he continued to play whenever someone invited him. By setting himself a limit for how much capital to use as a starting point and not exceeding this at any time, he managed to gather quite a little nest egg. As always, Lady Luck was on his side. So much so that his reputation quickly spread and he had to take even more care not to fleece anyone.

Quite how far his skills had become known was brought home to him when he ran into Miss van Sandt again one morning. She was coming down the stairs from the office just as he entered the warehouse. He looked up, surprised to see her there at such an early hour, and alarmed that she hadn't paid attention to Holm's warnings for her to stay away. Holm was obviously right – she was foolhardy and stubborn.

'Miss van Sandt, *god morgon.*' He bowed and waited for her to reach the bottom of the staircase. She hesitated for a moment, then nodded and said a frosty good morning as she swept past him on her way to the front door. Killian couldn't resist a comment, and he was also determined to give her a subtle warning, so he said, 'Give my best regards to your stepfather, won't you?'

She stopped dead and turned slowly to face him, anger and mistrust warring in her quicksilver eyes. Killian smiled as she walked the few steps back towards him. 'I thought I "paid" you not to mention my visits here to him?' she hissed.

'That was for last time and besides, he found out anyway. Although not from me, I assure you.'

Her right hand twitched as if she wanted to hit him, but he regarded her calmly, only raising his brows at her when she stuttered, 'Why you ... you ... oh!'

He took pity on her and shook his head. 'Don't worry, your secret is safe with me. If you found your so called "payment" so awful, I won't make you do it again unless you want to.'

'Why would I want to kiss a hardened gambler? You're

not exactly an acceptable suitor, are you?' she shot back, her cheeks slowly turning pink.

'Hardened gambler? You exaggerate, Miss van Sandt.' It annoyed him that such rumours had reached her ears, and he was determined to be even more on his guard in future. He didn't let these thoughts show, however, but stayed calm.

'That's not what the gossips say. I hear you are on a winning streak.'

'You really shouldn't listen to idle talk. Don't you know that for each person who repeats the tale, the item in question is multiplied tenfold?'

'So it's not true then?' she challenged, putting one hand on her hip. He smiled again, liking her spirit. It was obvious she was trying to divert his attention from the original subject of their conversation. She was doing a fairly good job of it too.

'I play a hand of cards now and again with my friends, who doesn't?' He shrugged. 'It's hardly my fault if Lady Luck seems to favour me above the others at the moment.'

'Hah, a likely tale.'

'Well, you can choose to believe whatever you want, Miss van Sandt. The truth is that I don't play beyond my means and never recklessly. If that makes me a hardened gambler, then so be it. What amusements do you pursue? Embroidery? Gossip? Meddling in affairs you have been warned not to stick your pretty nose into? I rather think I prefer a game of cards.'

'You're impossible,' she muttered and turned to leave once more.

'Ahem, did you forget something?' he asked and she glanced over her shoulder, her eyes widening in consternation.

'No, I did not,' she stated firmly, but she stayed rooted to the spot.

He took his chance and stepped close to her, after first checking there was no one else about. Quickly he bent to give her a swift kiss, chaste but lingering a touch longer than he should have. 'Please don't come here again,' he whispered. 'I mean it. It's too dangerous for you. Trust me.'

Her eyes flew up to search his, but he turned and left her there, hurrying up the stairs before he was tempted to do more than just kiss her. Her spirit had fired his blood, but he knew she wasn't for him. He had no time for dalliance at the moment.

He just hoped she listened to his advice.

Jess ran into her mother as soon as she entered the house, so there was no chance of disappearing up to her room unseen to think things over.

'There you are, Jess. Where have you been? Mrs Forbes has looked everywhere for you.' Her mother looked distracted, as always.

'Oh, I thought she said she was staying in bed this morning because she had a headache.'

Mrs Forbes never refused a glass of whisky the few times she was offered one. She was forever pining for Scotland and said this drink made her think of home. Last night had been one such occasion. Robert had brought out the bottle to celebrate some successful business deal he'd made that day, and he never liked to drink alone. Katrijna couldn't stand the 'vile stuff' as she called it, which meant that Mrs Forbes was usually invited to have a glass instead. Invariably, she had a sore head the next day, and Jess had expected her to stay in bed until lunchtime.

'No, she's been up and about for some time,' Katrijna said. 'She's quite cross with you, you know, and who can blame her?'

'I'm sorry to hear that, I just went to the market. There were some embroidery threads I needed.' Jess had bought these on her way back to the house, just in case anyone thought to ask where she had been. 'I wasn't alone, I had Margit with me.' That particular maid was Albert's niece, and therefore not likely to tell tales, so Jess knew she was safe in that respect.

'Oh, well that's good. Do go and find Mrs Forbes though. I really don't want to listen to any more complaints this morning.'

Jess did as she was asked and for once Mrs Forbes accepted her explanation without suspicion. Since her companion winced every time the sun peeped through the clouds and spilled into the room, Jess figured the old dragon was still suffering. This made her less inclined to think too much about what Jess had been up to.

'Did you hear any news while you were out?' Mrs Forbes's main interest was gossip, since nothing much happened in her own life. She made it her business to find out everything she could about any inhabitant of Gothenburg worth knowing. This was not a trait which endeared her to Jess.

'Not much. There was talk of an engagement between Miss Vallgren and a Mr Forslund, but no definite announcement.'

Mrs Forbes nodded. 'Yes, I heard that yesterday. Apparently he had to be forced into it. He had, shall we say, overstepped the bounds of propriety.'

'Really?' Jess wondered whether such a course of action would be the solution to her own problem, but somehow she didn't think it would work. To deliberately become pregnant would be a huge gamble. No doubt Robert would find some way of discrediting her instead of making the man responsible pay for his actions. She suppressed a sigh. 'There was also more talk of Mr Kinross's winning streak,' she added, wanting to see what reaction that piece of news would cause. It was Mrs Forbes who had told her of his gaming in the first place.

'Doesn't surprise me,' the woman snorted. 'He's a bad one, mark my words. He'll never stay employed with Mr Fergusson for long. Born to a life of leisure, that type, and probably never done a day's work in his life.'

A few weeks earlier Jess would have been inclined to agree, but that morning Albert had mentioned in passing that he was very pleased with the work Mr Kinross was doing. He said the young man was making huge progress. This didn't fit with the image of a dissolute gambler.

He could still be a scoundrel though.

She shivered, remembering with outrage that Mr Kinross had dared to make her pay for his silence yet again. However, she couldn't deny she'd had the opportunity to leave. So why hadn't she? An innate honesty made her admit to herself she had actually wanted him to kiss her again. She'd needed to know whether it would have the same effect on her as it had the previous time.

Well, there was no doubt about it now.

In fact, his touch turned her into a witless idiot, unable to so much as protest, but his next words had made her forget everything else. Albert had already begged her not to come again, but she had taken his words as those of an over-concerned uncle, dismissing his fears. Mr Kinross was a different matter. Did he know something she didn't?

It was disconcerting that he knew so much about her affairs. He'd only been in Sweden for a few short weeks. How had he found out about her circumstances so quickly? Even if he listened to gossip as avidly as Mrs Forbes, there shouldn't be anything to learn. Other than the old story about her and Karl of course. She wondered yet again whether Albert had let slip anything, but she simply couldn't believe him capable of breaking her trust. He wasn't a man who spoke without thinking. He was as loyal as it was possible to be. Besides, he had sworn to try to help her, although naturally he had to be careful unless he wanted to lose his employment.

Her thoughts returned to Mr Kinross, her mind's eye conjuring up a disturbing image of him smiling as he bent to kiss her, his extraordinary eyes intense. She shivered. Kinross was trouble with a capital T and he could protest his innocence all he liked – she still didn't believe him. He may not be a hardened gambler, but he *was* reckless. By his own admission he dared anything and she was sure he would come to a sticky end.

That wasn't her problem. She, for one, would take care not to be alone with him again. What he did on his own was none of her business. A thought struck her suddenly. Perhaps she ought to find out exactly what he knew? Another visit to the warehouse so soon after this one was out of the question. But there was one other place where she saw him regularly and where he had sworn to sit next to her whenever he could – at church.

She smiled to herself. So far she had thwarted his attempts, but she rather thought it was time to relent.

Killian continued to attend church every Sunday, because he didn't want to offend anyone until he was his own man. So far, Miss van Sandt had managed to avoid sitting next to him again and he had to endure the mind-numbingly boring sermons without any diversion. It didn't help that he now actually understood a lot of what the minister said. He would have preferred not to.

He had tried to outwit Miss van Sandt a few times, but she always found some excuse why it was necessary for her to move. Her mother needed help with the boys, Mrs Forbes was beckoning for her to sit somewhere else or the bench had a loose nail or some such. All very convenient, and naturally he couldn't protest since that would have been considered suspicious. In the end, he admitted defeat and stopped trying.

It was therefore a great surprise when he found her at the end of the pew the following Sunday. She even went so far as to move over slightly to make room for him. He raised his eyebrows at her, but she pretended she hadn't seen the question in his eyes. Instead she turned the pages of her hymn book with great concentration.

'Good morning,' he said and sat down beside her, intrigued by this new development. She nodded absently and turned to say something to Mrs Forbes. Killian decided to be patient. Whatever she was up to would no doubt be revealed in good time.

Her brothers were fidgeting as usual. The youngest soon managed to fall off the bench and scrape his elbow, although judging by his howls one could have been forgiven for thinking his entire arm was broken. Mrs Fergusson tried to hush him, since the minister glared in her direction. When that didn't work, she lifted the little boy into her arms and hustled him outside.

That meant Mrs Forbes had to move over to sit with the older boy, who seemed put out by his mother's departure. Young Ramsay started to kick the bench in front of him and refused to stop, despite being reprimanded both by his father and Mrs Forbes. In between each kick, the boy whispered the words, 'Want Mama', over and over again.

The result of all this disruption was that Killian found himself virtually isolated at one end of the pew with Miss van Sandt. He was just about to take advantage of this when she whispered, 'I need to speak to you. Please pretend you're concentrating on your hymn book or something.'

He threw her a brief glance, but did as he'd been asked.

'What about?' he whispered back.

'What you said the other day. Why were you so adamant I should stay away? I've done nothing wrong.'

'Your stepfather doesn't seem to agree. I heard him arguing with Mr Holm. I think you'll find yourself back in the forest for good if you don't stay away from the business. He was quite determined about that.'

She made a frustrated little noise and Killian was tempted to take her hand and squeeze it in reassurance. 'But why?' came her anguished question. 'What is he hiding?'

'You think he's hiding something? From you?' Killian hadn't considered that before. He thought the hostility between them had only come about because she disliked Fergusson usurping her father's place.

She nodded and told him briefly the true circumstances of the marriage proposal from Mr Adelsten the previous year. 'So you see, I'm sure he's up to something.'

'Why are you telling me this? How do you know I won't tell Fergusson?'

She shot him a quick look of fear, but he saw resolve in her eyes at the same time. Perhaps even a touch of desperation. 'What do I stand to lose?' she asked. 'I can't find the answers any other way, so I had to take a gamble you wouldn't betray me. You were kind enough to warn me earlier, so I thought ... but perhaps I was wrong? Will you tell?'

'No, I won't, but I can't give you any answers either. So far, the only proof of wrong-doing I have found are some properties owned by the company where the rent money seems to be going straight into Fergusson's pockets. That's nothing to do with your situation though. And although Mr Holm must know about it, he hasn't said anything so I don't suppose it's that much of a crime. The company is doing well enough that he should be able to provide you with your full dowry at any time.'

He sensed her despair and saw her shoulders hunch over in defeat. 'Then I don't know what else to do. I just feel there is something not right. Why would he go to such lengths to keep me away otherwise?'

'Don't give up yet. I'll let you know if I find anything, but please don't come to the warehouse again. It really is too risky.'

'If you say so.'

'Have you thought of looking in his study?' Killian suggested. 'If I was hiding something, I would keep it close to me, not at my place of work.'

'You're right. Perhaps I should, but ... what if he were to catch me?'

'Make sure you do it when he's not at home. He's out most days, isn't he?'

She nodded and he saw her clench her fists with determination. 'Yes. I'll have to try.'

'Well, sit with me again next Sunday so that we can communicate. I'd like to know what you find.'

'I will. And thank you, you've been very helpful. I'm afraid I can't repay you in any way.'

'Oh, I don't know, I'm sure I could think of something.' He smiled at her and saw understanding dawn in her eyes, only to be replaced by outrage.

'Why, you ...'

'Shhh.' He put a hand over hers under cover of her skirts, his smile widening. 'I was only teasing. You are delightfully easy to rile, you know.'

She relaxed a little, and even managed to smile back. 'Is that so? Well, I'll just have to be on my guard then.'

'You can always try.' He grinned at her, and just to prove she was no match for him, he kept hold of her hand for the rest of the sermon despite several attempts on her part to pull it away. Eventually, she accepted defeat and made a face at him, which made him want to laugh out loud. If they hadn't been in church he would have been tempted to kiss her. Instead, he contented himself with circling her palm with lazy thumb strokes, which made her blush.

He was looking forward to the following Sunday already.

The *Lady Madeleine* wasn't difficult to find and Farquhar strolled along the crowded quayside in the gathering dusk, slightly dazed at the sheer size of the vessel. Ever since Allan had reported the ship's return, he had been trying to think how best to incapacitate it. He'd come up with several ideas, but none of them seemed plausible now that he could actually see the ship for himself.

'Damn,' he muttered.

There was still a lot of coming and going, with men running up and down the gangplank loading a new cargo. Farquhar watched them for a while. It would seem his cousin had set up in business and was trading Scottish goods in Sweden. That was exactly the sort of thing Lord Rosyth would approve of, which meant Killian had to be stopped.

There was only one thing to do and that was to strike him where it would hurt the most – the cargo. If Killian had no merchandise with which to trade, he couldn't make any profit. A hazy plan took shape in Farquhar's mind, becoming clearer the more he thought about it.

'Yes, the cargo has to go,' he said to himself. 'All of it.'

He watched for a while longer, then went off to gather what he needed. He would do the deed himself this time. That way he'd avoid having to pay anyone for their silence, and he would do it tonight. It shouldn't be too difficult.

Farquhar smiled to himself. He was so intent on his plans he never noticed the shadowy figure that followed him wherever he went, watching his every move. It never occurred to him that two could play the same game.

Chapter Thirteen

Gothenburg, Sweden

The door to Robert's study stood slightly ajar and Jess paused on her way to the kitchen. The temptation to enter was irresistible. She knew he had just gone out and wasn't due to return until suppertime. It seemed too good an opportunity to be missed. Looking around quickly, to make sure she was really alone, she slipped inside and pushed the door to without shutting it completely.

With a pounding heart and her ears alert to the slightest sound, she tip-toed over to Robert's desk. It was neat and orderly as always, all the papers in tidy piles. When she riffled through them, she couldn't see anything other than ordinary business correspondence and lists of goods and prices. She made sure she put them back exactly as she found them.

Oh, Lord, oh Lord, please help me, she prayed silently, although quite what she wanted God to do, she wasn't sure.

Kinross' words echoed through her mind. *If I was hiding something, I would keep it close to me, not at my place of work*. It made sense and she knew he had to be right, but where to look?

A sound from the hallway made her freeze. Her heart stopped almost completely for an instant, but whoever it was moved on, the footsteps receding into another part of the house. She breathed out, shaking from head to toe, but was even more determined to continue her search. She had risked too much already to back out now.

She opened the drawers, one by one, but didn't find anything until she opened the middle one. A half-finished letter suddenly stared her in the face. Scanning its contents, she read

Dear Sir,

I am writing to you regarding that most delicate matter we discussed a few years ago now, upon the demise of my business partner. I am sure I do not need to urge you to keep our dealings to yourself. However, I must warn you there may be those who will seek to discover the truth and as you know, that would not be to either your advantage or mine. I would therefore advise the utmost caution, should anyone ask you any questions.

In the meantime,

There, the letter ended and Jess was left with an overwhelming sense of relief mixed with curiosity and utter frustration. Here was some tangible proof at last, but who was the letter for? And what else had Robert intended to write? She turned it over, but there was no name or direction, only the letters AM. That could be any number of people. She wanted to scream with vexation.

As she lifted the sheet of paper, however, she noticed there was a clean one underneath, upon which there was a faint imprint of Robert's words. She thought he must be one of those people who push very hard with the quill when writing so that it showed on the next page as well. This was definitely to her advantage. She snatched the clean sheet up and put it in her pocket. It might be possible to make the words visible by rubbing the paper with dirt or ash later. Since she didn't dare take the original, it was the best she could do in the circumstances.

The following Sunday, she would pass it on to Kinross to

see what he thought and he in turn could show it to Albert. Perhaps now they would believe that she wasn't imagining things.

'Captain Craig, it's good to see you again. How was the trip?'

Killian was pleased when Mrs Ljung ushered the captain into his sitting room one gloomy evening and he hoped for good news.

'The voyage itself was uneventful, but we had a bit of trouble before we left Edinburgh.'

Killian's stomach sank. 'What kind of trouble?'

'The cargo caught fire.'

'What? Oh, hell.' He clenched his fists. 'How did that happen?' A frisson of fear shot through him, laced with anger. Was he never to be allowed to prosper?

'Arson. Had to be, there weren't any lanterns on board at the time and certainly not in the hold. I'd never allow it and my men know better than to disobey my orders.'

Killian stood up abruptly and began to pace the room. If it hadn't been an accident, he knew only too well who was the likely culprit. Farquhar. *Damn him!* Quite how his cousin had found out about him owning the ship, he had no idea. He supposed someone present during his game with McGrath might have spread the word. 'So you're telling me you had to sail over here with no cargo?'

Captain Craig shook his head. 'No, I was asleep in my cabin, but luckily there was a witness who managed to alert me to what was happening. Together we put the fire out before it could do much damage. We only lost a few sacks of grain.'

Killian breathed out a sigh of relief. 'That was fortunate.'

'Indeed. When I thanked the young man, he said he was a friend of yours, name of Adair?'

'Ah, thank goodness for that. So he's doing his job then. I did have my doubts, since he's an idle young varmint.' Killian was happy to hear that Adair hadn't gone back to his thieving ways. At least not enough to stop him tailing Farquhar as he'd been asked to do.

'His job?' Captain Craig looked puzzled, so Killian filled him in by telling him about the bad blood between himself and his cousin, as well as the task he had set Adair.

'You should've told me before. I'd have posted guards, but I'll certainly do so from now on. Never occurred to me we'd need to do that. Everyone knows I sleep on board and that's always been enough in the past to guarantee the safety of the cargo.'

Killian nodded. 'Yes, I'm sorry. I should have guessed my cousin wouldn't leave me alone even when I was out of the country.'

'Why does he hate you so much? If you don't mind me asking.'

'I think he wants to take my place as my grandfather's heir and he's been putting spokes in my wheel for years. I wasn't aware he knew about the ship or I'd have warned you. I'd be grateful if you would be watchful from now on though. He won't be content until he's destroyed me completely.'

'Hm, well as to that, he'll have to find another way. Nothing more is going to happen to the ship, you have my word on that.'

Killian smiled at the man. 'Thank you, Captain. Thank you for everything.'

'Not at all. I've brought you the profits, and we didn't do too badly.' Captain Craig extracted a clinking pouch from his pockets and handed it to Killian. It was a lot heavier than he had expected.

'I'd say!' He tipped out the contents and counted the coins, then whistled softly. 'I guess you were right, there really is money to be made going back and forth between Sweden and Scotland.'

'Sure there is. As long as you buy the right goods and keep in well with certain merchants. Not to mention avoid the likes of your employer. Far too stingy, that one.' Craig grinned and Killian couldn't help but grin back.

'Have you paid the crew?' Craig nodded. 'Good, then tell me how much you need in order to keep the ship in good repair and to buy more merchandise, then we'll split the rest in half.'

Captain Craig's eyebrows rose. 'Half, Mr Kinross? Surely not.'

'But of course. You're doing all the hard work, so you deserve to profit from it equally.'

'Why, thank you. That's very generous. Very generous, indeed. I hadn't expected anything like as much.'

'It's only fair. Now let's plan the next trip.'

Killian knew he was being magnanimous towards the captain, giving him far more than he could ever have hoped for. He knew if the man was happy, he had even more of an incentive to make that profit larger. That in turn should make more money for Killian in the long run. At the moment he was pleased with any steady income, apart from the meagre salary Fergusson was paying him. It was much better than worrying about when his next win at the gaming tables would be.

Later, when the captain had gone, Killian added his share of the profits to his growing stash of money in a safe hiding place. A few more trips like that and he might be able to set up in business for himself. Then Mr Fergusson would have to find another clerk and good riddance, he thought.

'Er, Mr Holm, could I have a word please?'

It was Monday morning, and Killian had come in extra

early hoping to catch Holm on his own, which was exactly what had happened. The piece of paper Jess had passed to him at church the previous day was in his pocket and he was itching to discuss it with Holm.

'Yes, what is it?' Holm looked up from a ledger he had been working on and frowned. 'You here very early. You ill?'

'No, I'm fine, it's just, there is a matter I need to discuss with you and I didn't want an audience.' He nodded towards the warehouse proper, where soon the manual labourers would start to arrive for the day's work. 'It concerns Miss van Sandt.'

Holm's frown turned into a ferocious scowl. 'I thought I asked you to forget about her. If it's about her visit, I told her not to come back and she hasn't.'

'No, that's not what I want to talk to you about. The thing is, we often sit next to each other at church. For some reason she decided to confide in me about how matters stand between herself and Mr Fergusson.'

Holm tut-tutted with impatience and shook his head. 'Silly girl,' he muttered, then sighed and looked Killian in the eye. 'I tell you, is better for you not to get involved. Nothing good can come of it. She will soon accept her stepfather has control over everything and when he's ready, he will marry her to someone. That is all she can expect. I do feel sorry for her, but her father was foolish to give her hope for more.'

It was Killian's turn to shake his head. 'I don't think she disputes that, Mr Holm. She does feel Mr Fergusson has been less than truthful though and yesterday she passed me something which appears to confirm her suspicions. Take a look at this.' He handed Holm the piece of paper and the other man's eyes narrowed while he glanced at it.

'This is a copy of a real letter?'

'Yes. She, uhm, happened to find it in Mr Fergusson's study.'

'Happened to find it, eh?' Holm smiled ruefully. '*Envisa flickebarn*,' he muttered. 'And she gave you this in church? You sure no one saw her?'

'No. We "accidentally" swapped hymn books and it was inside hers. I didn't open it until I was back at my lodgings.'

'Hmm. Well, it does seem to confirm there's something going on, but it doesn't actually prove anything.'

'She said there was no address, but the letters AM were written on the back. Do you know who that might be?'

'Could be several people. There's Axel Månsson, the smith, Adolf Morgren, the merchant, Anders Milner, the magistrate, Arne Mattisson, the ...'

'Hold on a moment, a magistrate? He would be a useful ally to have, surely?'

Holm shrugged. 'He's been a friend of the family for a long time. I'm sure he would never do anything to hurt the van Sandts.'

'Maybe not voluntarily, but what if he was forced?' Killian had lived long enough with his cousin to know that blackmail was very tempting when everything else failed. He'd lost count of the number of times Farquhar had made servants and others do his bidding because he had spied on them and knew something they didn't want others to find out.

Holm looked bemused, but shook his head. 'I don't think so. There have never been any rumours about him taking bribes or anything. Not like some.'

Killian paced the office. Now that he had become involved with Miss van Sandt's affairs, he wanted answers. It was frustrating to be shown this tantalisingly small piece of evidence and not be able to go further.

'Leave it with me,' Holm said. 'You should stay out of this or you might lose your position. Jessamijn should never have involved you.'

'But I want to help. I can't stand injustice.' It made him think of his grandfather's treatment of him and he knew that Miss van Sandt was right to fight her corner. 'Shall I keep the paper for now? It might be safer.'

'Very well. Hide it in your rooms and don't show it to anyone else.'

'And will you let me know if you find anything? I can tell Miss van Sandt at church.'

'*Ja*, I will. But warn her not to expect too much. And, *för Guds skull,* tell her no more snooping. It could be very dangerous.'

And with that, Killian had to be satisfied for the present.

Chapter Fourteen

'Kinross, may I introduce Mr Colin Campbell, a true Scotsman like ourselves.'

Killian had once again been invited to the Fergusson household for supper, but this time it was more of a business occasion. The dreary salon contained a large group of ladies and gentlemen. Killian had seen some of the men around town or at the inn and knew they were all merchants or seafaring men, but he'd never been formally introduced to them. Presumably some were also colleagues of Fergusson's. Colin Campbell was one of these.

A pair of blue, intelligent eyes looked out from under bushy, greying eyebrows and regarded Killian with interest. Campbell had probably never been handsome even when he was young. His nose was on the large side, with a high bridge and long slightly rosy and bulbous tip, and his mouth, although curved in a pleasant smile, was rather thin. He made up for this with his jovial manner and he was smartly dressed in a russet-coloured velvet coat with matching satin waistcoat and buff breeches. On his head he wore a curled wig that matched his eyebrows, and Killian noticed that his linen was white and starched to perfection.

'Pleased to make your acquaintance, sir,' Killian said and bowed, receiving a nod and a smile in return. 'I hear you have recently returned from Scotland. How are things over there?'

'Much the same as usual,' Campbell replied. 'I'm glad to be back here though, as our great plans are coming to fruition.'

'Great plans?' Killian was all ears, although he didn't

want to seem too inquisitive. Fergusson never told him about any of the deals he struck. It was only through Holm that he sometimes learned about planned ventures.

'Those gentlemen over there,' Campbell nodded towards two others who were now talking to Fergusson and his wife, 'are Henrik König and Niclas Sahlgren, both well-to-do merchants. In June they received permission from His Majesty the King to form a Swedish East India Company. Since I have some experience of these things, I've been asked to act as advisor and supercargo on the first journey. I'm really looking forward to it.'

Killian knew by now that a supercargo was the person responsible for an expedition to foreign ports. He would be the one in charge of selling the cargo and negotiating a better one for the return journey. It was a position that required experience and a sharp brain. Mr Campbell seemed to have both. 'You've travelled a lot then, Mr Campbell? That must have been fascinating.'

'Oh, yes, I've had quite a few adventures, lad. Sailed for some years with the Ostend Company, although that's being abolished now. I know my way round foreign parts, indeed I do.' Campbell went on to talk about some of his journeys abroad, and Killian listened with rapt attention. An idea had taken root in his mind, and at the first opportunity he dared to ask some leading questions.

'Do you have a ship for the first trip yet?'

'There's one being made ready in Stockholm as we speak. It's called the *Friedericus Rex Sueciae* named after Sweden's King Fredrik I. It had to be either built or fitted out in this country. That was one of the conditions the company has to adhere to, otherwise we could have bought a suitable one.'

'That makes sense, I suppose,' Killian commented.

'Yes, it will benefit the Swedes, and he's been very magnanimous in other ways, His Majesty. Any foreigner sailing with us will be given Swedish nationality to protect them on the journey. The company also has sole and exclusive rights to trade for fifteen years.'

'That does sound incredibly generous.' Killian wondered what the Swedish King would get out of this deal, but didn't dare ask. He was sure some incentive had been put forward in order to obtain such concessions.

'Indeed it is, but that's not all. There are also benefits with regard to duty and excise charges, as long as we depart from and come back to Gothenburg. Not sure that will go down too well with the locals since they still have to pay, but that's not our problem. And of course they'll profit from it as well in the end. We'll be selling their goods abroad, won't we, and bringing merchandise back.'

'And will it be very profitable, do you think?'

'My dear young man, you have no idea! Staggering sums can be made in the East India trade, take my word for it. And lost, as I know to my cost. Yes, a risky business, but when a venture succeeds, the gains are enormous.'

'Really? And will it be possible to invest in this particular one, do you think Mr Campbell?'

'But of course. Anyone is welcome to contribute, so long as they have a minimum of five hundred silver *daler*. There's already been considerable interest. Why, are you thinking of investing? Didn't think young clerks had the resources for that.' Campbell chuckled, obviously not intending any insult by his words.

Killian smiled back. 'No, of course not, but my grandfather is Lord Rosyth and he can well afford it. If there's a profit to be had, he might be interested. Or I might persuade him to lend me the required sum against interest.'

This was an outright lie, since Killian had no intention of involving his grandfather. He still hadn't told anyone he was the owner of the *Lady Madeleine*, so he thought it best to hedge for now. Besides, his grandfather's title usually made people sit up and take notice, and Campbell proved this point.

'You're related to Lord Rosyth, are you?' he said, looking as if he found Killian much more interesting because of this connection. 'I've met him on occasion. A fair man and canny with it.'

'That he is.' Killian didn't mention that the old curmudgeon had been anything but fair to him.

'Well, if you can get money out of him, there will be profit aplenty,' Campbell promised. 'As long as the ship returns intact, any investment will pay for itself tenfold at least.'

'As much as that?' Killian felt excitement building up inside him. 'In that case I'd be very grateful if you could keep me informed about this venture.' He told Campbell where he lived, and the man promised to send word of any developments. Then another thought occurred to Killian. 'I don't suppose it would be possible to come along on this voyage, would it? Only, I'm trying to learn as much about trade as I can and it strikes me that this is an opportunity not to be missed. That is, if Mr Fergusson can spare me.'

'Why yes, I don't see why not. There will be four supercargos, and I believe the positions are all filled, but we'll need assistants. They are generally young men interested in learning the ways of their superiors. The pay isn't great, but then you'd receive a share of the profits, plus there's the *pacotill,* of course.'

'The what?'

'*Pacotill.* It means that everyone on board has the right to bring a small amount of goods to trade with for themselves. They're also allowed to buy merchandise in China to bring back and sell here for a profit. Obviously there isn't much space in which to store things, but if a person is clever enough and buys the sort of thing that doesn't take a lot of room but brings a pretty penny over here, it's possible to do quite well out of it.'

Killian vaguely remembered hearing of this custom and thought it seemed like a good way of making extra money. 'That sounds fair to me. Well, if you'd be willing to consider me for a position as assistant supercargo, I'll broach the subject with Mr Fergusson tomorrow. Perhaps we can come to some agreement. I take it he's an investor too?'

'Oh, yes, that's why we're here this evening. He wanted to hear more about it.' He winked at Killian and said, 'We Scots have to stick together, now don't we, lad? I should be glad of your company on the voyage, and so I shall tell Fergusson.'

Killian smiled back and nodded. 'Thank you, sir.'

He didn't tell Campbell that Fergusson was obviously not of the same opinion. So far he'd given Killian nothing but menial tasks to perform which would never give him the opportunity to earn any extra money. He hadn't been offered any chance of investing in Fergusson's deals either. He was barely told about them. It annoyed him in the extreme since he hadn't come here to act as someone's lowly clerk, although he had to admit he was learning a lot from Holm.

He watched while Campbell wandered over to the group on the other side of the room, and was startled when someone next to him whispered, 'And what are you plotting now, Mr Kinross?'

He turned to find Miss van Sandt standing in the shadows, not far from the entrance to the room. For once she was dressed becomingly in a light blue silk gown which Killian thought complemented her fair colouring to perfection. He wondered if she had overheard his conversation with Campbell. 'Nothing that concerns a mere female,' he said, a teasing note in his voice. He knew he was being deliberately provocative, as he had never been one to underestimate female intelligence, but some devil prompted him to continue to tease her like this. He wasn't disappointed in her response this time either.

'I am not a "mere" anything, I'll have you know. I'm sure my brain is every bit as good as yours. My father told me so.' Her eyes blazed at him and he thought again how they sparkled when she was angry. That made him smile.

'You should be in a temper all the time, Miss van Sandt. You look lovely when your eyes shoot sparks at me.'

'Well, really!' Words failed her and as if she couldn't think of anything else to do, she punched him on the arm. She then looked around, horrified, to see if anyone had noticed. Killian did the same, but thankfully even the dragon was busy chatting to some woman over by the tiled stove and no one was looking their way.

He raised his eyebrows at her. 'You want a fight, do you? I can think of better ways of using your energies. Besides, I was paying you a compliment. Were you never taught how to receive one gracefully?'

'You were doing no such thing,' she gritted out. 'You are forever teasing me, and it's very irritating.'

'You think so? That must be why you allowed me to kiss you then. Twice.'

'I did not.'

'Really? I don't recall holding on to you,' he said, knowing he was fuelling her anger even further. It was the plain truth, however, and he could see from her expression that she knew it too. He had merely bent his head to place his mouth over hers on the last occasion, and she hadn't done anything to ward him off.

'I ... I ... you're impossible.'

'So I've been told, many times,' he agreed good-naturedly. 'Now did you want to know what Campbell and I were talking about, or did you hear it for yourself?'

'You would discuss such things with me?' She blinked in surprise, her anger evaporating in an instant.

'I don't see why not, if your brain is as good as you claim. No doubt it will be the talk of the dinner table later anyway.'

'Then yes, please, I would like you to tell me more.'

Killian obliged, but he couldn't help wondering why she was so interested. If he hadn't known better, he would have said she was as excited by the East India venture as he was himself. That was intriguing to say the least. A girl had no hope of going on such a journey, and if Fergusson didn't even want to cough up her dowry, he would certainly never give her the money to invest in anything like this.

'Why are you so curious about this?' he asked at last, trying to understand how her mind worked.

'It seems to me this may be one of the reasons my stepfather is discouraging my suitors.' Her expression was still animated and he thought to himself that this was how she ought to look all the time, not demure and quiet.

'What do you mean?'

'If Robert wants to invest in this venture, he'll need as much money as possible. Therefore it's not in his interests to pay out a large sum to any future husband of mine.'

Killian shook his head. 'I doubt that's the case. Surely he has enough money for both? Otherwise he could borrow some if necessary. No, I think his dealings with you are entirely separate to this issue.'

'Maybe you're right, but the point is that we don't know and every possibility has to be explored. I intend to find out what he's up to, if it's the last thing I do.'

Killian smiled. She was definitely stubborn and possibly too headstrong for her own good, but he couldn't help liking her determination and her forthright ways. She'd make a formidable wife and perhaps one day ... but no, he wouldn't think of leg-shackling himself to anyone as yet. He had more exciting things to do.

Killian was wrong about one thing – nothing more was mentioned about the East India plans until the men were all left behind in the dining room with a whisky bottle and glasses. During the meal, the talk had all been on subjects suitable for the ladies. Killian wondered why such secrecy was necessary. He hoped Miss van Sandt could keep her mouth shut, since he obviously shouldn't have told her anything about it.

He didn't find out much more than what Campbell had already said, except for the fact that the company would have the right to use violence if they were threatened by other trading nations in any way.

'So we'll need some cannon on that ship of ours,' Niclas Sahlgren said to his partner. 'The more the better, if you ask me.'

'Aye, it's a cutthroat world out there,' Campbell added, looking grave. 'It's each man for himself, or each nation perhaps in this case. The English and the Dutch won't take kindly to any competition, nor will anyone else. It won't be easy, this venture, you know. Never think it. I'll try to avoid the Dutch as much as possible though, that's the best course of action. Not give them any provocation.'

'I'm sure you'll manage admirably, my good man,' Henrik König slapped Campbell on the back. 'We have faith in you.'

'Well, thank you kindly. I'll most certainly do my best.'

Killian was the last person to leave and Fergusson stopped him in the hallway just as he was putting his gloves on.

'One moment, Kinross,' he said. 'I wanted to warn you not to mention anything about this East India venture to anyone else at present. It's not exactly a secret, but the fewer people who know about it, the better. Until investors are formally invited, that is.'

'No, no, I won't discuss it with anyone who doesn't know about it already. What about Mr Holm?'

'Yes, he knows, of course. I've informed him of my intentions and he's all for it. Oh, and Campbell told me he had been speaking to you about the possibility of taking you on as an assistant supercargo. We'll need to discuss it, but I'm not against this in principle.'

'You're not?' For some reason, Killian had expected objections by the dozen and was surprised by Fergusson's words.

'No. I'm investing heavily in this venture. It would be to my advantage to have someone on board who can make sure my interests are served.' Fergusson looked down his aquiline nose at Killian, as if he was trying to put him in his place. Killian clenched a fist inside his glove, but kept his expression neutral.

'Ah, yes, I see. Well, I would certainly do my best.'

'Excellent. We'll speak more soon. Goodnight then, Kinross.'

'Goodnight and thank you for inviting me.'

Killian closed the door behind him and turned to make his way down the cobbled street in the direction of his lodging. Before he had gone more than a few yards, however, a shadow detached itself from the gate that led into the Fergusson's back yard and whispered, 'Wait, please.'

'Miss van Sandt? What are you doing outside so late?' He looked around to make sure there was no one else about. Then he followed her through the gate and into the yard, where he could see faint light spilling out from the kitchen windows. She stood shivering in a corner, her evening gown covered only with a shawl.

'I had to speak to you again and this was the only way.'

'Oh?'

'I wanted to thank you for not treating me like a dumb animal, the way my stepfather does. And for helping me with the letter and so on. I ... I'm afraid I misjudged you slightly when you first arrived. I apologise.'

'No need for that and you don't have to thank me, I was happy to help. I'd be grateful if you could keep the details about the East India venture to yourself for now though. It seems I should have kept my mouth shut. It's not common knowledge yet.'

'Of course I will. And I confess I did overhear some of your conversation with Mr Campbell anyway, so you only added a few facts.'

He looked down at her face, so earnest in the moonlight, and saw the fierce intelligence shining in her eyes. She was right, she wasn't a mere female at all. Killian knew a lot of women were empty-headed ninnies, thinking of nothing but their next gown or social gathering, but not this one. He had the feeling she would be a match for him in any intellectual task.

'You'd better go inside before they find you missing or you freeze to death,' he said gently. '*God natt, fröken* van Sandt.'

She hesitated for a moment, as if she was waiting for something.

He realised that she expected him to try to kiss her again and he wanted to, there was no doubt about that. It would definitely be a bad idea. The darkness, the moonlight and the stillness all around them would have been a potent mixture designed to lure them to madness. Killian didn't trust himself not to take advantage of her innocence, so he stood still, not moving so much as a muscle. When she saw that he was waiting for her to leave, she turned and headed for the back door. She disappeared inside with one last look of confusion thrown his way.

Killian shook his head and let out a long sigh. Never had he been so tempted by an 'untouchable' before, but too much was at stake. He couldn't afford to ruin his future by acting unwisely. For once in his life he was going to do everything right.

Jess was extremely angry with herself, but there was no denying she was bitterly disappointed that Mr Kinross hadn't tried to kiss her in the darkness. It was the perfect opportunity and for once she was charitably disposed towards him after his earlier fair treatment of her. Yet he had done nothing. Why? He really was the most contrary creature.

It irritated her that it should matter, but she had longed for his touch. She sensed that here was a man who didn't look down on her, despite his constant teasing. Knowing someone valued her as a person, not a chattel, was a powerful aphrodisiac. Had he kissed her tonight, she would have returned his caress in full measure. She raised her fingers to her lips, which tingled at the thought.

Not that she knew how. She had only ever been kissed twice before by Karl, who had managed to pull her into a dark corner on a couple of occasions. He just planted his lips on hers, then tried to grab her behind. She had submitted to the kissing part, but pushed his questing hands firmly away from any other part of her anatomy, not wanting to be thought fast.

'But we're as good as betrothed,' he had whispered in a throaty voice that had scared her somewhat. 'No one will think the worse of us … .'

'Nevertheless, I would prefer it if you didn't do that,' she told him firmly, dancing out of his way. 'Oh, I see Mrs Forbes looking for me, I must go.' That last had been a lie, since no one could be seen from where they were standing, but he hadn't protested further and allowed her to leave. That was the last time she saw him before her banishment. Had she perhaps offended him with her reluctance? Surely not, and besides, she knew well enough whose fault it was that Karl's interest in her had come to an end. The blame lay squarely with her stepfather.

She returned to her earlier train of thought. Kinross' kisses were different. They sent shock waves through her system even though he had never tried to touch her in any other way. Jess wondered why that should be so. It was a mystery, and one she obviously wasn't going to solve tonight. With a sigh, she took herself off to bed.

Chapter Fifteen

A month passed, during which Killian had several discussions with both Fergusson and Campbell. It was decided that he was definitely going on the voyage to China as assistant supercargo. Although he would have to work hard during the journey, he would be given the opportunity to learn everything Campbell had to teach him. It seemed like a fair deal to Killian, but after his initial enthusiasm for the idea, Fergusson began to have cold feet. He tried to withdraw his consent, but fortunately Campbell put a stop to that the moment he realised what was happening. This made Fergusson even grumpier, since he disliked being thwarted in any way, but Killian didn't care.

'It's almost too good an opportunity,' Fergusson grumbled whenever the subject came up. It was as though he was jealous of Killian's freedom to go on such a voyage. He glowered from under his wild eyebrows, like an angry badger that had been cornered and didn't know how to escape the trap. 'I had only just got used to having a second pair of hands here in the office,' was another of his complaints. 'Now Holm will be run off his feet again. I suppose I'll have to pay someone else to take over your duties. More money spent which I can ill afford.'

This last statement was patently false, since Killian had seen several fat pouches of silver in the strongbox. He didn't say anything, however, just exchanged a look with Holm behind Fergusson's back. The Swede had been very pleased for him and commended him on his quick thinking in asking Campbell for employment.

'You could do worse,' had been Holm's comment, which

for him was praise indeed. 'If I wasn't too old, I'd join you.' He raised his eyes heavenward now as if praying for patience while Fergusson ranted on, but remained silent as well.

'I expect you to do your utmost to further my interests,' Fergusson continued. 'If you think you're going to profit mightily from this yourself, then think again. Your share will be moderate, but then you're learning so much which will be compensation enough, I should think. You'll have to use most of your *pacotill* on my account, of course. I am after all the one allowing you leave to go, so try to spot some good bargains.'

Killian swore to himself that Fergusson would only ever see a very small percentage of any profit he made on his own trade goods. He was determined to maximise this. In order to find out the best goods to bring, he talked to anyone who had ever had anything to do with China trade. Holm made a few suggestions as well. In the end, he decided to buy finely wrought clocks, binoculars and other mechanical things. Apparently the Chinese liked those. He also bought some delicate silver and gold snuff boxes, which he was told were highly valued, and he very much hoped this was right.

Killian asked Campbell not to mention that he wanted to be an investor himself. 'My grandfather might not want it known,' he told him. The reminder of the connection with Lord Rosyth worked wonders. Campbell promised not to tell a soul, least of all Fergusson, whom he didn't seem to like very much.

The only other person to whom Killian revealed his plans was Captain Craig, who had returned yet again. 'And I'm sorry to leave you to do everything yourself for so long. Will you be able to carry on trading while I'm gone?' he added.

'Of course, I'll continue as we have begun.' Craig didn't seem fazed. 'There should be a tidy sum waiting for you when you return. Everything's been running smoothly so far and there's no reason there should be any problems. Don't you worry about a thing, your money and your ship will be safe with me.'

'And you won't tell anyone it's mine, unless I don't come back?'

'I swear to keep it a secret, if that's what you want.'

'Good. I'll draw up a will to say you're to have half the value of it in the event of my death. The other half, I want paid to my grandfather, just to show the old crosspatch I'm not the wastrel he thinks I am.'

Craig chuckled. 'Wouldn't that surprise him, eh? I'll see it's done, never fear, but I pray you'll return safely so it won't be necessary.'

Killian was grateful to have such a stalwart ally, and was sure the captain could be trusted. The *Lady Madeleine* would be in safe hands.

Having realised how much more profit could be made from investing in the China trade, however, he set about trying to increase his present capital as much as he could. He began to play for much higher stakes when he gambled. Soon his reputation increased to the point where even some of the young Swedish noblemen in town sought him out. One such came marching into *The White Hart* one evening and headed straight for Killian's table.

'I hear you don't play like your penny-pinching countrymen,' the man said by way of introduction and sat down without so much as a by your leave. 'That's if you're Kinross, of course?'

The man had addressed him in Swedish and fortunately Killian had now reached a stage where he could understand most things. Although his grammar and pronunciation still weren't perfect, he had no trouble joining in a normal conversation. Annoyance at the slur on his countrymen made him clench his jaw, but he decided against commenting.

'That's right, I am.' Killian looked the man up and down and didn't much like what he saw.

Tall and fairly good-looking, the Swede had an air of petulance and arrogance that grated. He raised Killian's hackles from the outset. He wore a coat of crimson brocade decorated with an enormous number of gold buttons. They must have cost a small fortune, and his silver shoe buckles were much larger than necessary. Killian decided the man obviously had more money than sense, which was all to the good. Such men were usually careless in the extreme and therefore precisely the right sort to gamble with. With this in mind, Killian bowed and asked politely, 'And you are ...?'

'Karl Adelsten.'

The name rang a bell and Killian soon realised who the man was – none other than Miss van Sandt's former suitor. He regarded Adelsten more critically, wondering what she had seen in such an oaf. He had to admit that to a woman he might seem like a good catch and his social standing probably had a lot to do with it as well. Still, he was surprised that Miss van Sandt should have fallen for Adelsten. Perhaps he had never shown her anything but his most charming manner, which was clearly not the case this evening.

'I'm pleased to make your acquaintance,' Killian lied. 'And do I take it you want to play a game of dice with me, or do you perhaps prefer cards?'

'Cards. Dice are for sailors and other scum.'

Killian raised his eyebrows at such rudeness, but didn't comment.

Adelsten looked around at Killian's companions. They happened to be James McEvoy and Graham Frazer, just like on his first night in Sweden. 'What about you? You want to play too?' Adelsten asked them.

They both shook their heads. 'No, he cleaned us out yesterday. We'll have to wait until next pay day now.'

Killian swore inwardly. He didn't need anyone advertising his luck any more than it was already. Fortunately, Adelsten didn't seem put off by this statement at all. He only guffawed as if he thought it a great joke.

'Well, what are you waiting for? Call for a new deck of cards, Kinross.'

Killian did so, and their game began. He was pleased Adelsten had chosen cards, rather than dice. That meant he would be able to use cunning and his good memory instead of just relying on Lady Luck. At first, he was careful not to wager too much. He wanted to lull Adelsten into a false sense of security. He ordered wine and gave the young nobleman the lion's share. The Swede didn't notice, he was so intent on their game. His face, a bit puffy from constant over-indulgence of all things culinary, became flushed with the heat of the room and his intense concentration. When he started to lose steadily, it turned ever more puce.

'Damn it all, man, you can't possibly have such luck,' he exclaimed at one point.

Killian shrugged. 'Not always, no. Would you rather we continued the game some other time? I really ought to be going anyway.' He didn't point out that some of Adelsten's ill-judged choices during the game were more to blame for his losses than any luck on Killian's part.

Adelsten glared at him. 'Oh no, you can't leave yet. You're staying until I've had a chance to win that little pile back.' He indicated the mound of silver coins currently lying next to Killian.

'Very well, as you wish.'

He played a few careless hands, allowing Adelsten to win back a little of the silver he had lost. Then he concentrated hard and won it all back and much more besides. When the taproom was almost empty of customers, Adelsten slapped his cards down onto the table with a bellow of frustration. He stood up, swaying slightly. 'Devil take it,' he swore. 'It's obviously not my evening, but I'll have my revenge another time. You'll not deny me another game?'

'Of course not,' Killian replied. 'I'm here most nights and I'd be happy to play whenever you wish.'

'Then I'd best go home and do the pretty to my wife, so she comes up with some more of her family's riches.' Adelsten sneered. 'Only thing she's good for at the moment, in her condition.'

From this comment Killian gathered that Mrs Adelsten was with child and her only function, in her husband's opinion, was to breed heirs and share her fortune. Such free speaking about a wife the man should have cherished gave Killian even more of a disgust of Adelsten than he already felt. He pitied the poor woman and could only be grateful on Miss van Sandt's behalf that she had escaped such a fate.

'I look forward to seeing you another time then,' he said, accompanying this lie with a smile. He waited until Adelsten had weaved his unsteady way out of the door before gathering up his winnings.

McEvoy, who was the only one to have stayed and watched the entire game, puffed out his cheeks and shook his head. 'What an arse,' he said succinctly. 'I'm surprised you managed to keep your temper with him. I would have punched him on the nose halfway through the evening, if not before.'

Killian grinned. 'I think I've hurt him much worse by taking all his silver. My guess is he'll be out of pocket for quite a while now. To have to go crawling to his wife for more will annoy him no end.'

McEvoy laughed and slapped him on the back. 'Aye, you're probably right about that.' He raised an arm to wave at Murdoch, who was yawning hugely, waiting for them to leave. As always, the innkeeper was reluctant to lose even a penny of possible earnings. 'Landlord, a drink to celebrate my friend's wisdom here, if you please.'

'Have you ever been to Sweden, Allan?'

Farquhar was sitting in the darkest corner of a rather seedy tavern with his spy. He'd made sure they were nowhere near anyone who could overhear their conversation. This was essential for what he had to say. He'd even gone so far as to wear a wig to make sure his ruddy hair wasn't noticed, although it wasn't such a violent shade of red that it stood out unduly.

'Sweden, Mr Kinross? No, I don't think as I have. Why would I want to go there?'

'Because it might be worth your while.' Farquhar paused while this sank in and understanding dawned on his companion.

'Ah, of course. Lovely country, so I hear,' Allan said with a grin.

'Indeed, and if you're willing to travel there, I have a little job for you. Could be worth a tidy sum.' Farquahar put his hand in his pocket and clinked a few coins together for emphasis.

Allan's eyes lit up with greed. 'Any time, Mr Kinross. I'm at your disposal, you know that. What would you have me do?'

'The thing is, my cousin Killian seems to have taken up residence over there and I quite like not having him around. Edinburgh is a much more peaceful place without him. I'd be even happier if Sweden should become his final destination, if you take my meaning.'

Farquhar stared at Allan to see whether the man would baulk at murder. He had made it his business to find out if there were any rumours of Allan having a hand in such things before. This had proved the case, so he was confident it wouldn't be the first time the man had done away with someone.

'Oh, aye, I see what you mean. Accidents happen, right? 'Specially on foreign soil. Never can trust foreigners, now can you? Bunch o' heathens.'

'Precisely my point. I'm glad we understand each other.' Farquhar extracted a money pouch from his pocket and held it out to the man. 'My cousin can be found in the town of Gothenburg. From what I hear it's not very large so he shouldn't be too hard to locate. Here is half the sum I'm willing to pay you for your services, plus expenses for the journey. The other half will be yours when the deed is done.'

'Fair enough.' Allan pocketed the money with almost indecent haste. 'I'll set about finding a ship then.'

'Very good. And Allan?'

'Yes, Mr Kinross?'

'You will be discreet, won't you? I don't want there to be any suspicious circumstances, you hear?'

Allan shook his head. 'You can trust me. Won't no one be any the wiser, I swear.'

'Good. On your way then, and report back to me as soon as you can.'

Farquhar watched as the man threaded his way through the tables towards the door and left without a backward glance. He had never taken quite such a drastic step before and a trickle of perspiration ran down his back as fear settled like a hard lump in the pit of his stomach. To his surprise he also felt a measure of regret. Somehow, he had always hoped Killian would solve the problem for him by dying young like his brothers. With the kind of life he led, it had seemed more than likely, but now Farquhar couldn't wait any longer. He hardened his resolve. This was no time for doubts. Killian had to be got rid of and like Allan had said, accidents happened.

'You're turning maudlin, man,' he muttered to himself. That wouldn't get him anywhere. No, the time had come for decisive action and there was no turning back now.

'Jess? Jessamijn, where are you?'

Hearing her mother calling from the upstairs landing, Jess came hurrying out of the kitchen. She had been helping the cook to prepare a list of provisions needed from the market the following day. 'I'm here, is something the matter?'

'James is still unwell and seems to be taking a turn for the worse. Could you send someone to fetch the apothecary, please? Tell them to hurry. James is as flushed as if he'd been in the fire and needs a physic of some sort.' Katrijna was wringing her hands, her forehead creased with worry lines and her pale blue eyes frantic.

'Oh, dear. Yes, right away, *Moeder*.'

Jess swallowed a sigh of impatience. Katrijna fretted at the slightest sign of illness in her two younger children, having lost three of Jess's siblings at an early age. This was probably yet another instance of her worrying about nothing. However, she knew there wouldn't be any peace until Katrijna had been reassured by a professional that James was not suffering from any fatal disease. Jess sent a maid out with instructions to bring the apothecary back at once. Then she made her way upstairs to try and keep her mother calm in the meantime.

The two little boys shared the nursery and when Jess came through the door she could see it was in chaos. Ramsay was sitting in the middle of his bed howling, while a harassed maid ran back and forth doing Katrijna's bidding. Katrijna herself was holding little James. The poor mite was flushed in the face and trying to cry in between bouts of coughing.

Twin rivers of mucus ran down from his nose into his mouth. He wasn't a pretty sight.

'Shall I take him for a while, Mama?' Jess never minded helping out in the nursery. She had come to love James as much as she adored Ramsay, and normally the youngster came to her quite willingly.

'No, he won't go to anyone but me. Could you see to Ramsay, do you think? He simply won't stop crying. And where's Mrs Forbes when I need her?'

'I'll go and find out.' Jess picked Ramsay up and began to croon softly to him, rocking him as she walked out of the room in search of her companion. He too was full of the cold, sneezing and coughing repeatedly, but he clung to her and calmed down slightly. Jess sighed. It looked like it was going to be a long night. She found Mrs Forbes coming up the stairs with a tray of hot drinks and all manner of other things that had obviously been ordered by Katrijna.

'Mama is asking for you,' Jess told her. 'She's in a bit of a panic.'

'Aye, don't I know it,' Mrs Forbes muttered darkly. 'Nothing new there and I'm coming as fast as I can.'

'Yes, I'm sure you are. I think I'll take Ramsay to my room, he'll never get any sleep otherwise. The apothecary should be on his way.'

'Fine, you do that.'

Ramsay soon settled down when tucked into Jess' own bed. He listened with drooping eyelids to the beginning of a story while she undressed and combed out her hair. Long before the end of the tale, he was sound asleep. She lay down next to him, listening to the sounds of footsteps coming and going in the corridor outside her room.

Ramsay was snoring, his blocked nose hindering his breathing, but Jess didn't think he was seriously ill as his forehead wasn't very hot. She prayed all would be well with little James too. The boy seemed particularly prone to disease, which was probably why Katrijna fretted over him so. Jess knew her mother would be devastated if anything happened to either boy. It wasn't something she wanted to even contemplate either, but she was afraid James wasn't very strong.

'Please, dear God, spare him,' she prayed. 'He is so small and innocent.'

She dozed off, but was woken some time later by Ramsay coughing as if his little lungs were going to burst. A series of short, hacking coughs came first. Then a long, deeply indrawn breath, which made a strange whooping noise. Finally more coughing until he gagged.

'Dear, oh dear, Ramsay.' She sat him up and made him bend forward in order to ease his breathing, while massaging his back with soothing motions. 'What are we going to do with you?'

He began to cry, muttering about his tummy hurting, which was no wonder she thought. He was probably using all his stomach muscles to help him cough and it was hard work for such a small body. She stroked his silky, dark hair and pulled him close to comfort him.

'I tell you what, shall I get you some warm milk with honey? Would you like that? It might soothe your throat and make you go back to sleep again.'

'Yes, please.'

'Right, well, you lie down again and I'll be back as soon as I can.' She put her own pillow under his in order to raise him up a little. She knew that helped when someone was suffering with a cough. Then she tucked the covers securely around him and kissed his soft cheek. 'All right?'

He nodded, looking tired and wan in the moonlight, and she wrapped her shawl around her and hurried off towards the kitchen. Ramsay was a strong little boy. Although she was fairly sure now that he was suffering from whooping cough, she wasn't too worried about him. James was a different matter. How was a tiny body such as his going to withstand that sort of coughing? She remembered having the disease herself as an eight-year-old. It had lasted for weeks and quite exhausted her. She shook her head and tried not to think about it. For now, all she could do was look after Ramsay until morning.

Chapter Sixteen

In the darkness of the early December morning, Killian made his way to the warehouse as usual. The weather had turned freezing in the last week and the fresh-smelling air was so cold it hurt the back of his throat if he breathed in too quickly. Huge flakes of snow swirled all around him. They blanketed the ground in a thick, lustrous layer that felt soft to walk on and made the normally dirty cobbles look pristine.

He huddled into his woollen cloak and felt grateful for the thick knitted sweater which Mrs Ljung had persuaded him to accept as a gift. She spent a lot of time making them for local fishermen and their families. When she saw him huddling by his tile stove every evening with a plaid around his shoulders, she decided to give her latest one to him instead.

'You'll catch your death if you're not properly dressed here,' she told him sternly.

'I'm wearing several layers of clothing, Mrs Ljung, just like I would in the Highlands.' But somehow it had never felt quite this cold in Scotland. Perhaps it was because Gothenburg was on the coast and there was a constant sea breeze. Or because Sweden was slightly further north. In any case, the scratchy woollen garment which he had hidden under his jacket was a godsend.

He opened the door to the warehouse with hands that were frozen despite the gloves he was wearing. Almost immediately he became aware of raised voices once again, and frowned at the sight of Miss van Sandt's maid standing by the bottom of the stairs. The girl was fidgeting and staring at the floor, obviously anxious. He ignored her and quickly made his way up to the office, determined to make himself known this time. As he stepped inside, he found Fergusson bellowing at the top of his voice at a defiant-looking, but very pale, Miss van Sandt. Her stepfather was almost incandescent with rage, his dark hair standing on end as if he'd been tearing at it with his fingers and the deep-set eyes scorching. Holm stood by the window trying his best to be inconspicuous, his thin frame almost blending in with the surroundings. The Swede's pale gaze, however, was lit up with concern and his forehead creased.

'And furthermore, you should be at home helping your mother, who is at her wit's end with the boys so ill. Not gallivanting about in the darkness on your own and poking your nose in where it's not wanted. I warned you about this before and you knew the consequences. Now go and pack your bags, we'll leave first thing tomorrow morning.'

Killian looked from one face to another, wondering whether to announce his presence or not, but just then Fergusson caught sight of him.

'Ah, Kinross, there you are. My stepdaughter was just leaving. Perhaps you'd be so kind as to escort her and her maid back to my house? And make sure she doesn't take any detours, won't you,' he added. 'I'm afraid I have some matters to sort out here this morning before a meeting with Mr Campbell, or I'd see to it myself.'

'Yes, of course.' Killian held open the door for Miss van Sandt and she stepped past him without saying a word, her head held high and cheeks burning. She threw her stepfather a look of loathing before descending the stairs, but he had turned away and didn't notice. Killian saw Holm shake his head at her and wondered what was going on.

This was not the time for questions, however, so he said nothing. Instead he concentrated on whisking Miss van

Sandt away from the warehouse. Once outside, he offered her his arm as any polite gentleman would and they set off towards her home. The maid followed without a word, trailing a few yards behind them out of earshot. Miss van Sandt was still in a temper and seemed reluctant to accept his help at first. In the end, she placed her gloved hand on his sleeve, a mere touching of fingers to cloth. But when she nearly slipped on an icy patch her grip became firmer and she took his arm properly.

'Careful, Miss van Sandt. The snow hides those treacherous pockets of ice,' he warned, judging it safe to speak by now, although he kept his voice low so that there was no possibility of the maid overhearing.

'I know, but they're not as treacherous as some people I could mention,' she muttered, her jaw set in a stubborn line.

'Possibly, but I thought we agreed you wouldn't come to the warehouse again. May I ask why you did so this morning?'

She stayed silent for a moment, and he wondered if she was going to refuse to reply. Then she sighed and it all came pouring out.

'Very well, I know it was ill-judged of me and I shouldn't have done it, but I acted on pure impulse. I found something last night, you see, and I couldn't wait to tell Albert. Since both my little brothers are ill and the house in an uproar, it was really easy to slip out for a while. Especially now Mrs Forbes is poorly as well and no one was paying attention to me. How was I supposed to know my stepfather would leave home when my mother is so distraught? He usually tries to comfort her, but of course I didn't know about his important meeting. He caught me in the office and ... well, you saw the rest.'

'Did he find you talking to Mr Holm?'

'No, luckily Albert had popped downstairs for a moment.

I was looking through one of the ledgers on his desk, just to pass the time, you know. I wanted to check whether I could still remember how to do the sums and so on as my father taught me. Robert thought I was snooping.'

'I see. And if he really does have something to hide, then I can understand his anger at finding you there.'

'Oh, but that's just it – he does! Last night I was looking after Ramsay and he started to cough a lot suddenly, waking us both. I went downstairs to make him a hot drink and when I passed Robert's study, the door was open. He must have forgotten to close it when he went upstairs. Well, with my mother in the state she's in, it's no wonder if he had to leave his work in a hurry.'

'That bad, is it?'

'Yes, my brothers are very ill with the whooping cough. Poor Ramsay is coughing his lungs out and as for James ... well, he's in a bad way and I'm very afraid for him.' She paused to wipe away a few sudden tears, then took a deep breath. 'Anyway, I could see Robert had left his desk in disarray, which is very unusual for him. You must know how tidy he is, and there were papers strewn everywhere. I went in and had a very quick look around. Would you believe it, right in the middle of his desk there was a letter from Anders Milner, the magistrate, assuring Robert that he'd never tell a soul.'

Killian asked, 'Tell a soul what exactly?'

'Well, he didn't say, only that Robert had no need to remind him of his obligations. And as long as Robert kept his part of the bargain, he could count on Mr Milner's discretion. I had the feeling he wasn't best pleased to be reminded. The tone was waspish, if you know what I mean.'

'Hm, interesting. That would fit in well with my blackmail theory.'

'Blackmail? You think Robert has a hold on Mr Milner

somehow?' She stopped and stared at him.

Killian nodded. 'Yes. Mr Holm told me Milner is known as an honest man and he's been a friend of your family for a long time. Therefore, the only way he would do you harm would be if he was being coerced. At least that's how I see it.'

'I'm sure you're right. That does make sense.'

They walked on in contemplative silence for a while, then Killian asked, 'Did you have a chance to tell Mr Holm then?'

'Only that I'd found something, but not what it was. He thought he heard a noise, so he went to check and then Robert arrived. Wretched man ...'

'Don't worry, I'll talk to Mr Holm as soon as I can.'

'Thank you.' She sighed deeply. 'I wanted to ask Albert about something else too, but now it's too late. I've been thinking about this East India venture you're going on.'

'Oh, yes. What about it?'

'I wondered if he could somehow get his hands on the same sum as my dowry so I could invest it. I know my stepfather would never consider that, but I thought it was too good an opportunity to miss. It's probably the only way I'd ever increase my money and my chances of a good marriage.'

'Hmm, it sounds reasonable to me, but I don't quite know how Mr Holm would manage that without someone noticing.'

'No, nor I, but could you possibly ask him for me? There might be some way.' She stopped again and raised hopeful eyes to his. 'Please? At least then I'll know I've tried.'

'I don't see why not. Leave it with me.'

'You're very kind.' Her expression turned bleak. 'Not that I'll have much use for money where I'm going.'

'And where exactly is that? You were told to pack, I heard, so I assume it's a fair way off.'

'He's taking me to Askeberga again, where I'll probably be staying for a long time. For ever maybe.' Her tone was bitter and she strode along the road, rather than walking with ladylike steps, showing Killian just how agitated she was.

'What or where is Askeberga?' he asked.

'It's our manor house in Småland, a county quite a way inland from here. You remember I told you I was sent away once before, after Mr Adelsten proposed to me? Well, that's where I was and it's a lovely place, but I really don't want to spend the rest of my life there all alone.' She snorted. 'To think I always thought it would be mine, but Robert owns it now of course, just like everything else.'

'And are you really a virtual prisoner when you're there? I mean, couldn't you just leave if you wanted to?'

'I suppose so, but where would I go, by myself and with no money? And Mrs Forbes will be with me again I'm sure. She won't be very pleased about going back either, she hates it there. Although perhaps since she's ill, she'll be spared for a while.'

They had reached the Fergusson dwelling and she turned on the steps and hesitated for a moment. 'Thank you for bringing me home and for promising to speak to Albert on my behalf. I – I don't suppose I shall see you again, at least for some time, so I wish you luck with your journey to China.'

Killian frowned, wanting to comfort her in some way, but he couldn't think of anything useful to say and with the maid now standing nearby, he could do nothing except bow to her. 'Thank you. I hope your banishment will be short.'

She gave a brittle laugh. 'Not much chance of that. *Adjö*, Mr Kinross.'

Jess ran all the way to her room and threw herself onto her

bed. She wanted to cry, but the tears were as frozen inside her as the weather outside. All she could manage were strangled cries of anger as she beat her pillow with her fists in frustration.

She had been so sure Robert wouldn't go out on a day like this when he was needed at home. Ramsay had been asleep at long last and she hadn't thought anyone would notice if she slipped out for a very short while. How was she to know Robert had a meeting with Mr Campbell that couldn't be postponed? Although she should have realised he wouldn't let his family stand in the way of any plans he'd made.

'Hateful, hateful man!' She hit the pillow again several times, wishing it was Robert's angry face she was punching.

The sound of someone calling her name intruded on her furious thoughts and she hurried to answer her mother.

'Yes, *Moeder*, I'm coming.' She took a deep breath and made her way to the sick room. It was boiling hot since the fire was kept going at all times. Both boys were lying tucked up in their beds, flushed with fever and coughing intermittently. Matters were definitely serious and her mother had been right to worry for once.

James's coughing bouts all ended with the same long drawn-out whooping noise that Ramsay made. Several times he vomited afterwards. Katrijna was kneeling by his side, trying to make him drink something, but he just turned his face away and whimpered. Katrijna looked at Jess, her eyes red-rimmed and dark with despair.

'There you are, I've been calling for ages. Please, will you try to make Ramsay take some broth? He simply refuses to listen to me and I can't leave James for very long at the moment.'

Jess did her best and managed to persuade her brother to take a few spoonfuls. He seemed listless and inclined to sleep in between the bouts of coughing, so she left him alone after a while.

'Moeder,' she began, wondering how to break the news to her mother that she was leaving the following day. 'I, er, had a slight disagreement with Robert this morning and, uhm, well, he's taking me to Askeberga tomorrow. Unless you could ask him to let me stay and help you with the boys?' she added hopefully.

'What? Oh, no, what have you done this time? Didn't I tell you to be respectful to him? Really, Jessamijn, you *must* learn when to keep quiet. And why now? I need you, you know that.'

'Well, then tell him he can't send me away. I haven't done anything wrong. I only went to see Albert. He was Papa's friend, you know that. Where's the harm in talking to him?'

'You went out all alone? Today of all days?'

'I took a maid with me, of course'

'Yes, but why now? This was not the time, Jess. I'm not surprised Robert is angry with you.'

Jess had to acknowledge that her mother was right, although she didn't tell her Robert had other reasons for being cross. She simply hadn't thought it through. The discovery of the letter had made her act on impulse, but she knew now she'd been very foolish. She hung her head.

Katrijna sighed. 'I'll speak to him, but if he's in one of his moods, I doubt I'll be able to sway him. Honestly, Jess, as if I don't have enough to worry about.'

Jess wanted to argue her case, but she could see that Katrijna's thoughts were all for the little boys at the moment, which was understandable. She thought that the best thing she could do was to go quietly and leave her mother to concentrate on the two patients. She couldn't expect Katrijna to help her at the moment. Perhaps when the boys were better again she would persuade Robert to allow Jess to come back. Swallowing down a lump in her throat, she went to begin her packing.

Killian was surprised to receive a summons to the Fergusson household later that day. When ushered into his employer's study, he could see immediately that the man was still agitated.

'Thank you for coming, Kinross. I have a favour to ask of you, and I wanted to do it in person.'

'I'd be pleased to help. What can I do for you?'

'Well, it concerns my stepdaughter.' Fergusson hesitated for a moment, as if he wasn't sure how to phrase his request. 'She and I ... well, in short, we're not on the best of terms and I've had enough of her misbehaving recently, as you probably gathered this morning.'

Killian nodded, but didn't comment.

'Jessamijn needs to be taught a lesson,' Fergusson continued. 'I've decided to send her to my manor house in Småland to rusticate for a while with Mrs Forbes. I was going to take them myself, but the apothecary's just been here. He tells us our little boys are suffering from whooping cough, which can be dangerous to the very young. Naturally my wife and I are both very concerned and I simply can't leave her at this time.'

'I'm sorry to hear that,' Killian said, feeling sad for Mrs Fergusson. 'But don't you need Miss van Sandt's help then in caring for her brothers?'

Fergusson snorted. 'Hardly. She's no help at all. In fact, she just makes my wife cross and gets in the way. No, I want her out of here, and that's why I would like to ask you to go with the ladies tomorrow, if you wouldn't mind? I don't want them to travel without a male escort, just in case anything should happen, although the coachman is capable enough in his own way. It's quite far, so of course you're welcome to stay for a day or so to recover, before making the return journey.'

'I'd be happy to. At what time do we leave?'

'As soon as it's light. Can you manage that?'

'Certainly, I'll be here.'

'Thank you, that's a weight off my mind. I shan't forget.'

Killian left the house, wondering why Fergusson was so desperate to have Miss van Sandt out of the way. Perhaps his intrigues weren't going as well as he had hoped? Or maybe what he perceived as her snooping had shaken the man's composure? Either way, Killian was looking forward to spending some extra time with Miss van Sandt. He had a feeling he wouldn't be bored at any rate.

'You're going to Småland, did you say? In this weather? You'll be frozen stiff before you're even halfway.' Mrs Ljung had brought his supper and found him packing a few necessities.

'Nevertheless, *Fru* Ljung, I have to go. My employer has asked me to, so I can't very well refuse. What do you suggest? Should I bring some extra blankets perhaps? Or my eiderdown bolster?'

She stopped to consider, then a smile spread over her face. 'No, I have the very thing for you.' She bustled out of the room and came back carrying what looked like a huge brown animal. 'Here we are, this belonged to my late husband. A big brute of a man he was, but that's all to the good. If this doesn't keep you warm, nothing will.'

She shook out a fur coat of enormous proportions, large enough to fit two grown men. Killian couldn't help but wonder exactly how big her husband had been. 'What kind of fur is that?' he asked, eyeing the garment and trying not to cough while dust motes danced all around them.

'Bear. As warm as they come. Take it, you can have it with my blessing.' Mrs Ljung had developed a soft spot for her young lodger and treated him like a hen would her only chick. Having missed out on motherly affection for so long, Killian quite enjoyed it and so he never discouraged her.

'I can't just take it, I'll pay you for it,' he said.

'No need.'

'I insist.'

'Well, pay me when you come back then, there's no hurry. Only promise me you'll wear this tomorrow or I won't rest easy. Wouldn't want you to catch pneumonia.'

'Very well, I promise.'

The following morning, when he saw the open carriage they were to travel in for the first stage of their journey, Killian was profoundly grateful for Mrs Ljung's kindness. He knew she had been right and without the bear coat he would most definitely have frozen to death.

Chapter Seventeen

Småland, Southern Sweden

Mrs Forbes was snoring loudly, her illness much worse. They had been travelling for three days now, starting off with a short boat journey up the Göta river and then continuing overland in stages by sleigh. Their only stops were to eat and sleep.

They had long since run out of topics of conversation, at least ones that could be discussed with Mrs Forbes present. The old lady kept interrupting with complaints most of the time anyway, making it all but impossible to talk. By the third day, however, she felt so awful she was quiet at last, which was a blessing.

Mrs Forbes had suffered continued bouts of coughing ever since they left the inn that morning. Each one left her exhausted with the effort, which was probably why she had fallen into a deep sleep. Jess could see her flushed face between the edges of her scarf and shawl. They were both wound round the woman's head and chin several times before disappearing into her tightly-wrapped cloak. A blanket was draped over everything else, almost obliterating her from view. She didn't look like she'd wake for hours, if she even survived the ride.

Pity for her gaoler briefly swept through Jess, but then she remembered that Mrs Forbes was in cahoots with Robert and the pity was replaced by anger. Despite Jess' pleas, Mrs Forbes had refused to try and change Robert's mind and allow them to stay, at least until the older woman was better.

'If he's sending you away again, it's because you deserve it. The Lord knows I'd rather not go travelling at the moment, but on the other hand I won't be sorry to leave for a while either. Could do with some peace and quiet. Your mother is a good woman, Jessamijn, but she drives everyone mad with her worrying and constant demands.'

'I'd say she was justified this time,' Jess replied angrily. 'The boys both have the whooping cough and that can be dangerous.'

'Only to newborns. The children will be fine.'

Jess wasn't convinced, but she prayed Mrs Forbes was right.

'Doesn't look good, does she?' The lazy voice beside her reminded Jess that she wasn't alone with her companion this time. At least not yet.

She turned to look at Mr Kinross, whose arrival to escort them that first morning had surprised her. She found his face right next to her own as he peered across her shoulder at Mrs Forbes. His nearness was disconcerting, but the sleigh they were travelling in was very narrow, so it wasn't as if the poor man could move over. Jess shifted slightly, but only succeeded in rubbing against him, which sent a frisson of awareness up her arm.

Feeling oddly flustered, she replied to his question rather grumpily. 'No she doesn't, but it's no more than she deserves.' One of the maids had told her that Mrs Forbes had been the one who alerted Robert to Jess' absence the day he found her at the warehouse. That was another reason why Jess was out of charity with the woman.

One eyebrow came up in quizzical fashion and Jess stared at Mr Kinross in fascination, before realising that this was probably rude of her.

'Saves us from her endless complaints at least,' he commented, a smile tugging at the corners of his mouth.

'I suppose so,' Jess replied.

She tore her gaze away, unwilling to be drawn in by his

charm. He may have treated her better than most men, trusting her with the secret of the East India venture and promising to speak to Albert on her behalf, but she still didn't quite trust *him*. He looked like another Karl, a handsome scoundrel, preying on innocent women. No doubt he spouted glib words and drew them in with eyes that promised everything but delivered nothing. Of course, she had no proof this was the case, but the fact that Mr Kinross was so good-looking had her convinced. Not to mention the way he was forever teasing her.

She glanced over at Mrs Forbes again, then at the blur of snowy forest speeding past the sleigh. She shivered and tried to huddle further into her cloak. It was woefully inadequate despite being covered by two shawls and a sheepskin rug over her legs. She cursed her stepfather's stinginess. He could well afford to buy her a fur-lined one if he wanted to, but he had refused. It was his fault entirely that her hands and feet were now beginning to go numb and it was a good while since she had felt her cheeks. She wondered if she would ever be warm again.

'Are you cold?' Mr Kinross asked. Jess was about to deny this, when a tell-tale shiver went through her. He smiled again, his eyes twinkling this time so that she found herself mesmerised against her will. They really were remarkable eyes, a clear cornflower blue and fringed with long lashes so dark they looked almost painted. 'We should share our body warmth,' he said, so quietly she thought she had misheard him at first.

'I beg your pardon?'

He indicated the huge bearskin coat he was wearing. 'If you come inside here, we'll both be warmer.'

'I couldn't possibly!' Jess looked at him again, to see if he was serious, but could see no sign of his usual teasing.

'Why not? It's one of the basic rules of survival, you know.

Shared body heat is the second best thing for keeping warm. Here, come inside.'

He undid the fastenings and opened the coat, making room for her to sit inside. 'Mr Kinross,' she protested, but before she knew what had happened, he had lifted her up as easily as if she weighed nothing at all and placed her next to him. Either he was very strong or her body had been colder than she thought. Surprised, she could only muster a token resistance and once she was enveloped in the bearskin, she no longer wanted to protest.

'Please, won't you call me Killian? We're in this together, so we should be on first name terms if you ask me.'

'No, really, I don't think this is a good idea.' Jess felt she ought to remonstrate with him, but the truth was that nothing could have tempted her away from the blessed warmth inside his coat. He pulled her nearer to his chest with one arm, while buttoning up the garment with the other, enclosing them both in its soft heat. Jess decided that a short warming-up session surely couldn't do any harm. There was no one to see her after all.

'If you try to relax a little, you'll find yourself a lot less cold as well,' he advised in an amused tone of voice.

Jess realised that she had been holding herself stiffly upright, while arguing with her conscience. Now she saw that he had been talking sense and she gave in, tentatively leaning her head against his chest. His chin came to rest on top of her head, which felt oddly comforting. Her nose was the only thing sticking out of the top of his coat. For the first time in hours she felt her body begin to thaw a little.

She sat in his embrace for a while, feeling guilty, but snug. She even began to enjoy the sleigh ride. It was smooth and comfortable in comparison to riding in a carriage on bumpy roads which was the case during most of the year. In the gathering dusk, the trees of the deep forest all around them seemed almost magical, their branches weighed down by thick blankets of snow that glistened in the light from the sleigh lanterns. The only sounds to be heard were the swishing of the sleigh's runners, the keening of the wind through the trees, and the jingling of the horses' harnesses. The animals' hooves made only a muffled crunching noise when they sank into the freezing cold road surface. The whole experience was somehow unreal. Jess burrowed deeper into the bearskin, forgetting for a moment who she was with.

Then Killian's chin moved a fraction, rubbing the top of her head in an affectionate caress, and she remembered. Sitting there being held by him in silence suddenly seemed even more intimate, so she tried to come up with a topic of conversation. 'Where did you get this?' she finally asked, indicating the coat which was several sizes too big for him.

'Won it off a gentleman who had been deserted by Lady Luck.'

'You were gambling again?'

'Not really, just playing a game of cards to pass the time. The gentleman in question was in his cups and insisted on a wager. Sadly for him, I won.' He chuckled and she felt the rumbling of it deep inside him under her ear. It was an unsettling sound.

'Are you telling the truth?'

'No.' He smiled. 'Actually, my landlady gave it to me. It used to belong to her husband, but he's dead now so he has no need of it. It would have been stupid to refuse, don't you think?'

'Oh, yes.'

Jess braced herself against him with one hand and looked up into his face, having just remembered something. 'You said this was the second best way of keeping warm. What then is the best one?'

His smile turned into a mischievous grin. 'You really want to know?'

'Well, I ... er, yes,' Jess stammered, although she was no longer sure.

'Very well, I'll tell you.' He bent to whisper in her ear. 'Lovemaking.'

Jess' eyes flew up to his and she gasped. But before she had time to object to his mentioning such a thing to her, he bent his head and kissed her full on the lips, his mouth moving slowly as if savouring the taste of her. Jess stiffened, her eyes staring into his, but she soon found out she should have closed them instead. He held her gaze and something in the depths of his azure eyes had her riveted. She couldn't pull away to save her life. Just before ending the kiss, Killian ran the tip of his tongue along her bottom lip, sending shockwaves throughout her body.

'Killian!' she protested, so scandalized she used his Christian name without thinking. She tried to pull away from him, but his arms were around her and he held her tight, chuckling again.

'Shush, it's all right, I was only teasing. I'm sorry, but it was just too tempting. I won't do it again if you don't want me to.'

'Most definitely not.' Jess felt her chest heaving with what she thought must be indignation, but which could have been something else. Karl's kisses had never made her feel even a flicker of desire. They hadn't involved tongues in any way either, but now here was this rogue, evoking sensations she didn't know existed. It was too much.

'You're sure?' She heard the teasing note in his voice again and couldn't resist another look, even though she knew it wasn't safe. 'Admit it, you enjoyed that.'

'Never.'

'That's a shame. I'll just have to try a bit harder then,

won't I,' Killian said and bent to kiss her again.

'No, I –'

Her protest was lost in a maelstrom of sensations as he did a more thorough job this time. Jess was virtually paralysed while he rained a succession of butterfly kisses on and around her mouth, until she opened her lips and he could deepen the kiss. She was shocked to the core when his tongue found its way inside her mouth. Even so, she melted into his embrace in the most unsettling manner and some instinct she hadn't known she possessed made her own tongue spar with his.

She felt him smile again, and almost pulled away. But the tingling waves shooting through her just because of this playing of tongues were so extraordinary, she simply didn't want them to end yet. At first she was too curious and soon she became caught up in the momentum, unable to break it off.

When he finally stopped for a breathing space, Jess' heart was beating like a wild thing and every fibre of her being was burning hot. He regarded her with a look of satisfaction and nodded. 'Told you so, didn't I? You're not cold any more.'

'That wasn't lovemaking,' Jess murmured. She wanted to dent his self-assurance somehow, but she didn't sound convincing even to her own ears. Having never experienced anything like it, she couldn't be certain. She had a feeling Killian was very practised in the arts of seduction, but to her mind, true lovemaking was when the heart was involved as well as the body.

'Well, whatever you call it, it does the trick. I, for one, am certainly feeling a lot warmer than I was. Now if only we could get rid of the old woman so we had more space, I could warm you down to your very toes.'

Jess felt herself blush and blessed the darkness which had now descended fully. 'You already did,' she muttered, and realised it was the truth. She could feel all her toes again.

'That was just the beginning,' he whispered and nibbled her earlobe which had somehow escaped from the confines of her shawl. 'You really are innocent, aren't you.'

'Killian, no, you've got stop this. I shouldn't have let you …'

'What?' His eyes glittered with mischief. 'I've barely touched you yet. Wouldn't you like me to show you more ways of keeping warm?'

'Absolutely not.' He shouldn't be talking to her like that. She was sure Mrs Forbes would have had an apoplectic fit if she'd heard the half of it, but having allowed him such liberties already, Jess knew she had brought it on herself. She tried to backtrack. 'I'll have you know I'm a respectable girl and … and besides, what else could you possibly do in a sleigh?'

'Push the old woman out and I'll show you.' His voice was as enthralling as his eyes, and for a mad moment Jess almost considered doing what he'd asked. Then she came to her senses.

'For shame,' she hissed at him. 'That would be murder.'

'Oh, yes, so it would.' He pretended a look of remorse, then grinned again. 'Never mind, we'll just have to hope she continues to sleep soundly.'

He lifted her chin with his fingers and bent to kiss her again. Jess' conscience was screaming at her to pull away, to tell him to stop, anything, but her brain refused to follow orders. Instead she submitted to another round of searing kisses, thoroughly enjoying every minute. *I must be a wanton,* she thought, as his hands began to roam under her cloak and she found she liked that too. He stroked her shoulders and back, then daringly, the underside of her breasts. Jess gasped at that, and pleaded with him to stop.

'Very well,' he murmured into her hair. 'I won't do anything you don't want me to, even if it's very tempting.'

Jess was grateful he didn't actually ask her what she wanted, because she would have begged him to continue. Instead, he returned to their kissing game. Somehow she felt slightly safer although even that turned her limbs to liquid fire.

Some time later, through a haze of desire, she registered that the horses were slowing down. She dragged herself back to reality. 'Killian, enough,' she whispered. 'We'll be there in a moment. I must get out from inside your coat. Quickly.'

'Hmm?' He seemed as dazed as she was and his breathing was uneven. It took a while before he reacted to her words and followed her instructions. It wasn't a moment too soon. Just as she had been returned to her previous position next to him and his coat closed around only him, the driver turned around and announced, '*Nu är vi strax framme, frun.*'

His stentorian tones woke Mrs Forbes. She spluttered to life among the shawls and gazed around in confusion. Then she erupted into a bout of coughing so violent it made Jess wrinkle her nose and move closer to Killian.

'Told you we should have pushed her out,' he breathed into her ear. 'Sounds like she'll cock up her toes soon in any case.'

Jess dug him in the ribs with her elbow, not daring to look at him in case she was overcome with a fit of the giggles. It wasn't a laughing matter, of course, but she felt happy and carefree all of a sudden. Even the thought of the coming incarceration couldn't dampen her spirits. She marvelled that a few kisses could bring about such a mood change.

With a hiss of the runners on the deep snow, the sleigh came to a halt in front of the steps to Askeberga's porch. Killian jumped out and reached into the sleigh to help Jess. Instead of taking her hands, he enclosed her tiny waist with his fingers and lifted her out, depositing her on the second step up. He then offered Mrs Forbes a hand and pulled her out, steadying her when she stepped out of the sleigh. While Mrs Forbes turned to thank the coachman, Killian followed Jess into the house.

'Let's hope she goes straight to bed, then I can show you how to keep warm in a freezing manor house,' he murmured from behind her. 'It's much more fun.'

'Killian, don't you dare ...'

Jess marched through the door, her back ramrod straight to show him that she was once more in control of herself. A frisson still shot up her spine and she knew she would have to use every ounce of willpower she possessed in order to keep from taking him up on his offer.

Nothing had ever sounded more tempting.

Killian followed her slowly into the house, breathing deeply to regain some semblance of control over himself.

'Hell and damnation,' he muttered. Who would have thought little Jessamijn was such a firebrand? She looked like an ice queen on the outside, but inside there were hidden depths. He had enjoyed teasing her with the occasional kiss before, but he'd never suspected she would fire his blood to this extent. In fact, he was quite shocked at how much he wanted her. The desire was somehow different and more powerful than any he had ever felt before. He didn't understand it, but knew it would be dangerous to continue this game.

It shouldn't have happened at all. He had promised himself he would leave her alone apart from verbal sparring. But after three days of sitting so close to her, it had all become too much. He smiled to himself as he recalled how easy it had been to entice her into his coat and then onto the next step. She was such an ingénue, but extremely responsive nonetheless. He knew it wouldn't take much to ignite her desire to the point of no return.

He shook his head to clear it of such thoughts. This was madness. He really must stop this. Soon he'd be on his way to China, and although that would temporarily save him from any consequences of seducing Jessamijn, he would eventually return and have to face the music.

Besides, could he really do that to her? She had enough to contend with. She didn't deserve to be treated badly by him as well.

No, he would have to leave her alone from now on. It was up to him to be strong for both of them.

Still, a little bit of flirting never did anyone any harm and they had to pass the time somehow. He would keep it light and not go too far. Surely, he should be able to manage that?

He ignored the little voice inside his head which told him he was a fool.

Chapter Eighteen

Askeberga, Småland

'Ah, pickled herring, how nice. There's nothing like a varied diet, is there?'

Killian tore off a bite of bread with perfect teeth and lifted a forkful of fish to his mouth. Jess caught herself staring at him, and turned away to concentrate on her own plate. A giggle welled up inside her and she had to turn it into a cough, but it was impossible to suppress it entirely. She couldn't help but enjoy his dry humour and the sarcastic comment about the herring was exactly how she herself felt about the food. Monotonous didn't even begin to describe it.

'Mr Fergusson believes one should only eat meat once a week unless one has guests,' Mrs Forbes informed Killian in a croaky voice. 'Fish is better for the constitution.'

'And cheaper,' Killian muttered.

'What was that?' Mrs Forbes was sitting at the opposite end of the long table and hadn't caught his comment, but Jess did. She spluttered into her bread and coughed again, then sent him a look imploring him to behave.

'I said, this herring is particularly tasty,' Killian said in a louder voice. 'Although it has been my experience that it's even better when washed down with *snaps*.'

'Alcohol? Oh, I don't think ...' Mrs Forbes stopped, then began again. 'Ah, yes, you gentlemen do seem to have a preference for such things, don't you.'

'You should have some too, Mrs Forbes. I've been told it's the best cure for colds and prevents congestion of the lungs. After that sleigh ride, you must be chilled to the bone.'

Killian gave Mrs Forbes his most charming smile and the older woman blinked.

'You don't say?'

'But of course. You must have heard that yourself, dear lady. In fact, I believe it was Mr Fergusson himself who told me.'

'Really? Well, in that case, perhaps I ought to try. Just a tiny measure, you know.'

Jess glanced at Killian. What was he playing at now? She had no doubt he was doing this on purpose. Jess had never seen Mrs Forbes drink anything other than whisky. The woman was forever preaching about the evils of drinking *snaps,* but here she was, ready to try some for herself.

The strong drink was ordered from the kitchen, and soon arrived with two small glasses of finest crystal. Jess wasn't offered any, but then she hadn't expected it. Killian kept his eyes on Mrs Forbes while he downed his measure in one go. She followed suit, apparently without thinking, but gasped and wheezed loudly. Soon after, she was overtaken by another bout of coughing.

'Dear Lord,' she spluttered eventually, overcome by the strength of the more or less pure alcohol.

'Don't worry,' Killian said. 'It tastes foul, but you'll soon feel the beneficial effects, I promise. One more, just to be on the safe side.'

'No, no, I couldn't possibly.' But as soon as her cough had subsided, Jess was amazed to see her companion swallow another full glass, after which she just hiccoughed. 'Oh, I say, it does warm you rather, doesn't it?' Mrs Forbes smiled, for the first time that week. Jess looked from Killian to her companion and back again.

He was enjoying himself, she could see that. The mischievous glint was back in his eyes and Jess narrowed her own eyes at him. She tried to send him another warning glance, which he ignored completely. Somehow, he managed to talk Mrs Forbes into having a third glass, then a fourth. Following this it was an easy matter to persuade her to retire early so that she could recuperate from the journey.

'Don't worry about Miss van Sandt,' Killian assured her as he escorted the old lady to the stairs, 'I'll look after her. Just you find your bed and recover from your ordeal. I really don't know what Mr Fergusson was doing, sending you out into the cold in your condition. Most un-gentlemanly of him.'

Mrs Forbes nodded and thanked him, and made no further protests. With an unsteady gait, she went off to bed without so much as a look at her charge. Jess stared after her and shook her head, then turned to give Killian an accusing glare.

'You, sir, are a complete scoundrel,' she told him.

He grinned and bowed. 'Why, thank you. I'm so glad my efforts meet with your approval.' He came round to stand behind her chair and bent to nuzzle her neck. 'Now where were we, Jessamijn?'

She swatted him away. 'We were finished,' she told him firmly.

'Oh, I don't think so. Not even close.' He kissed his way along her collar bone and although it was covered by the material of her dress, the kisses still burned her through the heavy wool.

'Killian, for heaven's sake,' she hissed. 'The servants will see you.'

He sighed deeply and stopped at last, sauntering back to his chair. 'Sadly, you're right. I suppose I'll have to behave for a little longer.' He picked up his glass and refilled it with another measure of *snaps*.

'Do you really like that stuff?' she couldn't resist asking.

'No, it's vile. I much prefer whisky or wine, but since this is all that's available, I'll have to put up with it. It takes away the taste of fish.'

She smothered a smile. He was incorrigible. She knew she ought to disapprove of his behaviour, but instead she was charmed. Probably just as he intended. Well, if he thought she would be an easy victim, he was in for a surprise. Charming or not, Jess had no intention of letting him go any further with his seduction. No man would get into her skirts before first putting a wedding band on her finger, and that didn't seem likely to happen any time soon.

She sighed wistfully. How she wished a man like Killian would marry her, if only to spite her stepfather and force him to hand over her meagre dowry. It would serve Robert right. Not that she wouldn't have married Killian for other reasons, if he'd asked. But that wasn't going to happen either, she knew.

She stared morosely at the leftovers of her pudding, congealing on her plate. Her appetite had deserted her and she almost reached for the *snaps* herself. Perhaps that would take away some of the bitter taste in her mouth at the thought of what her stepfather was doing. If only she could thwart him. If only she could find herself a husband without his knowledge …

She glanced at Killian, who also seemed lost in thought for the moment. Seeing him knock back another glass of alcohol, however, gave her brain a jolt. An idea began to take shape inside her head. She mulled it over for a while, and a plan formed, slowly but surely. It might work, or it might not. Either way, it was worth a try.

The *snaps* decanter was almost empty. 'Would you like some more?' she asked. 'I can have the servants refill it.'

He gave her a measuring stare, but she opened her eyes wide and stared back, feigning innocence. 'I suppose it will help to pass the time,' he replied.

Jess picked up the little bell placed on the table near where Mrs Forbes normally sat and rang for a servant. One of the maids came running and soon had the decanter filled to the brim once more.

'Will there be anything else, Miss?' she asked.

'No, thank you. That is all.'

Jess watched her leave, then turned back to Killian. 'Could I try a little please? I wouldn't mind getting rid of the fish taste myself.'

His eyebrows rose, but he made no comment, only filled the glass and passed it over to her. She took a small sip, then almost choked, her eyes watering while she fought for breath. 'Good heavens, how can you drink a whole glassful in one go? That's disgusting.'

'I told you so, but you get used to it.'

He took the glass back and finished its contents, before filling it again. Jess thought that must be at least his sixth one, and wondered if he was drunk yet. It was hard to tell with him. He wasn't swaying or slurring his words, the way her stepfather did when he'd had too much whisky. On the other hand, how could anyone drink that much and stay sober? It seemed impossible. Just the one sip had made her knees feel wobbly.

She made small talk until he'd had two more glasses, then surreptitiously checked for signs of drunkenness. Looking into his eyes, she thought they had a somewhat glazed expression. They weren't quite as focussed as before, but she still wasn't sure so she decided to test him.

'Shall we retire to the parlour for a while?' she suggested. 'That will give the maids a chance to clear the table here. Or would you prefer to go straight to bed?'

'Are you offering to accompany me?' The mischievous glint was back in his eyes and Jess felt her cheeks heat up.

'That wasn't what I meant, and you know it.' She stood

up and made her way to the door, turning round to watch his progress across the room. Were there any signs of unsteadiness, she wondered? To her delight, he stumbled on the edge of the carpet and had to grab the nearest chair to keep upright. Jess hid a smile and headed for the next room.

The parlour was a beautiful room, well-proportioned and with a row of tall windows facing a lake. However, the sheer size of it meant that it was freezing in winter. The fire didn't appear to have been lit since last time someone visited the house and a musty smell of damp wood and furnishings permeated the room. Jess ignored this and gathered her shawl around her for warmth. She went over to draw the thick curtains to stop the draughts that whistled in around the window frames. Then she sat down on a small settee on the other side of the room. She wished she could kick off her shoes and pull her feet up underneath her, because the wind was finding its way into the room in between the thick oak planks of the floor as well.

Killian threw himself down next to her. Although he was much too close for comfort, she made no comment. When he leaned his head on her shoulder and closed his eyes, she moved to accommodate him.

'Are you feeling all right?' she asked.

'Never better. The room is spinning a little, but if you don't mind me keeping my eyes closed for a while, that will soon stop.'

Jess waited to see whether the alcohol would have any more effect on him. She had heard it sometimes took a while, but once it entered the blood, the person who had been drinking would become virtually incapacitated. They often remembered nothing of their actions the following day. That would suit her just fine, she thought, although at the same time guilt at what she was contemplating shot through her.

'Why are you being so nice to me?' he asked and peered at her suspiciously.

'I'm just being polite. It would be impolite of me to tell a guest to stop leaning on me if he is feeling unwell, don't you think?'

'Nonsense.'

He levered himself up so that they were face to face, and Jess could smell the alcohol fumes on his breath. Normally, she would have found this offensive, but somehow she didn't this time. When he smiled and rubbed the tip of his nose against hers, a shiver of anticipation shimmered through her. She parted her lips, knowing what was coming.

She wasn't disappointed.

This time the kiss was positively indecent and the taste of the *snaps* made it extra intoxicating to her senses. The alcohol tasted so much better this way than straight from the glass, and she kissed him back with abandon.

'You're learning fast,' he breathed, sounding pleased. His hand came up to cup the back of her head, pulling her closer and stroking the nape of her neck. This sent little darts of pleasure down her spine and she brought both hands up to tangle her fingers in his auburn hair. The ribbon around his queue came undone and the mass of silky strands fell about his face. Jess revelled in the feel of it and gave herself up to the wonderful sensations he was creating with his mouth, kissing her, sucking her bottom lip and playing with his tongue.

The sound of one of the maids giggling in the dining room made her come to her senses and she tore her mouth away. 'Wait, no. Stop, please.'

She hardly recognised her own voice, so husky with desire was it. It was a shock to realise how close she had come to succumbing to Killian's lovemaking. He stilled, but didn't let go of her, just held her close while their breathing slowed down a little. She tried to think rationally and made herself focus on the plan she had hatched even though the mere thought of what she was about to do made her want to hang her head in shame.

'Killian?'

'Hmm.' He had his eyes closed again and was leaning his forehead against her bosom.

'Will you marry me?'

His head came up, his eyes wide open and he blinked several times. 'What did you say?' He let go of her and sat up, staring at her. Jess swallowed hard, afraid she'd made a mistake. He obviously wasn't as drunk as she had hoped, but he swayed slightly, which reassured her, so she gathered her courage and ploughed on.

'I ... I asked if you would marry me. That's the only way I'll let you continue with this ... this game.'

'I may be wrong,' he drawled, 'but I was under the impression that I was supposed to do the asking.'

Jess felt herself blush to the roots of her hair and looked away. This had been a bad idea. A very bad idea. She'd never felt so embarrassed or ashamed in all her life. 'I know, but I'm desperate,' she whispered. It was the truth, but guilt clawed at her insides. She shouldn't involve him in her problems, especially not in this underhanded way.

'You like me that much, do you? Well, that's gratifying.' The teasing note was back in his voice, and this helped her regain some of her composure. At least he wasn't completely outraged by her proposal and he hadn't yet refused.

'No, no, that's not why I asked, although of course I like you well enough. It's just that I need a husband ...' She floundered, realising this didn't sound very flattering.

He chuckled. 'Let me get this straight. You want me to marry you because you need a husband, not because you particularly want it to be me?'

'Er, something like that. I'm sorry, I know I shouldn't have said anything. It's just, I really am desperate.'

He frowned. 'Why? Are you with child?'

'No! I told you, I'm not that kind of girl. I mean, I've never ...'

'Calm down. I didn't think you had. Just thought I'd make sure. What is it then?'

'I'm afraid my stepfather won't ever let me marry. I told you what happened when Mr Adelsten proposed, but I didn't tell you that he'd already refused two other suitors on my behalf. And now I'm going to be stuck here again for goodness knows how long. For ever maybe.'

'So you want me to marry you and take you away from here?'

'Well, that is the only way I can escape his control. I simply have to marry someone, it doesn't matter who. If I don't, he'll soon find another use for my dowry and I'll be forced to stay a spinster all my life. You ... you've made me realise I couldn't bear that.'

Killian closed his eyes as if this was all too much for him to take in, but when he opened them again they seemed be seeing all too much. Jess turned away, even more ashamed now. She had thought it would be so easy to trick him into marriage, once he'd had too much to drink. Apparently that wasn't the case and it had been appalling of her to even contemplate such a thing.

'Jessamijn?' He put his hand on her cheek and made her face him once more. 'How do you know I won't squander the money instead? You thought I was a hardened gambler. As your husband, I would have the right to do whatever I wished with it.'

'Well, I was going to ask you to sign a document giving me the right to half my dowry. I can invest my share in the China venture perhaps. I don't care what you do with the rest. As long as my stepfather doesn't get it, it doesn't matter who does. I hate him!'

He was silent for a moment, then he said, 'Very well, why not?'

'I beg your pardon?' Jess was confused now. Killian was swaying again and nodding, then a chuckle escaped him.

'I agree to your proposal. Go fetch some paper and write out your agreement, I'll sign it.'

'You ... you will?' It was Jess' turn to blink. He ignored her and closed his eyes again, leaning back against the settee, smiling like he hadn't a care in the world. Jess looked at him, then saw that he was drunk after all, and probably didn't know what he was saying. Her plan had succeeded. She vacillated for a moment, guilt at taking advantage of him warring with the urge to jump at this chance while she could. Filled with sudden determination, she jumped up from the sofa. It really was her last recourse. If she didn't act now, she was doomed to eternal spinsterhood. She threw Killian one last look, but he clinched the matter for her.

'Go.' He flapped a hand at her, lazily, and smiled. 'I'll wait here. The room is spinning again.'

Jess hurried away before he changed his mind.

Killian watched her leave the room from under lowered lashes. As soon as she had gone, he sat up and rubbed his face with both hands, while taking a deep breath. He'd always been able to hold his drink and was nowhere near as inebriated as she appeared to think. It just suited him to let her think so.

'Well, this is a surprise and no mistake,' he muttered. He'd realised she was up to something when she plied him with *snaps*, and had waited with interest to see what she was about. But a proposal? That was the last thing he'd expected.

Marriage.

It wasn't something he'd ever seriously contemplated before. Certainly not for gain, but it couldn't have come at a better time. His half of her money would be very useful indeed when added to the rest of his hoard and invested in the East India Company. The way she'd made him feel today had also shown him clearly that being married to her wouldn't exactly be a hardship. In fact, if he had to marry at all, why not to Jessamijn?

She was pretty enough, had a neat figure, even better than he'd thought as he had discovered that afternoon, and was intelligent and resourceful. In short, she should make an admirable wife. There was something else too – she evoked feelings of chivalry inside him that he hadn't known he possessed. For some reason he wanted to protect her, keep her safe and pay Fergusson back for his mistreatment of her.

He shook his head and smiled. It had taken courage on Jessamijn's part to propose to him. He was astonished that she was prepared to go to such lengths in order to stop her stepfather from dominating her. He could only hope she accepted a husband's control a bit more meekly, although personally he would prefer a wife with spirit.

Killian frowned and wondered how Fergusson would react to this scheme. If the man had somehow cheated Jessamijn and used money which was rightfully hers, he wouldn't be too pleased. No doubt Killian would lose his job, but since he was leaving with Campbell soon anyway, it didn't much matter.

His thoughts returned to Jessamijn and her drastic measure of marrying a man she didn't necessarily want. He smiled to himself. Oh, but she wanted him all right. She just didn't know how much yet.

Desire stirred inside him again, but he quelled it. This

wasn't the time or the place. Much as he had enjoyed dallying with Jessamijn, he wasn't going to seduce her tonight. But once they were married …

He heard footsteps and hurried to lean back once more, pretending to be asleep. Jessamijn came to a halt in front of him and shook his shoulder gently. 'Killian? Wake up, please. I want you to sign this, then you can go to bed.'

'Hmm? What's that?' He focussed his gaze on her in myopic fashion. 'Oh, it's you. What's that you've got?'

'Just a piece of paper. You promised to sign it, remember?'

She looked very anxious and Killian had to hide a smile. Did she really think he was so drunk he'd sign an important document without reading it? She must be incredibly naïve. He struggled to sit up and squinted at the agreement she had drafted. He scanned it quickly, while pretending to have difficulty reading her handwriting. She had written down a set of rules which gave her complete control of half her fortune, while he was free to dispose of the rest as he saw fit.

He had to agree to marry her and stay married for at least three years. She also stipulated that the marriage should only be consummated if she so wished. His eyebrows rose at that, but he quickly hid his annoyance. So she thought she could keep him at arm's length, did she? *To hell with that*, he thought. He'd soon persuade her otherwise and it wasn't worth arguing over now. Besides, this agreement wouldn't be worth the paper it was written on because it wasn't witnessed. He would stick to most of its terms because they were fair, but as for the rest … He grabbed the quill she was holding in one hand.

'Very well, where do I sign?'

'Here, please.' She pointed at the bottom, and he signed with a flourish.

'There you are. Now, can we go to bed?'

She snatched the agreement out of his hand and danced away. 'I'll send the maid in to show you to your room,' she called out over her shoulder. 'Goodnight.'

He shook his head and smiled after her retreating back. 'Goodnight, little wife to be,' he muttered. 'Sweet dreams.'

Chapter Nineteen

Killian woke up with a pounding headache and cursed the Swedish *snaps*. He may not have been very drunk, but the wretched stuff had terrible after-effects. To make matters worse, the room he was in was so cold the water in the hand-basin was frozen. He had to bash it with the ewer in order to be able to wash and it wasn't a pleasant experience. Shivering, he dressed in a hurry and went in search of warmth downstairs.

He found Jessamijn alone in the dining room, looking nervous and jittery.

'*God morgon*,' he said cheerfully. 'How is my betrothed this morning?'

'You remember then?' she said, frowning and looking around as if she was worried someone would hear their conversation.

'Yes, of course. Why, have you changed your mind?'

'Er, well, no, but the thing is, I think we should keep this to ourselves for now.'

Killian poured himself some ale and took a healthy swig, hoping it would cure his sore head. 'Why?' he asked.

'If Robert should find out, he'd be furious and he'd do everything in his power to stop us. Surely you know that?' Jess scowled into her bowl of porridge. 'We can't risk it.'

'True, but he's not here and it might be a bit difficult to get married without telling anyone,' he commented. 'Besides, don't we need your stepfather's permission?'

'In theory, yes, but as far as I know the marriage would be legal even without his approval. He might decide to withhold my dowry though. I've heard of other cases where that has happened and there was nothing the bride and groom could do about it.' Jess sent him an anxious look. 'Then you would have married me for nothing.'

Killian thought for a moment. 'Let's just present him with a *fait accompli*. If he kicks up a fuss, we'll threaten to tell the world he's so greedy he wants to keep all your father's assets for himself. We can hint we know he scared off your former suitors by offering them only a fraction of the dowry he was supposed to give them according to your father's will. I doubt he'd want his peers to know he's been trying to do you out of what's rightfully yours.'

'But that would be blackmail!'

Killian shrugged. 'So? It's no worse than what he's done to you.'

'I suppose.' Jess stood up and began to pace the room, chewing her bottom lip in concentration. Killian found it an endearing sight and a longing to kiss away her worries swept through him, taking him by surprise. He realised the prospect of marrying her actually excited him, although at the same time it seemed like a huge and frightening step to take.

Jess stopped next to his chair and frowned down at him. 'What if he still refuses? You'd be stuck with me and have nothing to show for it.'

Killian grabbed one of her hands and pulled her round to face him so that he could look in her eyes. 'I'm not a complete pauper, you know. It just means we'll have less money to invest in the China venture, but I'm sure it will still be enough. I thought your main goal was to escape from under Fergusson's thumb? Although it would be annoying if we can't make him pay out your dowry, it's not the end of the world. Now stop fretting. All will be well, you'll see.'

Jess didn't look entirely convinced and flung away from him to start pacing again. 'That still doesn't solve the problem of how to go about it without Robert finding out.'

Killian mulled over their options. 'How old are you exactly?' he asked.

'I turned twenty-one a few weeks ago, but that's neither here nor there, is it?'

'No, but most people would consider you old enough to make rational decisions, so no one could say I took advantage of you. How well do you know the local minister?'

'Very well. He's always been very kind to me, especially since Papa passed away.'

'So if you tell him we have Robert's permission to wed, is it likely he'll believe you?'

'Maybe. He'd have no reason *not* to.'

'Than let's speak to him. We should be able to persuade him to marry us straight away. If necessary you'll have to hint there are circumstances which make it imperative we marry quickly.'

Jess stopped abruptly and her eyes flew to his. 'What? No!'

Killian grinned. 'It's not uncommon for couples to, er ... anticipate their marriage vows.'

Jess' cheeks turned an interesting shade of pink and she threw herself down on a chair, refusing to look at Killian.

'But even if we manage it, what about the banns? Mrs Forbes goes to church every week. Although her Swedish isn't very good, I think she'd notice if Mr Ekman read our names out loud three Sundays in a row.'

Killian sighed. 'Very well then, we'll have to go back to Gothenburg and go sailing.'

'How would that help?'

'I've been told that out on the open sea the captain of a ship has the right to perform the services of a minister if there isn't one to hand. I know a captain who'd be willing to marry us.'

'Hmm, I suppose that would work, although it's not very satisfactory. If we're to claim my dowry, we need proper papers.'

'Then my first suggestion is our only option. There must be a way of making it work.'

Jess opened her mouth to reply, but was interrupted by one of the maids who came into the room and curtseyed.

'Excuse me, Miss, but *Fru* Forbes is asking for you. She's not at all well.'

'Oh, dear, I'd better go back to her then.'

'It's probably the after-effects of the *snaps*,' Killian commented with a grimace. 'You were right, it's vile stuff.'

Jess shook her head. 'No, I don't think so. She's truly ill, even worse than yesterday actually. I want to send for the local wise woman, but she won't let me. Mind you, I don't know if Old Edith will agree to come out in this weather.'

'Is there no proper physician nearby?'

'Hardly. The nearest town is at least an hour away, and I'm not even sure there's one there.' She hesitated by the door, then asked, 'I ... you won't be leaving quite yet, will you?'

He looked towards the window. Outside, the most enormous snowflakes whirled around in a mad dance, coming down thick and fast. 'I'm not going anywhere, by the look of it. Besides, your stepfather gave me permission to rest here for a day or two before going back.'

'Oh, well I'll see you later then. We'll have to discuss ... uhm, our plans some more, but please, will you keep it to yourself for now?'

She looked genuinely anxious and Killian nodded. 'Of course. Who am I going to tell?'

Jess was very worried about Mrs Forbes. The old lady kept her in the stifling bedroom for at least half an hour, complaining about her aches and pains. Despite this, at first she refused to allow Jess to send for anyone, even though it was clear she was very ill. In the end, however, she had to give in.

'The old crone probably knows nothing,' Mrs Forbes grumbled. 'These provincials are backwards in every way, but I suppose she's all there is.'

In fact, Mrs Forbes looked so pathetic and small Jess had forgotten all her hostility towards her. The old woman's colour wasn't good, the coughing was rough and her breathing ragged. Her hazel eyes seemed sunken into the pale cheeks, their normally fierce gaze dull and listless. There was no doubt Mrs Forbes had caught the whooping cough off the two boys, but somehow that didn't seem the only thing wrong with her. She was running an extremely high fever as well, no doubt increased by the furnace she had instructed the maids to stoke in her fireplace. Her breathing sounded laboured even when she was free of the cough for short spells. Despite this, she refused all offers of tisanes and other healing draughts.

The wise woman, when she finally turned up, agreed with Jess. When they walked together to the front door after the consultation, Old Edith turned to Jess, her expression grave. 'I must tell you, Miss van Sandt, your companion is very unwell. At her age, I really can't say whether she'll pull through. I've done some blood-letting, which'll help reduce the fever. You must make her drink water and nourishing soup as much as possible, and have someone sponge her brow with cold water until she cools down. I'll call again tomorrow, weather permitting, but there isn't much more I can do.'

'Is it just the whooping cough? Only, she sounds much worse than my brothers, although perhaps that's due to her age.'

'No, I'm afraid she may have congestion of the lungs as well, but it's hard to tell. Just do as I said and pray, that's all we can do.'

'Thank you, it was kind of you to come.'

Jess paid Old Edith and insisted on giving her a blanket to wrap around her as a shield against the cold. It was a wonder such an old woman had managed to walk from the village, but she seemed indomitable. Jess was very grateful.

Mrs Forbes, however, was a different matter. She wasn't in the mood to co-operate, and refused to eat or drink anything. Nor would she allow the maids to sponge her burning forehead, complaining that the cold water hurt her brow. In the end, the only thing Jess could do was to leave someone to watch over the old lady while she dozed fitfully.

Jess found Killian in the parlour some time later, busy feeding logs onto the fire in an effort to take the chill off the room. He had pulled a sofa into position in front of the fireplace to catch the warmth and invited her to sit beside him.

'You look worn out. Is the old dragon running you ragged?' he asked, taking her hand for a moment to give it a sympathetic squeeze.

'It's not so much that, it's more that she won't do what's best for her. I've tried to follow Old Edith's instructions, but Mrs Forbes simply refuses to do as she's told.' Jess sighed and shrugged her shoulders in a gesture of defeat. 'What can I do? I can't very well force her.'

'No, you can only do your best.'

They sat in companionable silence for a while, staring into the soothing flames as the fire hissed and crackled its way up the chimney. Outside, a veritable blizzard was howling round the house. Jess prayed Old Edith had made it back to her home.

Despite the smell of disuse that still lingered in the room, she felt safe and snug ensconced here with Killian. She was also grateful to fate for bringing them together. It did seem to her as if it had been pre-ordained somehow, God's answer to her prayers perhaps, although she still couldn't believe how bold she had been in proposing to him the night before. It was lucky for her he had taken it so well. Now all they had to do was work out a way to marry without anyone being the wiser.

As if his thoughts had been running along the same lines, Killian said, 'I've been thinking about this marriage business. You know that saying about every cloud having a silver lining?'

'Yes, what of it?'

'Well, if Mrs Forbes is really ill, she won't be able to go to church for a while.'

Jess turned slowly to stare at him. 'You mean ...?'

'Precisely. If we can only prevent anyone else from telling her, then there's no reason we can't have banns read for the next few weeks. And even if she's well enough by the third week, she can't stop us from getting married.'

'But that would mean you'd have to stay here. At least, I think we both have to be present each time. What about your journey to China?'

'Mr Campbell said we're not leaving until mid-January at the earliest. Anyway, as I said this morning, doesn't look like I'm going anywhere for quite a while.' Killian nodded towards the window. 'Even with a sleigh, I doubt I'd be able to travel very far. Unless your stepfather actually comes looking for me, he'll assume I've been detained by the weather and will return as soon as I can.'

'It could work, I suppose. Perhaps if I tell the cook it's a secret and we want to surprise everyone, she'll ask the others to keep quiet?'

'And would they?'

'I think so. They've always been kind to me and when we were here last year they didn't get on terribly well with Mrs Forbes. She can be a bit domineering. Besides, they're all women and if I tell them we're in love they'll think it's terribly romantic. They adore tales of love with happy endings. I've heard them telling each other stories like that many times in the kitchen of an evening.'

Killian grinned. 'It shouldn't be too hard to pretend to be in love. All you have to do is gaze adoringly at me whenever they see us together.'

'Oh, really? I should think it's the other way round. Men do the courting after all.'

'Do they now?' He sent her a teasing glance to remind her of just who had done the asking in this case. Jess felt her cheeks flame, but he rescued her from having to answer.

'Very well, I promise to make eyes at you at every opportunity. Will that do?' he said.

Jess punched him on the arm and this time it almost felt as if she had a right to do so. 'There's no need to go overboard.'

He leaned over to nuzzle her neck and whispered, 'We can always let them catch us kissing. You'll have to pretend you can't keep your hands off me.'

She pushed him away, hoping he wouldn't see the tell-tale shiver that ran through her at his touch. Somehow she didn't think she'd have to do much pretending and that scared her. 'Be serious,' she admonished. 'Let's discuss this properly.'

He put on a mock-serious expression and sat up straight. 'Very well, madam. I'm all ears.'

'Killian!'

'All right, all right.' He subsided. 'Let's think now. What of the male servants, won't they betray us? There's a groom, a gardener and the coachman. Anyone else?'

'No and they never come in the house, so as long as Mrs Forbes is bedridden, they'll have no opportunity to talk to her.' Jess took a deep breath. 'You know, it might just work. Shall we give it a try anyway?'

Killian smiled. 'What have we got to lose?'

'Very well. Let's go to church early on Sunday and speak to Mr Ekman beforehand. I think I can manage to swear him to silence as well, even if Mrs Forbes should happen to send for him.'

Jess felt a frisson of fear slide through her, but ignored it. It wasn't a perfect plan by any means, but it could work. It must.

Jess and Killian passed the time that evening by playing chess and cards, trying not to laugh as it seemed somehow irreverent in the circumstances. However, despite the hush of illness which lingered over the house, Jess enjoyed herself immensely. Although she still considered him a rogue, she came to realise that being married to Killian wouldn't be too much of a hardship, as long as she didn't expect fidelity. Somehow, she doubted he'd be capable of that.

I'm going into this with my eyes open, she told herself. *We are both marrying for convenience. If we can enjoy each other's company from time to time, then what harm is there in that?* It would be an equal partnership, she was determined about that. She wouldn't allow him to make any decisions without her input and she would never, ever, fall under his spell the way her mother had done with Robert. She wasn't a weak-minded female like Katrijna who seemed unable to live without a man. No, if Killian was to bed her, it would be on her terms, not his.

If only her treacherous body wouldn't give her away ...

Chapter Twenty

The following morning, the snow had stopped falling at last and they woke to find an icy fairyland outside the windows. The sun's rays reflected off the sparkling prisms in the snowdrifts and almost blinded them. It was as if some giant had decided to throw out his vast collection of diamonds and covered the entire world with them. Both Jess and Killian were enchanted.

'Do you want to come outside?' he asked, before she had even sat down at the breakfast table. 'It's so beautiful, it's calling to me.'

She smiled broadly. 'Yes, irresistible, isn't it? I just have to check on Mrs Forbes and make sure she has everything she needs, then I'll join you.'

They met up in the hall, each having put on as many clothes as they could find. Especially all the stockings they possessed, for keeping their feet warm would prove the most difficult. Kerstin, the upstairs maid, happened to be crossing the hall as Killian put on his huge bearskin coat. She stopped and looked at Jess' much thinner cloak and shawl with a frown.

'Begging your pardon, Miss, but shouldn't you wear a fur coat as well?' she asked, bobbing a slight curtsey. She glanced surreptitiously at Killian as if she wasn't sure whether to run from him or gawp at him.

'Of course I should, Kerstin, but I'm afraid Mr Kinross is the only one who owns such a thing. Even if he lent me his, I wouldn't be able to walk in it. Just look how long it is.' The enormous garment reached all the way to the floor when Killian wore it, and he was a good foot taller than Jess.

'I doubt the old master's coat is quite as long,' Kerstin said, blushing as Killian smiled kindly at her.

'What old master? You mean my father?' Kerstin nodded. 'Well, he didn't have a bearskin coat as far as I know. Mind you, I never spent any time with him here during the cold season, we only ever came when it was summer.'

'He was here in January one year,' Kerstin said. 'And he bought himself a fur coat because it was one of the coldest Yuletides in living memory and he arrived just after. Shall I fetch it for you? I know where it is.'

'Really? Yes, please.' Kerstin scurried off and Jess turned to Killian. 'I do hope it will fit me or you'll be able to stay outside a lot longer than me.'

They didn't have long to wait. Kerstin came running back with an armful of fur, albeit of a different type and much lighter in colour. 'It's wolf,' she panted, trying to shake the coat and succeeding mostly in sending out a shower of dust. 'A bit moth-eaten, but not too bad. Here, try it on, Miss.'

Jess wrinkled her nose. 'It smells a bit musty,' she protested, 'but I suppose beggars can't be choosers.' She took off her cloak and shrugged into the wolf-coat. Thankfully it seemed to have been made for a normal sized man, not a giant. 'Oh, this feels wonderful! And it's so soft.' She ran her hands up and down the fur, which was grey, cream and black, with long hairs like a shaggy dog, but much smoother.

'When you've been outside for a while, I'm sure the smell will disappear,' Kerstin said.

'I hope so. Thank you anyway, this should keep me warm.'

They set off, slowly at first, trying to wade through the snowdrifts that had piled up on the road that looped in front of the house, forming an 'O' shape with a huge oak tree in the middle. The air was crisp and fresh and their breath emerged like plumes of smoke.

'Mmm, doesn't it smell heavenly,' Jess closed her eyes and

breathed deeply. 'So clean.' On impulse, she bent to scoop up a handful of snow and put it in her mouth. She let it melt on her tongue where the vaguely metallic taste lingered together with the chilling sensation. 'Tastes good too.'

'Look how deep it is. There's no way I could possibly leave any time soon,' Killian commented, and Jess had to agree. The roads would be impassable for the foreseeable future.

They turned to make their way across the white-blanketed lawns and round the corner of the house. Jess found it hard going with her long skirts, so she tried to walk in Killian's footsteps which made it a bit easier. Noticing her predicament, he turned and stretched out a hand to steady her, and then kept hold of it as they walked on.

Although it started out as a demure walk, it wasn't long before Killian picked up a handful of snow to throw playfully at Jess. Soon they were having a full-blown snow fight with much laughter and shrieking. Jess thought to herself it was just as well Mrs Forbes had been dosed with plenty of laudanum that morning, otherwise she might have reprimanded her charge for unseemly behaviour. She didn't dwell on this for long, however, she was having far too much fun.

'Just you wait, you scoundrel, I'll get you back, see if I don't,' she shouted at Killian. He had a great aim and hit the side of her head, showering her in a cascade of snow. Even though she was wearing a shawl tied under her chin, she still felt the cold of the snow penetrate to her scalp. She chased after him, both of them running full tilt down towards the lake, until he tripped on a boulder hidden by the snow and fell down, rolling onto his back.

Jess arrived seconds later, breathless and panting, with a huge handful of snow poised to hurl at him. Before she could do so, he hooked a leg behind her knees and brought her crashing down on top of him.

'Killian,' she protested. 'No, don't!' He held a pile of snow only inches from the back of her neck, while holding onto her with his other arm so that she couldn't escape. At the same time, he was laughing so hard he nearly lost his grip.

'What will you do to stop me?' he teased, moving the snow closer.

'I'll ... I'll hit you, no kick you.' He laughed even more. 'No, wait, I know.' Jess had hit on the one thing guaranteed to distract him and bent quickly to cover his mouth with her own in a searing kiss. He stopped laughing, his eyes widening. They were an intense blue in the bright sunlight and Jess felt as if she was drowning in their depths for a moment. Then he dropped the snow, enclosed her with both arms and kissed her back. What had been meant only as a diversionary tactic suddenly turned into something much more serious. It was a long while before Jess came to her senses and lifted her face up to stare down at him.

'I ... sorry. I didn't mean to ...'

He grinned. 'It's allowed. We are betrothed after all, aren't we?'

'Yes, but not in that way.'

'We'll see,' he replied, then rolled them both over so that she was the one trapped underneath. 'Just one more for good measure.' He kissed her again and Jess couldn't help herself. Her mouth responded as if it had been made only for this and she lost track of everything.

Her heart was beating even faster now, but not from the snow fighting. Killian smiled that slow smile that sent shivers down her back and she turned away abruptly when he let her go. 'I think you're safe,' she heard him say with a chuckle. 'At least from the snow.'

She got to her feet eventually and tried to dust herself off. She couldn't look at him, or she'd be tempted to throw herself back down on top of him again. It was incredible how her body reacted to such a simple thing as a kiss. Frightening too, she thought. She checked to see whether anyone could have seen them from the house, but they were quite a way off and there didn't seem to be anyone about.

He stood up and they helped each other brush the snow off their backs. 'Come, let's go and see if the ice will hold us,' he said, taking her hand in his and beginning to run towards the edge of the lake.

'It might not be safe,' she protested, but she allowed him to pull her along anyway.

'We won't go far,' he promised. 'If it's thick enough we could go fishing later. I used to do that on the loch whenever it froze over when I was a boy.'

'You lived by a loch?' Jess was intrigued. She had never heard him talk about his home before.

'Yes, but that was a long time ago. It's no longer my home.' His tone changed and she sensed it wasn't a subject he was comfortable discussing, so she let it go.

'We can ask the gardener, he might have what we need,' she suggested.

'Good idea. For now, let's just test the thickness.'

The ice was thick and strong. After locating the equipment they needed, as well as some bread for bait, they spent a happy afternoon fishing on the ice. They caught ten fat perch, a few roach and two small pikes. The roach went straight back into the lake, since they were inedible, but the rest of their haul they took to the kitchen for Britta, the cook, to deal with.

'My, my, you have done well,' she said, smiling at them. Jess had confided the secret of their marriage plans to Britta, who had promised she wouldn't breathe a word to anyone. She seemed genuinely pleased for Jess. 'Would you like these for your supper? Lots of bones in pike, but well worth the effort if you've a mind to pick your way through them.'

'Yes, please,' they said in unison, then looked at each other and laughed. Killian took Jess' hand and led her out of the kitchen. On the way, he gave her a kiss on the cheek in full view of Britta and the kitchen maid, who pretended not to see.

'Killian,' Jess protested, but he only raised his eyebrows at her with an innocent expression. Jess didn't have the heart to object.

'Please won't you tell me a bit about yourself, Killian? You know my family, such as it is, but I know nothing of you.'

They were sitting by the fire yet again a few days later, and although Jess had sensed he didn't like to talk about himself, curiosity finally made her ask.

He shrugged. 'What do you want to know? I'm the grandson of Lord Rosyth of Rosyth House, who's more or less disowned me. One day I'll have his title, but not much else. The rest will probably go to my sainted cousin Farquhar.' He snorted. 'Now there's someone who could show your stepfather a thing or two about ruthless machinations. He's married to a woman called Ailsa and has two daughters, but I've never met them. That's about it.'

'You have no parents? No brothers or sisters?'

His expression hardened. 'I have a mother, but we're not really on speaking terms. She left me with grandfather when I was ten, just after my father died.'

'Why?' Jess stared at him. It seemed a very callous thing for a mother to do.

'Who knows? She and grandfather didn't get on. She told me some nonsense about him wanting to raise me without mollycoddling so I could be a good laird. I didn't believe a word of it.'

'But she was kind to you before? I mean, she wasn't an uncaring mother?' Like mine is now, she wanted to add, but didn't because she knew that was unfair. She was sure her mother did care, but at the moment she was preoccupied with the little boys.

'She was almost overly affectionate, I'd say,' Killian replied, then smiled. 'Not really what boys appreciate at that age.' Then he sobered. 'But to go from that to nothing at all was a bit of a shock.'

'Sounds to me as though she was forced to go,' Jess said. 'Did your grandfather have some hold over her?'

'Not that I know. I have wondered, but since she supported herself after her departure, I couldn't see any reason for her behaviour.'

'Well, did you ever ask her?'

'No. I nearly did just before I came here, but then I decided there was no point. Forget it, I shouldn't have mentioned it. Perhaps one day I'll have it out with her, but for now, I'd rather leave it.' Killian stared morosely into the flames and Jess understood that this particular topic of conversation was now at an end.

'Tell me about Scotland,' she invited instead. 'I would love to go there some time. Mrs Forbes is forever telling me about the Highlands. Is it really as beautiful as she claims? She does seem rather biased to me.'

Killian smiled and said in a broad Scottish accent, 'Aye, lass, there's nae place like the Highlands in all the world.'

'Be serious.'

'I am. It's beautiful and wild, a bit like you actually. And craggy.' He leaned over to kiss the tip of her nose.

'Are you saying I have a craggy nose?' She tried to look offended and he laughed.

'No, no, it's lovely. I mean you have the same fresh look about you and your eyes are the colour of the clear water that flows into the lochs.'

He stared into her eyes as if he truly found them beautiful and for a moment Jess almost believed him. Then she reminded herself he was practised in the art of flirtation. He had probably said much the same thing to a dozen or more girls. Still, it was always nice to receive a compliment, so she smiled at him and said, 'Thank you, you're too kind.'

'Not at all, it's the truth. If you've heard all about the Highlands already, shall I tell you about Edinburgh? Now there's a place you should visit one day ...'

Chapter Twenty-One

In the end, it was all so much easier than they thought. Despite having to walk to church each Sunday through the deep snowdrifts, they had no trouble persuading Mr Ekman to enter into their conspiracy. A sweet, elderly man with a round, beaming face, Jess had known him for years. He therefore took her aside to ask her if she was sure this was what she wanted, adding kindly, 'I wouldn't wish to see you coerced in any way, Miss van Sandt.' But Jess was able to put his mind at rest.

'Oh, no, Mr Ekman, there's no need for you to be concerned. I'm in complete agreement with Mr Kinross about this and I know what I'm doing.'

At least I think I do, she added silently to herself. Although there were still times when she wondered if she had done the right thing.

To their delight, there were more blizzards, and they felt fairly sure no one would question why Killian stayed on for so long at Askeberga. There really wasn't any way for him to leave, other than on foot. Since no one would risk horses breaking their legs in the deep snow, there was no news from Gothenburg or anywhere else. They assumed no one could reach them either, which was the most amazing good luck.

Poor Mrs Forbes remained ill, and at first Jess thought she couldn't possibly pull through. Another visit from Old Edith, however, made a huge difference. This time she didn't mince her words and delivered a long lecture on the evils of stubbornness and not doing what was good for one. The result was that Mrs Forbes began to submit to having her face bathed with cold water. She also drank down the various nourishing broths brought to her sickbed without too much protest.

'I can't abide broth,' she muttered, but swallowed nonetheless. Jess and the maids ignored her complaints for the most part and just continued to feed her in silence. On the fourth day they were rewarded for their patience. Mrs Forbes began to look slightly better and even said 'thank you' once or twice.

'She must be feeling well,' Kerstin muttered under her breath. 'She'll be smiling next, and won't that be a miracle.' Jess hid a smile of her own and told Mrs Forbes they were all pleased she was on the mend.

'Aye, maybe I'll be able to get up soon and save you the trouble of looking after me. I know you must all be wishing me in Jericho.'

Old Edith, who happened to be there at the time, turned round and snapped, 'There will be no getting up for a long while yet. You're staying in that bed until I say you can leave it. If you put so much as a toe outside before then, you'll have me to deal with. You're as weak as a kitten, for heaven's sake.'

There was no doubt Old Edith was right. Mrs Forbes was still racked by bouts of coughing, which seemed to drain every ounce of her energy. They might even have caused her to crack a rib, since her side ached each time. Even holding a spoon for herself was too much.

'We don't mind,' Jess assured her. 'Just you concentrate on getting your strength back now, however long it takes.'

On the third Sunday, which was the twenty-third of December, Mrs Forbes was a lot brighter.

'I should like to go to church, I think,' she said, 'seeing as it's almost Christmas.'

Jess felt her heart do a somersault and her lungs

constricting, making it hard to breathe. She blurted out, 'Oh, but you can't!'

She realised this sounded a bit suspect, so she quickly added, 'You couldn't possibly walk all that way, Mrs Forbes, and the coachman says there's still too much snow to take the horses out.' That was a lie, as Jess well knew, since much of the snow had now disappeared. However, although Mrs Forbes could look out of her window, she wasn't able to tell the state of the roads from there, so Jess felt safe in deceiving her. 'Besides, you want to be well enough to celebrate Yule, don't you?'

Not that they were doing much celebrating, but Britta had been preparing special dishes all week. Jess knew there would be an elaborate meal and sitting up for it might tax Mrs Forbes.

'Very well, perhaps I'll wait until next week then. Do send my regards to Mr Ekman.'

'Of course.' Jess let out the breath she'd been holding and her heart went back to its normal rhythm. She sent up a silent prayer of thanks.

As Jess and Killian set out for church, a shiver of apprehension ran through her. Killian noticed, because she was holding on to his arm, and he put his hand on top of hers and gave it a reassuring squeeze. 'Don't worry, I'm sure all will be well. If no one has told Mrs Forbes by now, we're safe.'

'I know. I just have this vision of someone arriving just as we're about to be married and rushing into the church to stop us. It would be so humiliating.'

Killian smiled. 'No one here knows us well enough to object, surely? And I doubt anyone from Gothenburg will be arriving in the middle of a church service. They'd go straight to the manor and wait there. Stop fretting, everything will be fine.'

Jess nodded and tried to push aside her misgivings, but couldn't help asking in a small voice, 'You ... you don't regret agreeing to this now? I mean, fifteen hundred silver *daler* isn't really a lot of money. You could have done much better.'

Killian stopped and allowed the servants, who had been walking behind to overtake them before he spoke. He took both Jess' hands in his – she could feel the warmth of them even through their gloves – and looked her in the eyes. 'Jessamijn, if I didn't want to marry you, believe me, I wouldn't be here. Now, if you're getting cold feet, please say so and we can call it off. If not, let's be on our way.'

'I ... yes, Killian. I'm sorry, I just wanted to make sure.'

'Well, you can stop worrying. Everything will be fine. Trust me.'

Killian offered his arm to his betrothed once more, then marvelled that he could sound so sure, when in fact he was the one who had been getting cold feet. He had woken up that morning, wondering what on earth he was doing, marrying a girl without her family's consent, and one who might bring him more trouble than she was worth. And just as he was about to embark on a long and dangerous journey too.

He must be mad.

Whenever he looked at Jess, however, the certainty that he was doing the right thing returned. He only had to see an anxious expression on her face and some deeply rooted urge to protect her surged through him. Fergusson had treated her badly and Killian was her only hope of escape. How could he possibly let her down when she needed him?

Besides, what difference did it make who he married after all? He wasn't about to let his grandfather chose a bride for him and since he had never fallen head over heels in love with anyone, he may as well marry Jessamijn. At least he couldn't be accused of doing it purely for mercenary reasons. As she so rightly said, fifteen hundred *daler* was hardly an astronomical sum. In fact, he'd amassed much more than that himself through his gaming.

Outside the church, he stopped and waited for everyone else to go inside before them, as Mr Ekman had instructed. He took Jessamijn's trembling hand in his and, smiling, bent to kiss her full on the lips, as much to convince her as himself that this wasn't a huge mistake.

'Are you ready?' he asked, and together they entered the church.

The snow had begun to fall again outside. The huge silent flakes were few and far between and floated to the ground without a fuss, caressing anything they encountered with their cold softness. Jess had left a small opening in the curtains so that she could watch them shimmer in the moonlight. It was such a beautiful sight, she didn't want to miss it, and she was sure she wouldn't be able to sleep anyway, after the day's happenings.

She was married. She was Mrs Kinross.

It didn't feel real, but it was. Just to reassure herself she felt for the ring Killian had put on her finger. It was his signet ring which was a bit too big, but it had been the only thing he had to hand at the moment.

'I'll buy you a better one as soon as we're back in Gothenburg,' he'd promised. 'This will have to do for now, I'm afraid.'

Jess didn't mind. Whether or not she had a proper wedding band was the least of her concerns.

Standing in front of Mr Ekman with Killian that morning had felt so right in the end, as if it had somehow been meant. Jess didn't know why. It was purely a business arrangement, there was nothing remotely romantic about it at all, despite the kisses he had given her both before and after the event. And yet ... a part of her had wished there was more to it. Much more.

Don't be such a ninny, she told herself. Killian wanted her money, as much as she wanted to escape from Robert, and together they would achieve their aims. Nothing more, nothing less. Only fools married for love and hadn't she proved to herself what happened when you fell in love? Believing in the sweet nothings murmured by scoundrels like Karl gave you nothing but heartache and tears. No, far better to marry for other reasons without involving emotions in any way.

She sighed and closed her eyes, trying to drift off to sleep. Life was never quite the way you thought it would be, but at least being married to Killian would be interesting, to say the least. She had a feeling life with him would never be dull.

The timbers of the old house creaked as they tried to accommodate the cold that whistled in through numerous cracks. Floorboards groaned as if they bore the weight of hundreds of feet, long gone. The eiderdown on top of her sheets and blankets kept out the freezing draughts and Jess burrowed underneath it, revelling in the warmth and comfort. She was used to the sounds of Askeberga. The familiarity of them soon lulled her into that half-state between waking and sleeping where it's impossible to be sure what is real and what is a dream. When a floorboard creaked somewhere near her bed, therefore, she didn't react, only sighed in satisfaction. Moments later, however, a gust of cold air entered her sanctuary, followed by a body which slid into her bed so quickly she didn't even have time to protest. Jess opened her mouth to cry out, but a hand descended on it and cut the sound off before it left her throat. Her eyes flew open.

'Shh, it's only me.'

Killian's words were unnecessary, because she had known it was him even before he said a word. It scared her to realise that she already recognised his scent and found it intoxicating. Her body reacted to his presence next to her by a sudden tingling, and she gritted her teeth, angry with herself. So much for her resolve to stay aloof from him.

He took his hand off her mouth, seemingly confident she wouldn't raise the alarm, and she gave vent to her feelings in a furious whisper. 'What are you doing here? You agreed to a marriage in name only.'

She could see him clearly in the shaft of moonlight still spilling in through the chink in her curtains and she tried to scoot away from him towards the edge of the bed. He stopped her by putting both arms around her and without answering her question, kissed her thoroughly.

Emerging breathless from this, Jess tried to remonstrate with him again, but he put a finger on her lips and shushed her once more. 'I had to come,' he whispered. 'We must finish what we started this morning or it won't be legal.'

'What? But ... no! You signed the contract, remember?'

He smiled and began to rain kisses on her cheeks, nose and mouth, while murmuring soothingly. 'I know, I know, but even you must realise that if we don't consummate our marriage, Fergusson can have it annulled. You don't want that, do you? There must be nothing he can do about it otherwise he'll find a way to keep the money. Just this once, that's all it will take, then he'll be powerless.'

'I suppose you're right, but ...'

'And I seem to remember your contract said the marriage could be consummated if you so wished.' His fingers glided slowly down the front of her nightshift, which had somehow come undone at the top, and caressed her breast, sending a shockwave through her stomach down into her legs. 'Are you sure that's not what you want?' he whispered, following his hand with soft lips that burned her nipple through the flimsy material before he flicked it with his tongue.

Jess felt herself dissolve, as if her limbs had no will of their own whatsoever. His hand was now travelling lower, while his mouth continued to work its magic on her breasts. She forgot all her reasons for not wanting to consummate the marriage except one.

'No, wait, Killian, please. We can't do this. What if I become with child? I don't want to be left a widow with a child to support if anything happens to you during the voyage. It would be too much.'

'It won't happen that quickly. We'll only do it this once and there are things I can do to stop you from conceiving. Trust me.'

He kissed her on the mouth again, preventing her from voicing any more protests, and the truth was she didn't want him to stop any longer. Her body was crying out for something, what she wasn't sure, but she knew only he could give it to her. She wanted him, desperately. The weeks spent in close companionship, with him teasing her senses at every turn, had left her with a hunger for more. Here was her chance to find out what that was. She couldn't resist.

His fingers caressed the inside of her thighs, having bunched her shift up somewhere around her middle without her noticing. When he found her most sensitive spot, she almost cried out, so intense were the sensations he was creating inside her. A crescendo built and waned, as his fingers came and went, and she heard him murmuring encouragement and words of love. She found herself believing him.

'You're so beautiful. That's right, relax and let me give you pleasure. There is nothing to be afraid of, you know you want this as much as I do, sweeting. I want you, only you ...'

With a sigh, half-pleasure, half-protest, she gave herself up to the enjoyment. She allowed him to do whatever he wanted until he positioned himself on top of her and entered in one swift stroke. As if he had known she would cry out, he put a hand over her mouth to stifle any sound, but her eyes opened wide and the spell was broken temporarily while pain penetrated her fog of pleasure.

'Killian, I ...'

'Shh, love, just wait a moment. It will pass.' He kept still inside her and instead inserted a finger between them, finding that spot which had so entranced her earlier. Slowly, the pleasurable sensations began to build inside her once more. When he moved again in a slow rhythm, the discomfort faded away.

Somehow, her body knew what to do now and she followed his lead in an ever faster crescendo which ended on a tidal wave of sensations, her mind splintering into a thousand fragments. She wanted to cry out again, with pleasure this time, but he covered her mouth with his and they swallowed each other's cries.

When it was all over, he took her in his arms, wrapped all the blankets and sheets around them like a cocoon, and just held her until their breathing returned to normal. At first, Jess felt languid and content to stay there, but as her senses returned, so too did her misgivings.

It had happened, exactly what she didn't want – she had fallen under a man's spell, unable to withstand him in any way. She had allowed Killian to do whatever he wanted with her, had been prepared to give in to his every command as long as he didn't stop what he was doing. She had, to put it baldly, been helpless, the way her mother was helpless to resist Robert.

She understood now the hold her stepfather had over Katrijna. If this was what he did to her, she could quite see that a woman as weak as her mother would be unable to refuse him anything. But Jess was made of sterner stuff and this must never happen again.

'You have to leave now, Killian,' she murmured.

'What?' He sounded drowsy and content. She could almost hear the smile of victory in his voice – he had won. Only this time, though, she promised herself.

'I said, you should go back to your room. It's done. Our marriage is legal in every way, so there's no need for you to stay.'

He frowned at her. 'You don't want to try again? It always gets better with practice, you know.' He trailed a hand down to cup her breast, but she pushed it away, despite the enjoyment even that small caress gave her.

'No. I didn't enjoy it and I don't want to do it again. You said once was enough. If you don't leave now, I'll scream.'

He sat up and scowled at her. 'The devil you didn't enjoy it. You're lying.'

She sat up too, ignoring the shiver that went through her when the cold night air hit her bare shoulder. 'You can't possibly know what I felt, so you'll have to take my word for it. Now please, go away and don't come near me again. We have a business arrangement and you have signed a contract to that effect. Kindly stick to it.'

He stared straight into her eyes, as if he could see into her soul and she was very much afraid he could. 'I have no idea what maggot has got into your brain now, but I know for a fact you're lying and I could prove it to you. However, I don't stay where I'm not wanted, so have it your way. Next time you want to be pleasured, you'll have to ask me. I won't come begging.'

He snatched up his shirt with angry movements and dragged it over his head. She heard it rip, but he didn't seem to care or even notice. After sending her a penetrating glare, he stalked to the door and disappeared as silently as he had come.

Jess gathered the covers around herself and lay down, shaking with emotion and cold. Tears gathered at the corners of her eyes, but she dashed them away with impatient fingers.

So what if he was right? So what if she had enjoyed his lovemaking immensely? She couldn't let him have that hold over her. It would only be the first step and before she knew it, he would be controlling everything the way Robert did. She had to stay firm.

Why then did she feel as if her heart was breaking?

Killian was furious with himself.

He should have been less impatient and given her more time to get used to having a man in her bed. She was a virgin after all, a complete innocent. Instead, he had blundered straight in and treated her the way he would have any other woman. The way he pleasured experienced women.

'Damn!' he muttered, punching his pillow in frustration.

He could have sworn she'd enjoyed it. In fact, he would almost take an oath to that effect, but perhaps it had all been a bit too overwhelming? For someone who had probably never even seen a man without his clothes on, what they had just done could have seemed disgusting or immoral or ... he didn't know what else.

But no. She had been content afterwards, he would swear to it. It was only after she'd had time to think about it that she came out with her demand for him to leave. Something had spooked her. Or was it simply that she didn't find him to her liking?

He almost laughed out loud. Well, that would be a first. How ironic if the one woman who *didn't* want him was the one he'd married. *Lucky at cards, unlucky in love* ... The silly phrase ran through his mind and he frowned into the darkness. That was complete rubbish.

Either way, he now found himself with a wife who didn't want him in her bed. He'd been so sure he could persuade her to tear up that ridiculous agreement she had made him sign, but it would seem he was wrong. No point staying at Askeberga any longer. He might as well go back to Gothenburg and confront his new mother-in-law and her husband and try to squeeze the money out of them that was his due. No, his and Jessamijn's. His wife had her part of the bargain, he would have his.

He ground his teeth in frustration. This was not at all how he had imagined his wedding night, but as he'd told his *wife* – the word made him take a deep breath – he refused to stay where he wasn't wanted. In the morning, he would leave, snow or no snow.

Chapter Twenty-Two

Gothenburg, Sweden

'Mr Kinross, am I glad to see you again! I thought something bad had happened to you.' Mrs Ljung was overjoyed to have her protégé back and ushered him into the house with a beaming smile. 'And you have a visitor too. He's been waiting for days and I didn't quite know what to say to him.'

'A visitor?' Killian was exhausted from the journey, which had been accomplished at great speed since there were no ladies to take account of this time. He certainly wasn't in the mood to be sociable. 'Who is it?'

'A young lad. Doesn't speak Swedish, so I've not been able to talk to him much, but I think he understood when I told him to wait. I put him in your rooms and fed him. I hope I did right?'

Killian smiled reassuringly at her. 'Yes, thank you, Mrs Ljung, you've been very kind. I think I know who he is now and although I've no idea why he's here – he shouldn't be – he is almost like family to me.'

He took the stairs up to the first floor two at a time and, just as he'd suspected, found Adair sitting in front of his tile stove staring into the flames.

At the sound of the door opening, the youth turned around. A huge grin spread over his thin face and the amber eyes lit up. 'Mr Kinross, ye're back at last. I was fair worrit ye was dead.'

'Not yet, varmint. Although where I've been it was certainly cold enough to freeze to death. But what are you doing here? I didn't send you permission to come and I thought we agreed you'd wait until ...'

'I ken,' Adair interrupted, 'but I *had* tae come. I heard one o' yer cousin's men buyin' passage tae Sweden. When I told yer friend, he said it were best I come and warn ye. We werenae sure why he was goin' ower here, but he cannae be up tae nae guid. 'Specially since I seen him pocket a bag o' coins from yer cousin.'

'I see.' Killian shook his head in exasperation. Did Farquhar never give up, he wondered. He'd have to have it out with his cousin once and for all to put a stop to his intrigues. If he made it back from China, that was. With a sigh, he went to sit by the tile stove next to Adair and held out his hands towards the welcome warmth. It had been a while since he'd felt his fingertips and they tingled back to life now with painful needle pricks. 'In that case, thank you. At least now I can be on my guard. I wonder if the man is here to put a spoke in my wheel or to do me physical harm?'

'He looks like a thug if ye ask me. Name of Allan. I asked aboot an ' he's no' a fellow I'd like tae mix wi', if ye ken wha' I mean. I heard some verra nasty things aboot him.'

'That's all I need right now. As if I'm not in enough trouble ...'

'Ye're in trouble, Mr Kinross?' Adair was all ears, presumably since it was usually he who was the troublemaker.

'You could say that. I'll tell you about it in a minute, but first I believe I hear the lovely Mrs Ljung coming up with some supper. If it's some of her pease pottage, I swear I shall love her for ever.'

The following morning, Killian made his way to the warehouse by a different route to the one he normally took. As an extra precaution Adair followed some way behind him, keeping his eyes open as always. Killian doubted this Allan person would attack him in broad daylight, but since he didn't know what the man had planned, he decided it was better to be careful.

It was very early still, and the warehouse was empty. When he entered the office, he found Holm already there before him, his spare shoulders hunched over a ledger.

'Ah, good morning. I should have known you'd beat me to it.'

'Kinross! Where on earth have you been? We heard about the heavy snowfall inland, but surely you could have made your way back sooner than this?' Holm looked disapproving, as if Killian had been evading his duties, which he supposed he had, even if it was in a good cause.

'No, it's been impossible to leave until now. I'm sorry, but there it is. And there were other reasons as well why I couldn't go.'

'Other reasons?'

'Yes, well, uhm, is Mr Fergusson due in this morning? I'll need to have a word with him. It's about his stepdaughter. Oh, and Mrs Forbes. She's been very ill.'

'Jess is ill?'

'No, not her, Mrs Forbes. Caught the whooping cough and then it turned into congestion of the lungs, but she's better now. Just a bit weak still.'

'Thank goodness for that. I thought for a moment there we'd lost another poor soul.'

'Another?' It was Killian's turn to frown.

'Of course, you don't know, do you? Little James ... I'm afraid he didn't pull through. So sad. He just wasn't strong enough.' Holm shook his head and looked down, overcome with emotion.

'Oh, no, Jessamijn will be devastated. She told me how much she loves her brothers.'

'Yes, well, that's nothing compared to how her mother feels. The poor woman has gone to pieces and Mr Fergusson's fairly cut up about it as well. As a matter of fact, he hasn't been near the warehouse for two weeks. So to answer your question, I doubt you'll see him today.'

Killian sat down, beginning to see just how difficult it was going to be for him to break the news of his and Jessamijn's marriage to Fergusson. They had agreed, in cold, clipped sentences the day after their marriage, that Killian would return to Gothenburg and confront Jess' stepfather first before fetching her back to town. Since Mrs Forbes wasn't in a fit state to travel in any case, Jess thought it best to stay behind. But how could he break this news now, when Jess' mother and stepfather had other things on their minds?

Holm had stood up without Killian noticing it and come round behind him to put a hand on his shoulder. 'What's the matter? You look upset, but surely you barely knew the baby?'

'What? Oh, no, that's not why ... The thing is, well, I was going to inform Mr Fergusson first, but I may as well tell you now. Jessamijn and I are married.'

Holm's mouth fell open. 'Married? But you said you weren't interested in her.'

'I wasn't. Well, not in that way, but she asked for my help. Said it was the only way she could escape from Mr Fergusson because he wouldn't let her marry anyone else. And with Mrs Forbes so ill, there was no one to stop us.' Holm was glaring at him. 'You don't have to look at me like that. I swear, I didn't marry her for her money. By all the saints, I'm in line to inherit the entire Rosyth estate one day. I don't need her measly dowry!'

Holm seemed to consider this for a moment. 'I apologise,' he said. 'I know you're not as frivolous as you first seemed and I confess I had begun to like you a lot. I'm afraid you shocked me, that's all. I thought perhaps I had misjudged you after all.'

Killian shook his head and raked his fingers through his

hair, closing his eyes. 'No, please don't apologise. I'm not a saint. In fact, I can't really explain it even to myself. It just … happened. And now we have to break it to Mr Fergusson.'

Holm looked thoughtful. 'Could you wait a while? That is, unless Jessamijn has returned with you?'

'No, she's still at Askeberga. I said I'd fetch her when things had calmed down a bit here.'

Holm smiled ruefully. 'That might be a long time.' Then he turned serious again. 'The thing is, I've been doing a little bit of investigating. You remember you told me about Mr Milner before you left? Well, it seems he does have something to hide. A mistress and several illegitimate children, to be exact.'

Killian blinked. 'How did you find that out?'

'Spying. Not something I would normally do, but it seemed important.' Holm shrugged. 'I just followed him around whenever I could. In fact, I'm surprised he's been able to keep it a secret for so long, he wasn't exactly circumspect.'

'But no one else knows?'

'I don't think so. Except Mr Fergusson, of course.'

'Yes. So we were right then, but what is it they've colluded at? That's what I don't understand.'

'Me neither. It's a shame we can't search through Mr Fergusson's study properly, but I couldn't ask Jessamijn to take such a risk. He must have a secret hiding place there. There could be some more clues.'

Killian smiled. 'Oh, we don't need to involve Jess in something like that, because I know just the person to help us. Hold on a moment, let me introduce you.'

Not long afterwards, Holm made Adair's acquaintance. Although he was doubtful at first, he was soon persuaded to allow the boy to help them. As a demonstration of his skills, Adair produced Holm's pocket watch which Killian had told him to steal at the first opportunity.

'See, he's quick as a flash,' Killian said proudly, while prodding Adair surreptitiously into giving the watch back. 'If anyone can do it, Adair can.'

'I really shouldn't let you risk it. What if Mr Fergusson catches him red-handed? He'd hand the boy over to the nearest magistrate and the punishment would be severe.'

'Dinnae wirry, sir, I'll no get caught,' Adair said confidently. 'If anyone comes, I'll jump oot the windae. I always open 'em first so's I can escape.'

Holm shook his head, but in the end it was agreed Adair would try that very night.

'You'd best keep out of sight until then,' Holm said. 'Go back to Mrs Ljung's and stay there. I'll come and see you tomorrow morning and if you've found anything, you can show me then.'

'Agreed.' Killian and Adair started to leave, then Killian remembered something. 'Oh, and Mr Holm? If anyone Scottish should come looking for me, would you please tell them I've gone to China already?'

'If you wish. Why?'

'It's a long story. I'll tell you some other time, but I'd be grateful for your help. Thank you.'

It was a dark night and Killian and Adair both dressed in sombre clothing in order to blend into the shadows as much as possible. There were hardly any people out and about, just a few late-night revellers singing at the top of their voices and a courting servant couple huddled in a doorway. They made it to the Fergusson residence without being seen. Adair walked fifty paces behind Killian and they met up in the yard just inside the gate.

'There was no one following us?' Killian looked around to make sure the coast was clear.

'No. I told ye I saw that Allan fellow sittin' half asleep at the inn earlier. He'd bin drinkin' and won't be goin' nowhere on a cold night like this.'

Killian shivered, still feeling uneasy. 'I hope you're right. Now, are you sure you remember what I told you about the layout of the house?'

'Aye, dinnae fash, Mr Kinross. I'll be fine. Just ye wait oot here by the windae and if I jump oot sudden, run like the wind.'

It sounded easy enough, but Killian had more misgivings than he'd let on to Holm. Normally he would never allow Adair to break into anyone's home, only follow them around and keep his eyes and ears open, but this was different. His future might be at stake here.

He stayed crouched under the window to the study and watched while Adair made his way to the back door. Once there, the youth made short work of picking the lock, which was probably a fairly simple one. He disappeared inside, closing the door behind him without a sound. Killian gritted his teeth and prayed for the boy's safety. If anything happened to him, it would be Killian's fault and he couldn't bear to think of that.

It seemed an absolute age before the window above him opened a fraction and Adair hissed, 'Here, tak these an' have a look-see. I cannae read Swedish like, but these looked important.' A bundle of papers slid out into Killian's waiting hands.

'Wait there unless someone comes. I won't be a moment,' he whispered and made his way over to the privy. Once inside, he tried not to breathe in the noxious air and concentrated on lighting a small lantern which he had brought. Quickly, he scanned the papers. They were mostly official contracts between Fergusson and other merchants for various things, all completely legitimate as far as Killian could see. He didn't really know what he had hoped to find – something to incriminate Fergusson in shady deals perhaps, especially with Milner – and he was disappointed but not entirely surprised. However, at the very bottom of the bundle he found something infinitely more interesting. His breath caught in his throat and his heart began to pound.

It was an official looking document written in Swedish, and the top proclaimed in large letters: '*Testamente. Aaron Vilhelm van Sandt. Anno Domini 1725.*'

Killian had by now learned enough Swedish to be able to understand most things. Although this document was written in complicated legal terms, he still got the gist of it, if not the exact wording. Skimming past the beginning of the will, which seemed to contain the usual legal phrases about being of sound mind and so on, he studied the important part further down where bequests were detailed.

> *'... och till min Dotter Jessamijn Katrijna van Sandt överlåtes härmed full kontroll av Messrs. Van Sandt & Fergusson, på villkor att hon låter sig tillrådogivas av Herr Robert Fergusson i den mån hon behöver tills dess hon når en ålder av tjugo-fem år eller ingår giftermål. Vid sådant tillfälle skola halva denna firma tillhöra henne och halva hennes make och de två skola råda över allt gemensamt ...'*

He felt his head reeling. If he understood this correctly, the entire company belonged to Jessamijn outright and if she married, half of it would still be hers and the other half her husband's. In other words, Killian's. He sat down on the privy with a thump, forgetting where he was for a moment.

'Good Lord,' he muttered. 'No wonder the man didn't want Jessamijn to go poking around.'

The will went on with various other stipulations, but as far as Killian could make out, there was no mention of

Robert Fergusson other than in the role of advisor. He had no right to any of it.

The thought stunned him, and he understood everything all too clearly now. Somehow Fergusson had managed to keep this will a secret and had taken over the company himself. How could that be?

He could only think that the will had never been proven, or Fergusson had shown a fake one to Milner and blackmailed the man into declaring it legal. No one except Jess had questioned Fergusson's actions. Everyone else thought he had a right to run things as he saw fit and marrying the widow had been a masterful stroke.

It was an outrage.

Killian suddenly remembered he was in a smelly privy and poor Adair was still waiting in the study. He gathered together the rest of the papers in a rush, while pocketing the will, and made his way across the yard back to the window.

'Are you there?' he whispered.

'Aye.'

'Put these back where you found them and make sure you don't leave any trace of your visit.'

'O'course I won't.'

The papers disappeared inside and the window closed with a soft click. Not long after, Adair emerged from the back door and made his way over to Killian as quickly as he could.

'Anythin' guid?' he asked.

'Tell you later. Let's go.'

They left the yard one at a time, moving as stealthily as predators on a hunt. Then they made their way back to Killian's lodgings by separate routes, meeting up outside Mrs Ljung's front door. Once safely inside, Killian breathed a sigh of relief and sank into a chair.

'Thank you, Adair, you did well, but let's not do this sort

of thing again in a hurry. I feel like someone's wrung me out. The tension was unbearable.'

Adair grinned. 'But it were worth it then? Ye found somethin'?'

'Oh, yes. And I think Mr Holm is going to be very interested in this. Very interested indeed.'

Chapter Twenty-Three

Askeberga, Småland

Several weeks had passed since Killian had left and each day Jess found herself sinking further and further into depression. She missed the companionship, she missed his teasing ways and mischievous grin, but most of all she just missed him. And it was her own fault that he had gone away so abruptly.

She knew well enough that matters had to be sorted out in Gothenburg and her mother and stepfather informed of their marriage. However, she had expected Killian to stay with her for a bit longer, so they could get used to being married and have time to make plans. She had no idea where she would live while he was away, for instance, and what she should do now she was someone's wife.

Wife. Even the word mocked her.

What kind of wife had she been, practically kicking her husband out of her bed on the first night? *A prudent one,* she tried to tell herself, but a little voice inside her told her she'd been a fool. Did she really want a marriage of convenience? He had shown her what it would be like as a real wife, not just a business arrangement. Although she still doubted his ability to remain faithful, with hindsight it seemed a much better prospect than the kind of marriage she had thought she wanted, whether she had to share him with others or not.

But now it was too late and she no longer had that option.

Would he even return for her, as he'd promised? Or would he stay in Gothenburg, taking his share of the dowry before sailing off to China. What if she never saw him again and all that was left to her was his name? Mrs Kinross. It still sounded strange to her.

She stared into the fire, the same one they had sat next to so often during his time at Askeberga, and tears welled up in her eyes. She dashed them away impatiently. What use were tears? No, she had to make the best of the situation and pray to God He would keep Killian safe. If He'd only bring him back from his journey, maybe Jess could somehow make amends. Once he returned they could start afresh. Or not …

Kerstin, the maid, came into the room, looking a little furtive and Jess frowned at her. 'Yes, what is it?'

'Britta needs you to look at something in the kitchen, Miss, er, Madam. If you please?'

'What, now? But it's late. She should have finished her duties by now.'

'It's just a small matter, won't take a moment.'

'Oh, very well.'

Jess wasn't in the mood to discuss supplies or food of any kind. In fact, she wasn't hungry at all at the moment, hadn't been for days. With a sigh, she followed Kerstin to the kitchen and then stopped dead inside the threshold.

'Good evening.'

As if conjured by her earlier thoughts, Killian was standing by the back door, wearing his bearskin coat and looking impossibly handsome. Even more so than she remembered, despite the fact that he was scowling. He bowed to her formally, but didn't move forward to greet her in any other way. Jess' heart sank.

'Killian, I … why are you here? Have you come to fetch me back?'

He nodded. 'Yes, but I'm afraid we'll have to leave Mrs Forbes behind.'

'Why? She's still very weak, but I think if we go slowly, she'd be able to manage.'

'No, I'm sorry, but we're going back alone and no one must know.'

Confused, Jess stared at him. 'I don't understand. Did something happen when you told my mother and Robert?'

'I haven't told them yet. In fact, I haven't seen them at all.' He looked at the floor and cleared his throat. 'I'm afraid I have some bad news. Your youngest brother passed away. He was too weak to survive the whooping cough. I'm sorry.'

Jess heard a cry as if from a distance and only vaguely realised it had come from her. Her hand flew to her mouth and there was a buzzing noise in her ears while she blinked to clear her vision. Black spots danced in front of her eyes and she felt as if the floor was moving. 'Oh, no! Dear God, no! Little James ...' She began to sob, unable to take in the enormity of this disaster.

Killian moved forward and put his arms round her, patting her back. 'I'm so sorry,' he repeated, his voice low and compassionate. Jess leaned her forehead on his shoulder and allowed the tears to flow.

'I ... I knew he wasn't strong, but the physician said ... only tiny babies died from it. He said, he said ...' She couldn't continue, the words sticking in her throat.

'Usually, that's true, but James was apparently weakened by other illnesses, or so Mr Holm said. Children are fragile things. There was nothing the physician could do. I really am very sorry, I know you loved him.'

Jess felt comforted by Killian's presence and he held her patiently, murmuring soothing words until she had cried herself out. Despite this, she was aware of a constraint between them that had never been there before their wedding night. As soon as she had her crying under control, more or less, she disentangled herself and stepped away from him. 'Poor mother, how will she cope?' she asked sadly, thinking of Katrijna fretting over her chicks.

'I don't know. No doubt, time will lessen her grief, and she still has Ramsay to think of.'

'Yes, of course. He must be bewildered, it's difficult for someone so young to understand.' She wiped her tears away with the back of her hand and drew in a steadying breath. 'So you've not seen them at all?'

'No, and I think it's best if we keep our marriage a secret for now. Mr Holm knows and approves, but there are other matters we need to discuss. Not now though. We need to leave at first light. Can you pack tonight, please? Write Mrs Forbes a note saying you've left because you couldn't stand to be banished any longer and you want to make a new life for yourself somewhere else. Don't tell her where you're going, that way she can't inform anyone else. I'm sure Fergusson will send for her in due course.'

'But why can't she come?'

'I'll explain it all tomorrow. We don't want anyone to know you're in Gothenburg and don't tell her I'm here now either. I'll sleep in the stable with the grooms for tonight and I've bribed them to keep it to themselves. Agreed?'

'Very well, if you think it's necessary.'

'I do. I'll see you tomorrow then.'

With that he was gone, and Jess was left to stare after him, her thoughts in a jumble.

Britta came into the kitchen and Jess turned to her. 'Did you hear any of that?'

'Some, but I won't tell. I trust Mr Kinross to know what he's doing. Shall I help you pack?'

Jess sighed. 'Yes, please. We have to be quiet although I think Mrs Forbes is already asleep.'

She wished she could have as much faith in her husband as Britta obviously did. Why all the secrecy?

'So you see, the entire company belongs to you and me, apart from a ten percent share which your father gave Fergusson when he became a junior partner in the business. We can do whatever we like with it. It's all ours.'

They were in a sleigh once again, although this time they were sitting with a good foot of space between them. Several times Jess thought longingly of their last journey together when he had kept her so warm. She banished such wistful thinking and concentrated on his momentous news.

'I *knew* he was hiding something.' She slammed her hand down onto the seat beside her, white-hot fury slicing through her. 'And I was sure my father would never have left the company to my mother. But Robert made it sound so plausible when he told me about it, I began to doubt myself.' Jess was reeling from Killian's revelations. On the one hand she was thrilled, while on the other she wanted to tear Robert limb from limb for what he had done to her.

'Well, your instinct was right. Albert – Mr Holm said I could call him that now – anyway, he's been to see Mr Milner. Between them they're going to sort out the legal side so there is no doubt who is the owner of the Van Sandt & Fergusson company. Fergusson had a hold on the man, but now we've found out what it is, Mr Milner has realised others might do so as well. He simply has to face up to it.'

'I'm glad. Poor man, I wouldn't like to be blackmailed by Robert, that's for sure.'

'No. What we have to do now, though, is work out what to do. Albert thinks we should take things slowly and not let Fergusson know we've found him out yet. Not until all the legal documents are ready. But because I'm off to China soon, he said we could perhaps gather together as much of the company's capital as possible and invest it all in the venture. He doesn't think we should sell any properties though. That way, if the venture should fail, there will still be something to fall back upon. What do you think?'

Jess was very pleased to be asked. Killian was still obviously angry with her and had so far not referred to the state of their marriage even once. Nevertheless, he treated her as an equal when discussing everything that had happened with regard to the business. It was wonderful to be spoken to as if her opinion mattered, and she considered her reply carefully before answering.

'Yes, I think that's a good idea. How much money does he think there is?'

'He wasn't sure, but he thought perhaps five thousand *daler*, since there were some payments coming in soon. If the legal papers aren't ready by the time I leave, and Fergusson finds the money gone, Albert said we could pretend it had been stolen by you. That's why I wanted you to write a note to Mrs Forbes to say you'd gone to make a new life for yourself somewhere. It should make him look for you in Småland instead of closer to home and by the time he realises what's happened, it'll be too late.'

'But surely someone will see me?'

'No, you'll have to stay at my lodgings until everything is ready and you and Albert can confront Fergusson together with Milner if I'm gone. There's no saying what he'd do if he found you in the meantime. I'm sorry, but you'll have to go into hiding for a while.'

'I suppose that makes sense. When do you leave? Have they set a date?' The thought of Killian leaving soon made Jess' heart sink.

'I'm to be on board the ship in a week's time. Mr Campbell is hoping to leave no later than the twentieth of February.'

'But what if there's ice?'

Killian shrugged. 'I'm told it's possible to saw through it until the ship is in open water, but it may not come to that. The weather has been milder lately.' He turned to look at her. 'Do you agree with what Albert has suggested then?

It might be taking caution to extremes, but there are other reasons as well for keeping a low profile.'

'What do you mean?'

'Well, a young servant of mine, Adair, arrived from Edinburgh recently. He came to tell me my cousin had sent a thug by the name of Allan to Gothenburg, presumably to do me harm. He might have left by now, because Albert told him I'd already sailed for China, but if he decides to investigate a bit more thoroughly, he'll find out I haven't gone yet.'

Killian had already told Jess of the enmity between himself and his cousin, so she wasn't too surprised to hear Farquhar had sent a henchman. 'But what has that to do with me?' she asked, puzzled.

'If Allan finds out I have a wife, he could decide to hurt you in some way too. Who knows? Farquhar won't be very happy to hear that piece of news, I can tell you. He won't know it's a business arrangement only. Any child of mine would be another spoke in his wheel.'

'As a matter of fact, I've been meaning to speak to you about that.' Jess drew in a deep breath and tried to gather the courage to explain that she now thought she'd been wrong to insist they follow the contract to the letter, but Killian held up his hand to stop her.

'Don't worry, you made your views quite clear and I won't be troubling you in Gothenburg, if that's what you're afraid of.' He sounded curt again and Jess bit her lip.

'No, that wasn't ...'

'There are two rooms in my lodgings and I've arranged for myself and Adair to sleep in one of them, while you're in the other. So you see, there's no need for further discussion. Now about the investments ...'

He continued to talk only of business matters, and although Jess was still pleased he took her views seriously, she would have preferred to discuss their marriage instead. It seemed, however, that he now regretted their wedding night as much as she'd thought she had and there was no turning back.

She swallowed down a lump of misery which had risen in her throat and tried to concentrate on money matters. Perhaps she would find a more opportune moment to try and mend the fences between them. For now, it was a lost cause.

'My dear girl, it's wonderful to see you again.'

Albert gave Jess a bear hug, which was very unusual for him and she had to blink back a few tears of emotion. She didn't know what was the matter with her, she wasn't normally such a watering pot.

'It's lovely to be here, although Killian tells me I have to hide for a while.'

'We think that might be best, yes. It wouldn't do to underestimate your stepfather and if he got wind of our plans, there's no saying what he'd do to stop us. He would try to destroy the evidence for sure, and could even hurt Mr Milner or us. Who knows? His entire life is about to crumble.'

'I have to say it serves him right, although I'm worried what it will do to my mother. I know she's already in a bad way. I wish I could go to her this instant.'

Holm nodded, his expression sad. 'Yes, poor woman. But I remember she was the same when your other siblings died young and she recovered from that, so perhaps in time she'll get over this too. So very tragic.'

Jess nodded, not trusting herself to speak.

'But there's cause for celebration too, right? I've forgotten to congratulate you on your marriage. I hope you'll be very happy together. I think you've chosen a good man, my dear.' Holm smiled at Killian, who looked embarrassed by this praise.

'You ... you do?' Jess was slightly stunned by Albert's words. She hadn't realised he liked Killian that much.

'Oh, yes. If only he returns from his journey safe and sound, he'll be a great asset to the company and I'm sure the two of you together will make it prosper. It will be a pleasure to work with you. That is, if you'll still want me?'

'But of course we do.' Killian, who had until that moment stayed silent, agreed with Jess about this and they said the words at the same time, which made Albert laugh.

'You see? You even think alike. Excellent.'

Jess thought it was a shame they couldn't think alike in other ways too, but she supposed business would have to do for now. She should be pleased she had been vindicated with regard to Robert and soon she would be free of him altogether. She *was* pleased. Wasn't she?

'Right, now tell me exactly what we're doing,' she said, trying to sound businesslike. 'Are there any papers for me to sign?'

'There are indeed. I've brought them, so let's begin.'

Chapter Twenty-Four

Edinburgh, Scotland

'China? Are you serious?' Farquhar stared at Allan, unable to believe what he was hearing.

'Yes, Mr Kinross. The man your cousin works for told me himself. He'll be gone for at least a year and a half, so I didn't think there was any point in hanging around waiting for him. I can always go back later.'

Reluctantly Allan handed over the pouch of money Farquhar had given him, but Farquhar pushed it back across the table with an irritated sniff. 'No, no, keep it. I'm sure you've earned at least that much. But China? What on earth does he want to go there for?'

'Good profits to be made in the China trade, so I heard. I spent some time listening to the Scotsmen at the inn in Gothenburg. Those who could afford to had invested in the venture. They said they expected a return no less than tenfold on their money.'

'As much as that? Dear Lord, he must be stopped.' Farquhar was lost in thought for a moment. 'Well, seems there's nothing for it. I'll have to go to China myself. I couldn't ask you to go that far on my behalf.'

Allan squirmed and looked as if he was considering it, but then shook his head. 'No, sorry, but I've never been tempted by foreign parts. Don't think I'd survive another sea journey neither. Never been so ill in my life.'

Farquhar nodded. 'Very well, so be it. Thank you for the information anyway. I trust you'll keep this to yourself as usual? That's if you want to do business with me again in the future?'

'Nat'rally. You have my word.'

For what that's worth, Farquhar thought. Well, if Allan proved difficult, he'd have to be eliminated too. Lord, but things were becoming very complicated. *Damn Killian to hell!*

Killian had been dreading spending time with Jessamijn in such close quarters as his lodgings. He found it impossible to be in the same room without wanting her, but to his relief Mr Campbell claimed most of his time and he was spared this torture. He was needed to help with the preparations for their journey and consequently he barely saw Jess at all.

'You have to help me make sure everything I've ordered is brought on board,' Campbell told him. 'I don't want even a single item to be missing, or we could be in trouble. I've prepared very carefully for this venture and should anything go amiss, it will be my responsibility.'

'Don't worry, Mr Campbell, I'll make sure all is in order.'

Killian went on board the ship and oversaw the loading of both the cargo and all the provisions. A ballast of iron ore was brought out first and put on the lowest deck. This was covered with planking, then the rest of the cargo was placed on top – tar, copper, wooden items, iron products, followed by innumerable casks of fresh water and the food. It seemed to Killian that an inordinate amount of victuals were needed. Nearly two hundred sacks of ship's biscuits were loaded, together with barrels of salted pork, stockfish, dried peas and barley-grain, not to mention butter and cheese. Naturally they couldn't sail without the ubiquitous salted herring as well, and sacks of porridge oats by the dozen were necessary for their breakfasts.

Water wasn't the only beverage; small beer, *snaps* for the crew members and wine for the captain's table and the supercargos were stowed away. When all this was done, it was time to load the live animals which would be slaughtered along the way. The poor creatures – sheep, pigs, geese, chickens and even a milking cow – were put in pens, swine on the lower deck, the rest on the middle deck and none of them looked too happy about it, complaining loudly of their lot. The ship's carpenters were kept busy fencing them in so that they would be safe in case of high seas. Killian wondered inconsequentially whether animals suffered from seasickness too.

Just when he thought the ship couldn't hold any more, further supplies arrived. 'What's all this?' he asked Campbell, who was working alongside him, checking and re-checking everything.

'Extra wood, tar and building materials, in case anything will need to be mended, and ammunition for the cannon and other weapons. Candles for the lanterns, wood for cooking with, animal feed ... the list is endless.' Campbell sighed. 'But we'll soon be done and then we'll be off. I just hope I haven't forgotten anything.'

Amen to that, Killian thought.

A cold draught and the momentary dancing of the flames in the fire alerted Jess to the fact that the door had opened silently behind her. She turned to see Killian standing just inside the room, his expression inscrutable, his eyes narrowed. A sudden longing to be held by him shot through her and she had to swallow a gasp.

'I'm leaving in the morning so I've come to say goodbye. I'll be spending the night at the inn with the supercargos,' he said. 'I shall do my very best to bring home as large a profit as possible for our company, then upon my return you can have your share and do whatever you want with it.'

Jess felt a huge weight of grief settle in her stomach, as if he were already dead. He was certainly lost to her, she could see that now. A week had passed and he'd kept her at arms' length the entire time, not giving her the chance to so much as mention the word marriage. She had obviously driven him away with her stupid behaviour and there was no going back. She nodded, trying to accept her fate with good grace, but the pain of it gnawed at her insides, making her wrap her arms around herself to contain it. 'God go with you,' she said quietly. 'I ... I hope you return safely.'

'Do you? Perhaps it would suit you better if I didn't.' He removed a package of documents from an inside pocket and threw it down onto the nearest table. 'This contains my last will and testament, leaving you everything I own apart from the *Lady Madeleine*. Captain Craig knows what to do with that. I've also included a letter for my grandfather, telling him about you. If I don't come back, I'd like you to visit him and tell him I wasn't quite the wastrel he thought I was. Who knows, he might believe you.'

'I ... yes, of course, if that is what you want. I sincerely hope it won't come to that though. And I would be ... saddened if you didn't return.'

'Well, that's comforting to know.' She wasn't sure if his words were sarcastic or bitter, but she didn't like it either way. 'God keep you too,' he added. 'Pray for us all.'

And with that he was gone, leaving Jess feeling completely numb.

She had lost him.

'Jessamijn? Jess, are you there?'

A knock on the door woke Jess from a deep sleep and she stumbled to her feet and went to open it, forgetting to ask who it was. Luckily it was only Albert standing outside, shaking snow from his hair and looking a bit embarrassed.

'Albert, I didn't expect to see you here so late.'

Three days had passed since Killian left to board the

ship, but she had barely noticed since time seemed to have no meaning for her at the moment. She frowned at him. 'Is there some news?' She caught up her hair, which had tumbled down while she slept, and twisted it into a loose knot at the nape of her neck, then tried to smooth her gown.

'No, it was you I wanted to see.' Albert shuffled from one foot to another, as if unsure what to do.

'Well, come in.' She motioned for him to enter. 'It's a bit of a mess, but I haven't had time to tidy up today.'

Albert took a deep breath and walked over to the window, where he stood with his back towards her, staring into the darkness. The fresh smell of snow followed him and Jess realised she missed being outdoors. Surely it couldn't be long now before everything was ready and they could confront Robert. Standing by the tile stove, she waited for Albert to speak. She knew he liked to think before he said anything, so she didn't prompt him.

'I don't know if you're aware of it, but the wives of the supercargos and higher ranking members of the crew are allowed to go on board the ship to say goodbye,' Albert said at last, turning to give her a searching look. 'I noticed you and your husband seem to be at loggerheads, but this is a dangerous journey he's going on. You might want to think about settling your differences before he goes. Just in case ...'

He let the last sentence hang, although Jess had already caught his meaning loud and clear. Killian might not be coming back and this could be her last chance to make peace between them. She sighed.

'I know that, but I don't think he'd be too happy to see me,' she replied quietly. 'The, er, misunderstanding between us is such that ... well, it's complicated. Besides, I thought the ship had left already?'

'No, not yet. The winds have been contrary. The thing is,

if something should happen to him, you might regret it for the rest of your life if you don't speak to him now,' Albert insisted. 'I know. It happened to me.'

Jess' eyes flew to his. 'It did? When?'

'My brother.' Albert's jaw was clenched tightly, the words coming out in short bursts. 'Went to sea. Never came back. We'd had a disagreement before he left. I wish ...' He stared at the floor. 'It was all so unnecessary.'

'I see.' Jess didn't know what to say, but she realised he was right. She had to try and apologise to Killian before it was too late. 'Very well, I'll go. How do I get there?'

'At midday, be down by the bridge at Stora Hamnen. There'll be a carriage to take all the ladies to Fiskebeck, out by Rive Fjord. A boat will be waiting to ferry you out to the ship from there. Just say you're Mrs Kinross, they won't ask anything else. Oh, and dress warmly, it can take over an hour or so if the wind is up.'

He turned to go, but she put a hand on his arm to stop him. 'Thank you, Albert. You're a true friend and I really hope we can sort all this out soon. You won't regret helping us, I promise.'

He smiled, although sadness still lurked in his eyes. 'I'll never regret it for a moment in any case,' he said, putting a hand on top of hers and giving it a squeeze. 'Aaron was a good man, I owe it to him to look after you and I'm only sorry I didn't suspect anything before.'

'It wasn't your fault, you were duped just like everyone else.'

'Perhaps, but I shouldn't have made it so easy for the whoreson to take over. I should have asked more questions. Never mind, he'll get his just desserts now, I'll make sure of that.'

'Thank you.'

The carriage ride to Fiskebeck seemed to take forever and Jess' head ached from listening to the chatter of the other wives. They seemed to have a never-ending supply of meaningless gossip with which to while away the time, but it was all so inane. She tried to concentrate on the scenery, but there wasn't much to look at apart from the odd house or copse of trees. Snow flurries made it difficult to see much anyway, so Jess soon gave up trying.

By the time she squeezed into the boat between two rather large ladies, she wanted to scream at them to be quiet. Thankfully the motion of the waves silenced them before she disgraced herself by being rude. The waters were rather choppy, and although this didn't bother Jess at all, she huddled inside her wolf-coat for warmth. Albert had been right, it was freezing out on the sea, but the lovely fur kept her snug.

She stared straight ahead, lost in thought. She hardly noticed the bits of ice floating past or the biting wind that soon had the other ladies complaining non-stop. What was she going to say to Killian? How on earth should she phrase her apology? And what would his reply be? Would he even accept her olive branch?

Perhaps the best she could hope for was that they parted as friends at least. She knew they had never been lovers in the emotional sense of the word, but a part of her couldn't help but yearn for something other than friendship. He was her husband, bound to her until 'death did them part', and she couldn't bear the thought that this might come to pass sooner rather than later.

Despite the help of a small sail, it took them the best part of two hours to reach the ship and by then it was already getting dark. Jess wondered how the rowers would find their way back, but assumed there would be lights on shore to guide them. As they came closer to the ship, the *Friedericus*

Rex Sueciae, Jess marvelled at the sheer size of it. It towered over them, its three tall masts reaching towards the sky, although from where she was sitting, Jess couldn't see the top of them. The figurehead, a rampant lion, bared its fangs at them menacingly and a strong smell of tar wafted into her nostrils, almost making her recoil.

They bobbed up and down next to the hull while each woman in turn was helped to climb up on deck. Jess was the last one, deliberately skulking behind the others in order to delay her confrontation with Killian for as long as possible. She heard the captain asking the wives who they'd come to see. Each woman said her name and was assigned a member of the crew to take them to their husband. While she waited, she looked around at the forest of ropes, some as thick as her calves, that hung everywhere or lay coiled into tidy heaps next to the railing. Up here, the ship didn't seem quite as large any more. The conditions were cramped with crew members swarming all over the place.

'Mrs Kinross,' she mumbled when it was her turn.

The captain nodded and told the young sailor waiting to escort her, 'Downstairs, second cabin on the right.'

'Yes, sir. This way, Ma'am.'

She followed him down a short flight of stairs to the deck below and over to a cabin on the right hand side of the ship. The man knocked, but there was no answer, so he opened the door to look inside.

'He might be up in the main cabin, Ma'am. If you'd just step inside and wait here, I'll see if I can find him for you.'

'Thank you, that's very kind.'

Jess closed the door and leaned her back against it. She shut her eyes for a moment, trying to gather her strength. What could she say to Killian? *I've come to apologise for lying to you. I did enjoy your lovemaking, very much so, but I was afraid you would have too much of a hold over me if*

I let you do it again. It sounded silly, even to her, but it was how she felt and somehow she had to make him understand they needed a compromise.

The cabin was tiny, with a narrow bunk on either side and only one small porthole. She walked the few steps over to it to look out, but couldn't see anything except water and darkness. There was nothing of interest inside the cabin either, so she sat down on one of the bunks to wait, trying to calm her nerves as best she could.

It seemed to be taking the sailor an extremely long time to find Killian and she started to wonder if her husband was avoiding her on purpose. Well, too bad, she wasn't leaving until she'd seen him. She became bored and smothered several yawns. The long night before, when she'd tossed and turned, unable to sleep after Albert's visit, was catching up with her. Resigned to a long wait, she decided to lie down for a moment and close her eyes. Perhaps that would make time pass more quickly.

Both bunks had a pile of blankets, folded neatly and stacked at the foot end. She shook out the ones on the left bunk and lay down. It was cold in the cabin and she shivered despite her fur coat, so she pulled the blankets over herself until only the tip of her nose was sticking out. Warm and snug at last, she drifted off.

Killian didn't have a chance to return to his cabin until late in the evening. At first, he was busy overseeing the stowing of more goods below decks, where he helped Colin Campbell to personally check everything one last time. Then the captain asked all the supercargos and their assistants to dine with him in the main cabin. There was no time to go back and change, even if he'd wanted to, which he didn't. It was so damned cold, he refused to remove any clothing unless he absolutely had to. In fact, he wore the bearskin coat all the time except when in the main cabin, which was heated by braziers.

'We'll be off with the tide at first light,' Mr Campbell informed them and raised his glass. 'To a successful voyage, gentlemen.' His blue eyes were sparkling with excitement and Killian felt some of it rub off on him. They were going on an adventure.

'To a successful voyage,' they all chorused.

They dined well on fillet of beef and several other delicious dishes prepared by the cabin cook who only catered for the higher ranking members of the crew. The excellent food was washed down with a very tolerable red wine, and everyone's spirits were high. Killian suppressed all thoughts of Jessamijn and the battle with Robert she would have to face on her own. It was no longer his problem, he had helped all he could. His main task was to stay alive and to bring back as much profit as possible, so their marriage hadn't been entered into in vain.

Then, and only then, would he be able to turn his thoughts to taming his wife. And tame her he would, he was determined about that. He wanted to stay in Sweden to build up the merchant business and he would prefer to do so with Jessamijn at his side. He was sure she would be a great asset. Now that he was married, he would honour the oaths he'd taken and 'cleave himself only unto her', like the Bible said. In order to achieve this, however, he had to make their marriage work somehow.

It surprised him how strongly he felt about this. No woman in particular had ever mattered to him before, they simply came and went when he needed one. Being married to Jess felt different though and he hadn't made the vows lightly. No matter what, he was going to stay faithful to her. After all, he thought, he wasn't like Farquhar who apparently treated his wife like dirt.

Feeling bone weary, Killian made his way to what was to be his home for the next year and a half at least. He had a lantern with a single candle, which he put down on the sea chest containing his belongings that had been placed on the floor between the two bunks.

'Make sure you blow it out as soon as you reach the cabin to minimize the risk of fire,' Campbell had told him, so he did. In the dark, he sat down on the right-hand bunk and pulled off his boots. Then he lay down, covering himself with first his bearskin coat, then the blankets. It was narrow, hard and uncomfortable. He thought it was a shame there wasn't just one large bunk instead of these two smaller ones, but he supposed that sometimes the cabins had to be shared. No doubt he would become used to it.

On that thought, he was asleep in seconds.

Chapter Twenty-Five

When he woke at last, Killian could see daylight outside through the coating of frost on the porthole. It was freezing cold inside the cabin too, and he was reluctant to leave the warmth of his cocoon, but he had a feeling he was late. Mr Campbell would be expecting him. The motion of the ship had definitely increased, and he guessed they had begun their journey at last. They were lucky the sea hadn't been frozen, he thought, which was all too common this time of year.

He shivered and turned around, only to come face to face with his wife.

Jess was lying on the opposite bunk, blinking sleep from her eyes and peering out from under a mountain of blankets. They caught sight of each other and both shot bolt upright, blue eyes colliding with silver grey.

'Oh, no! Is ... it's not morning already?' Jess stammered, staring at the brightness outside.

'What the devil are you doing here?' Killian asked, gripping the edge of the bunk in an effort to keep his temper under control. He didn't bother to answer her question because any fool could see it was morning. He checked his pocket watch just to be sure and realised that it was, in fact, closer to midday. He wondered why no one had called him, but perhaps they had and he hadn't heard them since he slept deeply.

'I came with the other wives to say farewell. And I also wanted to ...'

'We already said our goodbyes,' Killian snapped. 'You couldn't wait for me to leave, as I recall.'

'That's not true.' Jess looked stung by his remark and

frowned. 'You were the one who couldn't leave fast enough.'

'Well, I didn't exactly feel welcome. It was a relief to go on board the ship.' He stood up, pulling the bearskin coat around him with angry, jerky movements and then bent to put on his boots without looking at her.

'No, Killian, I ... it's not like that.'

He glared at her. 'What is it like then? You're sorry you married me and you resent having to give me half your money? Well, don't worry. I told you, I'm going to make us both very rich and when this journey is over, I'll pay you back every last coin. Then you can go and live by yourself or with whoever you prefer. That blond oaf perhaps, whose wife might have died in childbirth by then if you're lucky. And maybe I'll return to Scotland so you don't have to see me again. How does that sound?'

He didn't know why he was saying such hurtful things to her, but he was so angry he didn't particularly care. He only wanted to make her feel as bad as he did himself.

Jess scowled at him. 'I should have known you'd be unreasonable. You always twist my words to suit your own meaning. Well, fine, have it your way. I'm sure it's what you prefer yourself anyway.' She turned away and lay down again with a thump. Her voice slightly muffled by the blankets, she added, 'Come back and tell me when there's a boat to take me back to town.'

Killian stared at her for a while longer, then drew in a sharp breath as her words pierced the fog of rage swirling around inside him. 'Hell and damnation!' he swore, then tore out of the cabin at high speed, slamming the door shut behind him. He climbed the steps up to the main deck in seconds, then raced over to the railing. He turned his head this way and that, scanning their surroundings.

Water, just water all around them. Nothing else. Not even a faint smudge of land on the horizon.

He cursed again and grabbed a passing sailor by the arm. 'Are we anywhere near land?' he asked, his frantic expression making the man stare at him.

'Land? No, sir. We left before first light, on account of the wind being fair and the currents good. We're prob'ly halfway to the Shetlands by now.'

Killian groaned. 'Oh, no ...'

The sailor gave him a concerned look. 'You all right, sir? If ye're feelin' queasy, best thing is to go and stand at the front o' the ship, like. Just stare at the horizon.'

'No, I don't feel queasy, I'm fine. It's just ... oh, never mind. Where's the captain?'

'In his cabin, I s'pose.'

'Yes, of course. Thank you.'

Killian approached the captain's cabin with some trepidation. Although normally unfazed by most things, he really disliked unpleasant scenes. As he'd already noticed, the Swedish Captain Trolle was a bit of a loose cannon. There was no telling how he would react to the news that there was a female on board his ship. One who would have to be returned to Gothenburg, thereby delaying the journey by at least a day.

He knocked on the cabin door, but there was no reply. Instead he heard raised voices and recognised the guttural tones of the captain mixed with the loud and unmistakeable Scottish burr of the first supercargo, Colin Campbell. Although Killian couldn't make out any individual words, there was no doubt the discussion was somewhat heated. He hesitated, wondering whether to return later, but then decided the matter simply couldn't wait. He knocked again, louder this time. There was still no answer, so he opened the door and stepped inside, clearing his throat loudly.

'Excuse me,' he said, 'could I have I word with you both please?' He shut the door behind him to make sure the conversation was private.

The two men, who both wore scowls of frustration and annoyance, stopped in mid-sentence and glared at Killian. 'Yes, what is it?' the captain barked.

'Erm, there is a slight problem.'

'What's the matter with you, man?' Campbell put in impatiently. He seemed to be in a foul mood, his agitation demonstrated by the fact that his curled wig was askew. 'Can't you see we're in the middle of a discussion here?'

'Yes and I'm very sorry to intrude, but it's my wife, sir. She's in my cabin.'

'She's what?' The two men stared at him, their expressions almost identical – horror mixed with disbelief, turning quickly to anger. 'What do you mean? You know very well women aren't allowed.'

Killian held up his hand. 'Yes, I do know, and believe me, I didn't ask her to come. In fact, we parted on fairly bad terms and I didn't expect her to come on board with the other ladies to say goodbye.' He shrugged. 'Apparently she changed her mind and she arrived yesterday. Since I spent the afternoon with you, I never saw her and this morning I found her in my cabin, asleep. Someone had put her in there and forgotten to tell me.'

'Devil take it, Kinross, didn't you notice her last night when you went to bed?' the captain spluttered.

'No, I put the light out as soon as I got there, like you told me to. Then I went straight to sleep. She must have been there already and didn't hear me come in.'

'Lord help us.' Campbell and the captain looked at each other.

'What do we do now?' Trolle asked.

'Nothing we can do,' Campbell replied. 'She'll have to stay. Perhaps we can find a ship in Cadiz to take her back?'

'All alone? Surely not. No, we'll have to turn back.'

For some reason, the captain was now looking smug, and Killian wondered why until Campbell turned on the man and almost shouted.

'We are *not* turning back and that's an end to it! As I've told you repeatedly this morning, the wind may not be ideal, but it's an off-shore one and it's propelling us forward. That's good enough for me. I'm the Swedish East India Company's representative on board and therefore my decision is final. I say we've waited too long already.'

'But we can't sail with a female on board, it's impossible.' The captain looked mulish now.

'The stupid woman can stay in her husband's cabin and not set foot outside it. No one will know.'

'For seven or eight months? Preposterous!'

'Oh, I'm sure she can be exercised from time to time.'

'Exercised?' Killian was outraged to hear Jess spoken of as if she were an animal in need of exercise when out of its cage, but the other two men ignored him.

'And what of the other supercargo who was to share the cabin with Kinross after Cadiz?' Trolle asked.

'He can sleep somewhere else.' Campbell said, the bulbous tip of his nose even redder than usual. 'Now stop thinking up excuses and get on with sailing this ship to China. I've had enough procrastinating to last me a lifetime!'

'If that's your final word, then so be it, but I'm warning you, we'll not get far without the right wind.' The captain stalked to the door and slammed out of the room, while Campbell sent a look of loathing after him.

'Pig-headed mule of a man,' he muttered, then sighed and dry-washed his face, looking very tired. 'Kinross, the woman is your responsibility. See to it she's not a nuisance.'

Killian decided not to argue for the moment. There didn't seem to be any point. 'Very well, I'll make sure of it,' he said.

'You do that.' Campbell sighed again and shook his head, calmer now he had prevailed over the captain. 'Females, eh? Never know what they're going to do next.' As Killian reached the door, he added, 'You'd best find her some food, or she'll be screeching the place down because she's hungry next.'

Killian nodded. 'Very well.'

'Oh, and you know what? Why don't you dress her up as a boy and tell everyone she's your brother, stowed away because he wanted to come with you? Might work.'

Killian doubted that very much, but couldn't think of a better idea so he bowed to Campbell and said, 'I can try.'

He cursed all the way back to his cabin.

'What do you mean, there's no turning back?'

Jess stared at her furious husband, her stomach twisted into knots of anxiety. She wished herself a hundred miles away at the very least. Why, oh why, had she listened to Albert? She should have known it wouldn't be any use. Killian hadn't wanted to hear what she had to say in any case.

'Exactly that, you can't go back to Gothenburg. You'll have to come with us, at least as far as Cadiz. The ship set sail during the early hours of this morning and Mr Campbell is refusing to go back just for your sake.'

Jess could see he was keeping his temper in check with enormous effort. He was holding onto the door latch so hard his knuckles were white. No doubt he was sorely tempted to beat her, even though he'd sworn he would never do that. Hearing his news, she had to agree he would have been well within his rights. She had acted very foolishly.

'Dear Lord, I never thought ... but then, the sailor said he was going to find you straight away. I had no idea he was going to take so long. Why didn't you come and speak to me?'

'Because no one told me you were here. The dolt was probably distracted by some other duties and forgot all about it.' Killian sat down on the bunk opposite and sighed. 'It never occurred to me you would come or I would have been waiting for you.' He shook his head. 'What a mess, but we'll just have to make the best of it.'

'How long will it take to reach Cadiz? And how can I return to Sweden from there?'

'It'll take a month perhaps, or so I'm told, but I have no idea how we're to send you back. For now, however, Mr Campbell has suggested you dress as a boy and pretend to be my brother.'

'What? You can't be serious. Why, that's, that's ... scandalous!'

'Not if no one knows you're a woman. After all, it's no use antagonising the other crew members unnecessarily.'

'What do you mean? Why should it matter to them?'

Killian raised an eyebrow at her. 'Surely you're not as innocent as all that? Why, they'll think I brought you with me on purpose because I can't be without a woman for the duration of the journey. They'll be imagining me swiving you at every opportunity while they have no one. They don't know the truth, do they.'

Jess felt herself blush to the roots of her hair. Of course he was right, but she honestly hadn't thought of that. 'There's no need to be crude,' she snapped. 'Besides, no one will believe I'm a boy, will they?'

'Maybe not, but it's worth a try. I'll get some clothes off Adair, he's about your size. And you can wear one of my waistcoats. It will fit you loosely and disguise your shape. We'll have to cut your hair and tie it into a queue – a pity, but it will grow again.'

Jess remembered that he had admired her long, straight

flaxen hair on more than one occasion and had stroked it in the aftermath of their lovemaking. She turned away to hide another blush as the memories of that night returned to haunt her.

'This is ridiculous. There must be some other way.'

'I'm sorry, but you have no choice in the matter. We have to do as Mr Campbell says. His word is law on this ship.' He sighed again. 'I think it's probably best if you stay in this cabin as much as possible. I'll tell everyone I'm making you help me with my paperwork as a punishment for stowing away. Then I'll take you up on deck after dark so you can have some fresh air and exercise. Agreed?'

Jess nodded, miserably aware that she should be grateful he was trying to arrange things to suit her, despite the fact that it was all her fault. 'Thank you,' she whispered, but he was already on his way out the door and didn't hear her. Either that or he chose not to acknowledge her thanks.

Jess just wanted to lie down and die.

To Jess' immense surprise, and perhaps Killian's as well, no one questioned her presence on board, at least not openly. Whenever anyone asked, she was introduced as his younger brother, a naughty stowaway caught too late to be returned to dry land. Since it was always dark the few times she left the cabin, she was able to pass for a boy fairly easily. She spoke only when asked a direct question and luckily her voice wasn't too high-pitched.

'I suppose we should be grateful you're so tiny,' Killian commented after their first outing on deck. 'Unless they see you without your clothes on, there's no difference in build between you and Adair. And his idea to smudge your face with a bit of dirt helps too.' Jess had been against this at first, but had to admit it worked.

Adair's clothing fitted her reasonably well and as Killian

had predicted, wearing his much larger waistcoat hid her feminine shape. At first, it felt odd to be wearing male clothes. The way the breeches clung to her backside and legs was definitely indecent, but she became used to it and soon began to enjoy the freedom of movement without skirts. Most of the time she also wore her wolf-fur coat, since there was no heating in the cabin or anywhere else. She wouldn't be able to discard it until they went further south.

Killian set Jess to work copying logs, journals and ledgers, a job he was supposed to have done himself. His casual compliment, 'I know you're as capable of doing it as I am,' made her feel better, but most of the time she felt very down and spent her free time just staring into space.

She also suffered from seasickness most mornings, although her stomach seemed to settle down in the afternoons. Adair brought her food, since Killian spent his time with Campbell and the other supercargos or with the first mate learning about sailing. Killian had also volunteered to take his turn at keeping watch each night. As the first supercargo's assistant he could have been excused from this duty, so Jess was sure he only did it in order to spend less time in the cabin with her.

'Please don't tell Killian about me being sick all the time,' she begged Adair. 'He's already so cross with me, I'm sure he'd be disgusted to find I'm such a poor sailor as well.'

Adair stared at her for a moment, as if he was on the point of making a comment, but then just nodded. In the short time she'd known him, Jess had grown to like him a lot. She appreciated that he acted as a buffer between herself and Killian. As long as Adair was present, they managed not to argue openly, and his cheeky ways gave them something to talk about other than their predicament. Most of the time, however, Killian stayed away from the cabin altogether, so that no conversation was necessary at all. This should have pleased Jess, since she told herself she'd rather not see him, but at the same time it made her angry that he avoided her.

One way or another, it was going to be an interminable journey.

Chapter Twenty-Six

The beginning was certainly not auspicious. Unfavourable winds forced them to anchor somewhere off the coast of Norway for several days. The captain and Campbell were heard to argue non-stop about whether they should attempt to continue or not. Indeed, the battle between these two strong personalities proved the only diversion, apart from reading.

'I don't know if these are of any interest to you, but I'm afraid that's all there is,' Killian said one morning, dumping several tomes on ancient Roman history onto Jess' bunk. 'Unless you'd like to read about astronomy?'

'No, thank you, the Romans will do just fine.' She was grateful he'd thought about her at all, although perhaps he was only trying to stop her from complaining about being bored.

The food was as monotonous as the weather. Although Jess was only hungry when she wasn't feeling seasick, she found the fare unappetising and was soon fed up with watery porridge for breakfast every day. Adair agreed.

'It's a shame we cannae eat wi' Mr Kinross,' he commented. 'He and they other high heid yins get different food from the rest o' us. They've even brought their ane cook an' there's a steward tae serve 'em.'

'Yes, but I'm sure their food will spoil just the same as everyone else's once we've been at sea for months,' Jess said.

It was well-known that even the water went bad during long journeys, and had to be sieved in order to sift out the worms and other insects. Jess hoped this wouldn't happen until after she had left the ship at Cadiz. The mere thought of it was enough to make her stomach heave. As for the food, she ate most things and didn't really care whether Killian had better food or not.

They passed through the English Channel, although Jess didn't see much of it since it was night at the time, and then continued south towards the Channel Islands. Up to that point they hadn't met any other ships, but once past Alderney, they sighted several that looked threatening.

'Could be Sallee pirates,' Campbell muttered. 'We'd best hoist English colours, since they usually don't fight with them.' This ruse appeared to work and fortunately nothing bad happened. They were left to continue their journey in peace.

Not that there was much peace on board.

Jess had never imagined a ship would be so noisy. Even at night, with the changing of the watch, there seemed to be a never-ending cacophony of sounds, all clearly audible from within the cabins. There were craftsmen of every kind – carpenters, sail-makers, a smith and a cooper among others – who laughed, joked or told stories while plying their trades. The many sailors kept up a steady stream of chatter as they worked, swearing frequently, shouting joking insults to each other or singing. Then there were all the live animals on board. They were clearly unhappy at being shut up in the hold and they let everyone know about it with their loud bleats, moos or squeals. On top of that chickens clucked, cocks crowed and geese honked.

Even the ship itself made a constant noise as it ploughed through the waves. Timbers creaked, sails snapped in the wind and the block and tackle clanked and groaned while the water splashed and sprayed up around them. And once a day the ship's bell rang out. This was the sailors' favourite sound as it meant it was time for their daily ration of *snaps*, a bonus Jess very happily declined. It all made her long for the quiet and solitude of the deep Småland forests.

Fine weather and fair winds brought them quickly down the coast of Portugal. After rounding Cape St Vincent, they reached Cadiz on the twenty-eighth of March. A pilot came to steer them past some cliffs and other hidden dangers into the large, deep harbour and they anchored in Cadiz Bay early in the morning. Soon after, Adair brought Jess her breakfast as usual, but almost dropped it when an almighty boom shook the ship to its core. This was followed by seven more.

'By all the saints, what a racket,' Jess exclaimed, putting her hands across her ears.

Adair grinned, his light brown eyes dancing with excitement. 'The eight gun salute tae greet the other ships moored here. Never thought it'd be quite tha' loud. Wish I could help wi' firing the cannon, but Mr Kinross won't let me go onywhere near them.'

Jess shook her head at him with a smile. He was still such a child in many ways even though in others he was wise beyond his years. 'Very sensible of him. You'd be a menace.' Another eight shots were fired off and Jess made a face and shouted, 'Wasn't eight enough?'

'They hae tae greet the city itself too, but I think tha's the end of it.'

Jess ate her breakfast while staring out the porthole. The view was lovely – beautiful houses surrounded by large city walls, all built of the same type of stone and bathed in brilliant sunlight. She wondered if she would be allowed to go ashore to explore a little before being sent home. There was a fort to the south with towers and fortifications and the countryside around it was covered with trees of a kind she had never seen before. Their dusky green leaves fluttered in the almost constant breeze.

A boat came into view and Jess felt her spirits plummet. Although she was happy to have reached harbour, she was worried about what was to happen to her now. Was this it? Had they come for her? And how was she to travel all the way back to Sweden on her own?

It didn't bear thinking of.

Killian watched the smaller vessel come up alongside the ship. Several men climbed up onto the main deck and Campbell went over to them. Killian followed, although he stayed in the background.

'You must be Mr Graham,' Campbell greeted the first man affably. 'I've had good reports of you, pleased to meet you.'

'How do you do? And this is Mr Pike.' Graham, who had a pleasant smiling face, introduced his companion, a rather thick-set man with a double chin who looked a bit discontented. Campbell greeted him too, but in a more reserved manner, and introduced them to Killian as the final two supercargos for their journey.

'You're very prompt, I must say,' Campbell commented.

'Yes, but I'm afraid we bring bad news,' Graham said. 'There's been an embargo placed on all merchant ships by order of the Court here. We've heard that even foreign ships are being forced into service on behalf of Spain on some sort of secret expedition into the Mediterranean. We thought it best to warn you immediately.'

'Forced into service? Goodness! Oh, no, we have to avoid that at all cost. That would be disastrous.' Campbell thought for a moment, then waved at the captain, who was standing over to one side. 'Captain Trolle, could you order the man-of-war's pennant to be hoist immediately, if you please?'

'Why?'

'Because we're going to pretend we're not here as merchants, that's why.'

'But we're a merchant ship.'

'Yes, I know that, but we must *look* as if we're not.'

It took Campbell a while before he made the captain understand what he meant, but Trolle finally went off to do his bidding. Campbell shook his head in exasperation, but didn't comment this time. He turned to the others. 'I think it's best if we don't let anyone come aboard, nor allow anyone to go ashore for now. Apart from ourselves, of course. Then hopefully no one will question our status. We won't unload the cargo until we know more about this situation. Has everything been arranged for our arrival, Mr Graham?'

'Yes, indeed. Mr Gough, our local contact, is at your disposal and we're all lodging with him during our stay here. He already has the necessary silver *piastres* which he'll give you in exchange for whatever goods you have brought from Sweden.'

Killian had learned from Campbell that the Chinese refused to trade with anything other than pure silver coins. The best way of obtaining these was to bring goods to sell here in Spain. With their rich South American colonies, the Spaniards had a seemingly endless supply of silver, unlike countries such as Sweden. They would be taking away dozens of chests filled with the shiny *piastres* or 'pieces of eight' when they left Cadiz.

'Excellent,' Campbell said. 'I'll just tell the captain no one is to leave the ship, then we can proceed into town.'

'So Killian has gone into the city then?'

Jess was still staring out the porthole, since there was nothing else to do at the moment. Adair was lounging on

Killian's bunk, taking advantage of his master's absence by being idle.

'Aye. He said he didnae ken how long they'd be, but we've tae stay here 'til he comes back.'

'I suppose he'll be trying to arrange passage for me.' The thought was depressing, and Jess realised a part of her wanted to continue this journey instead of returning to Sweden. Having come this far, it seemed a shame to have to turn back.

'He didnae say, but I reckon he will.' Adair sighed. 'A pity we cannae go ashore. I'd love tae feel land under ma feet again.'

'Yes, me too, but we'll have to be patient.'

'Fancy a game o' cairds? Nothin' much else tae do.'

'Very well, but I'm not playing for money. I leave that sort of thing to Killian.'

'Ye're jus' afraid I'm goin' tae beat yer,' Adair smirked. 'He's taught me a thing or twa, ye ken.'

'We'll just see about that. Now deal the cards.'

A week passed with no sign of Killian. There was a constant bustle, with boats coming and going, unloading the ship and bringing new provisions. There were more live animals to replace the ones that had been slaughtered already, fresh vegetables and fruit, barrels of water and sacks of grain. It seemed to be a never-ending stream and Jess wondered how it could all possibly fit in the hold.

As the days wore on, her nerves stretched to breaking point while she waited to hear what arrangements had been made for her. Killian stayed in the city with the other supercargos, presumably kept busy by Campbell, and there were no messages for her.

'How can it possibly take so long?' she complained to Adair. 'All he has to do is book my passage on a ship going north, surely?'

'But there might no' be ony goin' tae Sweden.'

'Well, then I could sail to England first, perhaps, or Holland, and find another ship there. I'm not completely helpless.' She knew this wasn't quite true though. She'd rather not have to fend for herself in a strange country.

Finally, at the end of the second week, Killian came into the cabin after knocking only briefly.

'At last. I thought you'd have been back long before now,' Jess burst out, the moment he stepped inside.

'I'm sorry, but I've had a lot to do.' He scowled at Adair, who hurried to gather up the playing cards and make himself scarce. When the door banged shut behind him, Killian sat down on his bunk and looked at Jess. He came straight to the point. 'I'm afraid you'll have to come with us. Mr Campbell and I haven't been able to find you passage back to Sweden. I'm sorry.'

'What? But surely there must be a way, if not directly, then via another port?'

'Well, yes, but there's no one to go with you unless we hire a local woman. Mr Gough could recommend someone, but how do we know she doesn't abandon you somewhere? It's one thing putting you on a Swedish ship which we know would take you straight home, or at least to somewhere in Sweden. But there aren't any of your countrymen here right now and we can't wait.'

'There's really no one who could take me?'

'No. You'd be at the mercy of a stranger, who might just take the money and return from the first port the ship reaches. You simply can't travel by yourself, it would be too dangerous. I talked it over with Mr Campbell and he agrees with me.'

Jess drew in a deep breath, trying to stay calm. 'But the alternative is just as dangerous, if not more so.'

'I know, but at least you won't be alone or with people you don't know.'

Jess digested this for a while, then bit her lip. 'I'm sorry. You must think I'm a great nuisance, but I swear I didn't mean to cause trouble.'

He shrugged, his expression bleak. 'I'm sure I'm equally to blame, but it doesn't matter.' He was silent for a moment, then added, 'Believe me, I would much prefer to send you back so that you'd be safe. You're right, this journey is going to be long and hard. There's no saying we'll even make it to China.' He dry-washed his face. 'I'd better just forget about going myself and take you back.'

Jess could see that he was genuinely concerned for her, but she knew how much he'd wanted to go on this journey. She tried to reassure him. 'No, I'm sure I'll be fine and if anything happens, it will happen to us all and that will be that.'

'But you're a woman.'

'So what? I'm every bit as healthy and strong as everyone else. Adair is as small as I am and if he can stand it, then why can't I?'

Killian nodded. 'I suppose when you put it like that, it makes sense.'

'I'm not a child. Let's not worry about what may be, it might never happen.'

'Very well, so be it. I'm glad you're taking this so calmly. I have to admit I had expected a major tantrum.'

'Then perhaps you don't know me as well as you thought you did.'

He threw her an enigmatic look. 'Maybe not. We'll have plenty of time to do something about that though, won't we? But for now, I have to go and help Mr Campbell oversee the loading of the silver.'

When he'd gone, Jess sank down onto her bunk and

closed her eyes. She was shaking, but with relief, not fear, and she felt strangely at peace. She was staying with Killian and even if they were at loggerheads, she knew in her heart this was where she wanted to be.

'I'm very sorry, sir, but all the ships bound for China have left for this year. There won't be another one until after next Christmas now. You just missed the last one, I'm afraid.'

Farquhar stared in disbelief at the East India Company clerk. The man had to be lying. 'Not a single one? Surely you're not serious?'

'The ships can only sail at certain times of the year, sir, otherwise the winds will be blowing in the wrong direction. No point going then, they'd only have to kick their heels somewhere for months on end.'

Farquhar ground his teeth and felt like punching the officious little man. Although outwardly polite, he looked as if he was pleased to be able to thwart Farquhar. 'Is there another way of reaching China?' he asked curtly. 'Via India perhaps?'

The man considered this, then shook his head. 'I don't think so and overland is not an option. Just a moment though ...' He scurried off to confer with a portly man sitting at a desk behind him and came back, nodding. 'Yes, it may be a possibility.'

'What?' Farquhar was fast losing what little patience he had and the man sent him a nervous glance.

'We heard a couple of ships were leaving from Ostend rather late. It may be they've not gone yet so you might be able to catch them.'

'Ostend? Fine. How do I get there then? I suppose you're now going to tell me there aren't any vessels bound for the continent either.'

'On the contrary, sir, as luck would have it, the *Porpoise* is just about ready to leave and her first port of call happens to be Ostend. If you'd care to make your way down to the docks, I'm sure the captain will be able to take you with him.'

'I'll go immediately.' Farquhar added a perfunctory, 'Thank you,' as an afterthought, although he didn't much feel like thanking the man.

As he headed towards the London Docks, he cursed silently to himself. If he didn't reach the Ostend ships on time, he might as well stay at home and wait for Killian to come back. Why did he always have such bad luck? Surely, it was his turn now for a helping hand from Fate.

'It had better be,' he muttered.

Chapter Twenty-Seven

Friedericus Rex Sueciae

They left Cadiz the following day and headed for the Barbary coast. There they hoped to pick up the northeast trade winds and the current that quickly drove ships southwest towards the Canary Islands. The weather was good and the sea relatively calm. Killian was therefore surprised to find Jess retching into a bucket when he returned to the cabin to fetch a ledger he'd forgotten.

'Jessamijn? Haven't you found your sea legs by now?' he asked, putting a hand on her shoulder. She looked up with a stricken expression, her face ashen. He felt very sorry for her, it must be miserable to suffer *mal de mer* for so long. Most people became used to the motion of the ship after less than a week.

'Apparently not. Perhaps the stay in Cadiz fooled my body into believing the journey was over and now I have to start all over again,' she said, attempting a light tone despite her obvious discomfort.

There was a knock on the door and Adair entered with a tray. 'I've fetched ye some bread an' cheese fer later. Shall I leave it here?'

'Yes, please.' Jess nodded and lay down on her bunk, no longer retching, but still very pale. 'Thank you.'

Killian glared at Adair. 'Don't be an oaf. I really don't think my wife wants to look at food right now. Can't you see she's ill?'

'Oh, no fer long. She'll be in fine fettle in an hour or twa,' Adair said cheerfully. 'An' then she'll be hungrysome, trust me.'

'How do you know she'll be better so quickly?' Killian looked from Adair to Jess and back again. Jess avoided his gaze by looking at the ceiling, then shivered and curled up on top of the blankets, almost as if she was afraid. What was going on here, he wondered. Did she have some illness she didn't want him to know about? Something catching? 'Tell me,' he barked, sudden fear making his tone sharper than he intended.

Adair stared at Killian as if he was a half-wit. 'Ye really dinnae ken?'

'Know what? You're not making sense, boy.' Killian was getting angry now at Adair's insensitivity and felt like clouting him around the ear.

'Lord gi' me patience,' Adair muttered. 'She's wi' child. Your wife's havin' a bairn.'

'What?' Killian sat down abruptly on his own bunk and blinked. He was completely pole-axed and his brain couldn't seem to take in what Adair had said. A child? How was that possible? No, it couldn't be. He wanted to protest that they'd only made love once and surely that wasn't enough, but he knew it was a ridiculous argument. It was perfectly feasible and he remembered now he hadn't been as careful as he'd intended to be. At the time, he'd been completely carried away by the wonder of finally making Jessamijn his.

He looked at Jess, but she was still studying the ceiling while fiddling with a tress of blonde hair as if she couldn't quite keep still.

'Adair, I think you'd better go,' she said, her voice quivering slightly.

Adair ducked out the door without another word, leaving them in an uncomfortable silence. Killian didn't know what to say and Jess seemed just as lost for words. The enormity of the situation hit him with full force and he felt as if someone had punched him in the gut, knocking all the wind out of him.

'Dear God, why didn't you say something?' he exclaimed at last.

She sat up and sent him a wary glance from under her eyelashes. He could see she was trembling with emotion now and he had a sudden urge to take her into his arms to reassure her. She looked away and murmured, 'I wasn't sure until recently and it didn't really make a difference anyway.'

'Of course it bloody makes a difference! If I'd known, I'd have ...'

'What?' She faced him with a frown. 'You think you would have found me passage back to Sweden more easily if you'd known?'

'Yes! No, I mean ... damn it all, woman, what do we do now?'

To his utter amazement Jess smiled at him ruefully. 'I imagine we wait for the birth of our child, just like everyone else. There's really nothing else we *can* do, is there? Nature will take its course.' She sent him a pleading glance. 'Please don't be angry. I was going to tell you, you know, but sometimes things go wrong in the first few months and I didn't want to scare you for nothing.'

'I'm not angry, but Jessamijn – we're going to China!'

She shrugged again, some colour returning to her cheeks. 'Women have babies all the time, even in China, I suppose. I just hope the poor mite isn't born here on the ship.' She counted quietly on her fingers. 'I'm guessing it will be a September baby. Will we have reached our destination by then, do you think?'

'I have no idea. Good Lord, this is a disaster.'

Killian tried not to think of all the implications – a pregnant woman travelling thousands of leagues across the oceans, possibly giving birth in a ship full of men who would have no idea what to do. Then the baby, small and vulnerable – his imagination ran riot and supplied him with images of suffering he didn't want to see. He shuddered. So much could go wrong, it didn't bear thinking of. There was also the fact that they couldn't possibly continue to pretend Jess was a boy.

'You don't want to be a father? Well, you should have thought of that before our wedding night,' Jess replied sharply, misunderstanding his words.

'No, it's not that. I'm just thinking of everything that can happen. How can you be so calm?' Killian was sure that in her shoes, he'd have been terrified. In fact, he was petrified now, on her behalf.

'Babies don't scare me. My mother has given birth to at least eight children that I know of, and she never had any problems birthing them. There's no reason I should either. And I know how to look after little ones, I've had plenty of practice. Besides, if something's going to go wrong, it would do so on land as well. It is God's will, isn't it? I mean, look what happened to poor little James …' She blinked away sudden tears, then shook her head. 'But we mustn't think like that. We have to be positive.'

Killian closed his eyes and tried to think logically. Of course she was right. He had just been thrown off balance by the surprise. If she wasn't frightened herself, there was no reason why he should be either. Except for the fact that this was a huge responsibility, which he wasn't sure he was prepared for. He was going to be a father. *Dear God in heaven …*

Looking at his wife, he was suddenly flooded by feelings of protectiveness. He had to keep her safe, and the child too, his little son or daughter. He went over to sit on her bunk and put a hand on her arm. 'Do you … can you feel it?' he asked, glancing towards her belly which was hidden from view by the waistcoat. It seemed no different than before.

'No, it's probably too soon. Perhaps in another few months.' She swung her legs over the side and sat up next to him, leaning her head on his shoulder for a moment. Without thinking, he put his arm around her and pulled her close. It felt good to hold her and for once she wasn't bristling at him but accepted his touch as if she needed to depend on him. He realised that was what he wanted, frightening though it was.

'You will tell me, won't you?' he said. 'I mean, I'd like to be a part of this, somehow.'

She smiled up at him. 'Yes, of course I will.'

'And if there's anything you need, you've only to say.'

She raised her eyebrows at him. 'Now don't go too soft on me, or I won't recognise the man I married,' she teased.

He smiled back. 'Don't worry, I'm going to be very stern with you and to begin with, I'm ordering you to rest this morning. No more writing, do you hear?'

'I'm not sick, you know. The queasiness will pass by lunchtime, like Adair said.'

'Maybe so, but I won't have you over-tiring yourself. Now lie down, please, or I'll have to push you down myself.'

'Aye, aye, sir, anything you say.'

Killian left her to rest, still feeling as if someone had punched him too hard, but he couldn't help a silly grin from spreading across his features.

He was going to be a father.

The following morning Jess was surprised to be woken rather later than usual, and by Killian instead of Adair. He put a plate of bread and cheese on the sea chest between their bunks, then produced a napkin containing a bunch of grapes from one pocket.

'Good morning,' he said. 'Has the nausea passed yet or would your rather I put this somewhere out of sight for now?'

'Uhm, no, I'm fine thank you, but ... where did you get those?' She nodded towards the grapes.

Killian winked at her. 'A leftover from the captain's table which just happened to disappear.'

'Killian! You didn't steal them?' She sat up and stared at him.

'I wouldn't call it that exactly. Don't worry, no one will miss them and I thought they might be lighter on your stomach.'

Jess felt a warm glow spreading inside her at his thoughtfulness. 'Well, thank you, but I don't want to get you into any trouble.'

'You won't, trust me.'

He surprised her again by not leaving immediately. Instead he sat down on his bunk and pulled a handkerchief out of his other pocket. It seemed to be tied up and Jess watched with interest as he undid the knots.

'I, uhm, believe I owe you something,' he said with a little cough of embarrassment that was most unlike him.

'You do?'

'Yes. I promised you this, but never had the opportunity to give it to you. Besides, I wasn't sure you still wanted it.' He pulled out a small gold ring made of several strands twisted together in an intricate pattern which made it shimmer. Holding it out to her, he added, 'But since there's no going back now, I thought perhaps you'd like to have it. Am I right?'

Jess' mouth fell open and she had to make a conscious effort to close it. 'Killian! I ... I don't know what to say. It's beautiful, thank you.' She took it from him and put it on after first pulling off his signet ring. 'Here, you'd better take this back.'

'Yes, thank you. Are you sure you like it? If not, we can always get another.'

'No, it's perfect.' Jess swallowed several times to stop the tears that welled up. 'Thank you.'

He smiled and stood up. 'My pleasure.' He took her hands and pulled her to her feet so that she stood chest to chest with him. 'Truce then?'

Jess could feel his heart beating, almost as fast as her own, and nodded. 'Yes, absolutely.'

He gave her a quick kiss on the cheek and left the cabin. Jess stood where he'd left her and put a hand up to the spot his lips had touched. She wondered whether his peace offering had been made just because of the baby, but either way, it made her happy that they were definitely not at odds with each other any longer. Friendship was better than nothing.

Jess could only marvel at the difference in Killian's attitude towards her from that day onwards. As they continued towards the Canary Islands, he spent all his free time with her, talking, playing cards or reading out loud while she rested on her bunk. He managed to cajole or bribe the captain's cook into giving him all sorts of tasty treats for her, such as fruit or newly grilled fish. In short, he seemed like a different man, but he still kept his distance physically.

About a week after they left Spain, the Canary Islands came into view and that evening Killian brought her up on deck for her usual outing. They stood side by side, leaning on the railing and looked at the dark smudge of the islands as they sailed past. There was no one else about and the only sound to be heard was the shushing noise of the waves as the prow pushed its way through the water and the flapping of sails above them.

Jess fanned herself with her hand. 'It's getting much warmer now, isn't it? Adair said one of the sailors told him it will be almost unbearable soon.'

'Yes, that's what I heard too. The cabin will be stifling, but I don't know what we can do about it.'

'I'll just have to wedge the door open a little and keep the porthole uncovered. Perhaps that will give me a slight breeze?'

Jess was very aware of Killian's forearm, which was resting next to hers on the railing, his warm skin touching hers. A frisson ran through her as he moved a fraction, and she had to curb a sudden impulse to reach out and run her hand along the hard muscle of his arm. Breathing in the warm, sultry air, filled with the scents of fresh greenery, lemon trees and habitation, she felt at peace, standing there with her husband, their child growing inside her.

Suddenly a light appeared in the sky like fire, and they both gasped in unison.

'What was that?'

'I don't know, but I did hear someone say there's a volcano on one of the islands, so perhaps that's it.'

'You don't think it will erupt, do you?' Jess had just been reading Pliny the Younger's account of the eruption of Mount Vesuvius when it destroyed the towns of Pompei and Herculaneum. The horrors of that were fresh in her mind.

'No, and even if it did, I don't think it could reach us here.'

'I wouldn't be too sure of that.'

'Don't worry.' Killian moved behind her and put both arms around her in a protective gesture. 'We'll soon be gone from here, the wind is strong.'

Jess leaned back against him before she'd even had time to think about it. It felt so right, as if that was where she belonged. She had an urge to turn around in his arms and simply give herself up to his embrace. If he had moved then, kissed the top of her head or even nuzzled her neck, the way he used to do at Askeberga, she would have dragged him back to their cabin by force and begged him to make love to her again. He didn't. Instead, he just continued to hold her without moving, as if he were made of stone. Jess wasn't sure what to make of that, so she stood still too, confused and longing for more, but afraid of being the first one to make a move.

The truth was, she had no idea how to entice her husband into bed. She wasn't even sure if he'd want her again. After all, that wasn't why he had married her. He was probably only being nice to her now because she was pregnant, but at least he wasn't angry with her any more, which was a relief.

She had to be happy with that.

Killian breathed in the scent of Jessamijn, who felt tiny and fragile in his arms. A bolt of desire shot through him and he would have liked nothing better than to make love to her right here, under the deep blue night sky, but he knew this wasn't the time. He was very tempted to at least kiss her, but he couldn't trust himself not to take it further if he did. It was better to resist altogether.

For one thing, she wasn't supposed to be a woman, although he was pretty sure there were quite a few people who suspected as much by now. And if they did know, he couldn't be seen to be enjoying her body when everyone else had to go without. It simply wasn't fair and would cause no end of trouble. Cabin walls were thin and no doubt any lovemaking, however furtive, would be noticed by someone. It wasn't an option.

Another problem was that he didn't want to jeopardise the baby. He had come to realise how precious this new life was to him – and his wife too for that matter. There was no way he would risk either in any way. If anything should happen to them because of his own base desires, he would never forgive himself. It was as simple as that.

He had to admit that God's ways really were mysterious. When the ship left Cadiz, he had decided to put the long months at sea to good use and try to woo his wife properly so that their marriage was no longer a sham when they returned to Gothenburg. Although the pregnancy had stopped his plans to drive her wild with desire for him, he now found himself courting her in a much more gentle manner, which she seemed to like. Obviously, this was God's way of showing him he had been going about it all wrong.

He breathed in the warm smell of her skin one last time, then said, 'Shall we go to bed now? It's late and you must be tired.'

She murmured assent and as they made their way down to the deck below and their cabin, Killian found he was content to just sleep in the same room as her. As long as they were together, that was all that mattered.

Chapter Twenty-Eight

The high, tree-less mountains of Tenerife faded into the distance and the ship set off into the Atlantic. Obliging winds pushed them in a huge arc towards South America first and then heading down to the southernmost tip of Africa. The debilitating heat did become almost unbearable. Jess spent most of her time trying to cool down with a crude fan Killian persuaded the English carpenter to make out of thin sticks of wood and some leftover sail canvas. It helped a little, but not much. Mostly she lived for the evenings when Killian was able to escort her up on deck and a welcome breeze cooled her overheated body.

'It's a good thing the queasiness has passed,' Killian commented, as they sat side by side in a corner of the sundeck, enjoying the fresh night air. 'You're sure you feel well in every other way?'

'Yes, I'm fine, just hot. Don't worry.'

'Of course I worry, so much can go wrong.'

'With the baby, you mean?'

'Not just that, but people seem to be dying of all sorts of things. Why only yesterday, two sailors went down with a putrid fever. It could be contagious and the barber-surgeon is helpless to prevent it.'

Fevers weren't the only things that killed. Conditions on board were so cramped that other illnesses, like dysentery, were rife. Despite a daily scrubbing of the decks with water and a weekly cleaning out of the lower deck where the sailors slept, it was almost impossible to keep the ship clean. As the days wore on, the food supplies dwindled and a lot of the food turned bad. Maggots or mould in the ship's biscuits were so common only a few people grumbled about it. The salted meat and fish tasted rancid and even the drinking water was disgusting. As the beer was all gone, however, there was no choice but to drink the water or die of thirst.

Then there were the fleas ... Jess scratched at a particularly itchy patch on her skin and tried to remember a time when she had felt comfortable. The journey already seemed interminable and they weren't even halfway yet.

'I wonder how my mother is coping?' she said. 'I wish Robert hadn't sent me away just when she needed me most.' She thought of her small brother whom she would never see again. Life could be so cruel sometimes. Although she'd told Killian they had to be positive, it was difficult not to be afraid for her own baby when she remembered how fragile James had been.

Killian took her hand and plaited his fingers with hers, giving them a gentle squeeze. 'Little James will live on in her heart, and although it will be hard for her at first, time does lessen the grief eventually. Besides, she has Ramsay to think of and for all his faults, I do believe Robert will do his best to console her too. He was just as distraught, Albert said. Together they'll cope.'

'I hope you're right.' Jess took comfort from the warm sensation of his fingers around hers. It gave her a feeling of security, as if she was safe with him next to her. 'I wonder what Albert is doing now?' she said to distract herself from thinking about how close Killian was.

'Yes. I sent him a letter from Cadiz, explaining what had happened, but I don't know whether he'll have received it yet.'

'Let's hope he's not having trouble with Robert, but with Mr Milner's help he should have been able to prove that the company belongs to us. I signed all the papers before I left and Albert will keep it running for us until we return, don't you think?'

'I'm sure he will. If there's one man we can trust, it's Albert.'

Jess just wished she could be sure they would be coming back at all.

Ten days after first spotting the Cape doves and other sea birds such as the huge albatross, they began to take soundings in the green, muddy water. This was in order to avoid running aground on the bank that surrounded the Cape of Good Hope and Africa's southernmost tip, Cape Agulhas. Campbell had no intention of stopping to replenish their stores, however, as this part of the world belonged to the Dutch. They didn't even sail close enough to see land.

'No point advertising our presence,' he said curtly. 'It would be too risky.'

The weather turned steadily colder and stormier, and winter clothing had to be found and put on again. Jess and Killian weren't alone in wearing fur – most of the sailors had sheepskin coats that seemed to keep their suppleness even when wet. Without them Jess didn't think they would have survived.

Although the cold was a blessing in many ways, the sudden drop in temperature also brought on chest infections and head colds. Jess woke up one morning to find Killian still in his bed, his face flushed and his breathing uneven. She rushed over to his bunk and shook his arm.

'Killian? Killian, are you all right?'

He opened his eyes, which were bloodshot and fever-glazed, their usual bright blue dulled with pain. 'Throat hurts,' he croaked. 'So hot. Head aches fit to burst.' Jess had never seen him anything other than healthy and she was suddenly terrified.

'Hold on. I'll get Adair to fetch some broth and some cold water and cloths.'

Killian didn't respond, which made her even more anxious, but when Adair finally arrived with the broth, Killian managed to sit up and take it. 'Ouch,' he muttered and it was clear he was having trouble swallowing. When he'd finished every last drop, Jess started to sponge his forehead with cold water, hoping to bring his fever down. It seemed to work for a while, but then he started to shiver instead.

'S-so co-cold,' he muttered, his teeth chattering. 'More b-blankets.'

Jess had already given him all hers and she didn't think anyone else would have any to spare. She looked at Killian and suddenly remembered his words to her during that sleigh ride so long ago. *Shared body heat is the second best thing for keeping warm.* 'Of course,' she said out loud and pushed Killian further towards the wall. 'Move over, I'll make you warm.'

'What?' he croaked, but she ignored him and lay down, wrapping her arms and one leg around him. There was barely room for the two of them in the narrow bunk.

She could feel him racked by violent shivers, but after a while they subsided until finally he was still. 'Nice,' he murmured, then startled her by opening his eyes and staring straight into hers. 'Guess I should be ill more often.'

His husky voice sent a tremor down her spine and Jess blinked. Her gaze flickered to his mouth, which was only inches away. She was overcome by a sudden urge to kiss him, the temptation so strong she almost gasped out loud. He smiled as if he could read her mind, that teasing smile she knew so well, but then she remembered he was feverish and probably not aware of what he was doing.

'Don't you dare be ill again,' she said firmly. 'My nerves

couldn't stand it.'

'Why is that then?' He was staring intently at her now, as if her reply really mattered. Jess wasn't sure what to make of this, so shrugged and pretended indifference.

'I don't want to be left alone on this ship with just Adair for company.'

'Is that the only reason?' He extricated one of his hands from under the blankets and put it round her waist, pulling her closer. Jess looked away from his penetrating gaze.

'Well, no. I ... I don't want to lose you. I mean, I want our child to have a father.' She added half jokingly, 'I wouldn't wish a stepfather on anyone, you know that.'

He kept his arm around her for a moment longer as if he was waiting for more, then let go. Jess had the feeling he was disappointed by her answer. She wondered if she should tell him there was another reason too, one that was much more important. But she found it impossible to bare her soul when she didn't know if he'd want to hear what she had to say.

'Don't worry. You're not getting rid of me yet,' he said and closed his eyes. 'And now I'm hot again, so you can get up and continue with that infernal sponge instead.'

Jess raised herself on one elbow and stared down at him, but he didn't look up again. She sighed and sat up.

Why was everything so complicated?

Killian soon recovered. Others were not so lucky and more crew members died before they began the long trek across the Indian Ocean, where the climate changed yet again.

They sighted the island of St Paul's at the beginning of July and sailed fairly close to land, although they didn't try to go ashore.

'We can't afford to lose any time,' Campbell said emphatically. 'If we don't make it into the China Sea by

August, we could be stuck waiting for favourable winds for nearly six months. Unthinkable.'

The island seemed to be fairly sterile in any case, hardly worth exploring, so no one complained. Everyone was eager to reach Java, where they knew they would be able to replenish their supplies and stop briefly.

Jess grew bigger every day, or at least it felt that way. 'I'm turning into a whale,' she complained to Killian, but he was entranced by the kicking of his child which could be clearly felt and didn't take any notice. She let him lay the palms of his hands against her abdomen whenever they went for their evening walks around deck. They were both amazed at the strength of the baby's kicks.

'It's a wild one,' Killian commented with a smile. 'I hope it's not a girl or she'll be a real hoyden.'

Adair's shirts no longer fitted Jess and she had to resort to borrowing Killian's. Soon it became impossible to hide either her pregnancy or her sex, but to their surprise most of the crew members took the news calmly. So too did Campbell, when they informed him about the baby. This was mostly because Killian hit on the idea of telling the supercargo that Captain Trolle was sure to disapprove. The two men were still at odds and this ignited the fuse again.

'It's nothing to do with the captain,' Campbell growled. 'This ship is under my command and it was my decision to allow your wife to stay on board. It's unfortunate she is *enceinte*, but if, as you say, this was something that happened long before she set foot on the ship, it couldn't have been avoided obviously.'

'No and I would have taken her back to Gothenburg myself, if I'd known.'

'No point in thinking about it now. It's happened and that's that. I will inform everyone and make it clear your wife is to be treated with respect.'

Despite his ongoing battles with the captain, who seemed either unwilling or unable to acknowledge that Campbell had the final say in everything, the Scotsman ran the ship with a firm but fair hand. For the most part, he was obeyed.

Killian had also made himself popular by his willingness to help out with the most menial of tasks. He wanted to learn everything there was to learn about sailing and trading and the men respected him for it. This meant that he only received the occasional envious glance when he finally dared to escort Jess up to sit under an awning on the sundeck during the day. No one complained openly.

He hoped it would stay that way.

The final part of the journey passed unbearably slowly for Jess, who was praying they would reach China before her time came.

She couldn't help but be enchanted by what she could see of Java, however. There were endless coasts bathed in bright sunlight and tightly covered with trees, their reflections giving the water the same deep green colour. Turtles floated in the water around them, and the small, dark-haired natives went around almost naked apart from cotton loincloths. Still, she didn't want to linger and was relieved when Campbell ordered the ship to sail on after only a brief stop to take on board supplies of food and water.

The milk from the strange coconuts refreshed her and made her feel stronger. Killian made sure she had a large supply of these, as well as various fresh fruits, the likes of which neither of them had ever seen before.

'I'm sure these are doing the baby the world of good,' she said to him, licking the juice off her fingers.

'Yes, and they're delicious too. Apart from this one, which tastes like soap.' He pointed to a greenish one and Jess laughed.

'I didn't realise you'd ever been so destitute you had to eat soap. Poor you.'

'Oh, there's a lot you don't know about me.' He grinned at her and she smiled back.

'I'm learning.'

And she was. They had plenty of time to talk about everything under the sun and although he showed no signs of wanting her as a lover, she felt they were now very good friends. She tried to tell herself she was content with that.

They passed into the China Sea at last on the sixth of August and entered the final leg of their journey.

'Thank the Lord for that,' Campbell muttered. 'Any later and we would never have made it. I only hope we're not too late as it is.'

Killian hoped so too. He was watching Jess' stomach increasing in size every day and prayed they'd make it to their destination before the baby was born.

Seven months after leaving Sweden, they reached the Chinese coast at long last. Campbell's fears proved right, however, when they sailed into a storm which drove them off course. It began with a strong wind, which increased as the day went on and then torrential rain arrived with a vengeance.

'It sounds so much worse than any rain I've ever heard in Sweden,' Jess commented as she huddled in the little cabin with Killian. She stared towards the port-hole which was covered with a shutter, but where the water still seeped in from time to time. 'And how can a ship possibly take such a battering and not sink?'

'They call this a *tai-fun*,' Killian said, 'and Campbell told me it's normal weather for this part of the world. Everything happens on a larger scale here.' That seemed to include the thunder and lightning, which reverberated all around them.

They listened to the waves crashing against the sides of the ship.

'Do you think the masts will break?' Jess asked, her voice quivering slightly.

Killian shrugged. 'The crew have done what they can by lowering the top masts and yards, furling and fastening all the sails and tying down anything that can move. Now all we can do is pray.'

It was stuffy and hot inside the little cabin, the sultry heat of early September nearly unbearable. Despite this, Killian sat down next to Jess on her bunk and put his arms around her. She didn't resist and leaned against him with a small sigh. Killian was content just to hold her and thought to himself that if they had to die this night, he wanted to do it with Jess in his arms.

Their prayers were answered, however, after an agonizingly long night and day, when the storm abated at last. On the third of September they arrived at Macao. Here a pilot came on board to guide them through the entrance to the Pearl River and four days later they anchored near the official entry of the river leading to Canton.

'So this is the famous *Bocca Tigris*,' Killian said. He was standing on deck with Jess and Adair, and the three of them studied their surroundings. There were two rounded forts, one on either side of them, surrounded by trees. These guarded the river entrance, which was a narrow space between a peninsula of the mainland and a small island. They could see soldiers inside the forts, looking back at them through openings that were presumably for shooting arrows, which was rather intimidating.

'What does the name mean, do you know?' Jess liked the sound of it and was curious.

'I read that it's Portuguese for *The Tiger's Mouth*, but apparently they got it slightly wrong. The Chinese themselves call it *The Tiger Gate*.'

A boat approached and some Chinese mandarins, high-ranking officials, came on board. Jess leaned over the railing to look at them more closely. 'What do they want? They're not hostile, are they?'

'No, but the Chinese make sure everyone follows their rules, otherwise we're not allowed to trade with them. They've come to inspect the ship and issue passes for us to continue upriver, I think. Mr Campbell told me there are lots of procedures. This isn't our country, we have to follow their laws now.' He glanced at Adair and smiled. 'That goes for you too, young man. I have no idea what they do to pickpockets here, but I'd guess it's not pleasant, so just you behave, all right?'

Adair tried to look offended, but failed. 'As if I'd try onythin' like that here,' he said.

'See that you don't. I'm serious, Adair, I don't want to lose you.' Killian ruffled the youth's curly black hair which was as wild as ever.

'Me neither,' Jess said. 'You're to be my baby's honorary uncle, aren't you, so don't get into any trouble.'

Adair smiled sheepishly, but she could see that he was pleased they cared.

Chapter Twenty-Nine

They were allowed to continue at last, up towards Whampoa, the ship's final destination. It was slow going because the current was strong and they had to be towed most of the way. Jess sat on the sundeck watching the beautiful view along the river. There was greenery as far as the eye could see and a soft, slightly hilly landscape with some trees. Mostly they passed meadows and rice fields. Interspersed with these were tiny villages, forts and several very high towers with strange roofs that tilted up at the corners.

'Those are pagodas,' Killian told her, settling himself beside her for a while.

'They're fascinating, but then everything here is,' Jess replied. 'You know, I'm really glad I came after all. This is something I'll remember for the rest of my life.'

Killian smiled, but shot a worried glance at her huge stomach. 'You're feeling well?'

'Never better. Don't worry, the baby's not due yet. He or she should be born on dry land.'

'That's good. Mr Campbell wants me to go on to Canton with him for a few days. Will you be all right staying behind? Apparently the Chinese don't allow foreign females in the city.'

Whampoa, where the ship would anchor, lay two miles downriver from the actual city of Canton, but the large European vessels couldn't sail that far because the river was too shallow. The supercargos and other members of the crew who were needed in Canton would have to continue by junk or sampan. It wasn't too far and Jess was sure she could get a message to Killian fairly quickly if she needed to.

'Yes, I'll be fine. I'll have Adair to watch over me and I'll bar the door to the cabin at night.'

Killian was reluctant to leave her, but at the same time he was eager to see the Chinese city he had heard so much about from Campbell. A large junk, flat bottomed and square, tall fore and aft, took them up the river. Killian looked around with great interest. As they came nearer the city, the traffic on the river increased and they were surrounded by other junks and the smaller sampans, a similar vessel but much simpler. The noise all around was almost deafening. The owners of the sampans all seemed to be selling something or other and were shouting in loud voices, waving their arms around for good measure. It was like a huge floating market and Killian was fascinated.

'Canton is more like three separate cities,' Campbell explained while they made their way through the confusion. 'There's the official city surrounded by walls, which we Europeans are not allowed to enter unless we're invited.'

Killian caught sight of the tall, thick sandstone walls with many towers, both round and square, and several gates. Nothing could be seen of what was inside, apart from rooftops, more towers and a pagoda. 'I hope we are invited then. I'd like to see it,' he said.

'Most likely we will, but you never know. The second part is the suburb, which is where we'll be spending most of our time. That's where the so-called factories are situated. They are the warehouses and living quarters of us foreigners. Most back onto the river and each country has its own factory. Our first task is to rent one. Sweden has never traded with China before and so doesn't have one specially built.'

'And the third part?'

'Ah, that's the "floating city". Look around you. There are houses built on stilts by the edge of the water and then all the junks and sampans here have been arranged into what looks like streets on the water. Whole families live on each one, although it must be terribly cramped for them.'

Most of the boats had what looked like little houses or huts built on deck. Some were only crude shelters made of bamboo, others much sturdier constructions. Killian wondered how the people survived in such conditions, but could only suppose they managed somehow. He was overwhelmed by all the unfamiliar sights and sounds. It was as if he had entered a completely new world, one where he didn't fit in. But he was determined to make the most of it and learn as much as he could of the Chinese people and their customs.

'Where do we go first, have you any idea?' he asked as he followed Campbell along the quayside. Although there were other foreigners here too, he felt incongruous in his European clothing. Wearing his grey wig as usual, Campbell stuck out even more, but he seemed unconcerned.

'Of course. We'll go and see Tin-qua, a wealthy and important merchant I did business with last time I was here. He should be able to rent us a factory by the waterside.'

This proved to be the case and the merchant seemed very happy to welcome them. He and Campbell greeted each other as was the custom by putting their hands together, bowing a little and saying something that sounded like 'haw-haw'. Apparently this meant 'I wish you all good' or words to that effect. Killian thought it a strange greeting, but copied Campbell. It wouldn't do to be impolite.

Tin-qua was dressed in a long robe made of dark silk. It was doubled across the breast and fastened with small, round buttons and it reached quite far down the leg. The sleeves were wide and long enough to cover the merchant's hands. Underneath he wore some sort of wide trousers and boots made of silk. When he turned to escort them to the factory, Killian caught sight of a long plait hanging down the man's back, all the way to his thighs. Perched on the top of his head was a round silk hat. It was more exotic than Killian could ever have imagined and he had to hide a smile of pure joy. He could hardly believe they were finally here.

The factory they were offered was a long, two-storey building which backed onto the river. At the other end it opened directly onto one of the main streets of the suburb.

'This will be excellent,' Campbell declared, and concluded his negotiations with the merchant while Killian listened. Good-natured haggling seemed part of the deal, just like it did at home in Europe. 'Now we'll send for supplies and men and get started,' Campbell continued. 'There's a lot to do and not much time. We can't stay more than five months, otherwise we'll miss the winds that will carry us south again. Let us begin!'

The crew had cheered when they dropped anchor at Whampoa, but as they and Jess soon found out, nothing very exciting happened there. Lots of other European ships were anchored nearby, and each one was assigned a *bankeshall*. This was a kind of large, but very basic bamboo warehouse built on the river bank especially for them. In it they stored the cargo and the ship's equipment, which was taken ashore for safekeeping. Some of the crew members slept there too since they had to guard everything night and day. It was also used as a workshop from time to time.

The ship had to be unloaded, cleaned up and repaired so that it was ready to face the long journey back to Europe. This meant a lot of work, especially for the ship's craftsmen. There were endless tasks – the rigging had to be repaired, the hull needed caulking, the sails were torn and had to be mended. Since the same type of work was going on aboard all the other ships around them, there was a constant racket that nearly drove Jess mad. She tried not to complain and instead thanked God she had reached China safely.

The supercargos and some of the crew went to the factory in Canton. 'They'll be takin' turns,' Adair told Jess, 'so's everyone gets tae set foot in the city at least fer a while. I cannae wait tae go!'

Jess would have liked to visit Canton as well, but Campbell vetoed this. 'You shouldn't really be here at all, my dear,' he said, firmly but not unkindly. 'I'm afraid foreign women are not allowed so it's best if no one sees you.'

Jess knew she couldn't argue with the man. He had been kind enough already and although it was frustrating to be so near and yet not be able to see the city, she had no choice but to follow his orders.

On the third day, Killian came back and told them a Chinese official was on his way to measure the ship.

'Measure it? What do you mean?' Jess was intrigued as this seemed an odd thing to do.

'We have to pay them some sort of tax and the price depends on the size of the ship and how much cargo we can carry, as far as I understand it. The thing is, you'll have to stay in the cabin and keep quiet. I don't know what the rules are about bringing women this far – hopefully there are no laws against it – but we don't want to take any chances. They probably won't measure the cabins, so please just hide in here until I come and tell you they've gone.'

'Very well.' Jess resigned herself to another boring afternoon and stood up to massage her back, which had been aching on and off since the previous day. The baby was growing very large and it was too heavy for her small frame. She sincerely hoped it wouldn't get much bigger or she'd never be able to push it out. She sighed and thought what a relief it would be when it was finally born.

A sumptuously dressed mandarin, whose title was apparently Hou Pou, arrived with great pomp. Killian stood to one side and watched while the official was greeted by Campbell and Graham. Hou Pou – or *The Hoppo* as most Europeans called him – was the chief director of customs in the province and had to be treated with the utmost deference. His visit was therefore a very formal procedure, including an exchange of gifts between him and the supercargos. The mandarin was then invited to take some refreshment in the captain's cabin, while his men got on with the job of actual measuring.

Killian chose to stay on deck and followed the Chinese men discreetly to make sure they didn't go anywhere near Jess. He watched as they chattered among themselves and made notes on paper. Their language was incomprehensible to him, and he wondered what they were saying. It felt strange not to be able to communicate at all and he was relieved when an interpreter – or linguist as Campbell called him – joined him and started to explain a little of what was going on.

'Mr Li calculating loading capacity,' the linguist told him. 'Special rules for measuring.'

Killian had noticed that they seemed to have rules for everything. Although this obviously made it easier for the officials to run the country, he wondered what the people who had to obey all these laws thought about it.

There were Swedish sailors working up above, finishing off the job of taking down all the sails and carrying them over to the *bankeshall*. Killian glanced up, admiring their fearlessness, then shuddered. He had climbed up to the top once, just to prove to himself that he could, but he never wanted to do it again. It had been one of the most terrifying experiences of his life.

As he watched, one of the men cried out and almost lost his footing, kicking out at a small spar in the process. This dislodged it, and Killian saw it falling rapidly towards the deck. A quick glance showed him that the man called Li was standing right where the spar was likely to end up. With lightning reflexes, he shot forward and pushed the man out of the way, both of them falling to the deck out of harm's way, just in the nick of time.

A great commotion broke out all round them, with Li at first shouting at Killian and glaring at him. Soon he fell silent when he realised what had happened. He said something to the linguist, who came over to help them to their feet, and then turned to Killian.

'Mr Li say to thank you very much. Save his life. Owe much gratitude.'

'It was nothing. I'm pleased he's not hurt.' Killian felt shaken, but tried not to show it. It had been a close call and could have ended in disaster, not just for Mr Li, but for their entire venture. There was no saying who the Chinese officials would have blamed for such an accident.

Li put the palms of his hands together in front of his chest and bowed deeply to Killian, and said 'Sank you.'

Killian copied him and replied in English, 'It was my pleasure.' To the linguist he added, 'I will make sure the men stop working overhead for now so that nothing like this can happen again.'

There was no need for such orders, however. The sailors had already climbed down and came hurrying over to him. 'Are ye hurt, Mr Kinross? We're right sorry, we'd no idea that piece was loose.'

'I'm fine, but the Chinaman could have been killed. You'd better wait until they're gone before you continue and make sure the deck is clear when you do so. Go and have a rest for now, I'm sure you must be as shaken as I feel.'

They nodded. 'Too right, sir. Will ... will there be money taken off our wages for bein' so careless?'

'No, accidents happen. I'm sure you didn't do it on purpose.'

'Thank ye, Mr Kinross.' They trooped off, looking relieved, and Killian returned to watching the Chinese officials as they continued their measuring.

A short while later, Mr Li made his way over to the stairs that led down to the deck below. Killian followed, beckoning to the linguist who came hurrying over as well. 'Where is he going?' he asked.

'Needs measure down where cargo is.'

'Oh, I see.' The man would have to pass the cabins, but not actually enter them. Killian went down the stairs after him, just to make sure, but his relief was short-lived. Just as Mr Li reached the bottom, they heard a sharp cry from their right. It sounded almost like an animal in pain, and before Killian could stop him, Mr Li had rushed over to the cabin that contained Jess and yanked open the door.

Mr Li stopped dead and simply stared, and when Killian caught up with him he could see why. Jess was standing in a puddle of water, clutching her abdomen while her face was twisted with pain. Adair was patting her shoulder awkwardly, an anxious expression clouding his features, obviously not sure what he should be doing.

Mr Li turned to Killian, his eyebrows raised and pointed between the two of them. Killian nodded and gritted his teeth. 'Yes, that's my wife.' No point pretending otherwise now that she had been seen.

He had forgotten about the linguist, but Mr Li turned to the man and uttered several rapid sentences, while Jess moaned again, although not as loudly as before. 'Are you all right, Jessamijn?' Killian hissed, while what sounded like a Chinese argument broke out behind him.

'Yes, I'll be ... fine. I was just surprised, that's all. I ... wasn't expecting this so soon. I ... ah, it's a lot fiercer than

I thought too.'

'Your clothes ...?' Killian gazed at the puddle by her feet.

'The waters broke. Must change. Can I borrow some of your breeches?'

'Yes, of course, but let me help you.' Killian moved forward, but she shook her head and shooed him and Adair away.

'No, leave me. I'll manage.'

She shut the door in their faces and Killian turned just as the linguist began to address him. 'Mr Li say your wife must come with him,' the man began.

'What? No! I mean, she's done nothing wrong. No one said she wasn't allowed this far.' Killian felt perspiration beading his forehead and almost panicked. He couldn't allow them to take Jess away now, that was unthinkable.

'No, no, nothing wrong, but Mr Li wife just have baby too. She can help your wife. Not safe here. Stay with Mr Li.'

Killian blinked. 'You mean, as a guest?'

The linguist and Li both nodded and Li bowed again and added something, which the linguist translated rapidly. 'Mr Li say owe you life. Repay by taking care of wife. Even.'

'Ah, I see.' Killian smiled at the two men, understanding dawning at last. 'Thank you, that would be wonderful. Do you mind if I accompany her as far as Mr Li's house? Just to reassure my wife?'

'Of course. Please let us go now. Baby come quickly perhaps.'

Killian knocked on the cabin door and when Jess let him in he explained what had happened. She agreed to go after some hesitation.

'I suppose being with another woman will be good, even if we can't communicate much. At least she'll know what to do if she's just been through it herself. Very well, let's go.'

A short while later they were on their way up the river.

Killian left a message for Campbell to let him know what was happening, and Mr Li excused himself from his duties. Killian sat next to Jess and took her hand and squeezed it.

'I wish I could stay with you,' he whispered. 'Are you sure you'll be fine with these people?'

She nodded. 'Yes. There wouldn't be much you could do anyway and I'll ask them to let you know as soon as it's all over. Don't worry if you don't hear immediately though. Some babies take days to be born, although I hope this one doesn't.'

'Amen to that.' He looked deep into her eyes. 'I will pray for your safety and that of the baby.'

He knew he would be devastated if he lost her. The mere thought made him feel cold all over.

Chapter Thirty

Mr Li's wife, whose name was Mei, took one look at Jess and hustled her up a narrow staircase into a small bedroom with a balcony that overlooked a courtyard. A couple of little dogs, so furry they looked like tufts of wool with legs, jumped off a cushion and came to sniff the newcomer. They wagged their tails, but were evicted by their mistress before Jess had a chance to make friends.

Mei then sat Jess down on a stool, before clapping her hands and issuing a series of commands to the stream of servants that came running. The sweet smell of incense hung over the room. Combined with the fragrance of flowers from outside, this made for a very pleasant atmosphere. Jess tried to breathe slowly and deeply, so as to help her body through the pains that came at regular intervals.

The room itself was fairly plain, with only a few items of furniture – the stool Jess was sitting on, a couple of clothes chests and a large bed. The walls were covered in white paper. At least it was clean, Jess thought to herself. She watched with gratitude while the servants started to bring all the things needed for childbirth, such as towels, hot water and cloths. She could see that they knew what they were doing, and this reassured her.

'Thank you,' she said to Mei with a smile, when the woman turned to her again. She stood up and bowed as Killian had showed her. 'It's the custom here and shows respect,' he'd whispered. Mei smiled back and indicated with gestures that Jess should sit down and wait for a while longer.

Soon after, an old lady came into the room, huffing and

puffing with exertion. She had obviously hurried to obey Mei's summons from wherever she lived, and listened intently while Mei explained the situation. Her little brown eyes widened at first when she saw that Jess was a foreigner, but she soon nodded and concentrated on the coming baby. She put her hands on Jess' stomach to feel the contractions which were coming harder and faster now. Jess bit her lip and tried not to moan out loud, but the old woman smiled kindly, and said, 'Aaaaah!' in a loud voice as if to show her that it was fine to cry out.

Jess could only hope she wouldn't have to.

Thankfully the baby was in a hurry, and arrived only a few hours later. Jess, dazed with pain, held her newborn son and said, 'Thank you, thank you,' over and over again to the Chinese women. They all beamed at her and chattered amongst themselves.

Servants cleaned her and the bed and tidied away all the paraphernalia of childbirth, while Jess settled down to try and feed her baby the way she had seen her mother feed James. 'Even if they don't get much nourishment at first, it will help your body to produce milk,' she remembered her mother saying. When she felt the strange pull of the baby's mouth on her breast, Jess understood what she'd meant. It was all a miracle, and so was her son.

'You're beautiful,' she whispered and kissed the downy head covered in tufts of blond hair. He took after his mother in that respect, but she'd already seen that he had bright blue eyes. Killian's, she thought with a smile.

'And so are you,' a voice said softly beside her.

She looked up and to her amazement Killian was kneeling next to her, an expression of relief on his face. There was also reverence as he gazed at her and his son.

'Killian! I thought they sent you away hours ago.'

He shook his head. 'No. Mr Li seems determined to repay me for saving his life and he let me wait in a room downstairs. I'm very grateful to him. But … are you well? And the baby, is he healthy?'

'We're both fine, I think. Here, would you like to hold him?'

She handed Killian the bundle and showed him how to support the baby's head. He sat on the floor and just stared at the little mite, who had now closed his eyes and gone to sleep. 'Amazing,' Killian muttered. 'Truly amazing …'

Their eyes met and Jess felt a deep connection, as if they were inextricably bound together through this child. They grinned at each other like a couple of village idiots and happiness bubbled up inside her. She had survived, the baby was fine and Killian had said she was beautiful. The world was a wonderful place.

'What shall we call him?' Jess asked after a while. 'Would you like him to be named after yourself or your father perhaps?'

'No, I don't think so. I'd prefer him to have my older brother's name, Brice. He was always very kind to me even though he must have thought me a nuisance. But you did all the hard work, it should be your choice. Would you like him to have *your* father's name?'

'How about both? Brice Aaron Kinross. That has a lovely ring to it and I like the name Brice.'

'Yes, why not. Here, you'd better take him back, my arm is going to sleep.'

She took the baby and snuggled down next to him. 'Now I think I'd better get some rest, because if he's anything like as lively outside the womb as he was in it, he'll be wanting food soon again.'

Killian smiled and reached out a hand to stroke her cheek. 'Thank you,' he said, 'for giving me a son.'

He stood up and to her surprise he bent to kiss her on the mouth before leaving. Jess stared after him, feeling more content than she ever had in her life. Then, overcome by exhaustion, she fell asleep.

'This is a strange place and no mistake,' Farquhar grumbled to John Ley, the first supercargo of the Ostend ship *Hertogh van Lorreynen,* on which he had at last found passage to Canton. They had left in April, but made good time and arrived just after the Swedish ship, to Farquhar's great relief. Now he had four or five months in which to find a way to eliminate his cousin.

'To be sure, it's not what we're used to,' Ley agreed. 'But intriguing, wouldn't you say?'

'I don't know. There aren't even any decent-looking women,' Farquhar continued. The tiny ladies he'd seen so far hadn't appealed to him in the slightest. He didn't see how they could tempt anyone else either, unless a man was desperate like the sailors. It was very aggravating, because he had come up with a vague plan to bribe a whore to entice his cousin. Then he was going to murder the woman in such a way that Killian would be blamed and hopefully punished for the crime. He'd heard the Chinese had very harsh punishments for their criminals and hoped this would take care of his cousin once and for all.

'Oh, I don't know about that. The little Chinese ladies are very sweet and obliging if you pay them enough.' Ley laughed. 'Mind you, there are others who seem to think like you. I hear someone brought his wife along and she's actually here in the suburb with us.'

'What? Who'd do a thing like that? I thought it wasn't allowed.'

'It isn't, but this fellow Kinross seems to have got round the rules somehow and –'

'Did you say Kinross?' Farquhar suddenly felt sick.

'Yes, what of it?'

'Oh, nothing, only I thought the name sounded familiar.' Farquhar managed to feign indifference. He was glad he'd travelled under a false name so that no one could connect him to Killian in any way. 'And he's brought his wife, you say?'

'Yes, as I was telling you, she's staying with some merchant or other and has just given birth. A boy I think, but I'm not sure. It's the outside of enough, wouldn't you say?'

Farquhar only nodded. He wasn't capable of speech at that moment because he was consumed by a rage so great he was afraid he might explode. Killian had brought a wife? Where had he found her? And the infernal woman had given birth to a son? It was more than 'the outside of enough', it was an outrage. His own wife had given birth to another daughter just before he left, and he'd been so angry he hadn't even bothered to choose a name for the baby. Three daughters and now here was Killian with a son at the first attempt. It simply wasn't to be borne.

Restless now, he stood up. 'I'm going out,' he said. He had to find the woman and her brat and do something, anything. He couldn't allow this state of affairs, it was an absolute disaster. And no doubt that whoreson would soon be busy making another child, another boy most likely. *No!*

'Very well,' Ley said, looking surprised at the suddenness of Farquhar's departure. 'Enjoy the sights.'

But Farquhar wasn't interested in any sights other than that of Killian's wife, preferably dead. He would find her if it was the last thing he did.

Killian was kept constantly busy and Campbell took him out every day on a never-ending quest to find a cargo at the best possible price.

First he contracted with a merchant called Hunqua for some silks. These had to be ordered straight away so that the weavers would have time to finish them to the right specification before their departure. He also negotiated a ballast of something he called *tutanego*, a metal whose ingredients they weren't entirely sure of, but which was heavy enough to steady the ship. Then he turned his attention to buying porcelain whenever they saw something that looked to be of good quality.

Most of their time, however, was spent arguing about the price of tea. Killian learned more about the various types of tea than he had ever thought possible or even wanted to know. By the end of September he was already heartily sick of it, as he told Jess at one of their meetings.

'I swear, even the smell of it is making me ill,' he said. 'Mr Campbell is unbelievably fussy about what he buys and he doesn't hesitate to refuse all the baskets which contain what he considers inferior tea. It's really tedious and the merchants aren't pleased. No doubt they're used to cheating the Europeans, but Mr Campbell is having none of that.'

'He sounds very canny,' Jess smiled. 'I hope you're listening and learning so you know what to buy in future.'

'Of course.'

Killian couldn't keep his eyes off his wife and son, who made as pretty a picture as he'd ever seen. Now that she'd recovered from her ordeal, Jess was positively blooming, and he had to stop himself from touching her at every opportunity. This was neither the time nor the place to try and tempt her back to his bed, even if it had been allowed. He knew women had to wait at least a couple of months before resuming their wifely duties, but he wanted to kiss her generous mouth every time they met. So far, he'd resisted because it would never be enough.

'It's a shame I can't come and see you more often,'

he sighed.

'Yes. Did you ask about that?'

'I did and although Li said I was welcome to visit at any time, Mr Campbell told me I shouldn't. It's probably better for Li if he's not seen to fraternise too much with us foreigners. He might lose face or something.' He shrugged.

'Never mind, time passes quickly and soon we'll be on our way home again,' Jess said with a smile. Nothing seemed to get her down at the moment and Killian was thankful for that.

'You're right. I'm sorry you can't at least go out to have a look around though,' Killian said. Chinese women, it seemed, were always kept indoors unless they had to work. They were hardly ever seen even in their families' booths. He had asked the interpreter if he could take Jess for a walk occasionally, but the man shook his head and looked worried, so he didn't pursue the question.

'It's all right, little Brice keeps me busy most of the time.'

'I'll tell you what, I need your opinion on what to buy to take back with us, so I'll bring you some samples and then we can choose together. How would that be?'

She smiled at him again. 'I'd enjoy that.'

'And shall I commission them to paint a dinner service with our initials? I'm told they can do that easily and it's fairly cheap. In fact, they'll paint anything we want. Perhaps you could make up a pattern?'

'I'll try to draw our initials entwined, but I quite like the Chinese patterns so I don't think we should do our own. It wouldn't feel authentic, if you know what I mean.'

'Of course, you're right. Well, let me know when you have finished the drawing.'

He was fascinated by his surroundings and spent as much of his time as possible wandering the streets of the suburb, which were made of square stone slabs and kept clean at all times. Any water or effluent escaped down little holes, presumably into some kind of sewer, and all rubbish was collected by the poorer inhabitants. Some streets were broad, straight and quite beautiful, but most of them were narrow, long, crooked and teeming with people.

Even for someone who had lived in Edinburgh, Canton seemed unbelievably crowded. Killian had to literally push his way through the mass of humanity that seethed around him, not to mention the various pigs, stray dogs and flapping chickens. Everywhere he went there were street entertainers, fortune tellers and even barbers carrying out their work in the middle of the street.

The Chinese people seemed to carry most things in baskets, often two at a time suspended on a bamboo pole over their shoulders. There were no carriages, only the odd palanquin for wealthier merchants and their wives. The houses were mostly two-storey dwellings made of mud or stone, with a booth at the front displaying the goods made on the premises and a workshop of some kind behind it and living quarters above. It all seemed very plain and functional, but lovely to look at and endlessly fascinating to an outsider.

Each street was aimed at a particular type of merchandise, with silk booths in one, clothes and hats in another, while a third would contain only food stalls. These were interesting, but not as pleasant since they stank to high heaven. The tea and silk merchants were the highest in rank, their area the finest. It all seemed very orderly to Killian, unlike either Edinburgh or Gothenburg where shops were opened wherever a merchant felt like it. The Chinese craftsmen also thought nothing of working openly inside their booths. They only put down their tools if a customer showed an interest in their wares, which were all arranged in neat rows.

'You're enjoying your stay here, I see,' Campbell

commented one afternoon, when Killian came back from yet another walk. Campbell's thin mouth curved in amusement, but the deep blue eyes sparkled with approval so Killian knew the older man was pleased.

'Yes, it's wonderful. I can't tell you how grateful I am to you for the opportunity to come here.'

'No gratitude necessary. You've worked hard to earn your keep and apart from the small matter of your wife, which wasn't your fault, I have no complaints about your conduct. In fact, you've been a great asset and I think you'll go far.'

'Thank you, you're very kind.'

'Not at all. I can't help but compare the way you pay attention to me as opposed to the laxity of some others I could mention.' Campbell's expression turned sour and Killian knew he was thinking of one of the other supercargos, who seemed to be spending all his time with the Ostenders rather than helping his superior. Killian had no idea why the man had become so friendly with John Ley and his crew, but he knew Campbell considered them ill-mannered. Killian thought it best not to even attempt to socialise with them.

'But let's not think about that,' Campbell continued. 'Tell me, have you found a buyer for the various mechanical instruments you brought with you yet? I would have thought there'd be plenty of interest.'

'Oh, yes. I showed them to several merchants and made them bid against each other.' Killian grinned. 'See, I've been watching you haggling and learned a thing or two.' Campbell nodded and smiled. 'And I sold them to the highest bidder only this morning. I've just kept a couple back which I'm going to give to Mr Li before our departure as a thank you gift for his care of my wife.'

'Good thinking. Now what will you buy with the profit of your sale?'

'Ah, now that's tricky. There's so much choice, isn't there.

I'll have to think about that some more.'

'Well, while you do that, let's go out and see if we can't find some more porcelain before the damned French buy all the best pieces. We really need to get that before everything else since it has to be stowed at the bottom of the ship and so has to be loaded first.'

Killian was very happy to go along with this. He was enjoying himself immensely and on the way to the porcelain merchants, he could look at all the other things on offer. Lacquer ware, mother-of-pearl boxes and gaming counters, carved ivory, and much more. He really was spoiled for choice and wouldn't decide what to buy just yet. There was plenty of time and he wanted to ask Jess' opinion too. He was sure she'd know exactly what a lady would like and what would make the most profit in Gothenburg.

He smiled to himself – they made a good team.

Chapter Thirty-One

The weather turned colder and Jess was grateful when Killian brought her a couple of thick, quilted silk jackets and matching long skirts. He had also bought warm baby clothes of silk and cotton for little Brice. They both laughed at the sight of him in a funny looking padded hat which protected his head, but made him look like a native baby.

'We'll have to call him Mandarin Brice from now on,' Killian joked.

'Don't listen to your papa,' Jess told the baby. 'He's mocking you when you look so handsome.' But she had to admit the only difference between him and Mei's son were the huge blue eyes and slightly paler skin.

She and Mei managed to communicate somehow with gestures and facial expressions, and from time to time Killian sent the linguist to help them for an hour or two. Jess soon picked up a few words of Chinese and her hostess tried English, both of which resulted in much laughter. Chinese was unlike any language Jess had ever heard before, and it confused her that one word could mean several different things depending on her tone of voice. She soon learned to imitate Mei exactly and proved better at this than Mei was at pronouncing English words.

Because they spent so much time together, looking after their children, Jess felt they were becoming friends. Mei also gave her some very useful tips, like how to tie Brice into a sling so that she could carry him and still keep her hands free for other things. Brice seemed to like it as well and often slept for hours like that while Jess paced the courtyard for exercise.

'He probably feels safe,' Killian said when she showed him. 'He can hear your heartbeat and it keeps him warm too, I should think.'

'Yes. It will be really useful once we're on the ship. Then I can walk around and still be able to hold onto things if it's windy without worrying about dropping him.' She handed him his son, who was thriving and putting on weight. Killian gazed at the baby as if he still couldn't believe his good fortune, and she smiled at this sight.

'What?' he said, catching sight of her expression.

'Nothing. It's just that I seem to remember you had quite a different reaction to babies when you first came to Gothenburg.'

Killian grinned. 'I'm still not interested in other people's children, but when it's your own, it's a different matter. He's just perfect, isn't he?'

Jess laughed. 'Of course he is.' She changed the subject. 'When the linguist came the other day he told me there's some sort of festival soon in honour of the god of fire. Have you heard of that?'

'Yes, apparently everyone hangs up lanterns and they make shapes out of them and there is light everywhere. It should be quite a spectacle.'

'Well, Mei has offered to let me go out and see it. She said we can go in a palanquin. That way hopefully no one will notice me. Do you think I should go?'

'I don't see why not. Keep your hair covered and people won't look twice at you if you're dressed the same as Mei. I can follow behind and keep an eye on your palanquin, just in case there's any trouble.'

'Thank you. I would so love to see it! I feel like I've been cooped up in here for too long.'

'That's understandable – you have.'

Farquhar felt as if he was being eaten alive by frustration. It gnawed at his insides and made him so restless he could barely sleep a wink, despite drinking huge quantities of *samfue*, a sort of Chinese brandy brewed with rice. Strictly speaking, this was forbidden to the foreigners because the Chinese believed it might encourage brawls. But Farquhar had found a Chinaman who was only too willing to supply him in secret and since there was nothing else to be had, he made do with that.

When he wasn't trying to drown his thoughts with liquor, he spent most of his waking hours prowling the streets. He hardly saw any of the wares on offer because he was constantly searching the crowds hoping to see Killian's wife. He knew where she was staying, but so far she hadn't set foot outside the door and he had no idea how to get inside.

As with most Chinese houses, Mr Li's home was long and thin, with the street end taken up by a booth selling porcelain. It was surrounded by other houses on all sides, and there seemed no way of reaching the back of it, short of going through someone else's house. Mr Li himself spent a lot of time away on business and had therefore hired someone to act as vendor on his behalf. Farquhar tried to talk to this man to see if it would be possible to bribe him, but the vendor only wanted to sell blue and white bowls. When Farquhar didn't show any interest in purchasing these, he simply turned to another customer.

Farquhar sometimes followed his cousin and watched from a distance while Killian wandered round, looking as pleased as punch. It made Farquhar's stomach curdle to see that expression of supreme contentedness. He wanted to wipe it off his cousin's face once and for all. Killian occasionally visited his wife, but never brought her outside, and Farquhar was beginning to despair of ever finding a way to see her.

Then John Ley told him about the coming festival.

'Everyone and his uncle will be out and about, I should think, just milling around and gawping. I saw it last time and it was fairly amusing. Helped to pass the time at any rate.'

Farquhar liked the sound of that 'everyone and his uncle'. It might mean that Killian's wife left the safety of her nest for at least a short while. If not, perhaps the rest of the occupants of Mr Li's house would leave her alone and vulnerable. He almost rubbed his hands together with glee, but restrained himself while in Ley's presence. The man probably thought him odd, but he didn't care. What he did was none of Ley's business.

On the night of the festival, he was out early and took up a position where he could watch the comings and goings of Mr Li's household. Sure enough, most of the servants soon trooped off, laughing and joking among themselves, leaving the house virtually empty. The vendor shut the booth early and left soon after dark. Mr Li himself came out and waited outside until two palanquins came down the street and stopped outside. He called out to someone inside, and two women came out, looking excited. They were both dressed in Chinese clothing, but to Farquhar, who was actively looking out for differences, one of the women immediately stood out.

Killian's wife. *Curse her!*

The women each had a child tied to their backs in a sling, but had no trouble entering the palanquins. Soon the little cavalcade moved off and Farquhar was just about to follow, when a movement to his right made him wait. Killian emerged from a doorway and walked behind the second palanquin, trying to look as if he had nothing to do with it, but it was obvious to Farquhar that he was watching it.

'Damn it all to hell,' Farquhar muttered.

Now what was he to do? He had never taken on Killian in a fight and won and he didn't think he would now either. Killian had always been bigger and stronger. With a deep sigh of frustration he accepted that he could only follow the group and hope the women would return to the house before everyone else, then he could strike somehow. It was his only chance.

Jess was enchanted. There was an atmosphere of celebration and it sounded like a thousand voices were speaking at once. Children ran back and forth, shrieking excitedly and comparing their little lanterns which all had different motifs. Hundreds of larger lanterns had been strung across the streets, almost forming a roof of light wherever they went. Many of the houses were lit up from within as well. Outside their doors, some people had placed figures made of paper – horses, humans, tigers and many others – and the whole scene seemed incredibly exotic to Jess, who drank in the sights.

Musicians played what sounded like plaintive tunes, but which must have been joyful because everyone seemed happy. Priests, dressed in long red robes of silk and tall hats, wandered the streets with incense burners and offerings. They went from house to house to bless them. Jess knew this was all in aid of placating the god of fire. The houses were all built so close together, fire was a hazard everyone feared and they hoped to be spared for another year.

When the palanquin stopped at one point because of the throng, Killian came up alongside it. 'Is all the noise bothering Brice?' he asked without actually looking at Jess.

She laughed. 'No, he's fast asleep. I think he'd sleep through an earthquake when his belly is full and his bottom clean.'

Killian's mouth twitched. 'Just as well. The ship is a noisy place and if he can sleep through this, he'll sleep well there too. Maybe he takes after his father?'

She heard the pride in his voice and felt happiness bubble up inside her. 'I doubt it,' she said to tease him. 'He looks more like my side of the family, he'll be a refined child.'

Killian snorted. 'Refined? Never! I'm going to teach him to be a fighter, not a namby-pamby sort.'

Jess smiled into the darkness. 'We'll see about that,' she said, but she knew that was what she wanted as well.

All too soon the palanquins turned back and stopped outside Li's house. Killian whispered a quick goodnight and melted into the crowds, while Li hustled Jess and Mei inside. They made their way up the stairs at the back of the house to feed the babies, who had by now woken up and were starting to grizzle. Both women were smiling broadly, pleased with their outing.

'Beautiful,' Jess said in Chinese – one of the new words she had learned – and nodded towards the outside world. Mei agreed and they settled down to nurse their children.

The rest of the house was unusually quiet and Jess guessed that Li had gone out again. He probably didn't want to miss the festivities now he'd done his duty by his wife and guest. She finished feeding Brice and burped him, then went to lie him down in the large tea chest she was using as his bed. Just as she was bending over, however, Mei's two dogs began to first growl, then bark in short, sharp bursts.

The little pets, who kept them company most days, were normally lazy in the extreme, and barely moved other than at mealtimes. Their squat, fluffy bodies were not used to exercise and their flat faces made it hard for them to breathe. They were very sweet and cuddly nonetheless and never aggressive. Now, however, they seemed on the verge of exploding with fury and wouldn't stop even though Mei kept shushing them.

'What's the matter?' Jess looked at Mei questioningly, but she frowned in puzzlement and shrugged.

'Let's go downstairs and look,' Jess said in English and gestured for Mei to follow her. She grabbed Brice and headed for the stairs, but when she opened the door she stopped with a gasp. Just below the stairs a fire raged, sending up clouds of smoke that made her cough instantly. She retreated into the room quickly, looking around for some means of putting the fire out.

Mei understood what she was doing and grabbed several covers off the bed and thrust them at Jess. She took them and handed her Brice in return. Then she drew in a deep breath, opened the door again and ran down to the bottom step, where she started to beat the fire with one of the covers. She threw the other one down and stamped on it, feeling it burning through her shoes, but she ignored the discomfort. She had to put the fire out or they would be trapped and die.

Coughing and spluttering, she managed it at last. Thankfully the fire hadn't had time to take hold properly and she saw to her horror that it must have been started deliberately. There was a pile of burnt cushions and door hangings on the floor by the stairs which had never been there before. If the dogs hadn't warned them, the fire would have flared up quickly and the flames would soon have engulfed the entire house.

Li came into the room from the opposite direction and stopped to stare at her, his eyes growing round with fear. He called out to his wife and Mei appeared at the top of the stairs, while Jess sat down on shaking legs. It had been a narrow escape.

She was alive and so was Brice, but who could possibly wish them dead? Dread settled in her stomach and for the first time since Brice's birth she was afraid.

'I really don't understand it,' Killian said with a worried frown. 'I've spoken to Li and to Campbell and as far as we know, we have no enemies. At least not to the extent they would want to kill us.'

There was something nagging at the back of his mind, but he couldn't think what it was and gave up trying for the moment.

'Didn't you say the Chinese call us *fan kwaes* – foreign devils? Perhaps there are some who really don't want us here.'

'Maybe, but it doesn't make sense. We are bringing them silver, making them rich, why should they mind? It's not as if we're staying for good. No, it's a mystery, but I'll keep my eyes and ears open. I think it might be best if you went back to the ship though. You'd be safer there among our own men.'

'Do you really think so?' Jess looked doubtful. 'We're closer to you here and surely now we know there's a threat, we can hire guards.'

'Yes, Li has already said he'll make sure you're guarded at all times. He's worried about his own wife being caught up in this. But still ...'

'Please, Killian. I want to stay here. It's much better for Brice not to be next to the water in a damp ship. Besides, I'll be spending more than enough time in that cramped cabin on the way home.'

'Very well, if you're sure?'

Jess nodded. 'I am. Li's guards will make me feel safer.' But not much, she added silently to herself.

Who wanted her dead?

Chapter Thirty-Two

Farquhar no longer slept at all. His brain gave him no respite from the murderous thoughts that swirled round inside his skull and he simply couldn't believe the women had escaped with their lives.

When he found the house empty, it had seemed like fate was on his side at last. With the two women shut into a room with only one escape route, they should have been burned alive or at the very least suffocated. Yet somehow they'd lived to tell the tale. He wanted to scream with frustration.

He thought up and discarded many different plans, but in the end there was only one that might work. He had to distract the guards, whom he had seen prowling outside the shop, and simply run inside and kill the bitch and her baby. He couldn't allow them to live. Even if he himself didn't survive this journey, he was going to make damned sure his daughters inherited Rosyth and not Killian or anyone of his blood.

It proved easier than he'd thought to distract the guards – he just started another fire late one evening outside the house next door by smashing a lantern against an awning. Everyone came running, while he hurried in the opposite direction and ducked into Li's house.

A serving woman came towards him, asking something in their infernal language, but he hit her hard and she crumpled to the floor. Before anyone else came to interfere, he headed for the staircase to the women's quarters and luck was with him again. When he threw open the door at the top of the stairs, the first thing he saw was Killian's wife, sitting on the bed cooing at her brat. There was no mistaking her, with her flaxen hair in a loose plait down her back.

'At last!' he cried, and pulled out a knife, rushing across the floor to lunge at her. She screamed, but before he could reach her, a pain shot through his leg and put him off his stride long enough for her to duck out of the way. He blinked and looked down, seeing a furry bundle with teeth that seemed to be attacking him. He cried out as the creature sank its sharp fangs into his calf one more time, then kicked out sending it flying. It landed with a whimper in a corner and went limp.

A bellow of female rage behind him alerted him to the presence of another woman, who must have been sitting out of the line of his vision. He turned to parry a blow she was aiming at his head with a heavy porcelain bowl. It struck his shoulder before falling to the floor, shattering in a shower of shards. He barely noticed. Enraged beyond reason now, he swivelled back to his original quarry. The blonde vixen was the only one he was interested in and the other woman could go to hell for all he cared.

To his surprise, she wasn't there any more and before he had time to turn his head to search for her, he heard her screaming, 'Take that, you whoreson!' A second before the world went black, he saw her out of the corner of his eye. She had a stool in her hands and was bringing it down on him, but there was no time to duck. He was helpless to prevent it from connecting with his skull.

Bitch! was his last thought and then he knew no more.

Jess stood panting over the man, the stool raised in case she'd need to hit him again, but he was out cold. She drew in a shuddering breath and registered the fact that Brice and Mei's son were both howling. Mei stood for several moments like a statue, staring at the intruder, before rushing to the corner to pick up her lifeless dog. After a short while, it whined and began to move. Jess was glad the man hadn't killed it.

'Killian,' Jess said. 'Mei, fetch Killian and Li.'

Mei nodded and headed for the stairs, ignoring her son's cries for once. Jess tried to block out the sound of Brice as well. She didn't dare move and kept her eyes fixed on the lunatic lying at her feet.

'Who are you?' she whispered. It was perfectly clear from his ginger hair and pale freckled skin that he wasn't Chinese and this surprised her most of all. Somehow she hadn't expected a fellow European to be the one harbouring a grudge against her and she couldn't understand it.

It seemed like hours before Killian and Li burst into the room, although it probably wasn't very long at all. Although Li rushed straight over to the man on the floor, Killian stopped dead and simply stared. 'I don't believe it,' he breathed. 'The whoreson!'

'What?' Jess said. 'You know this man?'

'Unfortunately, yes. He's my cousin.'

'Farquhar? You're not serious.'

'I'm afraid so.' He looked around, his mouth set in a tight line as if he was trying to stop himself from doing violence to the man even though he was already dead to the world. 'Do you have anything we can bind his hands with? He might wake up any moment and although I'd love to hit him, it's best if we just hand him over to the authorities. Otherwise I might be the one committing murder.'

Jess nodded and went to a clothes chest to find some belts. Li helped Killian tie Farquhar's wrists tightly and then looked at him, gesturing a question. Killian had picked up a few Chinese words as well and drew a little diagram in the air, saying, 'Man and man, brothers, son me, son him,' to indicate he and Farquhar were cousins. Li appeared to understand, although he still looked puzzled.

'I expect he's wondering why my cousin is trying to murder my wife,' Killian said. 'He'll have a deal of explaining to do when he wakes up.' He said the name of an official to Li, who shook his head and mentioned another. Then the Chinese man left the room, presumably to arrange to transport Farquhar to whoever was to take him into custody. 'This is a damnable business,' Killian muttered. 'Are you hurt?' he added to Jess, as if seeing her properly for the first time.

She was now trying to quiet Brice. The little boy was still upset that his cries had been ignored for so long and was having a hard time settling. 'No, just shaken.'

Killian went over to her and enveloped both her and the baby in a hard embrace. He buried his face in her shoulder. 'Dear God, but I want to tear him limb from limb for what he tried to do. What's the matter with the man? Why does he hate me, us, so much?'

'It must be jealousy, pure and simple. He can't be quite right in the head.' Jess sighed. 'What will happen to him now?' She glanced at Farquhar.

'I don't know. I'll have to go back to Campbell and find out. I need the linguist in order to make myself understood when I tell the authorities about this.' He stepped away from her and pushed his fingers through his hair distractedly. 'Can you tell me exactly what happened, please?'

Jess did, and soon after Li came back with several strong-looking men who carted Farquhar off. He started to come to and began to shout and swear, but everyone ignored him. Killian went over to Jess one more time and put his arm round her shoulder. 'You're sure he didn't harm you or Brice?'

'No, he didn't succeed.' She saw that he was torn between staying with her and going off to report what had occurred. 'Go,' she said. 'We'll be fine now he's under guard. Perhaps you can come back and see us tomorrow?'

'Of course I will.'

'Have you run completely mad?' John Ley was staring intently at the man who was officially in his care since he had come on the ship that was under his command. He looked as if he wished him at Jericho or possibly in hell, a sentiment echoed by Killian.

Farquhar said nothing. He just stared into space, the blue-grey eyes vacant, as if he was there in body only while his mind wandered elsewhere. His wide mouth hung open, although occasionally he muttered unintelligibly to himself.

'It's no use,' Killian muttered. 'I think he really has gone insane.'

'Well, what shall we do?' Ley asked, scowling now. 'The Chinese are saying he's my responsibility. If it was up to them he'd be executed straight away and I'm very tempted to let them do it, but I can't have that on my conscience. I could put him on trial on board my ship, but since this didn't happen while at sea, that doesn't seem a good option either. The only other alternative is to lock him up at the factory until we leave and transport him back to Ostend. You'd have to arrange for someone to pick him up there.'

Killian nodded. 'I suppose that might work. I could send word to my grandfather. He should sort out this mess since it's partly his fault for putting ideas in Farquhar's head.'

'You're not saying the old man put him up to this?' Ley looked horrified.

'No, no. I mean that if he had treated me the way a man normally treats his heir, Farquhar wouldn't have thought he had a chance to step into my shoes. Or that he was the rightful heir, not me.' He sighed. 'It's complicated, but trust me, it's indirectly my grandfather's fault.'

'Well, I'll take him into my custody and make sure he doesn't trouble you or your wife any more. It's only for two months, then hopefully we'll all be off for home.'

'Thank you, I appreciate your help.'

Killian threw one last glance over his shoulder at his cousin, but Farquhar was still lost in his own little world. There seemed no point jolting him out of it. Reality was obviously not to his liking.

The next few months passed almost in a blur and Killian felt as if he did nothing but look at tea, smell tea and watch others pack tea in chest after lead-lined chest. *Bohea*, *Pekoe*, *Souchong* and Green tea, all carefully weighed and stamped on by coolies, after he and Campbell had checked it to make sure it was of the quality they had contracted for. Inside the chests a second lining of paper added extra protection against humidity. Then it was covered with a piece of cotton material, a lead top and finally nailed shut by the carpenter before the whole chest was wrapped in oiled paper. Over and over again he watched this procedure. Hundreds of chests began to pile up in the courtyard of the factory and they all had to be brought indoors every evening just to be on the safe side. He was so sick of the stuff he refused to drink it.

Campbell was often annoyed with the merchants. 'They keep on trying to pass off inferior tea as top quality. Do they take me for a fool?' he muttered.

The only one who didn't was a man named Poan Key-qua, who seemed different from the rest and whose company Killian enjoyed. He had a longish face and a kind expression, unlike most of the others who often looked dissatisfied. He was also happy to answer Killian's many questions about China and its inhabitants.

Key-qua's perfectly trimmed moustache with pointy ends and an equally pointy goatee beard seemed to be the norm. He wore plain robes with embroidered panels on the chest and shoulders, together with a silk hat. Like most of his countrymen, he had high rounded cheekbones and a small, fairly broad nose and of course the obligatory long pigtail down his back. At first, the merchant's looks and clothing seemed very exotic to Killian, but he soon became used to it. He even bought a silk robe like Key-qua's for himself, finding it very comfortable and soft.

'He's the only one I trust,' Campbell said more than once. 'The rest of them are deceitful wretches.' Killian considered this too sweeping a statement, but there was definitely a lot of cheating going on. He and Campbell had to be constantly on their guard.

They often ate a meal with Key-qua before beginning the day's tea packing, sitting in a small courtyard outside his dining room if the weather was fine. It was very pleasant, a paved area filled with tiny trees, flowers and herbs in porcelain pots. There was even a glass bowl with little gold and silver fishes.

Chinese food was like nothing he'd ever eaten before, but as usual Killian enjoyed every morsel he ate. 'This is delicious,' he told the man. Key-qua seemed pleased that he appreciated what he was given.

The silks they had ordered started to trickle in and were sent down to the ship at Whampoa after they had bought as much porcelain as they wanted.

'It's not the right quality, but we simply can't wait any longer,' Campbell was heard to complain, but the blue and white china looked perfectly fine to Killian.

He was also very pleased with the silks, especially the ones chosen by Jess.

'You have an eye for colour and patterns,' he told her, making her smile with pleasure. 'Campbell ordered mostly taffetas, paduasoys and damask of different colours, as well as striped satin and some velvet. I think we've done better.'

'I hope so.'

Killian and Jess had opted for floral patterns and silks with embroidery. Crimson was the most expensive, but they had bought some anyway as they thought it would fetch a good price at home. They had also ordered some finished products like handkerchiefs and night caps, which Jess thought would be in high demand.

All in all, Killian thought they would do quite well out of this venture and he couldn't wait to see his grandfather's face when he told him he was a rich man in his own right.

The weather had turned colder, but a Chinese winter seemed less severe than a Swedish one and didn't cause them any hardship. Killian didn't see much of Jess and Brice, but knew they were safe and warm with Li and Mei. Now that Farquhar was under lock and key, there was no need to fret about them. Still, he was very much looking forward to going home so that he could spend more time with his family.

The last few days before their proposed departure date were even busier than usual. Killian had to concentrate really hard on the ledger he was keeping in order to record what had been sent down to the ship and what still needed to go. There was a Chinese man, commonly called the 'Comprador', who acted as a sort of accountant or steward on behalf of the Swedes. He had already added everything up, but Campbell wanted to make sure the man had done it correctly.

'Could you please go through it all one more time?' he asked Killian.

'Yes, of course.' Killian didn't mind. He admired the way Campbell always scrutinised everything and tried to anticipate any difficulties and prepare himself with great attention to detail in order to avoid them. It seemed to Killian exactly the way the person responsible for an expedition such as this should behave.

He sat in a small room overlooking the courtyard and was engrossed in his task, checking and re-checking his figures just to make sure they were right. One of the coolies had to say his name twice before he looked up. 'Oh, I'm sorry?'

'Man to see you,' he said. Killian realised this was the coolie who guarded the door to the street. He spoke a few words of English, enough to announce guests.

'To see me? Right, well, send him in.'

Killian wondered who it could be, but guessed it was either Li or perhaps one of the Ostenders. He didn't know anyone else, unless one of the merchants had come to offer him some last minute bargains. He looked up again when a voice said, 'I'm glad to see they work you hard, cousin. It's no more than you deserve.'

Killian swallowed a gasp and shot to his feet. Standing in the courtyard was none other than Farquhar, his pale eyes lit with a murderous light while he clutched a long knife in one hand. The reddish hair gleamed dully in the sunlight. 'Farquhar? How did you get out? I thought ...'

Farquhar laughed, a hollow sound entirely without humour. 'You thought they could keep me locked up, did you? You should have known better. It never worked when we were young, did it. I always managed to get out somehow, like I did today.'

Killian had to admit that was true, but he hadn't thought there was anyone to blackmail or bribe here in China. Obviously he'd been wrong.

'Well, you should have stayed where you were,' he said, anger flooding through him. 'You have no business here.'

'Ah, but that's where you're wrong, cousin. I have to kill you before you can escape me again and when I've done that, I'm going after your silly bitch of a wife. This time, she won't get away, I'll make sure of that, and neither will your brat.'

Killian didn't wait to hear any more, because a red mist of fury rose up in front of his eyes and he just wanted to shut Farquhar up. He didn't think he could stand to ever hear that hateful voice again, nor see the madness lurking in his cousin's eyes. This had to stop.

Killian threw himself at Farquhar, who was taken by surprise, but sidestepped at the last moment. He slashed wildly with the knife, forcing Killian to retreat, but the Chinese guard had heard the commotion and came rushing into the courtyard. One look showed him Killian's predicament, and he called out, 'Here!' before throwing Killian the bamboo pole he kept with him for defensive purposes. It wasn't perfect, but it was better than nothing.

Back and forth across the courtyard, the two of them moved, like dancers following an intricate set of steps. Killian was aware of others coming running to see what was going on, but when someone shouted out an offer of help, he waved them away. He would deal with his cousin and he would do it now.

'As always, you're too cowardly to fight me with your fists, eh?' he taunted Farquhar. 'You were a snivelling brat, hiding behind grandfather's coat tails and now you're hiding behind a knife. It's no more than I would expect.'

'Shut your mouth,' Farquhar snarled, but Killian's taunts threw him off balance and with a few quick thrusts of the bamboo pole, Killian managed to knock the knife out of his hand. Farquhar howled with frustration and launched himself at his cousin, fists at the ready.

Madness seemed to give him strength, but Killian had fought him many times before and knew where his weaknesses lay. He allowed him to get in a few punches, then sidestepped and landed a blow on the side of Farquhar's head. This was quickly followed by a punch in the gut that had him doubling over. He straightened up and tried to fight back, but Killian could see that his cousin was tiring now. Being locked up for the best part of two months had weakened him, and taken its toll on his muscles.

He waited a little while longer, making Farquhar chase him round the courtyard to tire him. Then he stopped abruptly and began to rain blows on his face, head and upper body. 'This is for trying to kill my wife,' he panted, hitting as hard as he could, 'this is for my son, and this,' he aimed a particularly vicious punch at Farquhar's jaw, 'is for all the harm you've done me.'

That last blow finished Farquhar off. His knees buckled and his eyes disappeared upwards until only the whites were showing, and then he fell forward. Killian bent over, panting hard from the exertion and from sheer relief. Graham, the second supercargo came and put a hand on his shoulder. 'Are you all right, Kinross?'

'Yes, thank you. I am now.'

'What do we do with him?'

'He's to be bound and taken to the Ostenders. I'll accompany him myself to make sure they lock him up properly this time. I'm afraid he's completely insane.'

Graham nodded. 'I'll come with you.' He turned to the coolie by the gate. 'You there, fetch us a palanquin please and quickly.'

Chapter Thirty-Three

It was with enormous relief that Jess and Killian boarded the ship on the sixth of January to begin the journey home. The horrifying attacks by Farquhar had put a damper on an otherwise enjoyable stay in Canton and they were glad to put it all behind them.

'I'll miss Mei and her little boy,' Jess said, waving to Li and his wife who had come downriver to say goodbye, 'but it will be wonderful to be with people I can talk to properly.'

'Yes, it's been interesting to say the least, but I don't think I'll be coming back in a hurry.' Li, pleased with the pair of binoculars and silver time piece Killian had given him as a thank you for looking after Jess and his son, had urged him to return soon, but Killian had no wish to do so. 'If we want to trade with China, I suggest we find a reliable supercargo to do it for us or perhaps we should stick to merely investing in these ventures.'

'Yes, now all we have to do is reach home safely. Let's hope we do so quickly.'

Jess' prayers were not answered immediately, however. Although they made good time across the China Sea, things began to go wrong as soon as they passed into the Sunda Strait. There they were surprised to find themselves blockaded by seven Dutch ships, who seemed hell-bent on hindering them from continuing their journey. Jess shivered at the sight of their menacing presence and tried not to imagine what this might mean.

Campbell ordered the Swedish flag to be hoisted and the anchor dropped, waiting to see what the Dutch would do, but nothing happened.

'Very well, let's try and sail away quietly during the night under cover of darkness then,' he said, but the Dutch caught up with them the following day fairly easily. Campbell ordered the ship to anchor yet again. Tired of this cat and mouse game, Campbell then commanded the second mate, Mr Bremer to take the launch over to the Dutch ships and ask why they were following them. Bremer took with him copies of their passes and Campbell's official letter showing that he was the Swedish Minister Plenipotentiary and Envoy to the Emperor of China, stamped and signed by the King of Sweden himself.

'That ought to show them,' Campbell muttered, but Killian wasn't so sure. There was obviously something wrong here.

He was proved right when Bremer never returned, and during the night they were surrounded by Dutch ships so they couldn't try to escape again. Finally, the next morning, the launch came back with orders for all the Swedish crewmen to go to the Dutch ships, except the captain and the supercargos. As a substitute, the Dutch sent over their own sailors and a captain to help sail the ship, although where to they didn't say.

'Must you go?' Jess asked anxiously, when Killian came to tell her what was happening. Brice grizzled as if he too sensed something was wrong.

'I'm afraid so, but I hope I'll be back soon.'

'Be careful and don't do anything rash. If anything should happen to you I … that is we …' She couldn't finish the sentence. There was so much she wanted to say to him and now she was afraid she'd never get the chance. They had shared a cabin since leaving Canton, but she hadn't yet worked up the courage to tell him she wanted him to be her husband in every sense of the word. And now perhaps it was too late.

'Don't worry. I will see you soon.' He gave her a quick kiss on the mouth, lingering a little too long as if promising more to come. She had to be content with that, but it wasn't nearly enough.

Campbell summoned her to his cabin soon after the crew had left. Mr Graham, the second supercargo, was with him and they both looked grave.

Campbell fixed her with his blue gaze in a direct, but not unkind way. 'Mrs Kinross, I understand you are of Dutch extraction and presumably speak their language. I just wanted to warn you not to let them know that, under any circumstances, because one of their accusations is they think we're harbouring Hollanders on board. I speak Dutch myself, but I'll not admit it unless I have to. I shall address them in Swedish.'

'Is that what this is all about?'

'Perhaps, although I think it has more to do with the Ostend company, which was officially dissolved last year. The Dutch didn't want competition from them and they suspect we've been sent out by the Ostenders, using the Swedish flag as a cover. The only two ships who had official permission to sail were the ones we encountered in Canton. It's all a lot of nonsense, and so I shall tell them. I've demanded to see the governor-general in Batavia and they're taking me there tomorrow.'

'And what of me and my son?'

'I'm afraid you'll have to stay here.' He gestured towards Graham, who had remained silent throughout. 'No need to fret, I shall leave the other supercargos here to watch over you. Now why don't you take a turn about the deck with Graham here? You look as though a bit of fresh air might do you good.'

Graham immediately came forward and offered his arm.

'I'd be happy to escort you, Mrs Kinross,' he said politely.

Jess didn't much feel like returning to her cramped cabin, and she liked the pleasant, friendly Graham, so she agreed. 'Thank you, that's very kind.' She nodded at Campbell. 'I wish you luck, sir.'

With Brice asleep in his sling, she ambled slowly from one end of the ship to the other with Graham. Some of the new Dutch crew members paused in their tasks to follow them with their eyes, and stared at Jess in particular. She heard one exclaim '*Godverdamme!*' – 'God damn it' – in surprise and assumed they hadn't expected to find a woman on board. No one spoke to them though, which was a relief.

'I do hope Mr Campbell is able to sort this out soon,' Jess said, trying to quell her anxiety.

'Don't worry. I have every confidence in him,' Graham replied. 'Mr Campbell will have us out of here in no time, you'll see.'

Jess sincerely hoped he was right.

She retired to her cabin, where she paced endlessly with Brice just to have something to do, but she was soon heartily sick of being confined. When Mr Graham came and offered to take her for another stroll after supper, she was more than happy to go with him.

'Has Mr Campbell gone yet?' she asked as they mounted the steps up to the main deck.

'No, he's leaving early tomorrow morning. He's hoping to speak to the Dutch governor-general as soon as he arrives in Batavia, so with a bit of luck we should be able to leave soon.'

She took his arm, as before, and they made their way to the fore. Along the way they passed a group of Dutch sailors who assessed Jess openly this time. She felt as if their eyes were boring into her back, which was very disconcerting and made her feel extremely uncomfortable. She took a deep breath and ignored them.

'She's a tasty piece and no mistake,' she heard one of them say in his own language as soon as she and Graham had gone past. The others chuckled and murmured in agreement.

'Yes, the captain ought to let us have some sport with her. Shall we ask him?'

'No point. He probably wants her for himself first, selfish whoreson!'

Jess felt her spine stiffen with outrage, but tried to keep her emotions under control. She gritted her teeth and although she understood every word, she pretended she hadn't heard, just as Mr Campbell had instructed. She couldn't entirely suppress a shudder, however, and Graham noticed.

'Are you cold, Mrs Kinross?' he enquired.

'No, no, I'm fine, thank you.' It was a balmy night with only a slight breeze and although she'd brought a shawl, it wasn't needed. Brice, on her back, acted as a sort of heater too, his tiny body snug against hers.

'I won't keep you up here for too long. Wouldn't want the little one to catch a chill.'

'I don't think there's any danger of that, but we might as well go to bed early I suppose.' Jess glanced towards the Dutchmen, but quickly averted her gaze when she found their eyes still resting on her. The sooner she was safe in her cabin, the better, she thought.

On the way back to the stairs, someone called out 'Mind that rope!' and Jess paused for a fraction of an instant before she remembered that he couldn't possibly be speaking to her. She hurried after Graham and breathed a sigh of relief when the bar was safely across her door.

By the afternoon of the following day, Jess was becoming seriously worried. There had been no word from Campbell and all was quiet on board the ship. It seemed like the calm before a storm, and Jess' stomach was turning itself into knots as she tried not to think about what might be happening to Killian. A soft knock on the door made her almost jump out of her skin, but she breathed a sigh of relief when she heard a familiar voice outside.

'Mrs Kinross? It's only me, Graham.'

Jess opened the cabin door a fraction. 'Yes? Has something happened?'

'No, no news as yet, I'm afraid. I just thought you might like to take another walk up on deck for a breath of fresh air?'

'Er, I don't know ...' Jess hesitated, remembering the crewmen of the night before, but she had been going nearly mad in the tiny cabin and a short outing sounded extremely tempting.

'It should be perfectly safe.' Mr Graham smiled. 'It's not as if we're prisoners, after all.'

'Well, it's very kind of you,' Jess said. 'It is rather stifling in here, I must admit.' He was right, no one had threatened them openly in any way. The Dutchmen didn't know she understood their idle talk.

Since Brice was awake this time, she carried him in her arms and followed Mr Graham up onto the deck. The Dutch captain who was supposedly looking after the ship in Campbell's absence was nowhere to be seen, but some of his crew members stood by the ship's railing again. Jess didn't know if they were the same ones, but either way, their presence made her uncomfortable. They studied her as she passed with the Englishman, but said nothing. Even so, the way they seemed to devour her with their eyes made her feel uneasy, particularly the gaze of a tall blond man who seemed to be their unofficial leader. A shiver darted through her and she stepped closer to Mr Graham.

'Are you sure this is a good idea?' she whispered. 'Those men don't look too friendly today. Perhaps it would be better if I just stayed in the cabin.'

'No, no, they can't very well do anything to you in broad daylight. The captain assured Mr Campbell we would all be perfectly safe in his absence.'

Jess remained unconvinced, but Mr Graham started walking round the deck and she didn't want to stand around by herself, so she followed him reluctantly. They made it from one end of the ship to the other without anyone bothering them, and then stopped to admire the view. The ship was anchored near a lush, green island, and it was a peaceful scene. Jess had just started to relax when she heard raucous laughter from the group of Dutchmen.

'I've a good mind to bed her, captain's permission or not,' Jess heard one of the men say with a lascivious chuckle. 'Though she looks to be the haughty kind, so she'd need some incentive no doubt.'

The others guffawed and suggested various lewd enticements that may or may not work. Jess concentrated on the view and hoped the colour in her cheeks could be attributed to the heat rather than embarrassment at their words. As long as it was just banter among the men, she had nothing to fear, she told herself.

'Ah, but I reckon the best way would be to threaten her son,' one of the sailors put in. 'Pretend to throw the child overboard and the bitch would do whatever you asked.'

'Yes, shark fodder! Although the sharks won't thank you for such a tiny morsel. Still, better than nothing, eh?' They all laughed at that quip as though they found it hilarious.

Jess froze and had to struggle not to turn around and snarl angrily at the crew men. Had they no shame? How could they even joke about something like that?

'Mr Graham, would you be so kind as to escort me back

to my cabin now please?' she said as evenly as she could to her companion. 'I do believe the heat down there is preferable to the actual sunlight after all.'

'Yes, of course. As you wish.'

They set off towards the stairs, but just before reaching them, their route was intercepted by the blond man. 'Going below so soon?' he asked in accented English, his eyes narrowed as he stared hard at Jess.

'Yes, the heat is too much for me, I'm afraid.' Jess fanned herself with one hand in exaggerated fashion.

'But you only just emerged, *Mevrouw*. I think you ought to stay a bit longer.'

Jess frowned at him. 'Excuse me, but I need to go and feed my son, if you don't mind.' She tried her best to stay calm, but her heart was beating uncomfortably fast and Brice must have sensed it, because he started to grizzle.

'You understood me, didn't you,' the man said.

'I'm sorry?' Jess felt fear churning inside her and settling like a heavy stone in her stomach.

'Don't try to fool me,' the man sneered in Dutch. 'I was watching you and you reacted when I said I'd hurt your brat. And last night, you heard the man yelling at you to watch out. Don't try to deny it, I saw you hesitate.'

'I don't speak your language so I have no idea what you just said,' Jess insisted in English. 'Now kindly let me go and see to my son.'

'I say, what's going on?' Graham protested. He'd been watching the exchange with a frown and finally found his tongue. 'My good man, this lady is Swedish. She hasn't the faintest idea what you're on about.'

The man ignored him and continued speaking Dutch, fixing his gaze on Brice. 'Tell me the truth, woman, or I'm going to wring his scrawny little neck.' Before Jess had time to move, he had reached out with lightning speed and put his huge hands round Brice's tiny neck. Jess cried out and went rigid with sheer terror. She forced her limbs to move and tried to push the man away, but he didn't let go of the baby and she realised there was nothing she could do without hurting Brice. She'd never felt so helpless in all her life and bile rose in her throat.

'Whoreson!' she hissed. 'Let go of him!'

'For the love of God, man, what are you doing? Are you insane?' Mr Graham came to her assistance and tried in his turn to get the man to let go of the child. But the blond man was much bigger and just pushed him out of the way with one brawny arm. Mr Graham stumbled on a huge coil of rope right behind him and fell headlong onto the deck, banging his head on the planking.

The baby started screaming, his little face turning bright red. 'Stop it! You're hurting him!' Jess screeched at the man. Panic gripped her and she tried to make her petrified brain come up with some way of rescuing her child without jeopardising her own situation.

'Not until you tell me the truth.' His eyes bore into hers with uncompromising fire and Jess knew he meant every word. She had no option but to do as he said or Brice would die. There was no way she was going to let that happen if she could prevent it.

'Very well,' she admitted, 'I understand a few words of Dutch and I heard you say something about a baby and throwing. That's all. There's only one baby here, so naturally I was concerned. Now let go of my son or I'm going to report you to your captain.' She glared at him, willing him to believe her.

The man took his hands away at last, but he was smirking now and Jess felt physically sick with fear, her legs and hands shaking.

'I think you're still lying, but we'll let the captain decide.

I believe the governor-general will want a word with you.'

'Don't be ridiculous. I'm not that important.' Jess had to speak loudly to be heard over Brice's wails since the baby was now almost hysterical.

'We'll see, won't we.' The man smiled again and leaned close to add, 'Unless you'd like to be extra nice to me? Then perhaps I'll keep my mouth shut.'

Jess shuddered and stepped away from him. 'Never.' She'd rather take her chances with the captain and the governor-general. 'Good day to you.'

Before he had time to grab hold of either her or the baby again, she rushed down the steps and tore into the cabin, pushing the bar firmly into place.

It took her a long time to calm herself and Brice, and even when he was quiet again at last, she couldn't stop trembling. She stroked his fuzzy head, the hair now almost as light as her own, and kissed his soft cheek, holding him close. 'I won't let them hurt you, my sweet, never fear,' she told him. But although he stared trustingly at her with his big blue eyes, so like those of his father, the truth was she didn't know how she was to keep him safe. If those men really tried to harm him, what chance did she stand?

Later that afternoon, she wasn't surprised to be ordered up on deck by the captain. 'Madam, you are under arrest and I'm taking you to shore,' he said through the cabin door, sounding very stern. 'Make no mistake, I will have my men batter this door down if you don't come of your own free will. Now pack a few essentials. You have five minutes.'

Jess knew there was no point arguing. Quickly, she stuffed what she would need into a bundle before tying Brice to her chest in his sling. He grizzled, still upset from the rough handling he'd received earlier, but she tried to shush him and followed the captain up to the main deck. A terrified-looking Mr Graham came rushing after them and when he saw her head for the railing and start to climb down to a smaller boat, he cried out, 'Where are you going? What's going on?'

'They think I'm Dutch, but don't worry, I'll soon put them right,' she replied with more confidence than she felt.

But how exactly was she to convince them?

Chapter Thirty-Four

She was taken to the walled town of Batavia and despite the dangerous situation she found herself in, she looked around with fascination at this strange city. Even though it was in the Far East, it looked almost entirely Dutch. Rows of gabled brick houses faced tree-lined canals, laid out in a straight grid just like the ones in Gothenburg. It was obvious Batavia had also been modelled on Amsterdam, and it felt almost surreal to Jess to be in such a familiar environment so far from home.

They approached from the sea and she couldn't fail to notice the massive shoreline fortress that dominated the surrounding area. Now it seemed that was to be her destination. She began to imagine herself and Brice rotting in some damp dungeon underneath the fort, but tried to suppress such thoughts. She needed to keep her wits about her and she knew that panicking would only paralyse her brain.

'Why are you taking me there?' she demanded to know, nodding in the direction of the fortress.

'It's where the governor-general is housed,' the captain replied, and although he wouldn't tell her any more, that was enough to calm Jess slightly. If she was at least given the chance to speak to the governor-general, she might be able to persuade him somehow that she was Swedish.

The place was teeming with people, and she gathered that other senior officials, as well as an entire garrison, lived at the fort. The captain handed her over to two guards and told them to put her in a locked room somewhere.

'I shall go and apprise the governor-general of your

presence,' he said to Jess. 'He's a very busy man, however, so it may be some time before he can deal with you.'

Jess hoped that meant hours of kicking her heels, rather than days, but as she went with the two guards, she didn't hold out much hope.

Killian stared in disgust at the bowl of food in front of him, which contained nothing but a small amount of rice and some old pork that was tougher than shoe leather. He wondered how on earth any man was supposed to survive on such meagre rations, let alone be able to do a day's work, but he didn't complain. Some of the other crew members had already tried that and been flogged for their trouble. Others had received the same severe punishment for barely any reason at all, and Killian could only hope Mr Campbell managed to talk them out of this dangerous situation before matters turned even worse.

He became aware of sniggering among some of the Dutchmen who were standing guard over the prisoners. He tried to listen to what they were saying, but although his Swedish was now very good, he found Dutch almost impossible to understand. He turned to the Swedish sailor sitting next to him and whispered, 'What are they finding so amusing, Almroth? They seem very pleased with themselves.'

Almroth looked slightly uncomfortable, but he was a forthright man and so he muttered, 'They're saying one of our women's been taken off the ship and into custody at Batavia. I think she's to be tried before the governor-general.'

'What?' Killian felt his mouth go dry. There was only one woman on board the *Friedericus Rex* and that was Jessamijn. How could she possibly have been arrested? This had nothing to do with her.

The thought of Jess, and presumably Brice too, in the sort of care he was on the receiving end of here made his insides turn to ice. Then he saw red. Without thinking about any consequences, he stood up with a bellow of rage. This had gone too far. Jessamijn hadn't done any harm and she had to be saved, no matter what.

He threw himself into the middle of the group of guards and attacked, closely followed by Adair who'd been watching and listening as usual. The youth had filled out a lot in the last few months and was handy with his fists. White-hot anger gave Killian extra strength, and having the element of surprise helped as well. Even so, it was a desperate struggle, but one he was determined to win.

Anything else was unthinkable.

Jess spent the night sitting on the hard floor of the little cell she had been taken to. She didn't dare fall asleep on the wooden bench which was all the furniture the small, airless space contained. She was afraid that if she lay down on the bench, Brice might fall off and she couldn't bear to think of him being hurt or worse. The place stank of excrement, vomit and rotting substances, but although this bothered her at first, she soon grew used to it. She found it harder to adapt to her uncomfortable position with Brice sleeping on her lap. Having only nodded off occasionally, she was in no mood to speak to anyone the following morning. The two guards who returned took no notice and ordered her to follow them.

She was taken to a grand room with large windows overlooking the bay, and after having waited a few moments, a man came walking in with brisk steps. He bowed, dismissed the guards and waited until they had left before addressing her.

'I am Dirk van Cloon, the Governor-General of Batavia, and I understand you claim to be a Mrs Kinross?' He spoke in Dutch and Jess saw no point in pretending she didn't understand. This man wasn't stupid and if she was to make him see that she wasn't a threat to him, she had to stick to the truth.

'I don't have to claim anything,' she said firmly, 'I *am* Mrs Kinross, Jessamijn Kinross. My husband is a former Scotsman, assistant to Mr Campbell, and we are all good citizens of Sweden, despite our varied backgrounds.'

'And yet you speak fluent Dutch and have a Dutch name.'

'I didn't know it was a crime to have a Dutch father,' she replied waspishly. 'Mine moved to Sweden when I was only a baby, but naturally he taught me his own language. I speak fluent English as well, but that doesn't make me English.'

He smiled fleetingly, acknowledging that she had a point. 'I'm sorry to have inconvenienced you then,' he said. 'Captain Backer is somewhat, shall we say, overzealous? We had been given information that Mr Campbell's ship was an interloper, an Ostend ship flying Swedish colours, and of course we had to find out whether this was the truth.'

'You don't believe that now?'

Mr van Cloon shook his head. 'No. I have spoken to Mr Campbell and read through his official papers. All seems to be in order and I have apologised to him as well. I do hope you can forgive us, but one can't be too careful. Is there anything I can offer you as compensation? I understand you may have had a less than comfortable night?'

'You could have my husband freed. He was taken away with the others when Captain Backer boarded us.'

'They will all be freed as soon as possible, including your husband. I ...'

Mr van Cloon was cut off in mid-sentence as a commotion broke out just outside the room and the door was thrown open. Five men came tumbling in, two of them landing on the floor, while one shouted in Swedish, 'I demand to see the governor-general. This is an outrage. Women and children should not be involved in any hostilities, and ...' The rest of his words were silenced by a blow.

'Killian!' Jess rushed over to the group and clouted the man who had just hit her husband. 'Leave him be, you oaf. And Adair, what are you doing here?'

The Dutchman turned to her in confusion, obviously not sure whether he should defend himself against a woman holding a baby. Meanwhile, Killian looked up from the floor and blinked, then a smile spread over his features.

'Jessamijn, by all that's holy. Thank the Lord, you're all right,' he muttered, trying to stand up. 'And Brice?'

'He's fine, we're both fine, but what are you doing here? I thought ...'

Before anyone could say anything else, Mr van Cloon's raised voice cut across everything else, icy with anger. 'What is the meaning of this? I thought I asked not to be disturbed. And can not three men subdue one man and a boy? What do I employ you for?'

'I'm sorry sir, but they escaped from the ship where they were being held and we've been chasing them ever since.'

'Do I gather this is your husband, Mrs Kinross?'

Jess nodded and held onto Killian's arm, despite the fact that one of the guards now had him in a firm grip on the other. 'Yes, it is.'

'May I ask why you have come, Mr Kinross?' Mr van Cloon looked Killian up and down with a scowl. He wasn't a pretty sight, dirty and dishevelled with quite a few bruises and one especially nasty-looking black eye. Adair didn't look much better. Jessamijn translated his words for her husband, who replied in Swedish.

'I've come for my wife. I don't care what you do to the rest of us, but a woman and child should be kept out of it. They are innocent of any wrong doing. Please let me take her place, whatever it is she's accused of.'

'Translate for me too please, Mrs Kinross,' van Cloon ordered tersely. 'I find the Swedish tongue somewhat difficult to follow.' Jess did so. 'There is no need, Mr Kinross. Your wife is free to go. I agree with your views entirely and although I admire your courage in trying to reach me to plead your case, I would like to know how you and the boy escaped from a well-guarded ship? And how on earth did you even know about your wife being here?'

Killian shrugged. 'The escape was easy. We, er ... hit a few people and jumped into a dinghy that was tied to the ship, then rowed as fast as we could. It took your men a while to lower the pinnace, so we had a head start. As for how I knew, the men guarding us were laughing about the fact that a woman had been found on board the *Friedericus Rex* and taken ashore. Since there was only one woman on that ship, I knew it had to be my wife.'

Governor-General van Cloon drew in a deep breath. 'Very well. I must say I've had enough of Swedes – or Scotsmen whichever you prefer – for one morning.' He turned to the guards. 'These people are free to go. Please convey them to their ship. And no more violence, that's an order.'

As if by tacit agreement, they said nothing on the way back, but when Killian took Jess' hand, she hung onto it as if she'd never let go again. She still couldn't believe everything had been so easily resolved, and could only be extremely grateful. Killian winced a few times and Adair clutched his head, muttering to himself. Jess wondered what they'd gone through in order to reach her. She longed to tend Killian's wounds, but had to wait a little while longer.

They found the ship mostly deserted, with only a few Dutchmen posted as guards. The blond man was nowhere to be seen, which was a relief. They made their way down to their cabin straight away after sending Adair off to his hammock. As soon as they were inside, Killian bolted the door while Jess put Brice down in his makeshift crib. Then she turned around and threw her arms around Killian's neck.

'Oh, Killian, I'm so glad you're safe. I've been so worried, I thought I'd never see you again.' Her eyes filled with tears and she tried to blink them away. She put up a hand to touch his bruised cheek. 'What did they do to you?'

Killian smiled and put his arms around her, holding her tight. 'I'm fine. A few scratches that's all, but did it really matter to you I might not come back?' He searched her eyes with his gaze.

'Of course it did. I ...' Although she knew without a doubt that she loved him, she still couldn't get the words out. What if he just laughed at her? He had only married her for convenience after all.

'Could it be you love me just a little, my wife?' The old teasing note was back in his voice and she felt herself blush.

'It could be, but I know it wasn't part of the bargain we struck ...'

'To hell with the bargain! Jessamijn, sweetheart, please tell me the truth, for so help me God, I love you more than I can say and I don't think I can bear it if you don't love me back.'

She stared at him, surprised at the vehemence in his voice. 'You ... you do? Well, of course I love you. I have done from the start, only I was too afraid to tell you. I didn't think you'd want to hear that.'

Killian groaned. 'Of all the hare-brained ... why wouldn't I? I realised early on I didn't want to follow your silly agreement, but you were so adamant I had no choice.' He grinned at her. 'Well, now we can make up for lost time and be damned to everyone on this ship.'

'What do you mean?' Her question ended on a little squeak, since Killian began to kiss her deeply and passionately until she felt as if her legs were melting. He ran his hands down her back and cupped her behind, pushing her close so she was in no doubt as to what he wanted, and she gasped.

'Killian, someone might come.'

'Let them. I don't care if the entire world watches. I've waited long enough. Please tell me you've recovered enough from childbirth?'

'Yes, of course I have. It's been four months or more, but ...'

He cut her off with another kiss and this time he didn't let up until she was long past making any more protests. When he carried her to a bunk and pushed her skirts up, she was only too happy to help him. Their only concession to propriety was to stifle each others' cries of pleasure with searing kisses.

Afterwards, she lay in his arms in the cramped bunk, sated and content as never before. 'I'm sorry for lying to you,' she whispered.

'Hmm? About what?'

'I did enjoy your lovemaking that first time. Too much, in fact. That's what frightened me. All you'd have to do was make me desire you and I'd do anything you asked. Like Mama with Robert. I didn't want you to have that sort of control over me.'

Killian started to laugh and hugged her close. 'You really are a goose sometimes,' he chuckled. 'Haven't you noticed by now that you have the same hold over me? Just a brush of those luscious lips over mine and I'm on fire. I'll do anything for you.'

She blinked at him, dumbfounded by this revelation. 'Really? I'd never thought of that.'

'Well, you'd better believe it. And speaking of luscious mouths ...' He bent to kiss her again.

'But we just ...'

'That was at least ten minutes ago. I told you, I've waited a long time.'

He didn't have to work very hard to persuade her, thus proving both their points.

Chapter Thirty-Five

At last they were able to set sail for home, but because of the delay caused by the Dutch, they almost missed the necessary trade winds and had a miserably long journey. It seemed to everyone on board as though it would never end and even the home stretch across the North Sea went unbearably slowly. Only one incident roused them from the general despondency – as they reached the passage between the Orkney and Shetland islands, a rather familiar ship was sighted.

A sailor came running to find Campbell. 'You wouldn't believe who it is, sir,' he panted, 'none other than the *Hertogh van Lorreynen.* The Ostenders!'

'You're joking?' Campbell and Killian went up on deck and sure enough, there was the ship which they had last seen in Canton. Killian watched while they sailed near enough to exchange news and a feeling of dread came over him. Somewhere on that ship was his cousin and soon Killian would have to write to his grandfather to ask him to make arrangements to collect Farquhar from Ostend. It wasn't something he was looking forward to.

John Ley, the first supercargo, was on deck and shouted greetings to Campbell.

'What an extraordinary coincidence! I thought you long home as you left before us.'

'We were detained in Batavia. It's a long story, won't bore you with the details. Most inconvenient though. And what of you, have you had a good journey?'

'The usual. We've lost a lot of men to various illnesses and I'm sorry to have to report that our prisoner passed away two weeks ago. Died of dysentery, although I think in part he willed it on himself. Refused to eat for much of the time, so he was already weak. Nothing we could do for him, I'm afraid.'

Campbell looked at Killian, who swallowed hard and tried not to show any emotion at this news. 'Thank you for letting me know,' he called over to Ley. 'I'll tell my grandfather as soon as I can.'

There seemed nothing more to say, and the two ships sailed on in different directions, while Killian went down to the cabin to share the news with Jess.

'I feel as if a weight has been lifted from my mind, but at the same time I'm filled with sadness,' he said. 'It should never have gone this far. I'm sure we could have come to some agreement.'

Jess put an arm round him and leaned her head on his shoulder. 'But he wouldn't have been satisfied with that. For him it was all or nothing. Some people are like that, there's nothing you can do to change them.'

'Yes, I suppose you're right.' Killian sighed. 'Still, what a waste. I wonder what grandfather will say?'

In the afternoon of the twenty-second of August, they finally came within sight of Vinga, the westernmost island in the archipelago outside Gothenburg. The relief on board was almost palpable and a cheer went up from the crew, which was echoed by everyone else. Unfortunately, the weather was so bad they were forced to anchor outside Marstrand, a small port north of Gothenburg. Although the purser was sent overland with news of their arrival, it wasn't until four days later that they were finally able to sail into the Göta river estuary.

'At last, we're home.' Jess breathed a sigh of relief. 'I don't want to even *see* a ship for a very long time.'

'I second that,' Killian said with feeling. 'I can't wait to be on dry land and have you and Brice safe.'

Their homecoming wasn't quite the joyful event they had envisaged, however. Going straight to the Van Sandt & Fergusson warehouse, where they hoped to find Albert before they saw anyone else, they were greeted by a totally unexpected sight. Albert was standing in the office looking utterly stunned, his lean body slumped as if in defeat. The place appeared to have been ravaged by something akin to a *tai-fun*. There were papers scattered everywhere, ledgers flung onto the floor and the strongbox stood wide open, its contents strewn all over the place.

'Albert! What on earth is going on here?' Killian stopped dead inside the door and reached behind him for Jess' hand, pulling her in next to him.

Albert looked up, the expression on his homely face a strange mixture of joy and sadness. 'Ah, Jess, Killian, there you are! I'm so pleased you made it back. We had the news from the purser, but ...' He spread his hands out to indicate the mess all around him and shook his head. 'I'm so sorry. This wasn't how I'd planned to welcome you.'

Killian went over to shake hands. 'But what's happened? Was the place burgled?' he asked, while Jess greeted Albert with a fierce hug.

'No, if only it were that simple.' Albert passed a hand over his eyes and sank onto a chair. 'Fergusson must have done this. Look, he's been through all the papers and taken any important ones. They're gone, every last one, and all the money too of course. This is all my fault.'

'How can it be?'

'When Jess disappeared, I decided not to tell him about us finding the will. Well, there seemed no point. Then when I received your letter from Cadiz, I thought I'd wait until at least one of you came back safely. But then this morning,

Milner and I thought it was safe to confront him when we knew you'd both returned, but he threw us out of his house. Utterly refused to listen to reason.' Albert sighed. 'He must have come straight here afterwards. I should have waited until you were here. I'm so, so sorry ...'

Jess put a hand on Albert's shoulder. 'You couldn't have known, don't worry. At least he won't get his hands on the profit from the China venture.'

Albert turned bleak eyes on her. 'But that's just it, don't you see? He will, because you can't prove you're the owner now. He's taken everything.'

'Not quite,' Killian put in. 'We've still got the original will. At least I think we do.'

'Really?' Albert looked up. 'I thought you left that with Milner and I'm afraid the same thing's happened to his office. I just had word from him.'

Killian gritted his teeth. 'No, I left it with Mrs Ljung and she promised to keep it safe for me. We'd better go and make sure she's all right. He's bound to look in my lodgings, although hopefully he won't think to check hers.'

'Let's hope not. He must be desperate to destroy it. He'll probably ransack my house too.'

'Then there's no time to lose. Albert, you go and make sure he's not at your place, then check on Milner. We'll take Adair with us. Come and meet us at Mrs Ljung's as soon as you can. And be careful.'

'Very well.'

'What about Brice? Should I take him to my mother's first?' Jess asked, her eyes wide and anxious.

'No, it's not safe. Fergusson might have gone back there. I want you both where I can see you,' Killian gripped her hand, fear for her safety and that of their son making him squeeze it so tightly she winced.

'Who's Brice?' Albert looked confused, then gasped as

Jess turned around to show him the baby who was sleeping in his sling on her back. 'Well, I never ...'

Jess smiled briefly. 'Our son, Brice Aaron Kinross. I'll introduce you later. For now, we'd better hurry.'

All seemed quiet at Mrs Ljung's house and at first they didn't think she was even at home.

'Adair, check her rooms carefully. We'll keep watch here,' Killian whispered, and Adair crept into the old lady's parlour on silent feet, pulling a long dagger out of his boot as a precaution.

Killian and Jess waited in the small hallway at the bottom of the stairs, their ears straining for any suspicious sounds. Brice began to stir and to prevent him from grizzling, Killian quickly extracted him from the sling and gave him to Jess to hold. She bounced the baby in her arms and shushed him.

Adair soon came back and shook his head. 'Empty,' he breathed.

A muffled noise from upstairs made them all look up. Putting a finger to his lips in warning, Killian tip-toed up, trying not to step in the middle of each stair tread where the wood creaked the most. The door into his rooms was slightly ajar and he peered around with caution. He caught sight of something on the floor and froze, swallowing an exclamation of outrage.

Lying on the floor was poor Mrs Ljung, her face almost unrecognizable with blood pouring out of her nose and her hair all matted. She wasn't moving, so Killian assumed she was either dead or unconscious.

In case it was a trap, he pushed the door open slowly and checked behind it before advancing into the room. He signalled for Adair to look in the second room, keeping Jess behind him just in case, but the youth soon came back. 'Nae one there,' he said. 'The bastard must've gone.' He looked at

Jess, whose face was white with shock at seeing Mrs Ljung's battered face and added. 'Here, gie me Brice. Gang sit doon the noo.'

Killian threw himself down next to Mrs Ljung and knelt on the floor, checking for a pulse. To his relief, the old woman stirred when he touched her wrist and opened her eyes with a moan. 'Hell and damnation,' he gritted out, 'is this Fergusson's doing?'

'You may be sure it is,' came a voice from behind him, and Killian turned around to find Fergusson standing by the door, with Jess in front of him, held in a vice-like grip. At her throat glinted the steel of a knife blade and Killian could see Fergusson's black eyes glittering almost as dangerously. He sucked in a sharp breath as the blood in his veins turned to pure ice.

'How the hell ...?' he hissed, but he knew the answer already. Fergusson must have been waiting outside the house and crept in behind them, catching them unawares just when they thought they were safe. He swore inwardly at his own stupidity in not thinking of this and swallowed down the bile of pure terror that rose in his throat. Taking a deep breath, he tried to think of a way to salvage the situation.

'Fergusson, there's no need for this,' he said, trying to keep his voice steady. 'I'm sure we can come to some arrangement.'

'I'm not interested in discussing anything with you, you snake,' Fergusson snarled. 'Go behind my back to take away what was mine, would you? You're beyond despicable, Kinross. Now give me the will or your little wife dies.' Pulling Jess with him, he moved sideways, away from the door and towards the tiled stove so that his back wasn't exposed to attack.

'The company wasn't yours in the first place,' Killian said. 'It belonged to Jessamijn and you know it.'

'She's just a girl. What does she know? Nothing, I tell you. She had no business learning anything about trade. I worked hard to earn my place there. Put up with her father's patronising partnership offer – ten percent, I ask you? Is that any way to reward a man who's worked for you for years? That company was my due and I *will* have it.' Fergusson's face turned red, and Jess uttered a terrified squeak as he tightened his grip on her.

'Well, perhaps if you hadn't been quite so greedy, no one would have suspected anything,' Killian replied, keeping a tight rein on his temper. 'If you'd paid out Jessamijn's dowry in the first place, she wouldn't have gone looking for answers.'

'Stupid little bitch. You should've just done as you were told.' He pushed the knife closer to her skin, making her whimper. 'This is all your fault.' Killian had been inching closer and Fergusson barked, 'Stay where you are or she's finished. I mean it.' Jess stayed silent, but Killian could see the terror in her eyes. He couldn't bear the thought of losing Jess, when he'd finally thought them safe. She and Brice were the most precious things in the world to him and even to contemplate life without them made cold sweat trickle down his back.

'Come man, be reasonable. Think of your own wife and child,' he whispered hoarsely, swallowing down the panic that was making it hard to come up with a plan of action. *Think, man, think!*

Fergusson snorted. 'My wife isn't interested in anything other than Ramsay. She hardly notices me any more. Hah! You can look after her now, play the dutiful son-in-law,' he sneered.

'Your son needs you. Surely you can't just abandon him?' Killian tried his best to sound persuasive, but Fergusson was too agitated to listen to reason.

'I'll come back for him when he's grown up a bit. Serve Katrijna right for monopolising the boy. For the last time, Kinross, give me the will.'

Killian held up his hands as if in surrender. 'Fine, but I'm going to have to come closer to you. It's hidden near the stove. Don't do anything hasty now.' He walked slowly towards Fergusson, who backed further into the corner.

'Keep your hands where I can see them.'

'I am. Look, I have to kneel now. There's a loose floorboard here and the will is underneath.'

'I checked all the loose boards already. You lie!' Fergusson shouted.

'No, you probably didn't put your hand in far enough. Hold on, let me show you.' Killian got down on all fours and crawled closer to where Fergusson was standing. Pushing the corner of a floorboard, it came loose easily and he pulled it out, sticking his left hand into the hole. 'It's in here somewhere, just a moment.'

He pretended to search around under the joists and saw out of the corner of his eye that Fergusson had moved slightly towards him, craning his neck to see what Killian was doing. Killian grunted with imaginary effort and surreptitiously gripped the loose floorboard with his right hand. Before Fergusson had time to step out of the way, Killian suddenly swung round and caught the man a heavy blow on the back of the knees with the piece of wood. Fergusson howled with pain and let go of Jess momentarily.

Killian shot to his feet and pushed her out of the way, then rammed into Fergusson's chest. The two of them crashed to the floor, with Killian on top. He raised his hand to strike his former employer, but suddenly noticed the man wasn't fighting back.

'It's a'right, he's oot cold.' Adair came rushing over and pulled Killian up with one hand, while still holding onto

Brice with the other. 'Hit his heid on the tile stove.'

'Thank the Lord for that.' Killian bent over to rest his hands on his knees in an effort to steady his legs. 'Watch him for a moment, please, will you? I'm going to tie him up and let Milner deal with him. Then I'll need to find an apothecary for Mrs Ljung.'

'Scum,' Adair muttered and went to stand guard over Fergusson, who showed no signs of stirring.

Killian took a deep breath and went over to Jess, pulling her into a fierce embrace. 'Are you all right, my love? Did he hurt you much?'

She was still pale as new snow and trembling almost as much as he was. She clung to him, but managed to shake her head. 'I'm ... f-fine. Oh, Killian, that was ...'

'Shh, I know. Too close. But it's over and we're safe. No one else is going to hurt you, I swear.' He kissed her hard on the lips, revelling in the taste of her, the feel of her in his arms. He promised himself he *would* keep her safe from now on, if it was the last thing he did. 'Perhaps now we can have some peace and quiet for a while,' he said. 'I don't know about you, but a few weeks without adventures of any kind would suit me just fine.'

Jess kissed him back just as fiercely. 'Amen to that.'

Epilogue

Rosyth House, Scotland

Lord Rosyth was in his private sitting room, resting on a day bed and sunk in gloom. Not even visits from his great-granddaughters could cheer him up these days and he felt as if he might as well just close his eyes and go to sleep for good. He'd lived too long as it was and there was nothing left to look forward to.

How had it all gone so wrong?

He sighed and closed his eyes, willing death to come and claim him, but his body had other ideas and his heart wasn't ready to stop beating yet. He was simply too healthy.

'Damn it all,' he muttered, and got up to poke at the fire with one of the irons, watching a shower of sparks fly up the chimney. He gave the nearest log another vicious jab, but it didn't soothe his frustration one bit.

A knock on the door made him turn around, and he frowned at the servant who entered at his call. 'Yes, what is it, McKay?'

'A visitor for you, my lord. Shall I show him up here or would you prefer to come down to the salon?'

'I'm not receiving anyone today, I told you earlier,' he replied testily. He couldn't understand why his neighbours persisted in trying to jolly him out of his bad moods. They should have given up a long time ago. Couldn't they see he just wanted to be left alone?

'This particular visitor is different, my lord,' McKay persisted. 'You'll be sorry if you send him away.'

Lord Rosyth stared at the servant, surprised by his impertinence. 'Well, really!' he exclaimed. 'Who is it then?'

'You'll see,' McKay said with a smug grin that annoyed him even more. The man had been with him for a long time, but never had he acted in such an infuriating manner. What was the world coming to?

'Make him come up here,' he shouted after the fellow, who was now heading for the door without even waiting for an answer. 'I'm not going downstairs before suppertime. And tell him not to stay too long, it tires me.'

'Very good, my lord.'

Lord Rosyth scowled after him. He'd have to replace McKay, the man was obviously getting above himself. People seemed to think that because he was old, he didn't have his wits about him. Well, they were wrong.

A moment later, however, he began to wonder if perhaps his wits had deserted him after all and he was seeing things. His eldest grandson came into the room and bowed to him, rather curtly. The grandson he hadn't set eyes on in over two years and who hadn't replied to a single one of his letters in all that time. *Damn his impudence!*

'Where the devil have you been?' Lord Rosyth snarled by way of a greeting. 'And what have you done with your cousin?'

'Hello, Grandfather. A pleasure to see you as always,' Killian replied.

'Don't give me any of your cheek, boy. Not a word have I had from either of you in years. Years! Surely you didn't expect me to welcome you with open arms?'

Killian shook his head and smiled somewhat ruefully. 'No, that was the last thing I expected. A leopard doesn't change his spots, as they say.'

'Well, good, because you're not getting so much as a farthing, either of you. Good-for-nothing scoundrels, leaving an old man to shoulder all the burdens on my own. I should have you horsewhipped for negligence, the pair of you.'

Killian calmly crossed his arms over his chest, a stance that exuded strength and confidence. 'You can always try.'

'Enough of this insolence! Just tell me what you've done with Farquhar and then you can go. At least now I know you're alive so obviously your avoidance of me was deliberate. Nothing more than I expected, but still ...'

'And what makes you think I've done anything with him? He didn't go with me to Sweden.'

'Well, I ...' he had no logical answer to that question, just a gut feeling that Farquhar's disappearance had something to do with Killian. 'The two of you were always getting into scrapes together,' he blustered. 'Stands to reason you'd know where he is. You were always the leader.'

'Not so. Just because I took the blame for most of our misdeeds doesn't mean I instigated them. But be that as it may ...' Lord Rosyth saw Killian take a deep breath and look away, before turning his gaze back to his grandfather. An expression of sadness and regret passed like a shadow over his features, then he said quietly, 'I'm sorry, but Farquhar is dead.'

'What? How?' He felt his head reeling. He had been afraid both his grandsons had perished, but now that he'd seen Killian, he had been lulled into false hope. 'What did you do?'

Killian's mouth tightened. 'Nothing, Grandfather. I didn't *do* anything, but I doubt you'll believe me, so perhaps it's best if we just leave it at that.'

'How did he die then?' He felt wrongfooted somehow, but that only made him more cross. 'If it wasn't you, what happened?'

'Farquhar died at sea, from dysentery I believe, on board the ship *Hertogh van Lorreynen*. You can verify that by writing to Captain John Ley of the Ostend Company.' Killian pulled out a sheet of paper from his pocket and put it on the nearest table. 'Here is his direction.'

Lord Rosyth blinked, still in shock at this news. 'I heard a rumour he'd gone to China, but I couldn't credit it. What in blazes was he doing on board an Ostend ship?'

'Following me.'

'Why would he do such a thing? I don't understand …' he trailed off. There were too many questions swirling around inside his head and he didn't know which one to voice first.

'No, that was always the problem.' Killian walked over to the window and stared out into the garden. 'You never noticed what was right before your eyes. It was easier to let Farquhar play his little games unchecked, wasn't it, than to deal with him once and for all. The sad thing is he would have been welcome to the estate because I want no part of it. You can give it to whoever you wish.'

The words were said with quiet determination, quite unlike the vehemence and acrimony with which their last conversation had been conducted. Lord Rosyth suddenly understood that he was no longer dealing with a petulant youth, but a man. One who knew his own mind and who couldn't be manipulated or coerced in any way.

Before he had time to think about this further, however, Killian turned and headed for the door. 'I will leave you now. No doubt you'll want to grieve in peace.'

'Grieving be damned! I want the full story and none of this mawkish rubbish. Playing games indeed. You're the one who was always doing that.'

Killian stopped and turned around, but he was scowling now and fixed his grandfather with stormy blue eyes. 'Me? I was never anything but honest in my dealings with you.'

'Hah! Running away to Edinburgh to force my hand – you don't consider that manipulation? Well, I called your bluff. Bet you were surprised when I didn't go after you and offer to have you back.'

'Not at all. I never expected that.' Killian walked over to the fireplace. 'May I?' he said and gestured to one of the two large wing chairs that flanked the hearth. 'If we have to have this tedious conversation, I may as well sit down.'

'By all means.' Lord Rosyth lowered himself into the other chair, feeling every one of his years weigh heavily on him all of a sudden. 'Now start from the beginning, damn it. What was it you think I never saw?'

'You really don't know?' Killian raised his eyebrows in disbelief. 'Farquhar always coveted the title of laird and the Rosyth estate. Surely you must have noticed that?'

'Of course I did, but it was just the natural envy of a little boy who wanted what he couldn't have. I thought he'd grown out of it. After all, he always knew you were the heir and I gave him a generous allowance for helping me run the estate.'

'Ah, but did he grow out of it?' Killian stared his grandfather straight in the eye. 'Can you honestly say you made him believe I was good enough to inherit anything? Me, the half-Irish grandson who never lived up to my brothers' memory? You didn't even make me believe it, which is why I left.'

'That's nonsense. You needed to sow a few wild oats, I could understand that, but I always thought you'd come to your senses. At some point, you would have come back here to learn how to be the laird properly. By cutting you off without a penny I reckoned you'd come crawling back sooner, but either way, it was only a question of time.'

'And be controlled by you? Never. I'm my own man. I thought I made that clear.'

'We could have worked together,' he said, but he knew he didn't sound very convincing even to his own ears. He *did* have a tendency to be domineering, that was true. And the boy had always had a stubborn streak. They were very alike really, come to think of it. Too alike perhaps?

'And all the lies Farquhar told about me? You swallowed every one,' Killian said. 'You even believed that story about Ruaridh's daughter until I convinced you otherwise.'

Lord Rosyth shook his head. 'Not all of them, no, but mostly they were corroborated by others. Can you deny you lived a life of debauchery at the card tables and in the gaming hells?'

'I did what I had to do to survive. You can't blame me for that when you gave me nothing.' Killian stared into the fire, a muscle working in his jaw the only indication that he wasn't as calm as he sounded. 'There were times when I couldn't afford to eat.'

'I expected you to come to me for help. We could've made a deal – for you to come back here and do as I asked during part of the year in exchange for an allowance.'

'It would never have worked.'

'Huh, maybe not. You're a headstrong boy.' He contemplated this in silence for a while, then decided there was no point arguing about it further. His thoughts returned to his other grandson. 'So you're telling me your cousin was plotting against you all along?' Killian nodded. 'And that is why he followed you to China? What were you doing there?'

'I signed on as assistant to the first supercargo on a trade journey to Canton. It was a great opportunity to learn how to be a merchant and since I'd also invested in the venture, it had the potential to make me rich. Farquhar must have found that out and set out to stop me. I suppose he didn't want me to outshine him in your eyes.' He smiled. 'As if I ever could.'

'I see. And did it?'

'What, make me rich?' Killian laughed wryly. 'Yes, although my wife had something to do with it as well.'

'You're married?' For some reason he was more surprised by this than any of the other things Killian had told him.

'Yes, to Robert Fergusson's stepdaughter, Jessamijn. I have a son too, Brice. He'll be a year old soon.'

This was all too much for him to take in at once and he found himself gaping stupidly like a fish. 'A son? You have a son? I never thought ... When you and Farquhar both disappeared, I lost all hope the direct Kinross line would continue. Well, thank the Lord for small mercies.'

Killian snorted. 'Small, is it? I'd say he's a huge blessing, myself. In any case, he's downstairs with Jess. If you like, I'll introduce them to you before I go, but we digress. Do you wish to hear the rest or not?'

'Yes, yes, go on.'

'As I was saying, Farquhar somehow found out about the venture and set out after me, intent on murder if I'm not mistaken.'

'Murder?' Lord Rosyth drew in a sharp breath. He had always thought Farquhar too spineless to do anything that drastic. He didn't like to think he'd been so wrong.

'Well, he tried twice to kill my wife and son, and then he attacked me in front of witnesses. I can obtain signed statements if you want.' Killian glared at him, obviously under the impression that his grandfather didn't believe him.

Lord Rosyth held up a hand. 'No, I'll take your word for it. I just can't quite understand it. He was always such a ... coward.' There was no other way to describe Farquhar, he had to admit.

'I think by that point he wasn't in his right mind. He tried to set fire to the house where my wife was staying. When that failed, he attacked her, then me. It was as if he didn't care whether anyone saw him killing me or not. That doesn't seem like the actions of a sane man to me.'

Lord Rosyth took another deep breath. 'Indeed. But he

didn't succeed, obviously?'

Killian's expression turned grim. 'No, luck was with Jess and as for myself, I managed to best Farquhar.' He shrugged. 'In the end, he was taken into custody by Captain Ley, who had brought him and therefore agreed to take him back to Europe again. That was the last I saw of him.'

Lord Rosyth was quiet for a while, then cleared his throat. 'I, er ... it would seem, uhm, ... I owe you an apology, Killian.' He found it hard to say the words, but he knew they were necessary if they were to move forward. He had been in the wrong, at least about some things. He took a deep breath and forced himself to continue. 'Can you forgive me?'

Killian looked at him as if he was gauging his grandfather's sincerity and Lord Rosyth held his gaze. Then Killian nodded, smiled cautiously and held out his hand.

'Very well. Truce?' he said.

'Yes, truce.' Lord Rosyth took the outstretched hand in both of his and felt the strength of it. This was somehow reassuring, but it annoyed him that he should feel this way. He might be old, but he didn't need anyone stronger to lean on. Of course he'd like to train the boy to take over one day, but he wasn't ready to relinquish the reins quite yet. *Perhaps a little help wouldn't come amiss, however,* he thought. *I do tire more easily these days...* 'So, do I get to meet your family?' he snapped, covering his unexpected feelings of weakness by bristling.

Killian stood up. 'Yes, I'll fetch them.'

Soon after, he returned to the room followed by a pretty blonde girl carrying an infant. A wave of emotion swept over him at the sight of his great-grandson, and he had to struggle to stand up and greet Killian's wife properly.

'I'm very pleased to meet you,' he murmured.

'And I you.' The girl smiled and curtseyed. 'This is Brice.'

She set the sturdy toddler on the floor and he immediately pulled himself upright with the help of the nearest chair. He was blond, like his mother, but with his father's cornflower eyes. He turned an inquisitive, fearless gaze on Lord Rosyth, who stared back.

'Hello, little one.' He looked at Killian. 'Calling him Brice was an excellent choice, if I may say so.'

'Yes, I thought you'd like that,' Killian muttered.

'Not because it's Scottish,' he said, bristling again. 'Only because it means he's named after a very brave young man who should never have been taken from us.' He smiled tentatively at Killian and forced himself to admit to yet another thing he'd been wrong about. 'But actually I think you'll make a better laird than he would have. He had no head for figures, fighting was the only thing he ever wanted to do. You have more sense.'

'Now he tells me,' Killian said with an answering smile, rolling his eyes.

Jessamijn shook her head at him. 'Behave,' she said, and Lord Rosyth was pleased to see a look filled with love passing between Killian and his wife. He'd never thought his grandson would make a love match, but there was no doubt he had.

He sat down in his chair again and Killian did the same, putting his arm around Jessamijn's waist and pulling her down to perch on the armrest.

'What are your plans?' Lord Rosyth looked at Killian and felt pride in his grandson for the first time. Definitely not a boy any longer, but a man grown, decisive and intelligent. He was exactly the sort of laird the Rosyth estate needed. 'Will you stay here?'

'Not permanently, no. I'm sorry, but Jess and I run a merchant business in Gothenburg. We enjoy that immensely and wouldn't like to give it up just yet. We recently made a profit of seventy-five percent on the China venture, so I'm sure you can see it would be madness not to continue. We could spend part of the year here with you, but mostly we'll need to be in Sweden.'

He saw the determination in Killian's eyes and knew that even though he'd prefer it otherwise, he had to accept his grandson's decision and be glad they wanted to spend at least some time with him.

He nodded. 'That will have to do, I suppose,' he said gruffly. He took the hand of the small child, who was now clambering around by holding onto his great-grandfather's legs, and sent up a prayer of thanks to God for this gift. It was more than he deserved and he'd be forever grateful, but he didn't need to tell his grandson that. Not yet anyway.

Two admissions in one day were more than enough already.

About the Author

Christina lives in London and is married with two children. Although born in England she has a Swedish mother and was brought up in Sweden. In her teens, the family moved to Japan where she had the opportunity to travel extensively in the Far East.

Christina is an accomplished writer of novellas, *Trade Winds* is her first novel.

www.christinacourtenay.com
www.twitter.com/PiaCCourtenay

More Choc Lit

Why not try something else from the Choc Lit selection?

New home, new friends, new love.
Can starting over be that simple?

Tess Riddell reckons her beloved Freelander is more reliable than any man – especially her ex-fiancé, Olly Gray. She's moving on from her old life and into the perfect cottage in the country.

Miles Rattenbury's passions? Old cars and new women! Romance? He's into fun rather than commitment. When Tess crashes the Freelander into his breakdown truck, they find that they're nearly neighbours – yet worlds apart. Despite her overprotective parents and a suddenly attentive Olly, she discovers the joys of village life and even forms an unlikely friendship with Miles. Then, just as their relationship develops into something deeper, an old flame comes looking for him ...

Is their love strong enough to overcome the past? Or will it take more than either of them is prepared to give?

ISBN: 978-1-906931-22-3

A modern retelling of Jane Austen's *Emma*.

Mark Knightley – handsome, clever, rich – is used to women falling at his feet. Except Emma Woodhouse, who's like part of the family – and the furniture. When their relationship changes dramatically, is it an ending or a new beginning?

Emma's grown into a stunningly attractive young woman, full of ideas for modernising her family business. Then Mark gets involved and the sparks begin to fly. It's just like the old days, except that now he's seeing her through totally new eyes.

While Mark struggles to keep his feelings in check, Emma remains immune to the Knightley charm. She's never forgotten that embarrassing moment when he discovered her teenage crush on him. He's still pouring scorn on all her projects, especially her beautifully orchestrated campaign to find Mr Right for her ditzy PA. And finally, when the mysterious Flynn Churchill – the man of her dreams – turns up, how could she have eyes for anyone else?

The Importance of Being Emma was shortlisted for the 2009 Melissa Nathan Award for Comedy Romance.

ISBN: 978-1-906931-20-9

Revenge and love: it's a thin line …

The writing's on the wall for **Cleo** and **Gav**. The bedroom wall, to be precise. And it says 'This marriage is over.'

Wounded and furious, Cleo embarks on a night out with the girls, which turns into a glorious one night stand with …

Justin, centrefold material and irrepressibly irresponsible. He loves a little wildness in a woman – and he's in the right place at the right time to enjoy Cleo's.

But it's Cleo who has to pick up the pieces – of a marriage based on a lie and the lasting repercussions of that night. Torn between laid-back Justin and control freak Gav, she's a free spirit that life is trying to tie down. But the rewards are worth it!

ISBN: 978-1-906931-24-7

All's fair in love and war?
Depends on who's making the rules.

Harry Watling has spent the past five years keeping her father's boat yard afloat, despite its dying clientele. Now all she wants to do is enjoy the peace and quiet of her sleepy backwater.

So when property developer Matthew Corrigan wants to turn the boat yard into an upmarket housing complex for his exotic new restaurant, it's like declaring war.

And the odds seem to be stacked in Matthew's favour. He's got the colourful locals on board, his hard-to-please girlfriend is warming to the idea and he has the means to force Harry's hand. Meanwhile, Harry has to fight not just his plans but also her feelings for the man himself.

Then a family secret from the past creates heartbreak for Harry, and neither of them is prepared for what happens next ...

ISBN: 978-1-906931-25-4

November 2010:

Money, love and family. Which matters most?

When Diane Jenner's husband is hurt in a helicopter crash, she discovers a secret that changes her life. And it's all about money, the kind of money the Jenners have never had.

James North has money, and he knows it doesn't buy happiness. He's been a rock for his wayward wife and troubled daughter – but that doesn't stop him wanting Diane.

James and Diane have something in common: they always put family first. Which means that what happens in the back of James's Mercedes is a really, really bad idea.

Or is it?

ISBN: 978-1-906931-26-1

November 2010:

If life is cheap, how much is love worth?

It's 1914 and young Rose Courtenay has a decision to make. Please her wealthy parents by marrying the man of their choice – or play her part in the war effort?

The chance to escape proves irresistible and Rose becomes a nurse. Working in France, she meets Lieutenant Alex Denham, a dark figure from her past. He's the last man in the world she'd get involved with – especially now he's married.

But in wartime nothing is as it seems. Alex's marriage is a sham and Rose is the only woman he's ever wanted. As he recovers from his wounds, he sets out to win her trust. His gift of a silver locket is a far cry from the luxuries she's left behind.

What value will she put on his love?

ISBN: 978-1-906931-28-5

Introducing the Choc Lit Club

Join us at the Choc Lit Club where we're
creating a delicious selection of fiction
for today's independent woman.
Where heroes are like chocolate – irresistible!

Join our authors in Author's Corner, read author interviews
and see our featured books.

We'd also love to hear how you enjoyed *Trade Winds*.
Just visit www.choc-lit.co.uk and give your feedback.
Describe Killian in terms of chocolate and
you could be our Flavour of the Month Winner!